WINDY CITY
DYING

WINDY CITY

DYING

ELEANOR
TAYLOR
BLAND

ST. MARTIN'S MINOTAUR........NEW YORK

www.minotaurbooks.com

Library of Congress Cataloging-in-Publication Data

Bland, Eleanor Taylor.
    Windy City dying : a Marti MacAlister mystery / Eleanor Taylor Bland.
       p. cm.
    ISBN 0-312-30098-0 (hc)
    ISBN 0-312-32048-5 (pbk)
    1. MacAlister, Marti (Fictitious character)—Fiction. 2. Police—Illinois—Chicago—Fiction. 3. African American police—Fiction. 4. Chicago (Ill.)—Fiction. 5. Policewomen—Fiction. I. Title.

PS3552.L36534 W46 2002
813'.54—dc21   2002069840

First St. Martin's Griffin Edition: November 2003

10 9 8 7 6 5 4 3 2 1

ACKNOWLEDGMENTS

Thanks to:

My editor Kelley Ragland, thank you for your commitment to Marti; to Ben.

My family: Kevin Todd, Sr., Melissa, Anthony, La Taja, Todd, Jr., and Antonia. You keep me grounded in reality.

Barbara Richardson, the real Janet Petroski, first recipient of the Ruth H. Rozenburg Victim Service Provider Award. You epitomize compassion.

Tara Boryc, GSD, ADC/PC, German shepherd extraordinaire. To my readers: Trouble is now a female, in honor of Tara's contribution to Trouble's character development.

The newest member of the Bland clan, Nathaniel Madden; Baltimore super fans: Shirley Johnson, Gloria Hilton, Ellen Gordon, Pat Ash, and Andrew Coles, who is a gift and a blessing. Everyone at Calvin College, especially W. Dale Brown and Annie Anderson, who is Mary's daughter and Joan's niece; the folks at the Kentucky Women Writers Conference, especially Shelda and Jan; Mary Alice Gorman and Richard Goldman at Mystery Lovers Bookstore; Sally and Doina, Mary Roberts Rhinehart Chapter, Sisters in Crime; John Doggett, the opinionated critic at Centuries and Sleuths Bookstore; and Shechter and Stu Shiffman, Stuart W. Miller, wherever you are, thanks much.

For enriching my personal experiences of modern-day adolescence, Dr. Howard Atlas and Mr. Herb King, and retirement congratulations to Dr. Kurtz, Superintendent, Waukegan School District 60; Rudy Martin, Arturo Hernandez, Lake County Juvenile Probation; Mike Schack, Marilyn Burden, Cindy Zina-veah, Neal Schilling, Anthony Payne, Debby Brosnan, Becky Raik, and Ralph Strickland at Joseph Academy. To Dr. Mehta and his staff: Anita, Sharon, Nida, Mary Ellen, Patti, Suzanne, and Jill. Dr. Holmberg and his staff: Alberta, Amy, Mary, Jenny, Sue, Dianna, Elba, and Sonya; Dr. Baker and Dr. Kirch.

Technical assistance: Hedy Hustedde, Bettendorf Library, Richard Hughes, former gubernatorial candidate, State of Iowa, Frank Winans, Lake County Sheriff, Retired, Shirlet Clark, R.N., Georgia Carrasco, Lake County Probation Department, Nanette Boryk, paralegal, Anthony Bland, teenager, Nathaniel Madden, adolescent counselor. Tracy Clark, copy editor, *Chicago Tribune*; Michael Allen Dymmoch, Phillip Corrigan, PADS Crisis Service; Patricia Jones, Supervisor, Waukegan Township; Diane Taylor, Director, Clara Weldon and Cynthia Alexander, Staben House.

WINDY CITY
DYING

TUESDAY, FEBRUARY 13

As Adrian Quinn entered the Geneva Street YMCA, a janitor just missed touching his shoes with a wide, short-bristled broom. Superstitious, Adrian backed away. Luck was with him tonight; being touched by the broom would have meant going home and remaining there until tomorrow. Safely inside, he could hear the sounds of people shouting and a whistle screeching in harsh blasts. He nodded toward the brown-skinned woman who sat at a desk behind a counter. When she raised her eyebrows, he said, "Sounds like I missed the tip-off," even though he wasn't there to watch a basketball game. Then he hurried toward the corridor where the noise was coming from.

Adrian was the only person in the hall until a young Hispanic boy rushed out of the gym where the basketball game was in progress. He stepped aside before the boy could bump into him, avoiding being touched by a stranger, another bad omen. Once again, he felt lucky. When he passed the open doors of a meeting room and saw the backs of about thirty people seated in folding chairs, he stopped close enough to listen to what was being said, and leaned against the cinder-block wall. The crowd was too small, the room too confining. And he assumed everyone in the room was Hispanic. He would be conspicuous if he joined them.

As he listened, Joseph Ramos said, "We must remember that we now represent forty-four point six percent of the population of Lincoln Prairie." There was not even a hint of a Mexican accent in his precise English. "It is time for us to be represented in city government. It is time for us to register and vote. We begin today." The people were silent until Ramos repeated "We begin today" in Spanish. Then there was rhythmic clapping as the small gathering took up the chant. *"Sí, nosotros comenzamos, hoy!"* Yes, we begin today!

They were fools, all of them. Anyone who listened to Ramos was a fool. They were being used by a man who promised much but accomplished nothing for anyone but himself. They were being taken in by Ramos just as he had been. Ramos would climb on their backs to get where he wanted to go. Adrian was going to put an end to that. Ramos would not be elected alderman. Ramos's people would not want him to be their attorney. He would see to it. He was going to take care of it tonight.

Continuing to speak in Spanish, Ramos said, "They do not want us here, but we will not go back where we came from. This is our country now, also. When you hear them saying code enforcement, that does not mean that the landlords will be required to make repairs, or that the city will fill in the potholes. Code enforcement means that brother and sister, mother and cousin, cannot live together in the same house." As Ramos's listeners agreed, they were drowned out by the crowd watching the basketball game, who cheered and stomped their feet on the bleachers. Adrian thought the eruption of noise might cause someone in the room to come and close the doors, but it did not.

"When my parents came to this country," Ramos said, "they lived with two of my aunts. It was crowded in that little house, built for one family, not two. But because of my aunts, my father and mother were able to work while there was someone at home to take care of their children. Soon, my parents could buy their own house."

Ramos spoke as if he knew what poverty was. He was wearing chinos and a cotton shirt tonight while Armani suits hung in his closet. Ramos, always pretending to be what he was not, still convincing others that he understood where they were because he had been there himself. Ramos was still promising to help people. All he would do was betray them.

"When Carmen and I married," Ramos went on, his voice rising, "we moved in with two of my brothers and their families and lived in the basement of a one-family house." As he spoke, his Spanish eased into softer cadences. "I helped my brother pay for that house until he could manage the payments on his own. Then I bought a house and my sister moved in with me. My parents raised nine children. Today we each have a house of our own." Ramos paused, then said, "But only by sticking together, by being family, by not letting things like code enforcement force us to live separately and remain in poverty."

Lies, all of it. Adrian fumed. Too bad he couldn't go in there right now and tell all of them what kind of man Joseph Ramos really was, but Ramos might recognize him.

"Separately, we can get nowhere. Without each other, we are alone," Ramos said, his voice strident. "Together we can achieve much. We begin today!"

Again the people clapped, and again they chanted *"Sí, nosotros comenzamos, hoy!"*

Their voices were louder this time, almost drowning out the screams of a crying child that came from the gymnasium. If only he could tell them how quickly Ramos would betray them. Instead he fingered the knife in his pocket. Even though it was closed, he knew the blade was razor sharp.

As Ramos began speaking again, Adrian walked away, passing the doors to the room without glancing in. He'd already listened to the same speech twice. He had timed it. Ramos would speak for at least another half hour, then he would spend half an hour laughing and joking and shaking hands as his people, ignorant believers that they were, drank coffee that was too strong and ate cookies that were not sweet enough. When he got to Ramos's house, he'd have almost an hour. If things went as planned, that would be time enough for what he was going to do.

*　　*　　*

Graciela Lara was in the kitchen of the Ramos home when she thought she heard a noise upstairs. She listened, wondering what it was, but the house was quiet again. The wind perhaps. This was her eleventh foster home in nine years. She had lived here since June. She was just getting used to the winter sounds of the house, the February sounds, when the wind blew the tree branches against the windows and the snow came. She felt safe here. It was the first time she could ever remember feeling safe. There were locks on the doors and the windows, and even an alarm system. But even if there were not, she would still feel safe here, although she did not know why.

Graciela turned the heat on under the kettle and got out a packet of cocoa. Always before she had to ask for everything and perhaps be told no, she could not have it. But here, in this house, there was always enough food and she could have whatever she wanted as long as it was not close to mealtime.

While she waited for the water to boil she put her backpack on the table, took out her school books and notebooks, then reached for the bag with the library books that she had just come home with. She had a desk in her room, but she liked working downstairs where they would not forget about her, where she could listen as the others made noise that was not fighting. She liked the smells here too, and how clean it was, and the bright red walls, and the cabinets and refrigerator where there was always enough for everyone to have as much as they wanted to eat.

Mrs. Ramos and the Ramoses' son, Francisco, were at their daughter, Micaela's, basketball game. José, in foster care here just as she was, did not trust any of the Ramoses. Although he would have said no, the same as always, when they invited him to go with them to the game, José had lied and told them he had forgotten a sweater at a friend's house so they would know that he did not need them, that he already had someplace to go.

The kettle began to whistle. She turned off the heat and got out a mug. While the cocoa was cooling, she began her math assignment. She liked to do the easiest work first. The quiet was unusual. Usually Francisco was demanding everyone's attention, talking and laughing and clowning, interrupting every time she tried to speak. She didn't mind being alone in the house. Until she came here, that was often the best and safest way to be. She liked it better when it was just her and Mrs. Ramos in the kitchen. She missed Mrs. Ramos, who talked or hummed almost all of the time. Micaela pretended she was not embarrassed by her mother's chatter and out-of-tune songs, and Francisco teased his mother. But Graciela would ask Mrs. Ramos the words to the songs, or ask her a question so she would talk to her. Mrs. Ramos didn't ignore her unless those other two butted in.

As Graciela put down her pencil and reached for the mug of cocoa, another noise interrupted, louder this time, a thump, as if something had fallen. José must have left his window open again. He was used to doing that when the room was too hot. Mr. Ramos had asked him to turn down the heat instead. José kept opening the window just to annoy him. Soon José would be sent back. He expected to be sent away, wanted to be sent away. But he acted first, giving others a reason to send him away so that he would not have to leave for no reason at all.

This Graciela understood. No matter how good she tried to be, or how many times she made the honor role, she too was always sent away. She was certain José wanted to stay here just as she did, and Mr. Ramos liked José the best, as bad as he was. He liked José better than he liked her. She had to be nice to José, because if she was not, she was the one who would be sent away, no matter what he did. She would go up now and close his window, keep him from getting into trouble again. If José did have to leave, she was certain she would have to go also. She really wanted to stay here.

The steps creaked as she went upstairs. A small night light greeted her when she reached the top step. There was another night light halfway down the hall, and one in each of their bedrooms. Although the light was dim, it was good to know that even in the middle of the night, she would not be alone in a dark place. She would not let anyone know, but she was afraid of the dark. Now she could see down the hallway. All five bedroom doors were open. Her room was at the far end of the hall. She frowned as she passed Micaela's room. It was always a mess. Graciela tried to imagine what it would be like to always be wanted, no matter what you did, but she could not. Francisco's room was worse than his sister's. Mrs. Ramos would just close their doors if their rooms got too messy. Graciela's was the only door that was always left open.

There was another noise as she stopped to smooth the bedspread on her bed. Everything was in order on her bureau, and all of her clothes had been ironed and hung in the closet or folded and placed in the hamper. She went to José's room, which was across from hers. That José. His bed was not made. And, just as she thought, his window was open. Papers were scattered about, but she could not see what had fallen on the floor, there were too many clothes everywhere. The window opened onto the porch and the Ramoses would not be pleased if they knew, but this time they would not find out.

As Graciela stepped into José's room a gust of wind made the half-raised blind bang against the window frame. Perhaps that was what she had heard. A cold blast of air made her shiver as she crossed the room to the window. As she stood there, pushing the curtains aside, she heard another noise right behind her. But before she could turn, she felt a sharp pain in her neck.

1

TUESDAY, FEBRUARY 13

Detective Marti MacAlister, and her partner, Matthew "Vik" Jessenovik, were completing a canvass of a neighborhood where a questionable death had occurred. The body had been found this morning. The preliminary report from the medical examiner indicated death by hypothermia. The state's attorney wanted to know if there was criminal negligence on the part of the absentee owner of the house where the body was found. When contacted at his office in Barrington, the landlord insisted that the man had died because he chose not to turn on the heat, or simply forgot, since he was over seventy. Marti didn't expect to prove anything one way or the other. The other two residents in the building had refused to speak with them. Those who lived in the houses on either side became fearful as soon as Marti and Vik identified themselves as police officers. They shook their heads and murmured "*Nada, nada,*" with nervous smiles.

Now Marti headed for the apartment building directly across from the one where the man had lived, stepping into the ruts made by tires in the snow-covered street. Ice had frozen in patches. She watched where she walked, careful not to slip and fall. Vik trudged along beside her. They had both arrived at the precinct before daybreak this morning and worked through the day without going outside. The only daylight she had seen had been through the window. Now it was dark again, and late to be knocking on doors.

"Damn, it's cold," Vik said. He had forgotten his gloves again and alternately blew on his hands and shoved them down into his pockets.

Winter had settled in early this year. There had been no January thaw and tonight's cloud cover concurred with the weatherman's prediction of snow. A few flakes were falling now. The wind blew hard and cold off the lake, making Marti's face tingle. She tugged at her scarf until it covered her nose. Her cell phone rang as she reached the curb. Another body had been found at a house on Julius Street. She glanced at her watch. It was a little before 10:00 P.M.

"Now what?" Vik asked. The brusqueness of his query implied that he didn't want an answer, and Marti understood why. It was only mid-February and so far this year they had investigated sixteen questionable deaths.

"We've got another one," she said.

"That's great, just great," Vik muttered. He sounded frustrated but didn't remind her that "this isn't Chicago," because she had worked on the force there for ten years.

"A suspect was found with this one and taken into custody," she said.

"You're kidding." Wiry salt-and-pepper eyebrows almost met across the bridge of his nose. His face was craggy, his beaked nose skewed from a break years ago. At six two, he was four inches taller than she was, but not more than ten pounds heavier than her 165. "Maybe our luck is changing."

"Let's not get optimistic. Nothing else has been going our way," she reminded him. "And nobody's been to the scene yet, except for the uniforms who got the call. They're waiting for the medical examiner and evidence techs. Janet Petroski is with the family."

Coroners were elected in Illinois and Janet believed that in that position, as a nonmedical professional, her initial responsibility was to the living. She visited with the bereaved and did whatever she could to help.

"Well," Vik said, "since there's nothing we can do there yet, we might as well finish up here. Not that anybody will know

8

anything about some old guy who froze to death, but at least they'll still have some idea of what we're talking about. By morning, he'll be history."

"It probably is a waste of time," Marti agreed. "But I don't think we'll have much time to follow up tomorrow."

Salt made pockmarks on the ice-crusted steps. Vik coughed as they approached the front door, then blew his nose.

"Can't shake this," he complained. "I wonder what a night's sleep would do."

It was a secure building, with a lock on the front door as well as an inner door just past the mailboxes. They had called ahead and the building manager was waiting for them. There were eight apartments, four up and four down.

"It's pretty late to be bothering people," the manager said. A down jacket gave him bulk, but his face was thin and his hands bony. Marti guessed his age at midtwenties, young for this kind of job.

"If you could answer a few questions for us, maybe we wouldn't have to bother anyone else," Marti said.

"Like what?"

"Like did the guy who owns that three flat across the street provide his tenants with enough heat?"

The man shrugged. "Look, I've got a job to hold on to, got a kid to support. Can't answer questions like that."

Marti thought maybe that was the answer to her question. Unfortunately, what people did not say could not be admitted into evidence.

"So, we talk to the tenants," she said. "Mind waiting here?"

He looked at her, brushed at thick blond hair, limp and oily, then nodded.

They started on the second floor. The first two people they spoke with didn't bother to hide their annoyance at being disturbed, even though they hadn't awakened anyone. There was no response at apartment 203. A woman opened the fourth door and looked up at them without taking off three security chains. She wasn't more than five feet tall and two of the chains were above her head. She looked to be at least seventy, and was wearing a puffy nylon cap. It was hot pink and decorated with flowers. Marti decided that it must be a sleeping cap since the woman had on a furry turquoise bathrobe that dragged on the floor and the white mask dangling from her neck didn't have any holes for the eyes.

"And just what do you two want, coming here at this hour of the night?" She sounded more interested than annoyed.

Marti glanced at Vik. From the way his face was scrunched up he had all he could do to keep from laughing. "We just need to ask you a few questions about the building across the street."

"You mean where old Jerry died. What about it?"

"Was he a friend of yours?" Marti asked.

"Yeah. He plays—played—a mean game of Scrabble. What killed him, the cold?"

"Yes."

"Now, why doesn't that surprise me. Law says you got to keep the place at sixty-three degrees at night. Most days his place wasn't that warm. And that landlord, always complaining how the furnace didn't work right." She called the landlord a few choice names.

Vik raised his eyebrows at the woman's profanity, but still looked ready to laugh.

"Ought to be a law against people like him owning buildings," the woman went on. "The one time Jerry called to complain about the heat, the fool had nerve enough to tell him that old people were always cold and to get himself a sweater. Didn't want to hear about the thermostat saying fifty-six degrees. Said it didn't work right. Some landlord." This time she added a curse to the names she called him. "The other two bought heaters, but Jerry, he was too worried about how much it would increase his electric bill." Her eyes filled with tears that spilled onto her cheeks. "Bad when you get old and the kids move away or just don't give a damn." Marti wondered if the woman was talking about Jerry now or herself. So far they hadn't been able to find any next of kin.

"Jerry has family?"

"No, not since his son died a few years back." She wiped at her eyes. "Poor Jerry. Damned shame. I gave him blankets, I did. Told him to call the city and complain, but it's too hard finding a place you can afford to risk getting put out."

Marti glanced at Vik. Clenched jaws and a scowl had replaced his urge to laugh.

"We'll get someone over there tonight," he said. "Have them check on the others and make sure they're okay. Those space heaters could be a fire hazard."

"You need to make that landlord live there for a week."

"I wish," Vik said, as they walked down the hall toward the stairs.

"Aha!" a voice said behind them. Turning, they saw a man brandishing a long, wide-blade sword.

"What the hell . . ." Vik said. He reached for his weapon. Before he or Marti could unholster their guns, the man stood inches away from them. He was pointing the sword at Vik's stomach. The edge of the blade was razor thin and looked sharp.

"Police," Vik said. "Put that thing down now."

"Sure you're cops," the man said. Two small horns protruded from near the top of his head. He was dressed in a black cape and tights.

Marti could feel her heart pounding. Bile rose in her throat. Her vest wouldn't stop that sword.

"I've got you now! You can't fool me. I told her that if she ever broke into this place I would get her."

They backed up as he jabbed the sword at them.

Marti realized that the chain that hung like a half-moon scar on his face was connected to a stud in his nostril and another in his earlobe. She spoke in a quiet voice. "Would you mind putting that down."

"So you can kill me? Do you think I'm stupid? I saw you snooping around. I heard you asking questions about me."

He kept jabbing as he spoke. As they backed up, Vik, to her

left, moved at an angle away from her. Sweat beaded on his forehead. Marti touched the wall and fought down the panic that came with being cornered.

"Let's talk about this," she suggested. "I'm not sure what you mean by that."

"You found out, didn't you? You know."

Maybe he was supposed to be on medication but had stopped taking it and she could talk him down.

"We really need to talk about this," she said. "Why don't you tell me about it?"

"I wouldn't tell you anything. I know she sent you here to kill me."

He was focused on her now. The tip of the sword was pointing at her midsection.

"I'm not here to hurt you," she said. "I just wanted to be sure that you were all right. That nobody was bothering you. I want you to feel safe here."

"Right, like Calunga Morgalota cares about that. I'm a Corigon. She wants me dead. She wants all Corigons dead."

"No, she doesn't," Marti said. It sounded like science fiction. "Not yet. You haven't been here long enough. She needs you to stay at least another six months so that she can complete her mission."

"She does?" He hesitated.

In that moment they both rushed him. Marti went to the right, got behind the man and grabbed his arms. Vik brought his fist down on the man's hands. The sword clattered to the floor.

It was almost midnight when Marti and Vik arrived at the house on Julius Street where the most recent death had occurred. Marti drove past the squad cars parked at the wood-frame house with the wraparound porch, and noted the scene-of-crime van and the medical examiner's vehicle. She circled the block and pulled into the nearest available parking space. The house was a large Victorian hemmed in by smaller well-kept homes on bigger lots. It was a densely populated part of town, but instead of a crowd, neighbors clustered on their porches, or stood in small, quiet groups with scarves wrapped to their noses, collars turned up, and hats pulled down over their ears. Snow, light but persistent, continued to fall, buffeted by the wind. Vik waited while she got her camera bag out of the trunk and they approached the house together. A uniform met them at the door. They wiped their boots on the doormat and stepped inside. The first thing Marti noticed was the quiet. She couldn't hear anyone crying.

"This was called in as an accident," the uniform told them. "An ambulance was dispatched and the paramedics were with the victim when I got here. There was nothing they could do. I cleared the room, then found out the suspect had been found at home, alone, with the body."

"Who's the victim?" Vik asked.

"Graciela Lara. Sixteen-year-old Hispanic female. Both she and the suspect were placed here by the state. We've got José Ortiz, age fifteen, in custody. Do you know Joseph Ramos?"

Marti thought the name sounded familiar but she couldn't place him.

Vik shook his head.

"It's his house, and he's running for alderman."

"What does he want?" Marti asked. Just their luck, a politician.

"Nothing specific, not yet anyway, but he's already making noises about how the investigation is being conducted."

"We'll handle it," Vik said.

"First door on the right."

Marti entered a room that looked like what her momma called the company room, a place for those infrequent guests you didn't know well enough to invite into the family room or the kitchen. Everything—furniture, carpet, walls—was a neutral off-white, relieved only by the figurines that curtsied and twirled in bright colored skirts on shiny mahogany tables. Pottery and vases, just as colorful, were lined up on the mantelpiece. The fireplace lacked smoke marks. There was a pile of unlit logs.

A woman, dry eyed and composed, sat on the edge of a chair. Her hands were folded in her lap. Her tan pant suit blended with the decor. A teenaged girl sat on the floor near the fireplace, head down, straight dark hair falling forward. When the girl looked up, her eyes were dry. A boy, short and rotund, who looked to be younger than the girl, was standing near a potted plant, as far away from the others as he could get and still be in the same room.

The man standing by the window turned to face them. He was several inches shorter than Marti and had the beginnings of a paunch. "So, this is how Lincoln Prairie's finest respond to a call from the Hispanic community."

The woman looked up at him, tight-lipped and silent.

Neither Vik nor Marti replied.

"I suppose I should thank you for not waiting until morning."

Vik took out his notebook and flipped to an empty page. "Mind telling us where you were tonight, Mr. Ramos."

"Where I was? What about . . ." He waved his hand. "There's a dead girl upstairs."

"There's nothing we can do there, sir, until the evidence techs give the okay."

Ramos's dark eyes narrowed. "They've been up there for over an hour. I bet it wouldn't take this long to process a scene if you were *east* of Sherman Avenue."

"This isn't about neighborhoods, sir," Vik said. "It's about following the correct procedures."

"Oh, sure," Ramos said. "Which is why you showed up two hours after I placed the emergency call."

"An hour and forty-seven minutes, sir."

"Your usual response time?"

"No, sir."

"Then I'm sure you'll be able to explain that lapse to your commanding officer."

"Yes, sir," Vik told him. "Now, if you could please tell me where you were."

When Vik had established that everyone in the room lived in the house, determined that they couldn't think of anything that was different about the place when they returned from when they had left, and made note of their whereabouts all evening, he said, "Let's make sure I've got this right. Graciela Lara and José Ortiz are foster children, placed here by the state. Tonight, about six-forty-five, Mrs. Ramos dropped Graciela Lara off at the public library. She was alone when she went into the library. None of you saw her again until Micaela found her upstairs. José Ortiz, who had gone to a friend's house at six-thirty P.M. to retrieve a sweater, was with her."

"Kneeling there," Ramos said, "covered with blood, crying."

Vik confirmed with Micaela that she had called to the others and not left the room and that neither she nor José had moved or touched anything else before her father came in.

"What did José say?"

"I told you already," Ramos said. "Nothing. He never said anything at all."

Marti followed Ramos's gaze as he looked at his daughter, who nodded, then his wife, who said, "Nothing."

"Had there been any disputes between them? Arguments, disagreements, fights? Anything?"

"No." Ramos spoke quickly. A look passed between him and his wife. She in turn looked at the children. It would be better to question them separately. When Vik looked at Marti and rubbed his earlobe, she looked down, then up. The questioning stopped.

Dr. Cyprian was waiting for them when they went upstairs. Marti was glad to see that he would be handling the case since Ramos seemed determined to find fault. Always calm and often reticent, the slender, middle-aged East Indian was well-known in the legal community and respected as a pathologist. Since Cyprian seldom discussed what he had not yet substantiated,

Marti didn't expect more than the most cursory information until after the autopsy.

Marti paused in the doorway and looked into the room where the girl's body lay. Jeans and shirts, underwear, socks, and sweaters were scattered everywhere. The girl was lying on some of the clothes and everything surrounding her head and shoulders was saturated with blood. There was very little spatter and that blood had splashed only on clothing near the body. Although the room was small, Marti didn't see any blood on the furniture or walls and wondered why not. She made a note to check the measurements the techs had taken of everything in the room in relationship to the body. Graciela lay on her left side, with her head near the wall by the window. Her eyes were closed. Her lips parted. She looked as if she had died before she had time to become afraid. Her body would be cool now, and in the early stages of rigor.

"Single wound," Cyprian said. "Throat. Here," and he pointed to the right side of her neck. "Knife. Can't say what length. No defense wounds. Bleeding and blood splatter indicate that he left the knife in until she was on the floor."

"Can you tell us anything about who did it?"

"Not yet."

Vik spoke from the doorway. "This is the boy's room," he said. "José's. Hers is across the hall. And look what we've got." Marti turned to look as he held up a plastic bag. Inside Marti could see something gray that was bloodstained. "A sweat suit," Vik said. "They found it folded and placed in that clothes hamper over there by the bureau."

Marti turned to the evidence techs. "Let's not take anything for granted here. Make no assumptions. Check all windows for signs of entry, check the perimeter of the house and all access to the property for footprints. And, you have taken measurements of the body in relationship to the room?"

"Yes, ma'am."

While Marti got ready to take her own set of photos, Vik decided to tag along with the evidence techs. "For God's sake, be thorough," he warned. "Ramos is already complaining."

Marti took a few wide-angle shots, then adjusted the lens and paused, looking down at the girl. Graciela. Grace. She was slender and wearing tight-fitting jeans and a light blue sweater. Marti guessed her height at about five three. Her fingernails were clipped short and polished a pale pink. She wore no shoes and her feet were dainty. Graciela. Grace. Graceful. It suited her. For a moment, Marti wanted to brush back the strands of soft brown hair that had evaded the clasp of a barrette. She wanted to hold Graciela in her arms and say, "Be all right now," something her own mother would say. Where was this child's mother? Would she care that her daughter was dead? Why didn't anybody in this house weep for her?

After the body was removed, Marti studied the room with practiced detachment. A few papers were also scattered on the floor. She squatted to look at them. School assignments, none with a passing grade. The bed was unmade. The drawers were empty, the surfaces of the furniture bare. More clothes were in a pile on the floor in the closet. She didn't believe the room looked like this because it was a boy's room. Her own son, Theo, who was eleven, was neater than his older sister. Not even her stepson, Mike, left a mess like this. It seemed odd that there were no other personal belongings, not a game, not a textbook, not even a comb or brush. She went to the window. It was closed but not locked. The curtains were damp, as if the window had been open earlier when a light snow fell. Turning, she looked at the blood-soaked clothing again. When she was killed, Graciela had been standing not far from where she was found.

When Marti went to Graciela's room she had to remind herself that José and Graciela were foster children, and that somehow had to account for at least some of what she saw. The two rooms could not have been more different. The bed was made. A pink bedspread that matched the curtains was tucked neatly around the pillows. Although there were no dolls or stuffed animals, a small array of inexpensive cosmetics, nail polish, and perfume was organized on a tray on the bureau. When she checked Graciela's drawers and closet, the girl's belongings were sorted by type and hung neatly or folded. Even the dirty clothes awaiting the washing machine had been folded before they were placed in the hamper.

A desk drawer yielded blank notebook paper, a few pencils and pens and several folders with completed school assignments. All had A's, many had comments from the teachers written across the top or in the margins. Marti thought of her own daughter's room. Joanna was about the same age as Graciela. Joanna's room was always such a mess that Marti couldn't figure out how the child ever found anything. Whenever Joanna began a sentence with "Where is my . . ." nobody answered. Now, just as Marti had wondered why José was such a slob, she wondered why this child was so tidy.

As she stepped into the hall, Marti paused and listened. She looked both ways, unsnapped her holster and held on to the grip of her gun. She kept to one wall, and checked out each room, looking behind her several times as she walked to the stairs. Damn. That incident with the sword would stay with her for days.

The closest place that Adrian could find where he could watch what was going on at the Ramos house while keeping out of the cold was a two-flat half a block away. The building was on the other side of the street and there was a bay window in the living room. Breaking into the empty first-floor apartment was easy. There was a streetlight out front, so he had to be careful in order to see without being seen. He chose a side window in the living room, where the view wasn't as good but being observed was less likely.

He had chosen to begin his mission in Lincoln Prairie because that was where Johnnie MacAlister's family lived. He wanted everything he did now to begin and end with a MacAlister. Just as his life had ended when Johnnie MacAlister arrested him thirteen years ago, his life would begin again with

Marti MacAlister's death. He had watched as she and another plainclothes cop made their way along the sidewalk and into Ramos's house. As he waited for them to emerge, he wondered how he would kill her and if he would kill her children also, or allow them to become orphans.

He had wanted to confront each person on his list, and let them know why they must die, but he had soon realized that the grief of a survivor was by far the worst pain. They had taken his life from him. Now as he killed the most important person in each of their lives, they would understand how precious, how fragile, how irreplaceable that life was, and like him, grieve for that life forever. Surprise and swiftness would be his ultimate weapons. Too much contact and the risk became much greater that someone other than the victim would see him, and remember.

Because Marti MacAlister was a cop, and because killing her would point the way to Johnnie MacAlister, and then to him, he had to kill as many of the others on his list as he could, then kill her. He had decided who must die and who could be allowed to live. With everyone on his list taken care of, he could fix the time of her death. He still had to decide how to kill her. Getting that close to a cop would not be easy. Killing her kids would be. He could slit their throats just as he had slit the throat of Ramos's daughter.

Too bad Johnnie MacAlister was dead. He would have derived immeasurable pleasure from killing him. If MacAlister were still alive, he would have killed his children one by one, and then his wife, and let all of the others on his list live. It was MacAlister's investigation that had led to his arrest. It was his testimony that had convicted him and had convinced the judge to give him the maximum sentence. If MacAlister were alive, though, once again he would have convinced the parole board that he should not be released. Yes, with MacAlister's death, luck once again was on his side. And with his wife's death, everything would be avenged.

* * *

19

Something about the suspect's name, José Ortiz, seemed familiar to Marti, but she couldn't figure out why until she recalled a young boy named José Martinez, from a case she had worked on not long after she came to Lincoln Prairie. Maybe that was who she was thinking of. She had no idea what had become of the five children in that case. She never followed a case beyond whatever court appearances were necessary, especially cases involving kids. The juvenile system as she knew it was not kind to children and too often unjust. She had a job to do—policing—where she could make a difference, not social work, which she had tried briefly before becoming a cop. Social work tore at her heart.

José Ortiz was a short, chubby kid with a major outbreak of acne. The small interrogation room where he sat hunched on a metal bench bolted to the floor made him seem even smaller. His round, full-moon face, and his dark, red-rimmed eyes, were not familiar, but when he looked up at her and Vik, something in his expression suggested that he knew them.

"Have we met before?" Marti asked. She sat across from him in one of two chairs reserved for personnel, while Vik distanced himself by leaning against the wall near the door.

The kid shrugged.

"I knew a José Martinez once," she said.

Another shrug.

"You've been advised of your rights?"

He nodded.

She turned on a tape recorder and went over the Miranda clauses with him again, explaining each and insisting on a verbal response.

"Now. You're willing to talk with us?"

"Why not."

"You have the right to say nothing. The right to have a lawyer present."

"They'll appoint one when I go to court." He had been taught at least a few things by being in the system. His attitude was one of defeat, not defiance.

"Tell me what happened tonight."

"I found her," he said.

"Found who?"

"Come on, you know who. Graciela."

"Tell me about it."

He thought about that, sniffled and wiped his nose with the back of his hand, then said, "In my room, on the floor." He paused again, then said, "Blood."

Marti considered that. The kid was still in shock, whether he had stabbed the girl or not.

"Was anyone else there when you arrived?"

"Not that I saw," he said.

"What did you see?"

"Nothing I hadn't seen before." He hugged himself, leaning forward, head down. "Except that Graciela left her stuff on the table."

"Why was that unusual?"

"She never left stuff laying around."

Marti thought of the girl's room. "Was she nice?"

"Perfect," José said. "Not that it would do her any good." He sounded sad as he said it.

"Did you like her?" Marti asked.

He looked at her for what seemed like a long time. "I didn't . . . hurt her," he said. "I wouldn't hurt her. I know—pretty girl, ugly guy, same house, he hits on her, she laughs, he . . . kills her. That's not what happened."

Marti hesitated, waiting to see if Vik wanted to jump in. When he didn't, she said, "Tell me what your room looked like when you went out last night."

When he described it, she wanted to ask why it was such a mess, but did not.

"Was anything different when you returned?"

"Yeah. Her."

"Anything else?"

He shrugged.

"Think about it," she insisted.

He did, then said, "The window was closed."

"They'll be taking you to the juvenile facility tomorrow," Marti explained. "We'll be seeing you there. If there's anything you need, call me."

He looked at her as if her last statement was a joke.

"No," she said. "I mean that, call me."

She didn't try to explain that she had kids of her own, or tell him that even if he had done this, he was still a child to her, and more in need of someone who gave a damn than most of the kids she knew.

"What do you think?" Vik said as they left the jail.

"The kid is a slob," she said. "For whatever the reason."

"You don't like where that sweat suit was found either," Vik said.

"No, or the fact that it was folded. Way out of character."

"No knife either," Vik said. "The techs went through every room. They turned that house upside down—without leaving a mess, of course. And nothing."

"Let's see what kind of a record he's got." If there was even one incident involving violence, things would not bode well for José Ortiz.

Instead of going back to the precinct she went back to the Ramos house. Without stepping on their property, she looked at it from the outside at every possible angle. There were no footprints in the snow, none of the snow on the eaves or any-place near any of the windows had been disturbed. As far as she knew, nobody except for José, Graciela, and the Ramos family had entered or exited the front or rear door from early this evening until the police had arrived. According to the can-vass reports so far, none of the neighbors had seen anything unusual or anyone lurking in the area.

Adrian spent the rest of the night in the vacant apartment and left before dawn. He took the 4:48 A.M. Metra train from Lin-coln Prairie to Chicago, then traveled by bus. He got off at

Roosevelt and Kedzie, and stopped at a liquor store to purchase a bottle of wine, then walked a block east to Troy. He'd been paroled from Joliet almost two months ago and had no intentions of letting his parole officer know he had moved from the room he had rented on the South Side to this two-room flat on the West Side. As soon as he did what he had to do, he would be on his way to Mexico. Nobody would find him there.

He walked along a narrow path in the center of the sidewalk that had been trampled down by many feet. Nobody shoveled here. The street was two blocks long and quiet now. Cold weather and snow tended to have that effect on everyone except the junkies. Even the gang bangers preferred to stay inside. He didn't have to watch his back but stopped anyway when a car came alongside moving slow. He watched the window, which was up. When it stayed up and the car passed him, he slowly exhaled.

Inside, his apartment was a little too hot but he decided against tampering with the thermostat again and opened the window a few inches instead. Then he got a long-stemmed glass and filled it with wine to celebrate his success last night. The rooms had only a bed, chair, table and small refrigerator with a hot plate when he moved in, to which he had added a clock, a few lamps, a CD player, and a bookcase. Breaking and entering and stealing came easy. He had acquired several small, framed paintings, expensive but not by anyone famous, and a few pieces of Waterford crystal. He was a long way from the Gold Coast apartment he had lived in before he went to jail, but at least now there were a few reminders of the way his life had been.

Unlike his jail cell, this was a safe place. He had moved the bed to an east-west position because sleeping north-south was unlucky, and pushed the bed near the wall so that he could not forget to get up on the same side he got in on. There was a .32-caliber gun under his mattress, not his weapon of choice but the only gun he had come across in his forays into other people's apartments. In each room, he had painted a wide circle on the floor with the curves touching each of the four walls. He was always careful not to step outside of the circles and everything he needed was placed within them. At least while he was inside, he didn't have to worry about bad luck or evil spirits.

He rang a small bell, just in case any demons were lurking outside the circles, then reached for the long-stemmed glass. As he sipped the wine he wondered what Ramos was doing now, with his daughter dead and his son accused of the crime. Too bad father couldn't defend son. That way the kid would be sure to rot in jail. He wondered if the boy were old enough to get the death penalty, then thought of Ramos, who wouldn't even be able to work as a public defender again once this hit the news. As the token Hispanic at his fancy law firm, any excuse would be enough to say adios to Ramos, just as the company where he had worked as a financial planning consultant had let him go as soon as he was convicted. And Ramos's family— daughter dead, son accused, wife distraught—not many marriages survived the death of a child. If Ramos's did, well, then his wife could always be found dead also—a suicide victim, of course, or so it would seem. Eventually he might kill Ramos, but there were other ways to die and he wanted Ramos to experience that kind of death first, just as he had.

2

If there was one thing that Marti loved almost as much as Momma's fried apple pies, it was paczkis. "Ummm, poonchkeys," Marti said, as she savored the apricot filling. Every year, on Fat Tuesday, Vik's wife fried these Polish pastries that looked like fat doughnuts and tasted wonderful. Vik always brought some in the next day.

"Ummmm," Vik agreed. He was polishing off a custard-filled paczki. There was a dark smudge on his forehead. He had gone to mass before coming to work and received his ashes. Unlike most people she knew, going to church services did not improve his disposition.

Marti decided to try the custard filling, too. As she munched she began reading through the information that had come in on José Martinez.

"So that's it!" she said. "He gave his name as Martinez because that was his aunt's name and he had been living with her when he ran away. His real name is Ortiz."

Vik looked up from his paperwork, frowning. "And?"

"José. He's one of the kids we found in the library."

"This José? He doesn't look the same."

"Well, it's been over four years. He weighs a lot more, and he's got all of those pimples."

She tried not to think too much about the five homeless, throwaway children who had made a temporary home for themselves in the old Carnegie library that winter four years ago. The children had lived there as a family, and foraged as

25

best they could to survive. One of them had witnessed a murder and put himself and the others in harm's way. José had been the youngest and the smallest.

Vik put his elbows on his desk and rubbed his forehead. "Kids," he said. "They never seem to go away. Especially not when you want them to."

Like her, Vik had been afraid of what they would find when they went into the library that cold December night. He had sent her upstairs because he was more concerned about her finding five children dead than the risk of her finding an armed killer alive. Although most adults found Vik's height, and his wiry eyebrows, crooked nose, and almost unblinking winter gray stare intimidating, the children went right to him. That night was the first time since they had begun working together that she had seen Vik smile.

Now he snapped a few pencils in half. "So, what's José been up to since the last time we saw him?"

"He hasn't done much of anything. No gang affiliation, no drugs. Or at least he hasn't been caught. Not much of anything else either. And," she counted, "only six placements interspersed with seven trips to a juvenile facility."

"Why, if he wasn't doing anything criminal?"

"Who knows. I'll put a call in to the most recent caseworker when their offices open."

"Must be nice to have a nine-to-five job."

"Nice and boring," Marti said.

"With all of those placements, there must be something about the kid that's not on paper."

"Well, it doesn't look like he was one for keeping his room clean."

"A lot of parents—and foster parents—would like to have a kid with a problem like that, MacAlister."

"But maybe not any of these."

"And Ramos was different?" Vik suggested.

"Ramos is going to be a real pain."

Vik scowled. "Too bad this town isn't big enough to alienate even a potential politician."

"No town is that big," Marti said. "It can always come back and bite you."

Lieutenant Sikich called Marti at five minutes to eight. "Your boss just called," he said. "He won't be in and I'm in charge. I expect to see you and Jessenovik in five minutes." He hung up before she could reply.

"Sikich!" Vik said. "Damn! Lieutenant Dirkowitz must be a daddy."

For a moment, Marti focused on that. "I hope everything is okay. That baby wasn't due for another three weeks." Then she said, "Dammit Vik, not Sikich again."

"You got any idea of what the policy is on having kids, MacAlister?"

"Maternity leave? Does it include men?" She knew as much about it as he did. "I hope this doesn't mean the lieutenant is going to be gone more than a couple of days."

Lieutenant Francis Sikich had been with the department thirty years too long. He was third in command thanks to circumstances years ago that had been within his control—the old boy network and brownnosing. He was in charge of procurement. His most memorable screw-up was a misplaced order for toilet paper that had them all bringing their own, his most recent the switch to a new telephone system based on the "If it's not broke, fix it," theory. When the second in command retired in December, nobody had considered Sikich as his replacement. The position remained open. And now this. On their way to Sikich's office, they confirmed that Lieutenant Dirkowitz's wife was in the hospital but had not delivered.

Sikich was waiting for them in a windowless room not far from the lieutenant's office, but a significant distance from Dirkowitz's secretary. Marti hoped he felt at home there. The only other time she had to work for him he decided that a command post near their office was in order.

"Not bad," Sikich said. "Seven minutes past eight. But in the future, I expect you to be on time." Sikich had spent two years in the army. The experience had left him with a permanent affectation of military bearing. He sat, stood, and walked ramrod straight. Behind his back, they called him the little general, not because of his height—he was six feet tall—but his personality. When Marti sat down, she leaned to one side, crossed one leg over her knee, propped her elbow on the metal arm of the chair, and rested her chin on her fist.

Sikich stood. "It's the middle of February, people, and already this year we've got sixteen death investigations. Five involving accidents, three suicides, one homicide/suicide, and six homicides, four of which are still open." He raised his eyebrows and stared at them for close to a minute. He was standing so still Marti wondered if he was holding his breath. "And that doesn't include the two cases that occurred yesterday." There was another dramatic pause.

Vik slouched in his chair and clasped his hands behind his head. "Our luck might be improving, sir. The last four cases have alternated, male, female, male, female. Maybe we're establishing a pattern . . . sir."

"If that remark was intended as some kind of a joke, Jessenovik, I am not amused," Sikich said.

"No, sir," Vik agreed. "It was just an observation."

"Well, if it's any indication of the best observations you can come up with, perhaps that is why we don't have a higher rate of closure on these homicides."

Vik didn't offer an answer to that. Score one for Sikich, Marti conceded, although she thought their closure rate was damned good.

"Which brings us to our primary problem," Sikich said. "Joseph Ramos is an attorney at a very prestigious Chicago law firm in addition to being an aldermanic candidate in next month's primary. As such, he is demanding more respect than it seems either of you have given him thus far." Sikich didn't smile as he said that, but Marti sensed an undercurrent of sarcasm.

"It seems that so far, *Mr.* Ramos has contacted our chief, who is also Hispanic, as well as the president of the Lincoln Prairie Mexican-American Business and Civic Association and the chairman of the Lake County Hispanic Political Coordinating Committee. Unlike other ethnic groups"—he looked at Marti as he said this—"the Hispanic community is not without influence. They organize and stick together. And"—this time he looked at Vik—"unlike some of our founding ethnic groups, they are not about to abandon this city. They'll take over everything in the next few years if nobody stops them. So, you two had better get in step with the times and demonstrate a little more savvy when it comes to community—translate that Hispanic—relations."

Marti did not want to see the expression on Vik's face, but she looked at him anyway, aware that his apparent passivity was disguising his anger.

"I advised our *chief* that every consideration would be extended to *Mr.* Ramos and his bereaved family."

"Sir, we are going to conduct a homicide investigation," Vik said, tight-lipped and precise. "Not a public relations campaign."

"And you will do that with the utmost respect for the minority population involved."

Vik didn't say anything else, another indication of the depth of his anger.

"Furthermore, Jessenovik, and you too, MacAlister, I want a complete report that includes everything you have on these most recent deaths on my desk by noon, and a complete summary of all other open cases with the most current information by the end of the day. And since we found the subject—this Lopez kid—"

"Ortiz," Marti said. "José Ortiz."

"Whatever. Since he was with the body, even though we have

not recovered the weapon, I expect that we will have an expeditious resolution and that charges will be filed forthwith."

Marti remained as silent as Vik while they walked back to their office. Vik could say what he wanted to about her being a big-city cop but she had learned how to handle the politics without compromising herself as a peace officer. She would do that now, and damn Ramos, Sikich, Chief Allendo, and anyone else who tried to tell her how to do her job.

After Marti checked the canvass reports again, she and Vik went out to talk with the neighbors who formed the perimeter around the Ramos house. Nobody had seen anything unusual, but it had been cold and windy, and even one woman who usually walked her dog every night had let it go outside unattended. Time and the weather had not been kind to the house on the next block that was directly behind the Ramoses'. White paint peeled from the wood frame, the steps leaned to one side, and holes at the top indicated where the banister had been. The screening had been ripped from the storm door and fluttered in the wind. An elderly Hispanic woman answered the door. She had a shawl wrapped about her shoulders. Marti thought about their most recent hypothermia victim. Concerned that the old woman might not have heat, she asked to come inside.

"*Sí,*" the woman agreed. Too trusting, Marti thought as she entered a hallway where the linoleum was worn and the wallpaper faded. The smells were familiar. Enchiladas, she thought, or maybe burritos. Both could be made without meat.

"Are you all right, little mother?" Marti asked in Spanish.

The woman nodded her head "*Sí, sí.*"

"We can go into the kitchen?"

"*Sí, sí.*"

The house seemed cool to her, not as warm as it should be, but not cold. The kitchen was so clean she could have eaten off any surface. Again, she detected the odor of food, but she wished she could check the small refrigerator and the cabinets.

When questioned about any activity at the Ramos house, the

elderly woman said she had already been asked these questions, but that she had seen nothing except the lights going on and off. She had not thought to tell that to the young officer who came last night. Why would something like that be unusual? she asked. Children lived in that house, children were always running up and down stairs. But she had noticed it, Marti thought. That made it unusual.

Before she left Marti ascertained that the woman owned the house, that she was not familiar with heating subsidy programs or services available to senior citizens. The woman agreed to speak with someone from the township office who could help her.

They were deciding whether to have lunch now or wait until after they interviewed Mrs. Ramos when Dr. Cyprian called. He had just returned from court and would be beginning the Lara autopsy in ten minutes. The state had not released any information to them about Graciela. Perhaps they would learn more about her now.

Carmen Ramos showed them into the company room again. Last night, Marti had asked if Graciela had brought home any books from the library, and if so, where they were. She had been shown into the kitchen. Walls the color of red hot chili peppers had greeted her, the bright red relieved by white cabinets and curtains. The room smelled of baked chicken. A basket filled with apples and pears was on the table and, along with Graciela's partially completed homework, a cup half filled with cocoa. As she remembered that, Marti tried not to think about the body they had found upstairs, or seeing that same young girl on Dr. Cyprian's stainless steel autopsy table.

Now Mrs. Ramos said, "My husband agreed that I could speak with you without his being here, if you would agree to everything being taped."

"No problem," Marti said, and waited while the woman turned the machine on and checked the volume. Then she asked, "Were these the first foster children you've taken in?"

"We've had seven others," Mrs. Ramos said. "José and Graciela were our first teenagers."

"Why did you take them?" Marti asked.

"We can always decide not to accept children, but José and Graciela were hard to place."

"Do you know why?"

"Their age, I suppose, but also, José, he was not easy to deal with. He asked for nothing, destroyed everything that was given to him, and disliked everyone. He never said please or thank you. He very seldom spoke to us at all. All of the children tested us, but José more than any of them."

"How did you feel about that?"

"These are not my children. I did not raise any of them. I cannot even guess at what their lives were like before they came here. The best we can do is accept them. Just keeping them safe and warm, well fed and clothed decently and giving them respect is almost all you can do. Eventually, most of them accept that. But very few trust you. Especially when your home is only one of many places they have lived."

"And Graciela?"

"She was a good girl. Perfect, you might say. Always helpful, always obedient, always pleasant, always mistrustful, always afraid."

"Afraid off what?"

"I don't know. Perhaps of not being wanted. Joseph, my husband, said it was because she had been abused."

Marti thought Mrs. Ramos had good insights about children in the system. What she didn't understand was this emotional detachment from what had happened here, in her home.

"Were José and Graciela friendly toward one another?"

"No. Although Graciela was friendly toward everyone else. José came to us first. When Graciela came, they disliked each other on sight. I have no idea why there was so much animosity between them. It was typical of José, but seemed very unlike Graciela."

"So you don't know of any reason for their attitude toward each other?"

"No. It was there from day one. Not that I ever thought it would lead to this."

"You don't seem too upset about what has happened."

"You learn," Mrs. Ramos said. "They live in your home for a while. They are secretive, distant, mistrustful. You have no control over their lives, the state does, so you . . . remember that."

"Will you continue to take in foster children?"

"Of course."

"Why do you do it?"

"Joseph, my husband, believes it is a good thing to do."

Marti wondered if that meant politically correct, but didn't ask.

"Who did Graciela go to the library with?"

"She went alone. I dropped her off. Ordinarily I would have picked her up, but I had my daughter's basketball game. The library is just four blocks from here. She said she would be back home by eight. I forgot to call and check."

Marti made a note to try to confirm what time Graciela had left the library.

"Did she meet anyone at the library?"

"No, Graciela kept very much to herself. She went to the library because she read a lot and also when she needed information that she couldn't get on the Internet. She was very thorough with her schoolwork."

"How often did she have friends over, or go to a friends' house?"

"Never," Mrs. Ramos said. "You are not listening to me. Graciela was at home most of the time. She did not have any social life, or friends. Very often they become that way. It is easier than always having to leave people you have come to like."

Marti nodded. That made sense. She would have to check it out anyway, but it did make sense.

*   *   *

Marti went to the high school next. The counselor she was referred to did not seem at all pleased to see her. Miss O'Reilly was tiny, barely five feet tall, with close-cropped dark hair with a few gray strands here and there. She had a pinched expression on her face, as if she were in pain.

"I was not informed that there would be any interviews with the police today."

O'Reilly took her place behind a desk that was clear of everything but a blotter, her name plate, a pen in a holder, and a small calendar. Her office was so neat, and looked so well organized, that Marti felt as if she were disturbing something by sitting down. There was one shelf of books. Marti wasn't sitting close enough to read the titles, but she was willing to bet they were in alphabetical order.

"Miss O'Reilly, I'm Detective MacAlister. I'm sure you know by now that Graciela Lara was apparently the victim of a homicide last night."

The woman nodded and folded her hands at the edge of her desk.

"What can you tell me about Graciela?"

"Not much, I'm afraid."

"Did you ever see her, speak with her?"

"Once, as an incoming student, to set up her class schedule. I don't actually recall doing that, but I did check my records."

"I see. Then I guess you can't help me."

"I don't appreciate your assumption that I do not have time for the students." Obviously offended, Miss O'Reilly sat rigid in her chair. Her spine was so straight that Marti wondered if sitting like that to express her displeasure caused back problems.

"Officer MacAlister, do you have any idea of what my caseload is like here?"

"With thirty-five hundred students and three counselors? Yes, I do. My daughter is a sophomore and you're her counselor, too. And you haven't met with Joanna at all this year. The difference is, my daughter has me, she has family to discuss school-related issues with. Graciela was in foster care. She had been in God knows how many schools before this one, and she did not have anyone to talk with on a consistent basis. She should have been more closely monitored. Did you keep track of her attendance, her grades, anything?"

"I will not sit here and be interrogated about how I do my job."

Marti sat back and waited to see what O'Reilly would say next. She wondered how long the woman could sit there, so close to the edge of her chair, without having a muscle spasm.

"Do you have any idea of how many Gracielas we have? How many homeless students? Over a hundred. How many illegals? We don't know. Do you know how many deserving students there are who need and can benefit from my attention?"

Marti assumed that meant that not only Graciela, the homeless, and illegals, were somehow not deserving of Miss O'Reilly's attention, but her daughter Joanna, as well.

"What makes a student deserving of attention?" she asked.

"Good grades, a willingness to be guided . . ."

That ruled out Joanna.

". . . academic excellence, extracurricular activities, good citizenship . . ."

"In other words, the kids who need you don't qualify?"

"I've asked one of Graciela's teachers, Mrs. Barrios, to come in," O'Reilly said, still rigid but ignoring Marti's last comment. "Also the student who has the locker next to Graciela's. There's only one; Graciela's locker is at the end of the row."

"That's it?"

"Graciela did not participate in anything. There have been no requests for grief counseling from any of the students, and usually there are at least a few who know the deceased well enough to feel badly about their death."

O'Reilly gave her a self-satisfied look, as if lack of student concern justified her own indifference.

"I would like to see each of them separately, and alone, in this office or whatever space is available that will provide privacy."

Now there was a look of affront. "Privacy."

"This is police business, Miss O'Reilly, not an extracurricular event."

When Miss O'Reilly vacated her office, she walked stiffly, with the same pained expression on her face that she had arrived with.

Mrs. Barrios was also short. Unlike Miss O'Reilly, she was plump and seemed friendly.

"Officer MacAlister. It is such a pleasure to meet Joanna's mother. She was in my college-placement English class last year. She always had something interesting to add to the class. Her observations, especially about people, about life, were mature and insightful. She thinks about things, analyzes them. That's always good to see in a student. But you're here to talk to me about Graciela."

Marti nodded. She was pleased with what Mrs. Barrios had said about Joanna.

"I'd like to be of some help, but I'm afraid the only reason I'm here is because I was Graciela's only Hispanic teacher."

"What can you tell me about her?" Mrs. Barrios's forthrightness gave more credence to what she had just said about Joanna.

"I teach communications, an umbrella definition that includes a variety of subjects. English, reading, speech, occasionally drama. There's usually some public speaking, debates, class presentations in most of my classes. Graciela did not like any of that. In fact, we struck a deal. She completed these assignments as required—which to me says a lot about her character and her determination—in return I let her sit in the back of the classroom, not away from the other students as much as . . . not feeling scrutinized by them. Occasionally I would substitute a written report for an oral assignment if I thought she was really going to get stressed out over it. And I always complimented and encouraged her—she thrived on it but it was deserved. She did exemplary work."

"Did she have many friends?"

"Many? 'Any' would be a better choice of words. She came and went and tried to attract as little attention as possible. Whenever I saw her in the halls, her head was down, no eye contact with anyone. I wish they would put something in their records so I would know they were in foster care, or had been abused, or were in the juvenile system, whatever. I guess that's some violation of their rights. But, if I had known, I have several other students in foster homes who have confided in me. Graciela might have been able to make friends with them."

"Do you know José Ortiz?"

"No. I know he was a student here. And now I know they lived in the same foster home."

"Is there anything else you can tell me about Graciela?"

"She did come to me sometimes, after class, but only because she needed me to explain something about an assignment that she didn't quite understand. She wouldn't call attention to herself by raising her hand."

The student who came in next was so wired that Marti wondered if she was on some kind of uppers. She was tall, so thin she looked anorexic, wearing too much makeup in Marti's opinion, and, Marti was sure, a skirt so short that it didn't meet the dress code. As she sat down, the girl tossed her head, and her long blond hair, expertly cut and styled, shifted and settled on her shoulders.

"How well did you know Graciela Lara?"

"I didn't. My locker just happened to be next to hers, so I saw her a couple of times a day."

"Did you ever speak to each other?"

"No. Why would we?"

The girl was kind of bouncing in her chair from the waist up, her upper body bobbing up and down as she if there was music playing that only she could hear. Her pupils looked dilated.

"Did you know José Ortiz?"

"Not to talk to. But . . . there was this boy . . ." She described him. When Marti agreed that the description fit José, she said, "Then he's the one who was always hanging around in the hall waiting to talk to her. She walked right by him. I mean it was obvious she couldn't stand him, but he sure did have a thing for her."

"Did you ever see them around school together? In the cafeteria? Waiting for transportation?"

"Look, no offense, but I don't care what those illegals do. They shouldn't even be here. I stay away from them. I asked to have my locker changed but they go strictly in alphabetical order. And it didn't do any good when my parents complained. At least she didn't try to break into my locker or steal anything." As she spoke, she bounced, patted her hair, smoothed her skirt, and twisted the rings on her fingers. "You're Joanna MacAlister's mother, aren't you? I think that's something, you being a real cop and all. And Joanna, she's awesome on the court. I don't go to softball games, too much dust. We even invited her to be on the yearbook staff, but she wasn't interested. Too intellectual for her, I guess. She is just an athlete. Anything else?"

Marti wanted to ask her what she was on. Instead she said "No."

"That's it?"

When Marti said that was all, the girl jumped up, grabbed her purse and her books, and rushed from the room.

Miss O'Reilly returned just as Marti was vacating the chair behind her desk.

"What did you say that girl's name was," Marti asked, even though she knew.

"Why, that's Brianna Laretson. Brianna is an outstanding student. National Honor Society, student council, yearbook staff, French Club, Drama Club . . ."

"You need to have her tested for drugs," Marti said. "Find

out what she's on. I'm not a narc, but I'd guess uppers."

"Why, how dare you!" O'Reilly said. "Even if you are a police officer. What gives you the right to make such a despicable accusation. Why, this is, this is—"

"Just a suggestion, ma'am, but to be on the safe side, I will be mentioning this to the principal."

"How dare you," Miss O'Reilly said. Her voice shook with outrage. "Brianna Laretson is one of our most outstanding students."

"Yes, ma'am," Marti said.

She left the high school with a slightly altered opinion of the student body and a better understanding of what it was like for Joanna to be considered "just an athlete" by some of the students, as if that made her somehow inferior. Then she thought of what Mrs. Barrios said, and felt better.

"Still nothing from the state on Graciela," Vik said, as they sat in the Barrister having a late lunch.

Marti rubbed her hands together as she prepared to dig into the thick burger and seasoned fries. Joanna, having lost one parent in the line of duty, was determined to hold on to her mother. Always efficient, Joanna seized on those few things she might be able to control, what Marti ate, which in turn controlled her blood pressure, and arteries, among other things. Or so Joanna hoped. Fatty foods were a no-no at home. Joanna had even convinced Momma to join her campaign.

"Mm-hmm," she said as she bit into the rare, juicy beef.

"Mmmmm," Vik agreed, his mouth filled with Swedish waffles and strawberry syrup. He invariably ate something gooey following an autopsy.

They were sitting side by side in a booth with their backs to the wall watching the other patrons as well as the front door. "Maybe we should talk to Denise Stevens," Vik said. "She runs juvenile probation. She must know someone who can speed things up."

"I do have a few questions for her," Marti said. "The laws

affecting juveniles have changed so much, and I haven't had to keep up. Their records aren't even sealed anymore. According to Dr. Cyprian, Graciela had an abortion. When this goes to trial, can that be disclosed? I don't think female minors have the same protection under the law as adult females whether they're living or dead. Will José be eligible for the death penalty? The court has discretion in treating juveniles as adults, and the state's moratorium on executions doesn't affect sentencing."

"I don't think the kid has a chance," Vik said.

"What if he didn't kill her? Sometimes people do take an instant dislike to each other."

"Like me and Sikich. I would like to kill him."

"Have you got any plans to get those reports to him that he requested?"

"Not anytime soon," Vik said. Red syrup dripped on his plate as he raised his fork to his mouth. "Maybe I'll e-mail what's been out there since yesterday, before I update it."

"We do have to prioritize," Marti agreed. "With such a heavy caseload and six open cases."

"Right now, we need to know if José and Graciela have any history. Give Denise a call when we get back."

A man at a nearby table caught Marti's attention as he started to rise, changed his mind, and sat back down.

"There was no struggle," Vik said. He nudged her and nodded toward the man she was watching. "Which could indicate someone she knew."

"But only one wound. Deliberate. Not something done in anger." The man motioned to the waitress. "And she left what she was doing to go upstairs. As if she was interrupted."

"I suppose that if José did leave the window open, someone could have come in," Vik conceded. "But if they did there should be footprints."

"And nothing is missing," Marti said. The waitress gave the man his check. She watched as he scanned it.

"That could mean anything," Vik said. "A deliberate attack, an interrupted burglary. A sudden impulse by a kid who was always mad about something. Speaking of which"—Vik checked his watch. "The Ramos kids will be home from school soon. I suppose Ramos wants those interviews taped too."

"Control," she said. The man was taking his time getting up. Why was he looking around first? "And Ramos is looking for something else to complain about." It was annoying to have both Sikich and Ramos looking over her shoulder. "And the kids will be too self-conscious to say anything if it's being recorded." She remembered the way Ramos and his wife had looked at each other, then their children, last night. Was there something Ramos didn't want them to know?

Marti tensed as the man stood up. She unsnapped her holster, then watched as he paid the cashier, pushed open the door, and went outside.

"At least they shipped our mad sword swinger to Chester," Vik said.

Marti rotated her shoulders to ease the tension. She was glad that the man was being sent to the only maximum-security mental-health facility in the state, and also the farthest from Lincoln Prairie, but they were cops, always a target and always exposed. There were too many other mad sword swinger types out there and this was just one more reminder.

Adrian stood on a side street near the driveway at the back entrance to the high school and watched as several dozen noisy, chattering teenagers came out of the double doors. Some headed for the parking lot. Others loitered, waiting until it was time for practice to begin for various sports activities. Several of the girls began talking on cell phones. Another took out a pack of cigarettes and passed it around. MacAlister's daughter was easy to spot. She didn't smoke; one long auburn braid hung down her back, and she was taller than the other girls and most of the boys.

He had watched her before and never seen her alone. Today he crossed between the cars parked in the schools driveway and walked toward the group she was standing with. He was wearing a woman's coat, and it was cold enough to wear a fur-trimmed hat low and a multicolored knitted scarf high.

"Excuse me," he said, when he was close enough for the MacAlister girl to hear him. He spoke in a quiet voice, but a higher pitch, like a woman, and tried not to attract everyone's attention, although he felt as if they were all looking at him.

MacAlister's daughter looked at him with calm, hazel eyes. There was something about her that made him uneasy.

"I'm looking for my daughter," he said. "Alisha Anderson."

The MacAlister girl raised her eyebrows but said nothing. A girl wearing glasses came closer and said, "There's nobody here by that name." She stared at him, hands on hips, as if she were daring him to say something else.

Bitch, he thought. He fingered the switchblade in his pocket. No respect for adults. Rude, like most kids today.

The MacAlister girl continued to look him.

"Thanks," he said. He would have liked to say something else.

As he turned and headed for the front of the building he heard one of the girls say, "I wonder what she really wanted?"

The girl who had spoken to him said, "Uuuugly. I don't think she's anyone's mother. Looked like a man to me."

"Keep an eye out and let me know if you see her again. Let's tell the others and alert security." It was the MacAlister girl. And she was talking loud enough to make sure he heard her. And from the way she had looked at him, she would not forget his face.

"Oh, Joanna. You take everything so seriously."

"Yeah, right," a boy said. "Like we need someone with a death wish coming on campus and shooting up the place or blowing us up with a bomb."

Adrian tried to act as if he hadn't heard them. It was all he could do not to walk faster.

When Marti and Vik returned to the Ramos house, Lupe Torres, a young Hispanic officer who worked as a community liaison, met them on the porch. Marti had known Lupe since she graduated from the academy and had watched her mature into a street-savvy, compassionate, no-nonsense cop. She enjoyed working with Lupe.

"The mother seemed apprehensive about us talking with her children," Marti explained. "Since you know the family . . ."

"No problem," Lupe said. She wasn't in uniform. "Having a sourpuss like Vik asking you questions is enough to make anyone nervous, and Joe is one of our more militant voices, as you've probably already found out."

"Sometimes you need troublemakers like him," Vik said.

Marti was surprised. He hadn't liked Sikich's attitude any better than she did, but he didn't like cowboys either, lose cannons who were cops or politicians.

Lupe grinned. She had a wide, lopsided smile that occasionally made Vik forget to scowl, but not today.

When Mrs. Ramos showed them to the company room again, Lupe said, "Oh, Carmen, can't we just go up to their rooms? And we won't need that tape recorder."

Carmen Ramos hesitated. Lupe said, "I'm sure Joe won't mind. Should we call him and ask?"

Mrs. Ramos nodded and Lupe made the call. "See," she said, after she spoke with him. "It's okay. Here, he wants to talk to you." There was no mistaking Mrs. Ramos's relief as she listened to her husband. "Yes," she said. "Yes. Okay. Fine." Then Vik announced that he would wait downstairs. Mrs. Ramos gave him a look that implied she didn't want to entertain him in their absence, but she sat down with a resigned if pained expression on her face.

Francisco Ramos was thirteen and still waiting for the growth spurt that would increase his height and redistribute his weight. He sat on the unmade bed with his back against the headboard, and Marti took the chair at his desk. Lupe sat Indian style on the floor. Marti looked about the room, saw a soccer ball, a uniform shirt hanging on the closet doorknob, a dozen posters, all of soccer players, boxers, or cars, and lots of magazines about the same subjects. She also noticed some clothes that had been shoved under the bed in an attempt to tidy up the room.

"My son plays soccer," she began. That wasn't a lie. What she didn't add was that Theo didn't enjoy playing soccer and only did so when he was required to at school. Since she didn't see any trophies or awards, she added, "He's not very good," which wasn't a lie either.

Francisco cocked his head to one side and said, "How old is he?"

"Eleven."

"I didn't like playing that much when I was eleven either. The parents argue with the coaches too much and yell at the referees."

"I'll have to remember not to do that."

"It's not so bad when you get older. You kind of ignore it."

"Did José play soccer?"

He shifted so that he was sitting farther away from her and looked about the room as if he wanted to leave. Marti waited. Francisco made wide circles on a navy blue blanket. "He was here longer than some of the others, but he was going to leave, sooner or later. They all do."

"How do you feel about that?" She didn't clarify whether she meant José leaving, or his being there.

Francisco shrugged. Marti's kids did that too. She found it annoying. She thought it must be some kind of universal sign, like a handshake or a high five, but she wasn't sure what it meant, or even if it meant anything, or if the meaning was always the same.

"My dad says it's no fun, not having a home or a family," Francisco said. "Maybe that's why José didn't like any of us."

"How do you know he didn't like you?"

"He was mad all the time. He never talked to anybody unless he had to. And he wouldn't play games or anything, not even on the Playstation. The last kid we had here played with me on the Playstation all the time."

"How did he get along with Graciela?"

The circles Francisco was making on the blanket became smaller, then he stopped. "He didn't like her either."

"How could you tell?"

"When nobody was looking, he gave her the finger. And sometimes he called her the B word when nobody could hear him."

Micaela Ramos was sitting at a dressing table and looking in the mirror as she brushed her hair. Gilt-framed pictures of her Quinceañera covered most of one wall. Marti could not imagine her athletic daughter sleeping in a room like this one. A ruffled bedspread with bouquets of tiny lavender flowers on a white background matched the canopy above the bed. There were lace dollies on the bureau and nightstand, and a lamp made from a doll with a frilly lavender dress and a lampshade to match. The walls and carpet were a deeper shade of purple. Aside from that, the room was a mess, almost as bad as José's.

Micaela put down the brush and swiveled around on the stool. "Hi, Lupe. I suppose you want to talk to me about what happened to Graciela."

"Kind of," Lupe said. Again, she sat on the floor. Since there wasn't a desk, and the bed was unmade, Marti asked if she could sit there.

"Yeah. Why not." Micaela seemed surprised that she asked.

The mattress was so soft she sank into it. She couldn't help contrasting this room with Graciela's room. But then, as Mrs. Ramos said, they were not her children. They were visitors in a guest room, much as she was a visitor in the company room.

"Are you Lupe's boss?"

"No. We're friends."

"And you brought Lupe so I wouldn't be nervous, or so that Daddy would let you talk to me without Mama being here."

"Yes," Marti said.

"Have you arrested José yet?"

"Should we?"

"He was here with her, wasn't he? Alone. He knew Mama and Francisco would be at my game and that Daddy would be away, too. And that story about having to get his sweater was a lie. I don't know where he went but I do know that José didn't have any friends."

"Why do you suppose that was?"

"Because he didn't like anybody, not even himself."

"Did he like Graciela?"

"All the boys liked Graciela."

"Did they have any particular reason to like her?"

Micaela raised carefully plucked eyebrows. "You mean was she putting out? Miss goody-goody? No way."

"Then why did they like her?"

"I have no idea, except that most boys are dumb."

Marti interpreted that to mean that the boys in question preferred Graciela to Micaela.

Micaela swung around to the mirror and picked up the brush again.

"Of course José and Graciela already knew each other when they came here. Not that they were friends or anything. I don't think Graciela liked José at all, not that she'd ever let on."

"Then how did you know?"

"Graciela was always making like she was helpful and friendly and nice, but when nobody was around, she was different. And she called José *disparatado* and *estúpido*."

Foolish or crazy, and stupid, Marti translated to herself. She wondered if that was because of his behavior now or from what Graciela knew of him from the past.

Marti walked Lupe to her car. It was cold outside, another gray winter day. Large, moist snowflakes drifted down. Lake-effect snow. This close to the lake it would stick and freeze, but maybe it would stop soon without much accumulation. "Is that really what they're like?" she asked.

"The Ramoses are a very traditional Hispanic family, with feminine women and macho men," Lupe said. "I'm not sure Joe could handle a woman who made it too obvious that she had a thought of her own. But don't get me wrong. Carmen is a very smart lady, and she does think for herself. She's just always had one hell of a time making decisions."

"It doesn't sound like Micaela and Francisco are too happy about having temporary strangers moving in and out."

"I'm sure the kids in foster care aren't too happy about it either. Francisco and Micaela are stuck in that irritating, self-absorbed stage as well as the center of their parents' universe." Lupe hesitated. Marti hoped she wasn't going to mention the mad sword swinger. So far, everyone was too busy thinking that his sword could have been pointed at them to say much.

"I hear you two are stuck with Sikich again."

Relieved, Marti shook her head. "That baby had better get here soon."

"I don't know," Lupe said. "I heard she's having a problem with the pregnancy."

"Then I hope everything turns out okay—ASAP." Marti liked Lieutenant Dirkowitz. He was a good man to work for. She hoped she'd still be in his employ when he returned.

As they drove back to the precinct, Vik asked, "What did Denise say about helping us get those records?"

"I had to leave a message. She's in the field today."

Sikich came into their office before they had a chance to remove their coats. "So, what have you got on the Ramos case?"

"The victim's name was Lara," Vik reminded him. "Graciela Lara."

"Yeah, right. Tell that to Ramos."

Marti hung up her coat. At least Sikich had got one name right. "We will, the next time we see him." Ramos was coming in to be interviewed at five.

"What about these other cases?" Sikich said. "We can't just ignore them, but we have to keep Ramos—and the *chief*—happy. I don't think you two can handle all of this. I'm going to assign—"

"Lupe Torres," Vik said. "She's worked with us before."

"Torres?" Sikich looked at them as if one of them had just passed gas. "A female Hispanic uniform with less than five years on the job working homicide?"

"What of it?" Vik was getting belligerent. "She's worked with us before. We don't have to break her in. And she works with this minority community you're so concerned about."

"I don't see how that qualifies her to work homicide."

"She knows the Ramoses," Marti said. "Ran interference for us so we could interview the kids without parental guidance."

Sikich stood there, mouth open. "Oh," he said finally. "Well, then, she can work with you on the Ramos case, but as for the others—"

"We'll work overtime," Vik said. "Be faster and easier than bringing someone up to speed and supervising them."

Marti yanked off her boots. Not tonight she wasn't working overtime. It was Valentine's Day. She had a surprise for her husband, Ben, and they were going into the city. There was no way she was going to hang around here any longer than she had to tonight.

Joseph Ramos called at two minutes past five to let them know that he would not be there for another hour. Marti said half a dozen choice cuss words after she hung up, speaking in English, Spanish, and Polish. Then she called Ben. Thank God he was a fireman and paramedic and understood delays and unexpected schedule changes.

"The boys and I are working on an itinerary for a road trip anyway," he said.

Intrigued, she asked if they were planning to traipse around in the snow.

"No, I think we'll save this for spring, and I think we'll just pack up and go."

"Sounds like a plan," she said, silently cussing out Ramos again because she couldn't go home.

When Ramos did show up, it was half past six. Marti was not in the best of moods and decided to let Vik handle the interview.

"Evening," Vik said.

"You've talked with my wife and my children," Ramos said.

"Yes."

"Is there anything they said that requires clarification?"

"No, not that I can think of."

Ramos didn't take off his coat. Marti hoped that meant he didn't plan to stay long but wished she had the time to detain him.

"Why do you take in foster children?" Vik asked.

"Because they need a place to stay."

"Of course they do, but why your place?"

"Because Hispanic children have fewer options than Caucasian children," Ramos said without hesitation. "Proportionately there are more Hispanic children in the juvenile justice system even though the majority of cases referred to juvenile court involve Caucasians."

When Vik held up his hand to interrupt, Ramos continued without pause. "Hispanic juveniles are adjudicated more often and referred to adult court more often. They are incarcerated for periods of time twice that of Caucasian offenders. They are referred less frequently to rehabilitative programs."

As Ramos took a breath, Vik said, "Why do *you* and *your wife* take in these children?"

"Because if we do, maybe other Hispanic families will also. They need to at least see a family that isn't dysfunctional."

"Good." Vik nodded. "What was your relationship with José?"

"There wasn't one. José was very alienated, very defiant, very oppositional."

"What effect did that have on your family?"

"There was no effect."

Marti would have liked to disagree but said nothing. Vik was on a roll.

"How did that make you feel, Mr. Ramos, not being able to reach José?"

Ramos didn't answer right away. "I didn't take him in to reach him. I took him in because he had no other place to go." He seemed to be choosing his words. "I didn't expect to be able to undo anything that the system had already done to these children. I wanted them to see an alternative way of life, a more normal, ordinary way of life. I hoped that would help them realize they had more choices when they had to make decisions on their own."

Marti saw a lot of what Ramos's wife had said in what he was saying now. Having spoken with Lupe, she thought maybe it was more a matter of Carmen influencing him than vice versa.

"What about Graciela?" Vik asked.

"She made my wife cry," he said.

"Why? What did she do?"

"Oh, it wasn't anything she did, not Graciela. It was what she didn't do. Carmen was concerned about her. Graciela would have ceased being a ward of the state in less than a year and be sent out on her own. She had two more years of high school. She was very bright but it seemed unlikely that she would ever make it to graduation, let alone college. And . . ." He hesitated, rubbed the back of his neck as if he were tired, then said, "Carmen didn't think Graciela had a snowball's chance in hell of surviving, and there was nothing she could do to change that, and that upset her."

Vik poured a cup of coffee. "What about José and Graciela?" He offered a cup to Ramos, who declined.

"You mean do I think José killed her? He was angry enough to. He probably had enough self-hatred to. But they had very little to do with each other. José kept to himself. Why would he harm her?"

That, Marti agreed, was the question.

Ramos was silent for a moment, then said, "We are given information when they come to us, whatever the state thinks we need to know. But only the child knows the details, the reality of his past. We can only see the results." He paused again. "So who knows. Maybe I should be grateful that it isn't my daughter, or my wife, or all of us who are dead today.

There's always that risk." The expression on his face suggested that this was the first time he had thought about that. "Of course statistically," he retreated again, "juvenile crime is down. Our perceptions are enhanced by sensationalism and the media, but juvenile crime rates are down significantly, and the rates for Hispanics are among the lowest of all."

By the time Ramos left, Marti had revised her opinion of him from pompous pain-in-the-ass politician to pompous pain-in-the-ass politician but possibly decent human being. Given his personality, she was almost certain her opinion of him would change again.

Before Marti could leave for home, she got a call from Ben. There was a major fire burning out of control in a neighboring town to the west. Lincoln Prairie was providing backup for the towns that had responded to the emergency. Ben was home, but on standby. There would be no trip to the city tonight. It was snowing again anyway, although she had no idea of what the accumulation might be.

When she arrived home, Trouble, their guard dog, had tamped down a trench in the snow along the six-foot-high chain-link fence.

"Good girl," she said as Trouble came over to her, alert but wagging her tail. She gave her a treat. "Good girl." Tail wagging, she followed her into the house.

Trouble was a working dog, not a pet. She and the house alarms were part of a security system that Marti knew was necessary but she wished she didn't have to have. When her best friend, Sharon, and Sharon's teenaged daughter, Lisa, moved into the apartment above their garage last fall, Trouble's territory had been extended to include that part of the yard. Sharon and Lisa could not go near Trouble though. Not even the neighbors could come near her. Trouble's family consisted of her, Ben, Momma, and three kids. Her job was to protect them. She did not recognize or accept anyone else. She was trained to attack and to disarm. She was a quiet, gentle dog, and intelligent. But anyone other than her family who came near that fence knew that Trouble was all business with strangers. Maybe she couldn't protect her children from all harm, but even if this house had to become a fortress, they would be safe in their own home. As soon as they were inside, Trouble began her inspection of each room.

The house was quiet when Marti entered. The kitchen was in shadows with only the light in the range hood turned on. She stopped and listened, heard the television in the den, then the sounds of her son, Theo, and Ben's son, Mike, laughing. She checked the stove. It was still warm and there was a casserole in the microwave. Then she checked her mail. There was another one of those letters, memos sent out by the Chicago department to advise her of subjects released from jail who she had been instrumental in convicting. Johnny used to call the released convicts the Whitmores for two brothers who had shot one of his partners in the back. She would think of the people on the lists as the mad sword swingers, at least for now, until someone worse replaced him. There were only four names. She couldn't remember them or anything about their cases and hoped their memories of her were also long forgotten. Anyone whom Johnny, her deceased first husband, had been involved with was also included. That list had dwindled in the four years since he died. The names listed for Johnnie, Jefferson Wilson and Adrian Quinn, didn't mean anything to her either.

Ben came into the room. "Hi." He took the letter, read it, then took her into his arms, smoothed her hair, then kissed her. He was a big man, solid, muscular, and taller than she was. He made her feel safe, secure, something she had never acknowledged needing until after she met him.

"Anyone here you're concerned about?" he asked.

"No."

"You sure?"

"I can't even remember them."

"Then they probably don't remember you either."

Even though the odds were slim that any of them had wasted any time thinking about her while they were incarcerated, she always felt a little apprehensive for about a week after the letters arrived.

"It's that guy with the sword," Ben said. "But a little fear is a healthy thing in our line of work."

She hugged him. It was good to have someone who didn't need her to be strong, the way Johnny had.

He led her into the dining room. There were candles on the table, a centerpiece of red roses, and a bouquet of heart-shaped balloons. "The kids and I had to come up with this on short notice, so the menu is . . . kind of interesting."

He seated her at the table and brought in the casserole dish. "Joanna has prepared this special vegetable casserole that includes broccoli and squash."

She made a face.

"I know, not one of your favorites, but it's got some vitamin or other that she thinks is important." He went back to the kitchen, returning with a large bowl. "The boys made a fruit salad and only ate half of it. The fruit came from cans, except for the jar of maraschino cherries and of course they added sugar and whipped cream. But no Jell-O. Momma Lydia made the biscuits. I stuck with baked potatoes and steaks with sauteed mushrooms and onions in a wine sauce."

They ate with a Roberta Flack album playing in the background.

"You're too quiet tonight," Ben said. "It's those kids, isn't it?"

"I remember José when he was a little boy with this makeshift family of children. Nobody, not even their families, wanted them. One of them, Georgie, rummaged through a Salvation Army bin to a find birthday present for his sister. A yellow sweater. Too big, but her favorite color."

"Do you know what happened to the others?"

"No, and I don't want to know. I saw Padgett a year or so ago. He was living with his mother. She's an alcoholic, but the kid loves her. Denise did some things that might have helped them, but what chance do they have? What chance do any of them have?"

"It'll eat at you until you find out about them," Ben said. He covered her hands with his own. "And then it will break your heart, but there's a lot of that in what we do. Our world is not kind to children, Marti. And it keeps filtering down. The court, the system, the school, the family, until the child stands alone."

There was such sadness in his voice that Marti leaned over and squeezed his hand. It was her turn to comfort Ben. She liked that.

Adrian forced the lock on the back door of the van, climbed inside, then secured the hatchback. He lay on the floor, partially under the rear seat, and waited. He had checked out this make and model at a dealership. The glass was tinted, so even if someone could make out a form or shape when they looked inside, it would be difficult to tell what it was. If they approached on the driver's side, he was positioned so they would not see him at all unless they opened the side door.

He had spent almost thirteen years in prison planning his revenge. It had taken a lot of thought to decide on a fitting punishment, to decide how to kill these people without their deaths being similar or traceable to him. Now that he was out, even though it was just a matter of locating them, and adjusting the timing to coincide with their routines, carrying out his plans had not been as easy as he thought. There were things he hadn't thought of, such as getting into Ramos's house last night without leaving footprints in the snow. So far, luck was with him. Getting to Judge Toner's house unobserved so early this morning, going through a window so he could disable the car would have been much more difficult if the weather hadn't kept people inside.

There were other things that he hadn't thought about yet, things he might not think about, things that would make taking care of the rest of those on his list difficult too. But being able to overcome these unexpected obstacles was a sign that he would succeed in killing all of them, just as he would succeed tonight.

During his trial, Judge Toner had overruled most of Ramos's objections, allowed questionable evidence to be admitted, accepted the jury's guilty verdict. She had not disguised her pleasure when delivering the maximum sentence allowed. Tonight Judge Margaret Toner would understand the full meaning of a living death. Tonight Judge Margaret Toner's husband of forty years would die.

Charles Toner headed for the parking garage in downtown Chicago with a feeling of relief. He had not been feeling well all day. He was coming down with the flu. If this dinner meeting hadn't been a regular weekly event, if he hadn't had a report to give tonight, he would have gone home right from work.

As he stepped inside the parking garage elevator and caught his breath, he wiped sweat from his forehead again. It was fifteen degrees outside and snowing and he was sweating. As soon as he got home he would take a hot shower to relieve the achiness, then take whichever of Margaret's many over-the-counter medications she considered appropriate. The upside of being married to a hypochondriac confined to a wheelchair was that although she was seldom sick herself, she was very good at managing everyone else's minor complaints.

The ache in his arm began creeping across his back and chest as he got into the van. At least it wasn't much more difficult to drive this than it was to drive his car. This morning had been a hell of a time for a damned near new car to die and have to be towed. With luck it would be back at home when he got there. There hadn't been time to check with the mechanic. He barely made it to work by nine this morning. A full schedule of clients, a meeting at five with a state senator and his aide, and this dinner at the Athletic Club had kept him on the run. And all the while these flu symptoms creeping up on him until now he felt more like vomiting than driving.

He exited on Jackson, headed east, and turned on Michigan Avenue, bypassing traffic on the Dan Ryan through the heart of the Loop. Not that things would be moving slowly this late, not unless there had been an accident, but so that he could decide whether or not to just stay in the city for the night. By the time he paused at the traffic light at Michigan and Ontario, his stomach felt queasy. Just the ginger and lime they had seasoned that salmon with, he decided. As much as he always enjoyed that, he should have had soup. As the light changed from red to green, he thought of Margaret. She enjoyed making a fuss over him. She would just love having him home tonight. It made her feel good to be in good health despite that wheelchair, and see others who could walk but were sick.

As he turned the wheel and made the turn onto Ontario, he felt a sharp pain that extended from his shoulder to the middle of his chest. Maybe he should go to the hospital. No, that would alarm Margaret, and besides, she knew enough about illnesses to take care of him, and she would like being able to compare similar, if imaginary, symptoms with him. There would be that endless chatter. As he thought about that, an impromptu visit to the hospital seemed a little less like a bad idea—except for the length of time he'd have to wait to be seen.

Suddenly chilled even though he was perspiring, Charles turned up the heat. He felt so cold, that bone-deep cold that only total submersion in hot water could alleviate. If only his shoulders didn't hurt. He passed the juncture where cars veered west toward O'Hare, and then the exit where I-94 merged with I-294. Within twenty minutes he would be home. He put in a tape as a distraction, *The Art of Healing* by Bill Moyers—not something he had chosen himself, a gift from Margaret. He drove along, soothed by the sound of a human voice rather than by whatever Moyers was saying. By the time he reached the Route 22 exit, he was wondering again if he shouldn't have turned east at Park Avenue and gone to Highland Park Hospital. Instead he headed west to Route 45 and his house in Lincolnshire.

By the time he got there he felt so exhausted he wondered how he was going to get out of the car. Maybe he would just lean on the horn. Using the remote, he opened the garage door, drove in, then closed it. Home. Thank God he was home. Margaret would be waiting for him inside. She would know what do for this flu.

"Good evening, Mr. Toner," a voice said behind him. He collapsed over the steering wheel as the pain in his chest intensified until he could neither see nor breathe.

The Toner house was east of the golf course. Once Adrian was certain the judge's husband was dead, he made his way to the nearby forest preserve. The sidewalks were clear, but it was beginning to snow. By the time there was enough accumulation for him to leave footprints he was too far away from the house for anyone to notice. It was so cold he didn't even come across anyone walking a dog. He followed a trail as far as Deerfield Road, then walked in a jagged east-south pattern toward the city. It took several hours but he didn't even feel tired. Those daily prison workouts to build his endurance were paying off. Buses were running when he reached Evanston, and when he reached the Chicago city limits, he caught a train. He would stop for breakfast, catch a few hours' sleep when he got back to his apartment, then review his plans for his next victim before going out again.

He was not pleased with the way Mr. Toner had died. No suffering, not knowing who had spoken to him or why. He had intended for him to remain helpless in that van, knowing that he would die. When he found out the judge was confined to a wheelchair, and realized how devoted her husband was to her, how much time he spent with her at home, how he took her places in the van on the weekends, it pleased him to know how lost, how bereft she would be without him. But he also wanted her to think about how close to her he was as he died, and how long it took, so that she could feel useless, and helpless, and guilty.

He must have scared Mr. Toner to death. There was satisfaction in that. In fact, the more he thought about it, the more it seemed as if luck had been with him. Now nobody would wonder why Toner hadn't just got out of the van instead of sitting there with the engine running until the fumes built up enough to overcome him. Adrian smiled. Yes, once again, his luck had been good.

3

Marti and Vik met with Denise Stevens for breakfast at the Sunrise Restaurant right after roll call. Vik suggested that they sit at a round table in the corner and Marti sat next to him, with her back to the wall. Marti noted that even in winter, Denise managed to wear hats that drew attention to her face. Today's was a roller-brimmed green felt with a scarf that tied under her chin. Like Marti, Denise was what Momma called healthy. She was about Marti's height but fifteen pounds heavier. Unlike Marti, she was not comfortable with her size. The hats drew attention away from her hips to her face and those strong, generous features that God sometimes favored African American women with, that made Denise so attractive; full lips—that space between the teeth that Ben thought was sexy—and wide eyes, long lashes, high cheekbones and prominent brows.

"No baby yet," Marti reported. "They say Dirkowitz hasn't left the hospital. I've got Momma and her church sisters praying."

"Another day with Sikich and we'll all be praying," Vik said. "I might even go to morning mass again. This Ortiz case has really got Sikich going crazy."

"I'll put a call in about those records on the Lara girl," Denise said as the waitress brought a tray laden with omelettes, hash browns, and toast. "And have a word with the social worker in charge of José's case. Those reports don't always tell you much. It probably wouldn't hurt to talk with the Lara girl's caseworker, too. They can also be closemouthed, and just not tell you anything. If you can catch them when they are answering their phone, it's much easier than getting them to return calls. Their caseloads are incredible." She spread jelly on half a slice of toast, then added, "I haven't had time to look at the paperwork on José. Fill me in."

Marti concentrated on her food while Vik brought Denise current.

"And you haven't talked with José since early Wednesday morning?"

Vik shook his head and began sectioning his omelette into small pieces instead of attacking it as usual.

"He's at the juvenile facility now," Denise said. "I'm going to have them do a psych evaluation based on what you've told me. It sounds like he's depressed."

"He's angry," Vik said. He eased a small bite of eggs and green pepper into his mouth.

"Part of the depression," Denise explained. "Although I'm not sure which triggers what."

"Does this mean he'll be medicated?" Marti asked. "Or can he refuse it?"

"Meaning that if he is on an antidepressant, he'll be competent?" Denise asked. "Charges haven't been brought yet. Let's take this one step at a time. If he is charged, depression could be a mitigating factor."

"The state's attorney is going to bring charges," Vik said. "Even if we don't have the weapon, he was found kneeling beside her body. Her blood was on his hands and on his clothes. There was no sign of forced entry, no indication that anyone else was on the premises when the homicide occurred."

"And Ramos and Sikich are both pushing for an adjudication hearing based on the evidence we have now," Marti added.

"Which is sufficient," Vik reiterated. He was hardly touching his breakfast. His cold had cleared up, so that wasn't it. The only other thing Marti could think of that could come between

Vik and food was his wife. Maybe she was sick again. Mildred had MS.

"Well," Denise said, signaling for a coffee refill. "What you want isn't always what you get. A lot of people want these kids charged, dispositioned, and locked up, but I don't think it's in anyone's best interest to be too hasty. It's far better to let emotions die down so that people can think about things more rationally. And, the state's attorney's office has a lot of confidence in you two. The fact that you're still investigating indicates to them that there is still something to look into."

Marti shook her head. "I haven't got much more than gut instinct on this one. Something just doesn't feel right. And maybe that's not it. José and I do have history. I remember when we found those kids in that library."

"Yes," Denise agreed. "I remember that, too. And we need to keep remembering that. Kids do not just go where José is. A lot of things usually happen before it gets this bad. A lot of things that we might be able to alleviate, even prevent, but do not. Remember those kids when they were in that library, Marti. I mean that. All three of us have to remember."

Marti chewed on some bacon. Vik was beginning to worry her. The waitress, familiar with Vik's eating habits, had brought extra jelly. He hadn't put any on his eggs or his toast and by now he was usually dipping his sausages in it.

"What's up, Jessenovik?"

"I was about to ask the same thing," Denise said. "I have never seen you take this long to eat anything."

"Sore throat."

"What?" Marti said. If he admitted it, he had to feel bad. "And you're sitting here giving us your germs? I've got kids at home. Denise deals with kids all day. What are you trying to do, become a one-man epidemic? Go to the doctor. Today. Now. You'll—"

Vik held up his hand. "I can handle it."

"Oh, I'm sure you can, but what about the rest of us? What

about Mildred? What about me when you're too sick to come in and Sikich gets to pick who I work with? We've got six open cases, partner. Sick is not an option."

"Okay, okay," Vik said, giving in.

"This morning," Marti insisted. "In fact, when we leave here we'll just swing by the hospital and flash our shields. It only takes a minute to get a throat culture."

They concentrated awhile on eating, then Denise said, "I can give you a run-down on the other kids."

"We don't want one," Vik said.

"There is one thing that could be interesting. LaShawna, the oldest, is missing."

"Missing?" Marti asked, dreading Denise's reply. "She was pregnant the last time I saw her." La Shawna was one of the children they found at the library. She was thirteen years old then.

"Well, she has a little girl now. She has become an emancipated teenager. The last anyone heard of her she was staying in a temporary facility for women with children. She took her little girl with her, said she was going to the public aid office, and never came back. And someone at the shelter became concerned. According to personnel at the home, LaShawna was devoted to her daughter, she had no history of drug abuse, but she was having a hard time making it on her own."

"When was this?"

"That's the interesting part. LaShawna went missing Tuesday morning. Apparently, José went somewhere Tuesday night. Do you think there could be some connection? Maybe he did meet a friend, even if he wasn't retrieving his sweater."

Marti speared a link sausage. Jose could have told the truth about meeting someone. But why LaShawna? And what connection could that have with Graciela's death? "Has anybody filed a missing persons report? There is a minor child involved."

"Not that I know of. And the child is with her mother. We hope."

"I'll take care of it when I get back to the office. After I get Mr. Epidemic to the doctor."

Sikich was waiting for them again. Marti forced herself not to bump into him as she went into the office. If he was going to keep pestering them, he might as well have a command post outside the door again, God forbid.

"Well, you two, what have we got on the Ramos kid?"

"Ortiz," Marti reminded him. "José Ortiz."

"Whatever. Are we ready to adjudicate?"

"We don't adjudicate anything," Marti said.

"That's just a formality," Sikich reminded them. "We give them what they need to bring a case. I talked with the state's attorney. He says you two are not ready to wrap this up yet. What's the matter? The kid is a killer. Adults kill. Therefore he's an adult killer. Let's get it over with."

"Juvenile is ordering a psych evaluation."

"Oh, sure, MacAlister, let him off the hook that way. After all, he's just a kid. So what if he killed somebody. Put him back on the street so he can do it again."

Marti almost wished Ramos was here to reel off some of his statistics. Then she remembered, Ramos was in agreement with Sikich.

"The chief wants closure on this, MacAlister. We've got too many open cases and this one is a no-brainer. Ramos wants to get on with his life, too."

Marti knew the chief well enough to know that Sikich was speaking for himself.

After he left, Vik said, "He just wants these cases closed on his watch, and damn guilt, innocence, or extenuating circumstances."

Marti raised her eyebrows as she looked at him, but said nothing. Vik was not a strong supporter of extenuating circumstances. The Lara case had to be getting to him because like her, he remembered finding José in that library. Was Denise right? Was that something they needed to think about now? Or would it just interfere with their job? Marti walked over and gave the rest of her coffee to the spider plant. Someone had abandoned it, half-dead, in their office several years ago. Vik had been all for trashing it, and scowled at Marti, who couldn't let go of something that was still alive and growing. Now the spiky leaves crowded the pot and grew toward the light. Vik had been too busy or to preoccupied to snap off the plant babies and at least a dozen were dangling. The plant thrived on neglect and abuse and bad nutrition. Damned shame when kids were asked to be that resilient.

Marti MacAlister lived in the kind of neighborhood that Adrian liked. Quiet, tree-lined, with large lots, empty driveways, and neighbors who either worked during the day or stayed indoors. There were no barking dogs and, as he walked down the street, no twitching curtains. While he was in prison, Adrian had tried every Web site he could identify to find out where Marti MacAlister lived. He still wasn't sure of exactly what he had done to find out that she lived in Lincoln Prairie, but once again, luck had been with him. He was on the computer, helping an inmate he was tutoring with research. As always, while he was accessing files, he typed in MacAlister, and an article about an arrest she had made had popped up. As soon as he was released, he came here and turned to the local newspaper, on microfiche at the library. That was where he found out that she had remarried. The phone number wasn't listed in the directory, and the telephone company would not release any information, but it wasn't that difficult to find out where Benjamin Walker, fireman / paramedic, lived.

The only problem today was the weather. It had cleared somewhat and wasn't as overcast as it had been. That was better than wind and snow, or worse yet, sunshine, but he would have preferred more clouds and less daylight. As he approached the cul-de-sac where the MacAlister house was located along with four other houses, he could see that one house needed its driveway cleared of snow and noted the address. He couldn't believe his good fortune. He was wearing workman's clothes today and carrying a small, portable snowblower.

MacAlister's house was big, and looked like a quad level. There were lots of trees in the back. He crossed the street so that he was entering the cul-de-sac on the side nearest the MacAlisters', and walked as if he had a specific destination.

Then he saw the dog. An old fear of being bitten always surfaced whenever he was around a dog. They could sense his fear and they reacted to it. Some growled, some bared their teeth, some just became wary. But they knew. He kept to the sidewalk near the curb, expecting the dog to bark and maybe even lunge at him. Instead, the big German shepherd just looked at him, almost as if he wasn't interested. Good, a pet, not a real watchdog. Then he noticed the sign. Beware of Dog. He almost smiled. He could probably walk right up to it and pet it. He slowed down and veered toward the fence as he walked. There was no reaction from the dog. It stood motionless as it watched him, but showed no signs of becoming aggressive. He walked until he was almost touching the fence. The dog tensed, but the change was so subtle that he wouldn't have noticed if he weren't watching for it. Then it backed up, as if it might jump the fence, but still there was no other reaction to indicate that it might attack. It must smell his fear. There was nothing he could do about that. The dog came closer to the fence when Adrian moved away and began walking alongside him.

Confident that the dog was not going to attack, Adrian slowed down and began looking around. When he noticed someone standing at the MacAlister window, he decided to ring the doorbell. The dog continued to follow him as he went up the walk. When he reached the door, he saw that the fence was lower there, and that the dog could easily jump over it. Still, the dog just watched him. Otherwise it did not react at all. When he rang the bell, the dog sat and looked at him expectantly.

"Yes?" A woman opened a small barred window in the door. There was a small sign that indicated the house had an alarm system.

He looked at the dog. It was in a crouching position now, but had not bared its teeth or made a sound.

"Can I help you?"

"I was wondering if maybe your neighbor there might want her driveway cleared."

"There is a sign that says no soliciting."

"I know, ma'am, but—"

"Please leave the premises now."

The woman raised her voice when she said "now" and the dog moved—just slightly—but it did rise up and lean forward.

Adrian turned, walked down the four steps slowly, and just as slowly down the walk. The dog escorted him to the edge of the property. He didn't know if the dog was harmless or well trained. For today, he didn't want to find out.

Marti was on her second cup of vending machine coffee when the odor of Obsession for Men preceded their office mates, who were vice cops, into the room. Slim swaggered in first, "tall, lean, mean, and brown sugar sweet" as he liked to describe himself. He wasn't too far off, although Marti didn't agree with the sweet concept. Conceited was more accurate. Slim flashed her a dimpled Cupid's-bow smile as he took off his coat. Cowboy ambled in behind him, wearing his trademark five-gallon hat, a sheepskin-lined jacket, and leather tooled boots with pointed toes.

"Morning, Miss . . . Mrs. Officer Mac," Slim said. Marti found the smell of his cologne more than a little annoying, but today she was glad to see both of them.

"I might have something for you," she said, and told them about LaShawna and her daughter. Even though they didn't handle missing persons, Slim and Cowboy had a whole network of sources to help them track down teenagers.

"Got a picture?" Slim asked.

"Not yet."

Cowboy tilted his hat back, exposing light blond hair. "We could head out to this temporary facility and check things out for you, but the women are usually uncooperative. Already had enough dealings with men."

"What?" Marti said. "That old Slim and Cowboy charm doesn't work all the time?"

Slim and Cowboy both grinned, and Slim shrugged. "What can I say?"

"Let us know what we can do," Cowboy said. "Sikich is hanging around like the pungent odor of cow dung. There's no way he'd approve of you working a missing persons case. Any word on Dirkowitz?"

"No baby yet," Marti said. It didn't sound good, and this baby was their first.

Cowboy began making coffee. "Having Sikich in charge makes me glad I'm just a lowly vice cop. For a *senior police officer* like Sikich—and I call him an SPO instead of an SOB only in deference to the presence of our female homicide dick—thank God live hookers are nowhere near as important as dead . . ." He didn't finish the sentence. "Sorry. We'll keep a look out for your missing child with child."

When Lupe came in, Marti ignored Sikich's directive that Lupe only work on the Lara case, and gave her the files on the other five cases first. "See if you can spot anything we've missed," she said. "I'll give you what I've got on Lara as soon as I take another look at it. That's the only case Sikich wants you to work on."

Lupe smirked. "Since when has anyone paid any attention to Sikich?"

"*Dupajas,*" Vik said. "*Skurvie sen.*"

Lupe looked at Marti.

"Polish cuss words," she explained, then turned to Vik. "*Skurvie sen,*" she agreed. She opened the file on the Lara case and began with all of the crime-scene photos, then went through the reports. That done, she put in a call to Dr. Cyprian.

"What else can you give me on the assailant in the Lara case?" she asked him.

"Nothing more than what you've got."

"There's no way the assailant could have been taller than five feet seven?"

"Well, if he was standing on something he could have been shorter."

"And everything you're processing for DNA comes from the clothing. There was nothing on the victim's body?"

"You know that, MacAlister. What is it that you want?"

"I don't know," she admitted. "Take another look at everything will you?"

"Sure thing. Anything else you want on your other open cases?"

"No. Not now, anyway. Lupe Torres is helping out with those."

"Good, another pair of eyes," Cyprian said. "Maybe she'll see something you missed."

His comment stayed with her as she went through everything again.

"Take your time with these, Lupe." she said as she passed her everything on the Lara case.

"In a minute. It looks like you can send what you've got on the hypothermia victim to the state's attorney."

"I don't think our little old lady will testify at a coroner's inquest."

"Not much you can do about that," Lupe said. "But it will close out one of your cases."

"Give me until tomorrow," Marti said. "Maybe I'll have another talk with the woman."

Vik gave her a look that suggested she was either slow or demented.

The call came in on José an hour later. He had been taken to Lincoln Prairie County General following a suicide attempt.

Denise met them when they got off the elevator at the hospital. "He'll be okay," she said. "Cut his wrists with a plastic knife that had been sharpened."

"While in a secure facility?" Vik asked.

"Not secure enough," Denise said. "But we're taking care of that as I speak."

It was an hour and a half before they could see him. The adolescent psych ward was secure. They had to pass through two locked doors before they reached the ward where José was being treated and another to get to his room. He was in the bed with his back to the door. Both wrists were bandaged.

Marti walked over to the window and stood where she could see his face.

"Hi, José. How are you doing?"

His eyes were closed and he didn't open them or respond when she spoke.

Marti looked down at him. He was about five foot seven. He weighed enough to overpower Graciela, although he looked more flab than muscle. And he was angry. Very angry. Even now, in the way his shoulders were set and his back rigid, his hands clenched into fists, his anger was apparent to them all.

The door opened and a nurse said, "It's been five minutes." That was all the time they had been allowed.

"I'll be back," Denise promised.

"We will, too," Marti echoed.

José didn't speak, and didn't move.

Marti decided to go by the apartment complex where the mad sword swinger had resided and talk to Jerry's friend. She parked across the street. As she and Vik headed for the building, she felt uneasy and looked around. It was a side street, away from a main thoroughfare. There wasn't any traffic and nobody was walking or loitering outside. Nobody was following her. Last night's snow had been swept from the front steps and salt granules scattered to prevent ice.

"Let me do the talking, Jessenovik. You've got strep throat and it takes the antibiotics twenty-four hours to kick in. You're still contagious."

"I don't feel like talking anyway," he said.

Marti rang the old woman's bell for the third time.

"Who are you?" her quavering voice asked again. She had gone from annoyed to apprehensive.

"The police officers who came to see you the night before last!" Marti shouted.

"Oh, oh, police. I thought you said 'please.' Just a minute."

The buzzer clicked on the outer then the inner door, but when they reached the apartment, once again the three chains were on. Today the woman was wearing a lime green polyester pants suit with bell bottoms that had been out of style for years, but seemed appropriate. Her short hair was fluffy and white. Two green bows attached to barrettes had been clipped above her ears.

"Oh, yes," she said. "I remember you. Shame about Jerry, isn't it? Have you heard anything at all about the funeral? Nobody here seems to know. Not that I can go out in this weather."

Marti couldn't think of a kind way to tell her that without next of kin or insurance, the funeral would be minimal and at the discretion of a local mortician. Nothing more than a cheap casket and a graveside prayer was likely.

"There's going to be a coroner's inquest, perhaps even a trial," Marti said. "Would you be willing to testify?"

"To what? That his apartment was too cold? Yes. Of course I will."

"The landlord will probably be there. His attorney definitely will."

"And? You think that's the only place he owns? That Jerry was the only one who was cold?"

"No, ma'am," Marti said. "But I do want you to know what you'll be up against."

"Hah," the old woman said. "They are the ones who will be up against me."

"Will testifying put you in any kind of jeopardy with your own housing?"

The green bows jiggled as she shook her head. "A woman owns this place. Takes care of her property and her tenants. It won't bother her at all."

"We'll keep you informed, then. And thank you. If you need transportation, let me know." Marti gave her a card.

"You wouldn't happen to know what happened to that loony down the hall, would you? I kind of miss him."

"He's being evaluated at a mental health facility, ma'am."

"Real nice man, long as he took his medication. Ran around wearing costumes and talking about aliens when he didn't. He wouldn't have hurt you, though. Got a little carried away sometimes, that's all."

"I'm sure you're right," Marti said. She could feel the goose-flesh rising on her arms as she turned and walked back down the hall. It was all she could do not to look behind her. Beside her, Vik did.

"Feisty old bird," he said as soon as they hit the sidewalk.

Joseph Ramos was waiting for them when they got back to their office. He and Cowboy were deep in discussion as to who was going to take the World Series this year even though the beginning of the season was several months away. First Sikich, now Ramos, Marti thought. Place was becoming busier and more accessible than a train station. She looked at the doorknob and wondered what the regulations were on locks. That old lady had the right idea, security chains and lots of them.

Ramos stopped midsentence when he saw her. "Have you seen José? How is he?" He seemed upset.

Marti pulled her chair over to where he was sitting beside Cowboy's desk. "He'll be fine," she said, wondering where this was going. Ramos was putting a lot pressure on Sikich, and probably the chief. Why was he here?

"I talked with the state's attorney today." Ramos said. "According to him, the case is still open. Why is that?"

71

So, that was what this was all about. They weren't moving fast enough to get José charged.

"These things take time," she said.

"Even for Hispanic youth?"

"Mr. Ramos, I'm a peace officer. I don't bring charges. I don't hear cases. I don't pronounce sentence. I gather evidence. That is my job, and I take a lot of pride in the way I do my job. I do not bring evidence to the state's attorney until I am satisfied that that is appropriate. I do keep his office advised as requested." So far, she did not have a motive or a weapon.

He looked at her for a moment, then said, "You mean that, don't you?"

She didn't answer. Perhaps he at least understood that he was leaning on the wrong person.

"Thank God," he said. His relief seemed genuine. "I know he must have done it, that everything points to him, but if there is any doubt, any possibility, any mitigating circumstance, anything that will help him . . . I don't want to see him get away with it, but I do want to see justice carried out, not just some kind of legal lynching."

Marti leaned back in her chair and looked at him. He meant it. He wasn't pressuring Sikich any more than the chief was.

"I can't keep them from adjudicating this whenever they want too, Mr. Ramos, not if they think there is sufficient evidence to proceed. I'm just saying that until I am convinced of José's guilt, and until I have sufficient evidence to support that, this case is open."

"I understand, and I appreciate that. As long as you continue to investigate, I will continue to do everything I can to see that José gets justice. I'm going to let the public defender handle things while José is in the hospital, but I will be retaining an attorney. And there is something about this in today's paper."

Just what she needed, publicity. Now Sikich would really turn up the pressure.

* * *

The reports on Graciela Lara were faxed in just as she was ready to leave for the evening.

"You go home," she told Vik. "There's nothing we can do with this tonight."

"No," he said. "I'll make a copy and take a look."

"I'll have a copy waiting on your desk in the morning. Go, I need you to stay healthy enough to come in, and your face is flushed. You've got a fever. Take some Tylenol when you get home."

For once he didn't insist on staying, which meant he must really feel bad.

The office was quiet. The whole upstairs was quiet. Traffic, their closest neighbor, had closed shop for the day over an hour ago. She wanted to leave too, just scan the reports and take a closer look tomorrow. Instead she got a cup of coffee that had been kept warm for hours, tested three doughnuts to see which seemed the least stale, and wished for an apricot-filled paczki as she returned to her desk.

Graciela's file was unremarkable. Marti skimmed over the early childhood abuse, the rape and sexual abuse when she was seven, and began matching the dates and locations of placements after that until she found one that matched the same time frame as José's, three years ago. It was a temporary facility, a juvenile home with fifty other kids in residence. Graciela arrived three months before José. They both left at about the same time six months later. Graciela's next stop was the hospital where she had the abortion.

Marti met Ben and the boys at the high school. Joanna's exhibition volleyball game was already in progress and she had to wait for a break in the action to join them on the bleachers. Marti was not an athlete like her daughter. She understood the rudiments of basketball. She thought softball games were much too slow but didn't have any problems following the action, such as it was. Volleyball escaped her and not just because getting a ball from one side of a net to the other didn't seem to make much sense. She had to watch the reactions from the team as well as the crowd to know when to cheer and she had to check the board to figure out which team had scored. Marti had never told Joanna any of this, but she was sure that when Joanna was hyped after a good game and she nodded and smiled as appropriate, Joanna was fully aware of her ignorance. None of that mattered tonight. She needed to be with her children, if only for an hour supper break since she planned to return to the precinct.

"You made it!" Theo said, all smiles. In profile he looked just like his father. Before she married Ben, Theo's narrow face, with his father's widow's peak and deep, dark eyes, was most often solemn. Now he laughed a lot. Her stepson, Mike, squeezed in beside her. Always affectionate, he gave her a hug.

"Joanna's team is winning," he said.

Ben leaned over. "Had supper?" he asked.

"Not yet."

"Bad day, huh?"

"Any day involving kids is a bad day, unless they're your own."

Ben reached under the bench and pulled out a small cooler. "Hot beef sandwiches," he said. "And enough for Vik. I stopped and picked up some frosted brownies too. Just in case you needed a chocolate moment."

She squeezed his hand and rested her head on his shoulder for a minute.

It had been dark for a long time when Denise Stevens got home. She had moved from the secluded house that she loved several years ago because it had become too small. She liked this house well enough. It sat back on a tree-shaded lot and her mother, Gladys, and her niece, Zaar, each had their own room. There was even a room for Zaar's mother, Terri, when she was well enough to leave the residential facility for the mentally ill for a visit. Her mother was in the early stages of Alzheimer's, but still able to care for herself and for Zaar, who was nine, in Denise's absence. As always, Denise hesitated in the driveway before pulling into the garage. She missed her other home, missed her privacy, missed the silence that sometimes didn't come now until she was in bed. Her old home had been a respite. There was little of that here.

She had worked without taking a break for supper, and stopped on the way home for Chinese. Gladys didn't cook anymore. The pot of coffee she had made this morning was almost full, but cold. She put on the kettle, wanting tea. This room always soothed her. She had gotten rid of the metal cabinets and replaced them with maple and had the walls painted a muted pastel gold. A vase filled with bronze and yellow and white chrysanthemums was in the center of the table. She took three mugs from the shelf, not certain if anyone would join her.

"Hi, Aunt Denise." Zaar always spoke in a soft voice.

"Hi, baby, how you doing?"

"Fine."

"Where's Grandma?"

"Up in her room reading her Bible. She didn't forget anything today."

So far, Denise's mother's forgetfulness extended only to not remembering what things were used for and what had happened recently. Denise prepared her breakfast and left a sack lunch in the refrigerator, which Gladys usually forgot to eat. The appliances were on a timer and could not be turned on during the day. For now, that would be enough. But they watched, she and Zaar, for the signs that would tell them things were getting worse. Denise knew she would not put her mother into a nursing home or assisted living facility unless she had no other choice. For as long as possible, Gladys would stay here.

"I'll get the tea," Zaar said. She was tall for her age, and thin, with long legs and bony hands. Even Denise admitted that Zaar was a homely child. She seldom smiled, and usually had a sullen expression on her face, although she almost never complained.

As they sipped peach tea, Denise said, "How was school?"

Zaar shrugged. She was an honor student, but only because she was smart. Zaar seldom showed any interest in her schoolwork and nothing seemed to excite her. Trips to the circus or the Ice Capades met with the same somber response as a trip to the zoo or the pumpkin farm. Zaar's psychologist said she was fine, given that she had spent the first four years of her life with a woman who was mentally unstable and incapable of showing her any affection. Denise felt guilty because she had minded her business and kept out of her youngest sister's life—and her niece's—far too long. So much for not intruding. Now they both had Gladys's encroaching senility to deal with.

"Don't forget," Denise said. "Carly is having her birthday party at play group on Saturday. We'll go out when I get home tomorrow and pick out a present. One of the church sisters is going to come and visit with your grandmother so we can have dinner, too." She didn't know what she would do without the support of their church. "Where would you like to go?"

"Red Lobster?" Zaar asked.

"Seafood. Sounds good." The last time they ate out, Zaar wanted Italian food. Maybe she was getting interested in what she ate. Maybe this was progress. Denise got up and poured more hot water for them both. She knew that later on, when Zaar and Gladys were asleep, she would think about those five throwaway children they had found four years ago in the library, and wonder—no, worry—about what was happening to them now. She was glad she had never married or had children of her own.

Adrian sat at the rear of the bus and read the Chicago *Tribune* article in the Lake County Metro section with increasing disbelief. He had killed a ward of the state, Ramos's foster daughter. And the foster son, not Ramos's own son, was accused of the crime. He had made a mistake and assumed all four children were Ramos's. And now, instead of being devastated by what had happened to his children, Ramos was gloating because they were unharmed. Instead of losing face as a negligent, absentee father, unworthy of public office, Ramos looked like a hero, taking in the unwanted and being betrayed by them. Adrian lit a cigarette, smoked it down to the filter, and lit another from the butt. He would have to continue with his plans and kill the others, then get back to Ramos. The next time all would go as planned. Now that one death had occurred, they would not be expecting any more misfortune. Then, Ramos's children could die in a house fire or some other accident. And Ramos, despondent, distraught, would kill his wife. Or so it would seem. The one essential element was that Ramos live and go to jail, and spend a very long time there, with no one to care.

At least the news about Judge Toner's husband was better, even if he hadn't lived long enough to think of his wife upstairs, helpless in her wheelchair as the fumes slowly built up and killed him. The newspaper confirmed that Toner was the victim of an apparent heart attack. Adrian smiled. Years ago, when he went to prison, luck had seemed to be against him. But he was finding out that was not true, that these others had just been more powerful than he was. Now he knew that the way to diminish their power, to control power and make it his own, was by surprise—the unknown, the unexpected, where luck could step in and work for him.

It was after seven when Adrian left the paper in his seat and got off the bus at Seventy-first and Racine. It was dark, a darkness compounded by broken streetlights and stores with plywood-covered windows that were closed for the night. And it was cold. He had not considered the weather in his plans, since he didn't know when he would gain parole. Now he saw the hand of fortune in the cold and the wind and the snow. The streets were all but deserted. Only the most determined drunks, whores, and junkies made their way outside.

The snow hadn't been shoveled and walking was difficult as he made his way south to Seventy-second using two canes. The woman's coat he was wearing flapped about his legs, the wool scarf tied at his neck itched. He waited in a doorway until the next bus came, and he could confirm that, as usual, LaPatrice Jenson—Letty Mae Jenson's daughter—was returning home from work. Then he turned the corner, gave her a few minutes to catch up, and, as he reached the alley, allowed himself to slip and fall, scattering the canes and groping for them. As he expected, LaPatrice Jenson rushed to help him.

"Ma'am, can I help you? Are you okay? Can you get up? Can you walk?"

As she bent over him, Adrian put his arm around her neck as if to help himself up. He took a quick look around and didn't see anyone else. He got to his knees, then before she could react, pulled LaPatrice into the alley. Looking at her, he saw her mother, Letty Mae, black as he was, but sitting in that jury box looking at him as though he were some new species of dirt. He punched LaPatrice in the face first, so that she couldn't scream, feeling nose cartilage give and teeth break. Then he punched, kicked, and hit her until her body was limp and he was gasping for breath. He checked the pulse at her neck and felt a faint throbbing, so he slit her throat. Then he took off the blood-spattered coat and zipped up his jacket. He rolled up the coat and dropped it and the scarf in a garbage can a few blocks away, then doubled back to Seventy-first and got on the next bus heading east.

FRIDAY, FEBRUARY 16

Marti knew she was avoiding Sikich when she left the house too late to make roll call and detoured to the address where LaShawna had been staying instead of going to the precinct first. A blustery wind blew snowflakes across the windshield. She hoped there wouldn't be any further accumulation. Even her kids were hoping for a cessation of snow. Theo and Mike and their best friends, Peter and Patrick, had an all-day trip planned with Ben tomorrow. She wasn't sure where they were going, but bad weather meant bad roads, which meant staying home.

The low-rise brick building she parked in front of was sandwiched between two others, with only a patch of yard in the front. A four-foot chain-link fence with an unsecured gate provided minimal security. There was a peephole in the door and she stood back so that whoever answered the bell could see her. After a moment, a window the size of an index card opened, and she could see cinnamon skin and dark brown eyes.

"Police," she said, and held her badge closer for inspection. "I'm here to ask a few questions about LaShawna Davis."

"About time," the woman said after she disengaged the security lock and was opening the door. "I called on Tuesday. That baby shouldn't be out in this weather. God knows if she's inside and warm."

"I'm Detective MacAlister," Marti said, as she stood in a small hallway.

"Tracy Williams," the woman replied. "Come on down here."

Williams led the way down a short, thickly carpeted hall to a large room with two bay windows that looked out on a snow-covered yard. Part of a swing set was visible. Round tables with plastic tablecloths indicated that this was the dining room. She counted the high chairs lined up along the wall. Five.

"How long was LaShawna here?" she asked.

"Came in Monday morning, left the next day. They can stay three weeks. Gives them somewhere off the street to catch their breath and begin figuring out what they can do for themselves. Usually by then we've helped find a place for them to stay or they've found a friend or relatives to stay with. We're sponsored by a church, don't provide much by way of social services other than referrals."

The woman sounded tired. Although she looked to be about forty, Marti thought she was closer to thirty.

"Do you have any idea of where LaShawna could have gone?"

When the woman hesitated, she added, "I'll keep anything you tell me confidential. I just need to find her and the baby, make sure they're okay, see what we can do to help her."

Again the woman hesitated, tracing her finger along the floral design on the plastic tablecloth. "They don't talk much, not even to each other. Street does that to you. Street does a lot of things to you. To the babies." Her voice was so sad Marti wondered if she spoke from her own experience. "You're tired, time you come here. Real tired. Just sleeping all night without worrying about someone stealing from you, or beating you, or raping you . . . sleeping is most of what they do for the first few days. That and eating three good meals a day." Her fingers moved from the table to her arm. She rubbed the back of her hand. "LaShawna didn't say nothing much to nobody. Sometimes a couple of the girls get real chummy, most of the time they don't. But she loves that baby. Best-cared-for baby I've seen in a while. And LaShawna's so skinny, I know who gets to eat when she has to choose. Says a lot for her. Some of them, the baby's just a burden. Bad luck. Bad news. Just plain bad. Not LaShawna, though. She loved that baby, she did."

"So she wouldn't do anything that would harm her child. Could the child have come to harm if she stayed here?"

"Can't see how," Tracy said. "I surely can't see how. We keep them safe and warm and fed if nothing else."

"Did she have any visitors? Receive or make any phone calls?"

Tracy shook her head. "No. I keep the phone hid or on me and they've got to have a real good reason for using it. And I sit right there and listen in. Some of these girls are coming from pimps, drugs, abuse, you name it. We don't need them bringing none of that here."

"Do you know where she came from when she came here?"

"Street. Came into the church off the street and they brought her here."

"Before that?"

"Couldn't say."

"And she said she was going to the public aid office when she left?"

"That's what she said."

"Did she leave anything here?"

"That's how I know she was coming back. Left everything she had."

Marti got a description of LaShawna and her child, then followed Tracy to a small room crowded with twin beds, cribs, and bureaus. Apparently they squeezed in as many women and children as possible. Marti went through LaShawna's belongings, all stuffed in a soiled, frayed backpack. A change of clothes for her and two pairs of socks and underwear. The little girl had six outfits, two blankets, and an extra pair of shoes. There was a doll the size of Marti's hand, and a small stuffed bear. In a side pocket she found little packets of sugar and crackers.

As Adrian watched from behind a tall fir tree with low-hanging branches, Marti MacAlister backed out of her driveway and headed for work. He checked his watch. She was late this morning. He had clocked her several times and this was the first time she had not left by 6:15 A.M. He waited until she drove out of the cul-de-sac, down the street, and turned the corner, then he headed for the precinct. She would get there before he did, but in order to choose the time and place when he would kill her as well as how he would kill her, he had to know as much as possible about her daily routine.

When he reached the precinct parking lot, her car wasn't there, but her partner's car was. Another aberration. He wondered how often this occurred. Not only was she late but she had missed roll call. Could this be her day off? He didn't think so, not a Friday. Just as he was wondering if she had called in sick or had a doctor's appointment or something to attend to involving her kids, she pulled in and found a parking space.

He wanted to know what had happened to cause her to deviate from her routine, but didn't see how he would ever find out. She was alone when she left the house, the same as always. Everything but the time had been typical as far as he could tell. What was different about today? He needed to know that. Since he didn't, it would be better not to plan to kill her on a Friday. And this was a much smaller town than Chicago. Gang and drug activity, not to mention the crime rate, were so much lower that he would have to make her death look like an accident unless he could lure her to the city where he would have more options. Once she was dead, he would have to leave the country right away, whether or not he had killed everyone else on his list. He gave her half an hour to come out, then walked across the parking lot, right past her car, and found a doorway where he could wait and watch unobserved.

Sikich was in the office when she got there. He checked his watch. "You're late this morning, MacAlister."

"Actually it's my day off and I'm early."

She could see that he wasn't sure if she was serious.

"Well, then, with your caseload I'm glad you made the prudent choice."

"Yes, sir. Every time we catch a suspect I tell them they

should obey the law. Not too many of them listen. Keeps us busy, keeping up with them."

Sikich looked a little flushed. "I assume you were working on the Lomas case."

"Lara, sir. Lara."

He shrugged. "Not important. We've got people breathing down our necks on this one. We've got what we need to nail the kid. No time for this kind of sentimentality."

Marti had gotten into the habit of ignoring offensive remarks, so she didn't respond to his suggestion that as a female she was soft when it came to kids. When Vik looked at her and raised his eyebrows, she blinked in agreement. Let him handle Sikich. He had been dealing with the man longer than she had, and in this instance, might have more patience.

"It's our case, sir," Vik said. "We're in communication with the state's attorney's office. I'm sure that when they feel there is sufficient evidence they will bring charges. You'll be the first to know."

"I am in charge here," Sikich reminded them. "Dirkowitz is much too hands-off."

"I'll let him know you feel that way, sir," Vik said.

Sikich's flush deepened. "You've not been turning in your reports on a timely basis, either of you."

"We'll get on that as soon as possible, sir."

"I'll expect something within the next hour."

"Yes, sir. We'll do the best we can, sir."

Again Sikich looked at both of them. He seemed about to say something, and Marti wondered if he was catching on to the fact that Vik's sirs were not as respectful as they sounded. Vik was using the same tone of voice and inflection that he used whenever he said *guuna*, which meant "shit" in Polish. Sikich opened his mouth as if he was going to say something, but turned and walked away. Less than a minute later, he returned.

"I almost forgot. I'll expect you to start keeping a daily log today, where you go, who you see."

"That information will be in our reports, sir," Vik said.

"A time log," Sikich said. "How much time you spend on each task."

This time he walked out and didn't return.

"A time log," Marti said. "He is out of his mind."

"I think he's beginning to figure out that he's not in charge here," Vik said.

"It's time he stayed the hell out of my way," Marti told him. "I don't need a watch dog at work. It's bad enough I have to have one at home."

"This does beat the hell out of establishing a command station."

Marti slammed her coffee mug down on her desk. If Sikich tried that again . . . Instead of commenting on what she might be driven to do, Marti filled Vik in on her visit to the temporary shelter.

"So," he said. "No LaShawna, no baby, and no intent to disappear, as far as we can tell. Damn, I thought we were through with those kids."

Ice-laced snow began making little pings against the window. The wind was picking up and according to the weatherman, the temperature would be dropping. She hadn't asked if the blue coat LaShawna was wearing or the red coat her little girl had on were warm enough, or if they had gloves or boots. Those were things she did not want to know since she couldn't do anything about it. She turned her attention to Graciela, and got through to her caseworker.

"Right, she's one of many, just one of many. We do the best we can." The caseworker sounded surly, perhaps because Denise had contacted her first.

"One less now," Marti said. "Graciela is dead."

"We take what we can get," the caseworker said. Marti wondered if she was just being flippant because she was angered over Denise's intervention or if she really felt that way.

"When is the last time you saw Graciela?"

"October. Things were going well for her at the Ramoses.'"

"She seems to have moved around a lot."

"Not nearly as often as some of them. She was quiet, well behaved."

"Then why did she leave so often?"

"Various reasons," the woman said. "Primarily, she was mean to the younger children when nobody was looking. And school reports indicate she had a real problem getting along with her classmates."

"And," Marti said, "she had an abortion."

"Yes. That's not that uncommon either. Let me check something." After a moment the caseworker said, "No. We tried to get her to identify the father but she refused. Most of them do, or else they say someone is the father whose DNA doesn't check out. Very protective of the fathers."

Or afraid, Marti thought. Was José the father? Had Graciela been afraid of him?

"I don't suppose anyone bothers with DNA testing when the child is aborted?"

"Why would they?"

"Is it typical to place them together for a second time the way José Ortiz and Graciela were?"

"This was a nice, Hispanic home, with people willing to take in adolescents who were difficult to place. There wasn't any reason not to, no indication that they either liked or disliked each other. Their first placement together was in a large group home. They probably had little or no contact. And they got along as well as could be expected at the Ramoses'. Or so I was told. The Ramoses didn't mind having two hard-to-place kids and they didn't complain about them while they were there. They were willing to keep Graciela until she graduated from high school, even knowing her background."

"What background?"

"There were several incidents of either rape or consensual sex, depending on who you asked. All the participants were minors."

"Anything else?"

The caseworker hesitated. "Other than being mean to the other children, no."

Marti waited.

"Graciela did everything possible to please the adults she was placed with."

"Are you telling me that there could have been sexual contact there as well?"

"If there was, nobody was talking about it, including Graciela."

Who would she have said anything to? Would anyone have believed her if she did?

"How did Graciela get into the system? How old was she?"

The caseworker didn't answer right away, then said, "I'm checking through her records," and was silent again. Eventually she said, "Here it is. Placed as a three-year-old. They were taken away from the mother because the boyfriend was physically abusing all five children."

"Graciela has siblings."

"Yes. I hope it's not important that you locate them. It could take weeks. All five were put up for adoption when the mother relinquished custody. I'm not sure how many I could locate, if any."

"Where is her mother?"

Again the caseworker flipped through Graciela's file. "Deceased," she said. "Fight while incarcerated. Head injury."

Marti wondered how anyone could deal with situations like this day in and day out. At least her clients were dead. Abuse or whatever life had handed out was over for them. She began to feel some sympathy for the caseworker. "Look, I need to talk with a few of the people she stayed with most recently. Adults, other kids if possible. Can you arrange that?"

"I'll see what I can do."

"I need to do this as soon as possible."

"I know. Everyone does."

Marti didn't bother to explain that the key to Graciela's death just might be found in her past, and most probably her recent past. She felt depressed when she hung up. She put a call in to Denise. "Who else can we talk to about Graciela and José? I mentioned this to the caseworker but I'm not sure she'll be much help."

"There must be a lot of adults. They were placed often enough."

"Did they ever see their parents, siblings, anyone in their families?"

"I doubt it. I'll see what I can come up with and get back to you."

Sikich was standing in the doorway when Marti hung up.

"Those reports," he said. "It's been an hour and fifteen minutes. Either you have them in my office in half an hour or I write you up for insubordination." He turned with military precision and walked away.

"He can do that," Vik said.

"Would anyone care?"

"It could mean a hassle until the lieutenant gets back."

"Could it mean having someone else put on this case?"

"Who?" Vik asked. "Unless they call in the sheriff's department. Not likely. We might have a little visit with the chief, though, or the deputy chief."

"That might not be such a bad idea, Jessenovik. Let's find out. Damn Sikich's reports and his time sheets."

When Sikich came in the next time, he had a copy of the *News-Times* in hand. Marti had forgotten Ramos's warning last night about a story in today's edition.

"This is exactly what we don't need," Sikich said. His voice was high and trembling. Marti wondered if that meant he was angry.

Vik took the newspaper. "Haven't seen it, sir." He read the article, then handed it to Marti.

There was a photo of the Ramos family, faces solemn. The article focused on Ramos's efforts to give Hispanic children a stable home environment and a second or even fifteenth chance at getting their lives together. With typical statistical precision, Ramos outlined the failure of the welfare system to help Hispanic youth, describing it as a system that frequently put them at additional risk while also destroying the Hispanic family unit, particularly where extended family was concerned. He then castigated the juvenile justice system. Marti didn't disagree with any of it. She was wondering if anyone would get around to mentioning Graciela when she began reading the final paragraph, "And now a sixteen-year-old ward of the state, Graciela Lara, is dead, allegedly at the hand of another Hispanic youth also trapped in the system. Where will it end?" aldermanic candidate Ramos asks. "When will my people be free?"

"And?" Marti asked as she handed the newspaper back to Sikich. Ramos hadn't mentioned the Lincoln Prairie Police Department, or either of them, or made any reference at all to the death investigation.

"This is just what we don't need. Publicity."

"We're not even mentioned. Nothing he said is directed at us."

"But it will be. Ramos is picking his shots, aiming at the welfare system first, the juvenile system. The next volley will be aimed at the legal system, that's us."

"Maybe we should deal with that if it happens," Vik said. He sounded so reasonable and unperturbed that Marti thought he was until she saw the way he was clenching, then extending his fingers.

Sikich hit the wall with his fist. "We'll deal with it now!"

"Any suggestions?" Vik asked, outwardly calm.

"Charges against the Ramos boy, now!" Sikich said.

"Ortiz," Vik said, sounding tired.

"What?" Sikich asked.

"The subject's name is Ortiz. José Ortiz."

Sikich gave him a look that suggested the name was of no importance. "This," he said, waving the newspaper. "This. Stop it! Now!" With that he all but marched out the door.

Marti stared at the doorway, waiting for him to return.

"I've had about enough of him," Vik said. "I think he ought to leave us alone."

As reluctant as she was to know how the other children they had found in the library had fared, Marti knew it was time to talk with them. One of them might have been with José the night Graciela died. One of them might know where LaShawna was, or why she had disappeared. She put in another call to Denise and got Padgett's current address. Denise was working on locating Georgie and Sissie. As far as she knew, they too were in foster care.

"First Sikich, now this," Vik said, when she told him where they were going. "At least we already know that Padgett's mother's a drunk and he's an enabler and they'll never make it up to poverty level. There's no telling with Georgie and Sissy. Too bad I just have strep throat and not pneumonia, then I could be home in bed."

Padgett had been a quiet child who was afraid of the dark and just about everything else when they encountered him at the old library four years ago. He had also been the child who was brave enough to lead the killer away from the four other children hiding inside. Padgett had moved several times since she last saw him a few years back. She remembered a clean but sparsely furnished apartment in a landlord-neglected house, but the house he was living in now was much worse. The street was a dead end in more ways than one, with houses in varying stages of neglect lined up along cracked, concave sidewalks that dipped at various angles with a pothole-filled street running like a faded black ribbon between. From the looks of the house, with cinder blocks replacing front steps, cardboard replacing broken windows, and an open Dumpster overflowing with garbage, nobody, including the building code inspectors, came here. Inside, the house smelled. It was a putrid combination of many odors, none of which she could identify.

Padgett came to the door. He was twelve now. His eyes, a startling blue, were bloodshot. His hair, black as coal, hung to his shoulders and needed shampoo, a comb, and some scissors. Marti couldn't believe how thin he was, how pale. He looked from her to Vik several times before he seemed to remember who they were. Then he stood aside and let them come in.

"What's wrong?" he asked.

"You tell me," Vik said.

"Is my mother all right?" He looked and sounded lethargic. "Did something happen to my mother?"

"Not as far as I know." Vik sounded more than discouraged. There was no hope in his voice at all.

Padgett walked to an upturned box that served as a table and took a generic cigarette out of a pack and lit it.

"I'd offer you a seat . . . ," he said, with a slow wave of his arm. Seating consisted of three piles of clothes and a stack of chair cushions. Two empty beer bottles and a few crushed cans littered the bare wood floor.

"Where is your mother?" Marti asked.

"Who knows?"

"When's the last time you saw her?"

"A couple days ago."

"Is that typical?" Vik asked.

Padgett nodded.

"Who's been drinking the beer?"

No answer.

"You working on becoming an candidate for AA?"

"Like mother, like son." Padgett sounded more defeated than defiant. "They say it runs in the family."

"Knowing that can give you an edge," Vik said. "How's school?"

Padgett shook his head. "You miss ten days and they suspend you for the rest of the semester. Ask me again in September." He took a few deep drags on the cigarette. "I suppose you're going to call that lady from Juvie now."

"Miss Stevens," Marti said. "Yes, I suppose we are. Meanwhile, we need to ask you a few questions about José."

He tensed but said nothing.

"Have you heard from him lately?"

Padgett looked at the wall somewhere behind her, then looked at her. "No. Never see the dude."

She didn't believe him.

"He's got himself into a little trouble. It would help him if someone could tell us if they saw him anytime Monday or Tuesday."

Padgett finished off the cigarette, ground out the butt on the floor, then said, "Yeah, well, we don't hang out together no more. Lost touch a long time ago."

"Well," Vik said, "if you remember seeing him, give us a call."

"Sure thing."

Marti put in a call to Denise Stevens on her cell phone before she left, but Denise was out of the office. She decided against asking them to send anyone else over, better to hope Padgett hung around long enough to see Denise.

"The Juvie lady's not in her office right now," she said.

Padgett didn't respond.

"She helped you and your mother the last time we called her."

He didn't look at her either.

"It doesn't look like those solutions are working anymore. She might decide to do something else this time."

"Yeah. So?"

"So will you hang around until she gets here? I don't want to call in anyone else. I trust her."

"I ain't got no place else to go. Too cold for the street."

Marti didn't think it was much warmer in here, but he was right. He'd have the wind and the snow to deal with outside and if the tennis shoes he was wearing were the only shoes he owned—and if there wasn't a pair of socks in the pile of clothes on the floor—Padgett wouldn't make it half a block without getting his feet wet, not to mention cold.

Vik took several deep breaths as they walked back to the car. "We're taking a chance on this. Think he'll stick around?"

"Depends. He will if he wants to survive."

"It's real easy to forget he's only twelve."

"Oldest twelve-year-old I've seen in a while," Marti agreed.

"I knew what it would be like if we got mixed up with these kids again, MacAlister. Damned shame I had to be right."

"What do you think he knows about José?" Marti asked. "If he did see him, why won't he tell us?"

"Maybe telling us would hurt José more than help him."

Marti was afraid of that, too.

Sikich was in their office when they got back.

"Now what?" Vik asked. "Sir."

"Your reports are still not on my desk."

Vik strode over to his computer, which he always left on, grabbed the mouse and hit a few icons and commands. "Damn," he said. "Why the hell would anybody mess around with this thing and screw up my files? I hate working for someone who doesn't have one damned thing to do. Sometimes I don't understand why some people around here are pulling a paycheck. I sure hope to hell we don't run out of toilet paper before Lieutenant Dirkowitz gets back."

He clicked a few more times and the printer began spitting out paper.

Sikich got red in the face but said nothing.

Maybe that's what they should do, Marti thought. Be more confrontational. She went to her computer, debated whether or not to make a big deal of finding her reports, and decided the faster they got Sikich out of there, the better. Her notes were not organized on forms yet and she was reluctant to give them up unedited, but it might be enough to keep Sikich out of there way for the rest of the day. Two things were certain, if he didn't get something, he was not going to leave them alone. And if he didn't leave them alone, things were going to get ugly.

"Anything else, sir?" Vik asked, handing him some computer printouts.

Marti wondered when Sikich was going to notice the emphasis on "sir" and realize that it was Vik's way of being disrespectful. She didn't trust herself to speak to Sikich at all, not now, anyway, and not anytime soon.

"This is not—"

Vik held out his hand. "If you can give me a couple of hours, sir, I might be able to find the time to rekey them."

"No, don't bother. I'll return this along with any questions I have. I still don't have your schedule for the day and I'll also need that daily log of your actual activities."

"Oh," Vik said. "I thought we were supposed to write that up after we did it."

"No, I would prefer knowing what you will be doing each day as well as having a follow-up report as to what you actually accomplished."

"I'll remember that, sir."

"Please have today's schedule on my desk before you go out. And in the future, have it on my desk first thing in the morning."

After he left, Vik said. "I wonder if our schedules should include what time we plan to go to the bathroom."

"Maybe I'll throw in how often I change my tampons. Then too, there is nose blowing, you've been doing a lot of that lately, Jessenovik."

Vik almost smiled. "Our schedule . . . those are great ideas. How about stopping for traffic lights and stop signs? And each entry should have the exact time, down to the second."

"If Dirkowitz doesn't get back pretty soon, Homicide might be on strike."

"Oh, come on, Marti. This schedule crap could be fun. I think we should have a uniform along to keep track of everything. We could even tell him what we did while we were in the bathroom. The more I think about it," Vik said, "having a uniform along doesn't sound like such a bad idea. Too bad we can't pull Lupe for that, but it would be too much of a waste of manpower. There must be some green rookie we can borrow. Maybe I'll check into it. The desk sergeants can't stand Sikich either."

Marti scanned the reports in her in-basket. Nothing much on Graciela yet. Forensics had some fibers they were trying to match. The blood on the sweat suit was Graciela's. All of the fingerprints had been identified, José, Graciela, the Ramos family. No strangers.

Marti and Vik joined Denise Stevens at the Barrister for a late lunch. Today Denise's hat of choice was a fawn-colored felt roller brim with a curving pheasant feather tucked into a brown velvet band. She was waiting for them at a table in the middle of the room.

"How about over here?" Vik said, and headed for the booth against the wall. Marti slid in beside him.

"What's with you two?" Denise asked. "What's got you so twitchy? Somebody get the drop on a uniform during a traffic stop?"

When they didn't answer, Denise said, "Closer to home, huh?"

Marti told her about the mad sword swinger.

"So I've got the view of the wall behind you to look forward to for at least a month."

It did take about that long to get over something like a razor-sharp sword pointing at one's belly, or a gun, or car, or whatever else the criminal populace had the opportunity and inclination to try when attempting to assault, maim, or kill a peace officer.

"You look tired, Denise," Marti said. Denise had seemed tired for a while now, almost ever since her niece and her mother came to live with her. "Everything okay?"

Denise poured creamer and measured sugar into her coffee before answering. "I'm looking for someone to stay with my mother during the day."

"That gets expensive. Something happen?"

"No, not yet, anyway. I've done everything I can think of to keep her and Zaar safe when I'm not there. But I don't know how fast her Alzheimer's will progress. Suppose she sets the house on fire? Or goes wandering off? There's a forest preserve with a pond two blocks from the house. I accept the fact that I don't have much love for my mother, but even so, I don't want anything to happen to her."

"What about a nursing home?"

"No. Not unless she gets so bad that I have no other choice. I deal with institutions every day. And at some point, no matter what the relationship, you have to take responsibility for being part of a family, even if you don't particularly like all the members. I know that sounds old-fashioned in these days and times, but I believe in it."

Marti reached across the table and squeezed her hand. "Me, too. How about one of those day care centers for seniors? Programs where they baby-sit them?"

"Have we got anything like that around here?"

"Be worth looking into."

The waitress brought their order and replaced the empty bread basket with another filled with warm rolls.

"That isn't real shepherd's pie," Vik said. "It's got ground beef instead of lamb. I think it's supposed to be lamb."

"Tastes good anyway," Marti said. It was her favorite. "Eat your bangers and mash and shut up. Those sausages look greasy. Joanna would have a fit." Vik chewed and swallowed slowly, but Marti thought his throat was beginning to feel better. "Are you taking those antibiotics as prescribed?" As far as Vik was concerned, her maternal instinct was one of her more endearing characteristics. He almost smiled.

Denise pushed the mashed potatoes that covered her pie into a pile at the edge of the plate, then picked at the green peas and carrots. "I located Georgie and Cecilia—Sissie."

Vik made a face as if a really rotten odor had wafted toward him instead of the delicious smell of pub food. "Damn, why did you have to spoil my lunch?"

Denise looked at him with a puzzled expression.

"We saw Padgett this morning," Marti explained. "He seems

to be participating in his mother's sole pursuit, the consumption of alcohol, and worse, he's been suspended from school for the rest of the year."

"The place they live in is a hovel," Vik said. "People live better than that in India and Africa. This is America."

Denise put down her fork.

"Eat," Marti urged.

"I think I'm more frustrated than hungry today. One of my best POs quit."

"Can't say I blame them," Vik said. "Not if they have to deal with the Padgetts of the world every day."

"The Padgetts of the world are the easy cases, Jessenovik. You haven't seen the tough cases yet, or at least not as many as I have."

"We told Padgett you would be over to see him today," Marti said.

"I'll get over there, try to figure something out. We might have to remove him if conditions are that bad."

"He really loves his mother, Denise."

"I know that, Marti, and I'm sure that she loves him. Sometimes that's not enough. We'll see." Denise reached for a roll, slathered it with butter, took a bite, and chewed slowly. Then she said, "José is still in the hospital, by the way. Severe depression. I've got a court order for a thirty-day evaluation. I'm thinking about sending him to a place that specializes in juveniles, but we've got some good people here, so I'll talk to them first, maybe bring somebody in to consult. We'll see."

"Did you find out anything else?" Marti asked.

"Nothing that you want to hear,"

"Tell me anyway."

Vik scowled. "Maybe you can save it for another day. We haven't met with Georgie and Sissie yet. I think my plate will be full after that."

"That's a good thing, since the one your working on now is almost empty," Marti said. "You want dessert?"

He signaled to the waitress and ordered ice cream and the

strawberry syrup that was poured over waffles and pancakes. He usually reserved gooey things for their postautopsy repasts.

"So," Marti said. "What's with José?"

"Jose is a real bad news kid," Denise told her. "He has a very hard time dealing with authority. He has gotten into numerous fights. Even when he is not actually in trouble, he is very oppositional. He was in a behavior disorder program at the high school. Mr. Ramos says he was never overtly disobedient with him or his wife, just passive-aggressive. José would do anything to avoid following the rules. He also said that José destroyed everything they gave him, Christmas gifts, clothing. Ramos seemed really hurt by that."

Fights, Marti thought. Violence. Just what she needed, violence in José's background. "Any record of him hitting females?"

"He's hit a few."

"Terrific. Did he ever get into it with Graciela?"

"We don't have any history on them, We know that they were at the same temporary facility for about six months but, there has been a complete turnover in personnel there, so I can't get anything aside from their records. There's not much on paper. Nothing that actually links José with Graciela, other than the time frame. Considering what we do know, that might be a good thing. Sorry, I'm not eager to make your case easy for you. I don't think José's such a bad kid. Of course, I could always be wrong about that. When you figure out what happened the night Graciela died, enlighten me. You know you always have my full cooperation, but even if you prove conclusively that José did it, I'm still not giving up on him."

"I wish to hell José would talk to us," Marti said.

"His public defender says he can't, not right now, anyway. The psychiatrist backs her up."

"Graciela sure can't talk." Vik reminded them. "Who speaks for her?"

"She'll talk to us," Marti said. "Through others, through her actions, through what we can learn about her life. I spoke with her caseworker again today. Asked if I could talk with a few people who knew her. The woman agreed, but I'm not sure she'll be of much help."

"Oh, yes, she will," Denise promised.

"She didn't seem too happy with your interference so far."

"Too bad. She will cooperate regardless."

Marti looked at Denise for a minute. Usually she was more laid back.

"Everything okay with you?" she asked again.

Denise massaged the length of her jaw with her fingertips. "They've taken over my refuge," she said. "I have no place to go."

"You mother and Zaar."

Denise nodded. "By the time they're settled in for the night and the house is quiet, I'm too tired to enjoy it. I've been reading the same book for two weeks now. Not enough time to finish it."

"Sounds to me like you need a little respite care. You talk to the reverend?"

They had a proactive minister at their church who saw to it that the church members responded to the needs of the community.

"The church sisters are very good about coming over evenings when I can't get home."

"Maybe you need one to come over on a night when you can come home."

"Marti. They do a lot. I really don't like to impose."

"Well," Marti said, "I'm going to talk to Momma about this. She knows a lot more about what's going on with the membership than I do. But it sounds to me like there might be more that we need to do. You do a lot for the church, Denise. They'll be glad to help out."

"I worry about Zaar worrying about her, trying to help watch out for her. Even though she's only alone with her for a short time, that's too much responsibility for a nine-year-old child. Maybe if I can find a day care program for Gladys, things will be better."

"Get on it," Marti said.

As they left the Barrister, and walked to where they had parked their cars, Marti noticed a vagrant nodding in the doorway of a rehabbed Victorian that now housed law offices. Although they were in downtown Lincoln Prairie, it seemed like an odd place for the man to sleep, especially during the day. Marti paused, and looked at Vik. He shrugged. He was getting used to homelessness now, just as she had gotten used to it while she lived in Chicago. Still, she wondered why nobody had noticed the man or made him leave. As she watched him, he looked up at her. His eyes were surprisingly clear and focused, with heavy lids and dark pupils. For a moment, their eyes held. Then the man got up, picked up a torn and dirty duffel bag, and shuffled away, his gait slow and unsteady.

Adrian felt pleased with himself as he hurried to catch the Metra to Chicago. He had seen her close up, and she didn't have a clue as to who he was or why he was here. He had talked to her daughter, gone to her house, and now he had followed her from the police station to that restaurant and looked her right in the eye. How he had wanted to tell her who he was and what he was going to do to her and why he was going to do it. He needed to get her alone, overpower her, and tell her all of those things before he killed her. She had to know why she must die. She had to know that. He would have to figure out how to tell her first, then kill her. He touched the gun that was in one coat pocket, thought about aiming it at her and watching her fall as the bullet hit her. He fingered the knife that was in his other pocket, and pictured a wide, gaping red smile as he drew it across her throat. It would be a tough decision, choosing between them, but he was up to it. He smiled.

School was getting out when Marti and Vik arrived at the home of John and Sarah Woods. They would have a few minutes with the adults before Georgie and Sissie arrived. It was a brick bungalow on a quiet tree-lined street, not more than five blocks from where the Ramoses lived, but on the east side of Sherman, near the bluffs that overlooked the lake. The house was on a narrow lot and sat back about thirty feet from the street. Someone had made angels in the snow in the front yard. The steps, walkway, and sidewalk had been shoveled along with the driveway that led to the garage. A portable basketball hoop was half hidden by a pile of snow.

A woman who looked to be in her midfifties opened the door. She frowned when Marti and Vik identified themselves as police officers and checked their badges before letting them in. The aroma of cinnamon mingling with lemon furniture polish greeted them. The living room was small but tidy and opened into a large dining room where books and games and a television set were crowded on a side board. Marti could see the controls for one of those video games on top of the cable box and a VCR. In addition to the dining room table there was a long, overstuffed couch and two beanbag chairs upholstered in corduroy.

"Are you Mrs. Woods, ma'am?" Marti asked. "Sarah Woods?"

The woman motioned them to two chintz-covered chairs and took a third chair that was wide and comfortable. The sofa partially blocked the view from the lower portion of a row of windows that faced the street. A gleaming large square coffee table took up most of the remaining space.

"I know you haven't come here to tell me anything about Georgie or Sissie doing anything wrong." There were laugh lines at the corners of Mrs. Woods eyes and mouth. Otherwise there were no wrinkles on her smooth brown face. Her voice was stern, but there was warmth in her dark eyes, and just a hint of amusement.

"No, ma'am," Marti said.

Since Mrs. Woods did not seem relieved by that, Marti assumed that she genuinely did not expect either child to get into trouble.

Marti explained about their encounter with the children in the old library. "How are they doing?" she asked.

"They've been with us four years now, and they are just like our own. We want to adopt them but the state hasn't approved it yet. My daughter and her husband never could have children and my boy died in an automobile accident, so they are a blessing to us all."

"And there are no problems?" Marti asked.

"They're on the honor roll, both of them. Come home, help out. I don't know what we would do without them. My husband, John, had surgery the end of November. They went right from school to the hospital the entire week he was there."

Marti glanced at Vik and could see the relief on his face. Before she could ask any more questions, the front door swung open and a young boy came in.

"Hey, big mama!" He went to the woman and put his arms around her and gave her a hug. Then he saw Marti and Vik and stiffened, his eyes filled with fear.

"They haven't come to get you, Georgie. Everything is all right."

Georgie relaxed. He had gotten taller, but had the same wary but kind dark brown eyes and close-cropped woolly hair that made Marti want to rub his head.

"Papa okay?" he asked.

"Papa's down in the basement getting the seeds for his garden planted. You know how he likes to start early."

Georgie sat on the edge of the sofa, waiting.

"We came to talk to you about José," Marti said.

"Is that all?" he asked. "I haven't seen him. Not lately. He lives around here somewhere, but I don't hang out with him."

"What do you know about him?"

Georgie looked puzzled, then shook his head. "We don't even go to the same school. He hardly speaks when I do see him."

"Where is that?"

"Last time I saw him was some time before Halloween at that little grocery store on South Street."

"Did he say anything?"

"No, not even hello. Just nodded."

The door opened again and a young girl came rushing in. "Big mama, I got an A on my science test!" She had the same walnut-colored skin and dark eyes as her brother. Her hair, unpermed, was plaited in thick cornrows.

"Lord, Sissie, an A!" She looked at the paper Sissie handed her. "There it is, the endoplasmic reticulum." Mrs. Woods looked at Marti. "She really studied for this. Now we both know all of the parts of the cell."

Sissie had been so excited when she came in that she hadn't noticed Marti or Vik until now. Her reaction was similar to Georgie's, except that he seemed afraid. Sissie was terrified.

"It's all right, child. It's all right. Nobody has come to take you away," Sarah Woods assured her. "They've just come to ask some questions about someone you know, a boy named José."

For a minute, Sissie had a blank look on her face, then she said, "Oh, José."

Sissie hadn't seen José at all. She didn't even know he lived nearby.

"How's Papa?" she asked Mrs. Woods.

"Downstairs getting things ready for the garden," Georgie said.

Mrs. Woods looked at Marti. "Papa had his prostate taken out. They got it before it was cancer and he hasn't had any problems since. But these children still worry about him so. It's a good thing, though. They got him up and moving around quick and in a hurry. He wanted them to see that he really was okay."

"I'm glad they caught it in time." Marti said. "That's good to hear." Three of their church members had died of prostate cancer in the past year. One was only fifty-four. For some reason black men were at high risk. She suspected it had as much to do with a reluctance to go to the doctor as it had with genetics or heredity.

"So," Vik said as they walked to their car. "At least two of them are doing all right."

There was a jauntiness in the way he walked that Marti

hadn't seen in a while. Nothing like a little good news to lift the spirit, as Momma would say.

As Adrian headed north along the lakefront, past Grant Park, the wind buffeted his face and the snow that covered the sand crunched beneath his feet. Despite the two sweaters he wore under a winter jacket, he was cold. The day reflected his mood—gray sky, gray water, frothing and foaming as waves crashed against the boulder-strewn breakwater. It was Thursday and he still hadn't decided which of two of them to kill tonight. He would have to make up his mind soon.

He paused as a man walking a large black chow approached, then he headed away from the animal and closer to the water. Dogs. He hated them. He tried not to think about MacAlister's dog as he kept a wary eye on the chow. Years ago, he had been set on by two neighborhood rottweilers. Nine at the time, he had yelled at first, then tried to run from them. When one knocked him down and he knew he couldn't get away, he had curled into a ball and stayed very still until they left him alone. He still had the scars from their teeth on his legs and shoulders, but they had gotten bored and gone away when he didn't try to fight them. Later, when he found out who they belonged too, and while they were tied up in a backyard, he had thrown stones at them, ignoring their yelps of pain, just as they had ignored his, until they were dead. That's what he would like to do to MacAlister's German shepherd. But something about the dog warned him away. That dog was too quiet, too calm, too watchful.

Now he turned, watched as the chow trudged through the snow, then squatted to do its business. Then he kept heading north along the shoreline until he reached the condo where he used to live. He counted up seventeen stories, found the window where he used to sip cognac as he watched the moon wax and wane, the water becoming violent and angry one night, then silent and watchful like a beast stalking its prey the next. He felt a kinship with the lake.

If. The word came to him again as it did so many times since he first realized as a child that he was black, discovered that the world had consigned a special place for black boys, and that he would always be a black boy to them, never a black man. He soon learned that whenever he tried to escape the place that had been assigned to him—a place where he was required to be subservient and grateful, a place where he was always considered inferior—they became fearful and struck out at him, sending him back to his place. The ultimate black man's place was prison and, whenever possible, death row. He had cheated them out of watching his execution, but they had taken everything else. He would never regain what they had taken from him, but he had learned how to take what they had and, like them, get away with it.

It was after four o'clock when Denise knocked on Padgett's door. She had a female caseworker with her from DCFS as well as Lupe Torres in uniform. This neighborhood was not on Lupe's beat but hers would be another familiar face. When Padgett opened the door, he did not look happy to see them.

"Oh. You." He stubbed out a cigarette on the floor.

"Where's your mom?" Denise asked.

"Don't know. Bar a couple blocks from here maybe. Ain't seen her in a couple of days."

"She take off like that often?"

He brushed oily black hair away from his eyes. "Sometimes."

"What do you do while she's gone?"

"I do okay."

"Do you like being alone?"

"Sometimes."

She checked his arms, concerned with his thinness, and found yellowing bruises.

"How did this happen?'

"Ma don't know nothing about it," he said.

"Who's her boyfriend?"

"Just some guy."

"Has he got a name?"

"Mickey. That's all I know."

"Does he hit her too?"

"Sometimes."

As Denise took a look around, caseworker in tow, she remembered what Vik had said about the place while they were at lunch. Looking at it, squalid seemed an inadequate description. Roaches were scurrying around in the kitchen and there were rodent droppings. Holes in the plaster revealed rusting pipes. The sink was piled with dishes that smelled and the stove crusted with burned-on food. The floor was sticky. Three paper bags held garbage. Padgett had been coping well when she saw him a few years ago, but he wasn't managing at all now. She returned to the living room. Lupe, arms folded, stood near a pile of dirty clothes.

"Okay, Padgett," Denise began. "This isn't working anymore. We're going to have to figure out what will."

"Does this mean you won't let me stay with my mother?" He sounded angry, resentful, but more than anything else, worn out. "I won't leave my mother. You don't have a court order to make me."

Denise recognized the plea for help.

"I have a DCFS worker, and an emergency situation."

"I knew those two cops would do this."

And he had done nothing to avoid or postpone it. He had opened the door almost before they knocked. Smart kid. He knew he was in over his head.

"I'm not going to any damned foster home. You can't make me."

"I have a place for you to stay for a few days, until we can sort things out."

"Juvie?" he asked.

"No. The hospital. I can't put you anyplace else until we know if you're clean or if you need rehab, and how your health is." His thinness worried her.

"What about my mother?"

"She's going to come home to an empty house with nobody but Mickey to take care of her," Denise said. "Is that good or bad?"

"Bad," Padgett admitted. "Real bad."

"You can't defend her, Padgett. You can't even take care of yourself, and at your age, you shouldn't have to do either."

"I'm staying here. We're doing okay. We're doing just fine."

"I can see how you're doing. We've tried that route, let you take care of her, or at least keep her company. It doesn't look like it's working out anymore, at least not for you."

"What about her?"

"Maybe she has to decide to look after herself."

"She can't," he whispered. "She can't. Can't you help her?"

"Only if she wants to be helped." Denise nodded toward Lupe. "Officer Torres will keep an eye out for her, and arrest Mickey as soon as he gives her a reason to. That's the best we can do."

Padgett retrieved a thin windbreaker from a pile of clothes and put it on over his sweater. He left the apartment without complaint, but Denise knew from experience that if anything happened to his mother in his absence, Padgett would always believe it was his fault.

Denise returned to her office. She should have gone home, but a stack of case folders was waiting on her desk. She still hadn't made much progress finding people Marti and Vik could talk with about Graciela, and time was becoming critical if one them had had anything to do with Graciela's death. She reached for the phone. An hour later she had contacted fourteen people. Three were willing to talk to the cops. That done, she did head for home. She was certain that Marti's next request would be for the same information on José, but she was tired, and Zaar had been alone with Gladys long enough. Finding people willing to talk about José would have to wait until tomorrow.

One of the church sisters met her at the door.

Zaar was right behind her. "Grandma's okay now, Aunt Denise," she said. "We called Aunt Belle like you said and she talked to her for a while."

"What was wrong, baby?"

"Oh, nothing much," the church sister said. "Miss Gladys put the dirty clothes in the oven."

"Did she turn on the oven?"

"No," Zaar said. "She was trying to figure out how when I got home from school."

"And Zaar called me right away and I came right over."

"Where is she now?"

"In the den. I fixed her a cup of sassafras tea and she's watching cartoons."

"She doesn't like the same ones I do," Zaar said.

Denise hugged her. "Oh, baby, I am so sorry I wasn't here. You could have paged me."

"No, you had to work, and I know what to do. Besides, I called Aunt Belle too. She does real good with Grandma, better than any of us. She says she'll be here tonight, after work."

Denise held Zaar for a few moments, feeling more comforted than comforting. Poor Zaar. First Terri, now this.

"Did you have supper? Do your homework?"

"We had grilled cheese sandwiches and tomato soup."

Good. That was Zaar's favorite.

"I didn't have any homework because its Friday, and you said if I took my bath first we could stay up late and watch a movie."

"Then go take your bath and we will. I'll even throw in cookies, popcorn, and cocoa."

She waited until Zaar went upstairs, then turned to the church sister. "Thank God nothing happened. And thank you for coming over and staying until I got home. You know you can always call me at work."

"I didn't have a thing else to do, and you, why, you've got plenty on your plate. You can call anytime. Sister Gladys has been a faithful church member for years. Never said no to anything anyone asked her to do. Now it's our turn."

Denise wished for the millionth time that Sister Gladys had

been as generous and considerate of her three daughters, as she had been with the church. Maybe if she had Zaar wouldn't be stuck with a mother who was institutionalized, Belle, who was a recovering alcoholic, and her. Her, what was she? A dysfunctional caregiver at best. As emotionally messed up as her sisters. Now just as she had done with her own daughters, Sister Gladys was putting her grandchild through hell. At least it didn't involve a man this time, Denise reminded herself. At least Zaar did not have to lie awake at night and wait for Gladys's man to visit her in her bedroom. Too bad that Sister Gladys probably didn't even remember any of that anymore. Too bad that she, and Terri, and Belle would never be able to forget. But, thank God . . . thank God Zaar would never know what that kind of abuse was like.

When Marti got home Joanna was waiting for her. Marti checked the pot, beef stew, thanks to Momma, with lots of turnip chunks and thick slices of carrots thanks to Joanna—and corn muffins, hopefully Momma and Joanna didn't collaborate on that and there was no canned pumpkin mixed in. Goblin, their cat, was curled up in her basket, asleep. Bigfoot, their Heinz 57 who was the size of a St. Bernard, padded in long enough to smell her stocking feet and nuzzle her hand for a pat. She could hear Ben and the boys upstairs. They lived in a quad level and the second floor above the basement had become the middle place. It was where everyone migrated when they weren't doing something else.

"Are they still planning their mystery trip?" she asked Joanna.
"Not tomorrow's adventure. The week-long event they're planning for spring."

"Hah! They've got Peter and Patrick in on it now, too."

Peter and Patrick were close to Theo and Mike's age and lived next door. There were other children in the houses that filled their cul-de-sac and the street that abutted it, but these four boys had quickly become best friends when they moved here last year.

Marti ladled stew into a bowl and discreetly sniffed a muffin. She couldn't detect the odor of nutmeg which would signal the inclusion of pumpkin so she put a couple of the muffins on a saucer.

"So, what's up with you?" she asked, while she waited for the stew to cool.

"It's this volleyball thing."

Volleyball? Now what had she missed. "What thing?"

"Oh, this camp, this traveling program, the scholarship opportunities."

"Oh?"

"You remember. We were talking about it last week, before the exhibition game."

She didn't remember. The conversation must have taken place in the den, with Momma and Ben, while she was dozing in her recliner. She waited, hoping Joanna wouldn't realize that she had been semiconscious during their previous discussion about whatever this was about.

"I like volleyball, Ma."

"I know you do."

"And I'm good at it."

"Very good."

"But it's not my life. I want to play softball and basketball too."

Marti wished she had been more alert the other night. She didn't dare ask what the problem was.

"I don't think I could devote my life to volleyball, that's all, not for the next six or seven years. And I don't know if I want to go to the Olympics or not. But that might be cool. I might be real sorry if I pass up the opportunity. But I have to decide now and I can't."

The Olympics? How did that become part of the conversation?

"How important are the Olympics?"

Joanna twisted a long strand of hair. "I don't know. And I

don't have enough time to figure it out. I have to decide now. Either I'm a member of the Invaders now, or I'm out."

"I think they'll give you a little more time than that to make up your mind."

"No. I have to decide now."

"Who's been talking to you about this?"

"That coach I told you about. She sets up all those camps and now she's in charge of this."

"Oh, her." Who was this woman? And this? This what? What was whoever it was in charge of?

"Yeah, her."

"She sounds pushy to me, Joanna."

"Assertive, Ma. Wait until you meet her tomorrow."

Tomorrow? "What time?"

"She's coming over at eight."

"Ben knows?"

"Yeah, Ma, he'll be here if you can't make it."

She knew so little about this that she thought she had better make it. "I'll be here. But Joanna, we need to talk about this."

"What do you think I'm doing, Ma?"

"I know but . . ." But what? Why hadn't she listened the other night? Was this woman talking contract or something? Could she? Joanna wasn't sixteen yet. Olympics? Was this some kind of scam?

"Sounds like a major commitment."

Joanna put her arms on the table and her head on her arms. "Right. Like the rest of my life."

"How do the other girls feel about it?"

"I've only met one of them."

So this wasn't a team thing. Or at least nobody else on Joanna's team was involved.

"What does she say?"

"Oh, God, she is little Miss Cheerleader. Volleyball is her life."

"Is she any good at it?"

"I don't know. She must be, but I haven't seen any of her highlight tapes yet."

Tapes? They taped them? During practice or while they were playing? And why? She would have to find out what Ben knew about this.

"Why are you hesitant?"

"Because, Ma, this is my life. I'm not sure volleyball is worth it."

"Even if it means going to the Olympics?" Marti thought accomplishing that would be a real stretch but she didn't say so. She knew Joanna was a good athlete. She didn't know if she was that good.

"I like sports, Ma. I love sports. But I just like to play. I like good competition, I like winning. But mostly, I just like to play. It's fun."

"And?"

"I'm not sure I want it to be more than something I enjoy. Everything in life doesn't have to be work, doesn't have to be a job, doesn't have to require . . . dedication, commitment. Volleyball is a team sport. I've never thought of it as a career." She sat back and clasped her hands behind her head. "Until now it was just fun. There's always some adult just waiting to change things. I know that if I go for it and I don't succeed, I'll feel a lot better than if I never try at all, and that's what really ticks me off."

So this wasn't about this lady or what she wanted. It was about Joanna, and the first major decision she had to make on her own, about her life.

Marti thought that she and Ben must be the only couple in town who had built a sunroom using bulletproof glass. It was their first anniversary gift to themselves. She had used some of Johnnie's insurance settlement, feeling uncomfortable with that at first. She and Johnny had never talked about either of them dying, or what might happen afterward, but they were both cops. The reality of death was always there, waiting. She wondered what would happen when she and Ben were dead, too. Would she have two husbands in heaven? Morbid thoughts, maybe, although they didn't seem so to her. Her thoughts nonetheless. She was as happy with Ben as she had been with Johnny, happier sometimes. She and Johnny had just wanted to be together and raise a family. They were both young. Maturity brought different perspectives.

Now when she visited Ben's parents in a suburb southwest of the city, saw that they were both getting older, more dependent on each other, with various ailments encroaching, and when she thought of Vik and Mildred, and the possibility of a debilitating illness, she realized how much more marriage was than she had been aware of when she was younger and married for the first time. Today she understood that all she had was now. And now Johnny wouldn't care about his insurance money or how it was spent, as long as there was enough left to send the kids to college. Johnny still loved her and wanted her to be happy. He always would. Just as she would always love him and knew that now he was happy.

Later, when she was in the sunroom with Ben, soaking in the hot tub, looking through the bulletproof glass at a cloud-covered sky with not a star peeking through, and inhaling the aroma of the vanilla-scented candles that provided a dim, flickering light, she said: "What's with Joanna and this Olympics thing?"

"Aha!" Ben said. "I thought you were too quiet to be awake when she was telling us about it."

"Well, I'm awake now. Kind of."

Ben stroked her thigh. "The woman's coming over tomorrow night. Let's talk about it then." His hand moved up to her breast.

"Yes," she agreed, "Good idea." She didn't want to fall asleep talking about the Olympics. There were better, more interesting ways to get tired.

Vik waited until nine o'clock to make the rounds of the Lake County shelters that were open Friday nights. By then the clients had washed up and eaten and most were asleep. Morning, a cold breakfast, and a bag lunch came early when you were homeless, and had to find a place to keep warm during the day. He went from one church to another, grateful that there were only eight in the county that LaShawna could reach easily. He knew he would spend the next several nights trying to forget the baby crying in the first place he went, and the woman in the wheelchair in the last. Just this church left and he could go home. He knocked on the side door that led to the basement and spoke quietly with the man who opened it. No, there was no woman there tonight with a young child, just one family with two school-aged children. Vik hurried back to his car wondering how homeless school-aged children went to school. He tried not to compare their lives with his own school days, when homeless children were unheard of, or at least not spoken of. No homeless people. No homeless children. That was the way he remembered it. That was the way he didn't think life would ever be again.

Mildred met him at the door. She was using her walker again. "*Moje cerca,*" he whispered, my heart. He kissed her mouth. He ran his fingers through her thinning gray hair and remembered it long and thick and blond, remembered her, strong and laughing. She didn't laugh as often now, although it didn't take much to tease a smile. Now she sat by the window more often, relied less on her cane and more on her walker, and needed their daughter, Krista, or her sister's help to cook. She had finally agreed to let a cleaning woman come in twice a week.

"Pasties," she said. "Still warm. And potato soup with dumplings."

He followed her into the kitchen and made sure she was settled in the well-padded rocker he had put by the window. Stephen had put up more bird feeders, even one that the squirrels could get at, pleased when the scampering rodents and squabbling blue jays amused her.

"So, what did you do this evening?" she asked.

He felt guilty for a moment, because he hadn't been home with her. "The job," he said.

She nodded. "It's all right, Matthew. Neither of us would be happy if you didn't do that job, and do it right."

"You were here alone."

"No," she said. "Not really. There's a peace to the quiet. And so many things to think about, and remember. So many good things to remember, Matthew. I was thinking about Door County. In the spring, let's go north, rent a place by a lake for a week. See if any deer come out early the morning or at dusk, looking for supper."

"Yes," he agreed. They would go, if that was what she wanted, even if he was in the middle of an investigation and a week could only be a long weekend. Marti and Lupe could manage while he was gone.

"*Moje cerca*," he said again. My heart. My heart.

Adrian shivered as he stood on the leeward side of the train station. Even though he was out of the wind, he had been standing there so long he was freezing. The Metra station was closed. The 10:10 train out of Chicago was due in seven minutes. If Douglas Grant stuck to his usual Friday night routine, he would detrain with enough alcohol in his system to make him just a little unsteady on his feet. He would then hurry across the tracks to get to the parking lot before the 10:15 train heading for Chicago was due to whiz past without stopping. Adrian knew he would have to act fast.

He didn't move from the shelter of the station when he heard the train approaching. Just in case. The two nights that he had been here watching, nobody else had gotten off the train. If tonight was any different, he didn't want anyone to see him. He couldn't see the red lights flashing, but the bell clanged and he heard the gates drop. If there were any cars or people about when he moved out of the shadows and toward the platform, he wouldn't be able to do anything.

He glanced down and noticed the penny near the toe of his running shoes. He didn't want to pick it up. Tails side up would mean bad luck and he would have to come back here next Friday. He wanted to be in Mexico by then. When he squatted to take a look at the coin, Lincoln was in profile, another sign that he was doing what he was meant to do.

Adrian smiled as the train pulled into the station, then stepped farther into the shadows as it departed. He pulled the metal pipe from his sleeve and held it at his side as he walked up behind Douglas Grant. No waiting cars, no other passengers. He caught up with Grant just as he was crossing the tracks. One hit took him down. He struck him again. Then he put Grant's head on one of the rails, and whistled as he walked back to the train station and stood in the shadows. The 10:15 bound for Chicago barreled past at sixty miles an hour. By the time the engineer began braking about half a mile away, Adrian was jogging in the opposite direction. He had counted on Jessica Grant to take his side. The way she kept looking at him, the sympathy in her eyes. Instead, they made her jury forewoman and she'd turned against him. Well, let her feel sorry for her own kids. Maybe she wouldn't turn on them the way she had turned on him. Time would tell. Jessica Grant and her three young children would never see Douglas Grant alive again.

5

Before Marti left home Saturday morning, she paused in the driveway and looked around. The street was empty. She backed out of the driveway, then drove slowly around the cul-de-sac twice, checking her neighbors' yards, then she went down the street and headed for work. She wasn't sure why she felt uneasy. Mad Sword Swinger syndrome she thought, but it wasn't that. She remembered that vagrant loitering in the doorway. There was something about him . . . something about the way he looked at her. She would have to keep an eye out, confront him if she saw him again, if only for her own peace of mind.

For whatever the reason, she was glad to be inside a secure building when she reached the precinct. Once in her office, she was more than a little surprised when she listened to her voice mail and there was a message from Graciela's caseworker with the names of three people she could talk to along with information on how to get in touch with them. Slim and Cowboy almost danced through the door before she had a chance to tell Vik.

"What's with you two?" she asked.

Slim dipped over in her direction, his caramel face all Cupid's-bow smile and deep dimples, and reeking of Obsession for Men.

"Remember that Internet sting?" he said.

She tried not to. Dealing with her own computer, which only involved internal functions like completing reports, filling out forms, and e-mail, was knowledge enough. She let Ben and the kids handle the Internet.

"What about it?" she asked. Circumstances were going to drag her into the world of computers sooner or later whether she liked it or not, and she was beginning to feel left out. Even Momma knew how to access a couple of Web sites.

"We got a hit! We got a hit!" Slim did a few dance steps and a doo-wop dip and spin. "Arrested a guy out looking for a little young meat. Thought he had an eleven-year-old prepubescent male and met up with us."

"Make my day," Marti said.

"Well, it sure as hell made mine," Slim said. "One less pervert out there."

Vik grunted. "And only nine hundred and ninety-nine million to go."

When Marti showed the social worker's list to Vik, he agreed that they would drive to Brookside first to see what they could find out about Graciela, since that was the town farthest from Lincoln Prairie. With road conditions the way they were, this was the best time of the day for distance driving. The sun was out at last, but that just meant that yesterday's snow would melt enough to freeze over and create hazardous driving conditions later on as the temperature dropped. As it was, they passed two fender benders and one tow job en route.

The residential facility where Graciela had lived for one school year was located in an isolated area that had probably once been some rich person's estate. The main building, a huge brownstone mansion, could house a hundred fifty children and adolescents. There was a barn in the distance, complete with a silo and white picket fence. Eight cottages were clustered around a large pond that was home to a flock of Canadian geese busy poking their beaks through the snow to get at the brown winter grass beneath. There were other outbuildings as well, including a garage that looked like something built during the days of horses and buggies, a gazebo, and a greenhouse.

A young man who identified himself as Jeff Willis, head counselor, met them at the door and led them into a cavernous main hall. Willis looked old enough to be just out of college and, by Joanna's definition, preppy, in Dockers, loafers, and a Tommy Hilfiger shirt.

"We left the great hall intact," Willis said, as if he had been in on the architectural conversion. "The classrooms," he pointed, "are in the west wing and the offices this way, to the east."

His office was small and one of many in a narrow warren off the hallway that looked as if it might have been one big room. Looney Tunes characters and toys filled a shelf and covered the top of a bookcase and at least half of his desk. Marti wondered how he made room for work.

"So you're here about Graciela. They told me it was okay to talk with you. She came here just before I did. That would have been about two years ago." Marti waited, but he made no reference to her death. "Graciela was always compliant, never a problem, aced all of her classes."

"Then why was she here?" Marti asked.

"As opposed to being in foster care?"

"Yes."

"Graciela seemed to find it much easier to adjust to institutionalization. That was always the placement that worked best for her. When she was in a home environment, she couldn't cope as well. She resented the attention paid to any other children who were there, and tried to monopolize the adults, not in any obvious way, but she wanted to be with them all the time, rarely spent any time in her room, was very helpful, but also hostile towards the other children. There are reports that she was physically mean to them, pinching and such, nothing that made her dangerous. She was much less suitable for private placements. I suggested a more intense institutional program, where she could receive psychological therapy, but that was never acted on."

"Do you know of anyone here who she made friends with?" Marti asked.

"No. She was in the recreation room most of the time, when she wasn't finding some way to assist the staff, but she didn't interact with the other clients."

"Did anyone dislike her?"

"No. I doubt it. Our clientele tends to be so narcissistic, so self-absorbed, that as long as you leave them alone, they scarcely notice you."

"There were no . . ."

"No conflicts, no confrontations. There was never any problem involving Graciela."

"No complaints about being pinched?"

"She didn't have to do that here. Being institutionalized is very different from private placement."

"In what way?" Vik asked.

"Sheer numbers, frequent personnel turnover, and some pretty tough, streetwise kids who would not be intimidated by her or take any kind of bullying without fighting back. I strongly disagreed with the decision to put her back into private placement, but she would have been legally on her own when she was due to graduate from high school. Everyone else felt it was more important to find a family who would be willing keep her beyond her eligibility."

"Does that mean you didn't think she could complete her education on her own?"

"Exactly. Latinas are not encouraged to get an education. It's cultural. Graciela would not have received any support within her community or from her peers. And she was a very intelligent young woman."

Their next stop was lunch, in an equally isolated restaurant made of logs with a sign that said Aunt Janie's Kitchen and hung at an angle as it swung in the wind. The parking lot was filled.

"Town meeting place," Vik grumbled as the went inside. The crowd, mostly older, sat at large communal tables that seated eight. The noise level was high. A senior citizen seemed to hold court at each table. Marti caught fragments of a conversation about World War I vets, led by a man with a hearing aid who looked as if he could have fought in it; a discussion on a quilt pattern; and a heated argument about a recent local election. The waitress waved them to a small table in a narrow space near the swinging doors that led to the kitchen. Not surprisingly, the food was made to order and delicious. Their sandwiches came with soup, coffee, and a trip to the salad bar and, tip included, they spent less than a total of fifteen dollars.

Their next stop was just northwest of Lincoln Prairie. Again, the house, although much smaller and a single-family, was somewhat isolated, sitting well back from the main road and at the end of a long gravel driveway. A woman met them at the door. She was balancing a baby on one hip. The child looked to be about six or eight months old, and behind her were three other children, all preschoolers.

"Hi, I'm Nina Rose Mansfield. Just call me Nina Rose. You must be the police officers. Come in." She held open the door with her free hand. The living room was a mess, toys everywhere, two playpens set up, but Nina Rose was a self-possessed and calm young woman. She did not apologize.

"Two of these just arrived last night." She jiggled the baby on her hip and reached out to hug one of the others. "Takes getting used to, such a sudden change, when you're this young. If you'll excuse me for just a minute, I've got a bottle warming for Carrie here, and Cody needs his pants changed."

Marti moved some unfolded laundry from the middle of the sofa to one end and sat down. An older girl who looked to be about ten came into the room and began picking up some of the toys and tossing them into laundry baskets, but said nothing.

"Oh, Lynnette, thank you," Nina Rose said when she returned. "Lynnette is such a big help. She reminds me of Graciela in some ways, but I don't have to worry about her pinching or teasing the children." She sat in a chair and rocked the baby who was wide-eyed and curious, trying to suck on her bottle and look around at the same time. "I am so sorry about . . . what happened." Her glance took in all of the children before she looked at Marti and Vik again. Marti nodded. They would not discuss what happened to Graciela in front of the children.

"When was Graciela here?"

"Oh, it's been a while." She thought for a minute. "About five years ago. She was eleven then. I try not to take in children who are more than nine or ten. I don't know what I would do with a teenager. My own are ten and twelve, so I guess I'll start finding out soon."

"Is that why Graciela left here?"

"This just didn't work out for Graciela at all. I tried. I did the best I could. I wanted to make a difference in her life, for a while at least, although I'm not sure that's always a good thing. Sometimes you're just a way station. That was all I was for Graciela. I had two other foster kids then, ages two and four. My own were five and seven. We were all miserable." She kept rocking the baby, who showed no signs of falling asleep.

"Was she friends with any of the neighborhood children?"

"Graciela was a loner. Kept to herself. Always around, in the kitchen, in here, wherever I was, like my shadow, but a loner for all of that. Very needy, very demanding, but in that quiet, undemanding way, just waiting, always waiting for you to pay attention to her."

"Was there anyone she didn't get along with?"

"Oh, she got along with everybody, with other kids her age by leaving them alone, with her teachers by being the perfect student, with me by never causing any trouble."

"But you were all miserable," Marti reminded her.

"I didn't know she was teasing the children. Not right away. I just saw them go from being reasonably happy to cranky and whiny. One day the window was open and I heard her telling the oldest foster child all kinds of things, why nobody loved her, why she had no parents, really mean things to say to another child. Then I understood what was going on and I called DCFS and told them the placement wasn't working. You want to help all of them. Realistically you cannot. But there is no reason to let them be even more unhappy or mistreated than they already have been."

Their final stop was on the far north east side of Lincoln Prairie. The ranch sprawled over a sizable piece of property. A middle-aged woman with auburn hair and a scattering of freckles answered the door. She smiled. "You're those two police officers, aren't you? I'm Anne Devney. Come right in," the woman offered, opening the door wider. "I was so sorry to hear about poor Graciela." She shook her head. "You never know what will become of them. I had five who have gone on to college." There were no children now, at least not that Marti could see, just four cats and two corgies.

The living room–dining room area took up the length of the south side of the house. Logs crackled in the fireplace. A white cat jumped up on Marti's lap while a marmalade cat sat beside her. Neither of the other cats made a move toward Vik. Children took to him right away, but animals tended to be wary. Marti stroked the cat and tried to ignore the white fur that was falling on her navy blue wool coat. When one of the corgis joined them, Marti could see that the dog favored one leg. Arthritis, she guessed. Neither dog could be considered young and frisky.

"When was Graciela here?" Vik asked. His voice was deep and gruff and Marti guessed that was why he spoke, to encourage the cats to keep their distance.

"Oh, about four years ago. A lovely child. So helpful. Quiet."

"What happened?" Marti asked.

"Oh, it was just the saddest thing. She just did not get along with the animals or my horse."

"Your horse, ma'am?" Vik asked.

"Yes, my horse."

"What seemed to be the problem?"

"Well, some of the children I've fostered have been afraid of him at first. Some never rode on him. But all of them liked him and eventually they would let him lick food from their hands and brush him down. But Graciela, I had to watch her. She would do all of those things, even ride him. But she was not kind to him and he shied away from her."

"What about the . . . cats . . . and dogs?" Vik asked, as if saying the words would cause them to befriend him.

"Do you see how quickly they took to Detective MacAlister? Well, they were the same way with Graciela, for the first few days. After that, when she came into the room, they ran out. And poor Shylock, here. Of course Graciela said it was an accident, but he hasn't been right since he took that fall down the basement steps. After that . . ." Anne Devney shrugged. "I really felt bad, sending her away. She loved to go the theater with me, and the Art Institute. She even tried the beginner class at the studio where I take ballet. As long as it was me and her . . ." Another shrug. "The only time I lived without pets was while I was in the navy. I couldn't do that now."

"I don't know what all of this tells us," Vik said as they headed back to the precinct. "What do we do now? Look for someone she was mean to without really seeming to be mean, who then got really mad at her for whatever she did to them?"

"Why not?" Marti agreed, ignoring Vik's testiness. "I think we better find someone who was at that juvenile facility when Graciela and José were there. See if we can find out what went on."

"There isn't anyone," Vik reminded her. "Turnover."

"Well, they'll just have to go through their personnel records."

They drove for a few minutes in silence, then Vik said, "What are you watching for?"

"I don't know, between that guy with the sword and that vagrant in the doorway yesterday . . ."

"Takes time," Vik said. "There are so many unpleasant possibilities in our line of work."

Marti agreed, but that didn't relieve her unease. Trust your instincts, Johnnie would have said. She had learned that that was the smart thing to do.

Vik didn't say a word when she checked out the area surrounding the county building, the jail, and the precinct.

When they pulled into the parking lot, he said, "Guess what? That old Saab over there belongs to Sikich."

"Damn. Not him again. Does he always drive that thing?"

"No. He's got a big pretty Lexus SUV. Wife must have it today."

Sikich was not in their office, but Slim and Cowboy were.

"I think he's looking for you," Slim said.

"Right, partner," Cowboy agreed, pushing back his five-gallon hat until a shock of white-blond hair fell over his forehead. "The man's got a problem. Came in here twice. When I suggested that he might have something going on with one or both of you he had the nerve to get in a snit."

The way he said it made Marti laugh.

"Then when he started walking past the door and looking in, I asked him if he thought you two were out somewhere doing the dirty—"

"Cowboy !"

"No, Marti, the man's a nutcase. Needs to be drummed the hell out of here. You should have seen him when I suggested running a DNA test on your underwear—"

"Cowboy, if you ever . . ." But she was laughing.

"Man's definitely got a problem," Slim agreed. "Wouldn't surprise me if we caught him in one of our Internet stings."

"Hell," Cowboy said, taking his booted feet off of his desk. "It wouldn't surprise me if we found him exposing himself in a public bathroom. If I ever see him going into one, I'm going to check him out."

Marti laughed again. "I hope you two can stick around for another half hour." She meant it. The odor of Obsession for Men didn't smell so bad right now, and it was strong enough to warn Sikich away.

While she entered her notes on her computer, Vik sat at his

desk and scowled. She hoped he was thinking of some way to get Sikich off their back short of killing him. She left a message for Denise, asking for help locating someone who had worked at that temporary facility, and made haste to leave when Slim and Cowboy got a call.

When they reached the sergeant's desk he called to them. "It's a girl, Angela Faith Dirkowitz, four pounds, two ounces. The little thing's got some kind of breathing problem. They medi-vac'd her to Chicago."

As soon as they were outside Vik said, "Well, Dirty Dirk might not be around for a while. We've got to go to plan B."

"What's that?" Marti asked.

"I don't know yet, but I bet I'll have it figured out by to-morrow."

Marti was going to get Momma's prayer group going at soon as she got home, and they wouldn't just be praying for Angela Faith.

The bright sunlight reflected off the snow and the glare almost blinded Adrian as he wound the transparent plastic wire around the tree trunk and made his way across the trail to wind it around the other tree trunk. There was no way to avoid the footprints, but he was wearing boots three sizes too big that he had picked up at a Salvation Army store for three dollars. He was also stomping so that he would make a deeper impression in the snow, as if he weighed more than he did, and taking long strides so he would seem taller. That should be enough to keep them looking for somebody else when they realized what had happened to Miss Sabrina Stanwick.

How sad her loss would be for her mother, Lureen Stanwick, chief prosecutor for the Cook County state's attorney's office. How tragic to lose her only child and such a gifted, brilliant child. Not only was Miss Sabrina an attractive young woman engaged to a state representative, she was also a much-sought-after expert in bioenvironmental chemistry as well as an accomplished pianist. Adrian smiled. Too bad she also enjoyed boating

and horseback riding in the summer and skiing and snowmobiling in the winter. Any one of them could be enough to kill
her. Today, one of them would be.

Adrian checked his watch and frowned. She was late today.
It would be dusk soon. Maybe she wasn't coming. Disappoint-
ment weighed him down worse than an onslaught of depression. She had to come. She had to. He had watched her too
long, planned this too long, looked forward to this for too long.
She would be up north skiing next weekend. He couldn't wait
two weeks for another chance. After her, there would only be
eleven of them left, plus Ramos's wife. And he didn't have to
kill all of them, just the most important ones. He could be on
his way to Mexico in another week, with all of this over and
done with.

He heard the engines in the distance and ran to hide among
a stand of trees halfway up the hill where he could watch. Three
snowmobiles came, not one. He saw the pink-and-white jacket,
the bright pink helmet, and knew the one in the lead was hers.
Then the bright pink helmet went sailing through the air, long
blond hair streaming behind it. The snowmobile, with the rest
of her body, careened off the trail and crashed into a tree. The
others veered off the trail just in time.

When Marti got back to the precinct, there were several phone
messages. The third one got her attention. "Detective Mac-
Alister, ma'am? I thought I'd better call you about LaShawna."
Marti didn't recognize the woman's voice. "LaShawna Davis?"
The woman repeated the name as if she was asking a question.
"You better find Reggie Garrett, ma'am. Before he hurts her
again, or does something bad to that baby. He said he'd kill her
if she left him. And she's left him. If he finds her, he will kill
her. Reggie is as nice as he wants to be until you cross him and
then he gets really, really mean."

There was a click as the woman hung up.

Marti listened to the recording two more times before she
handed the phone to Vik.

"Recognize the voice?" she asked, after he listened a couple of times and hung up.

"Nobody we talked to lately."

"But they must have my card. They called my private line."

"A lot of people have your card, MacAlister. A few of us have your number, too."

Marti ignored that, but noted that Vik's mood seemed to be improving. "She speaks of him as if she knows him. It doesn't sound like secondhand information, but it could be." Marti picked up the phone and waited until Records came on the line. "Get me whatever we've got on a Reggie Garrett and all variations. I don't have any spelling." She checked her watch. "I need it by five."

"It's quarter to six, Mac."

"I know."

Vik was checking out the coffeepot. "Damn," he said. "Cowboy's getting lax. Maybe we should complain to Sikich. Give him something important to worry about."

"Don't say that man's name," Marti warned. "He might hear you. If he comes in here right now . . . I'm in a mood to kill."

She listened to the phone message two more times. She wanted to hear some inflection, some nuance that seemed familiar, but she did not. "This woman is not disguising her voice and this is not someone who has spoken to me since I started looking for LaShawna. So how does she know I'm looking for her? And how did she get my card?"

"That place you went to this morning, maybe?"

"This phone call wouldn't be consistent with what the woman who runs the place told me about LaShawna not making any friends. We'll have to check it out, though."

The phone rang. Marti took notes as she listened. "Got a Reginald Edward Garrett. Eleven priors in the past seven years, misdemeanor battery, no felonies. Eight of the eleven arrests, and all of the most recent, involved women. We've got his last known address. It's his mother's."

She checked her watch again and phoned home. Ben and

the boys hadn't returned from their day trip. The woman who was going to talk to them about Joanna going to the Olympics was due at 8:00 P.M. "I'll do my best to be there," she promised Joanna. "If not, Ben can handle it if he's there. Or I'll talk to the woman tomorrow or as soon as she reschedules. I have to take care of something now. It can't wait."

But Joanna could, she thought, fighting down the familiar guilt. Everything, everyone, could wait, but not the Job. She didn't feel good about that, even though she knew Joanna would understand, or at least accept, her absence. How did Joanna really feel when she wasn't there for her? How would any adolescent feel? Any child? What was she doing to her children?

"Dammit, Vik. I hate working cases that involve kids."

"Tell me about it. We need to wrap up all of this, starting with José . . . and fast."

It was dark when they left the precinct.

Reginald Edward Garrett's mother lived in a nice ranch in a nice neighborhood on the northwest side of town. It was an older development, abutted on three sides by new and more expensive construction. Marti's stomach began churning as soon as she pulled up in front of the house. Every time she came to a place like this, where a known criminal had been raised by people who were at least middle class, she wondered what mistakes the parents had made, or if they had made any mistakes, and why children from a good environment went bad. Then she wondered about her own children.

The woman who opened the door didn't look anything like the woman Marti was expecting. Reggie Garrett was thirty-one. For some reason she had assumed that his mother would be at least fifty. If this mocha-complexioned, spandex-clad, shapely young woman was Garrett's mother, she looked young enough to have given birth before she was old enough to go to high school.

"Mrs. Garrett?" Marti asked.

"Used to be Garrett. Name's Garrett-Miller now, with a hyphen." The woman flashed sculptured blunt-tipped fingernails with pink, gold, and purple patterns as she patted her hair. The pink and purple matched the spandex. The gold matched the bracelets, necklaces, earrings, and diamond-crusted rings she was wearing.

They both showed the woman their badges.

"Cops! Hey! What's this all about?" She kept the door almost closed and didn't invite them inside, despite the cold. Marti wondered if she would have let them in if it had been snowing.

"Does your son, Reginald, live here?"

"Reggie? No way." The facets of a diamond ring trapped the overhead light as she touched her hair again. It was plaited in dozens of braids and pulled back into a ponytail.

"I let that boy lay on his lazy you-know-what for three years after he graduated high school. Boy never would have done a thing if I hadn't finally put him out. Still doesn't do any more than he has to. Look, I do not get involved with his life. He does his thing. I do mine."

Marti wanted to know if things were that way before Reggie graduated from high school, but that wasn't a question she could ask.

"So, what's he done this time? Did he beat up on somebody again? No way did I raise him to hit females. No way will I bail him out when he does. So you just go back and tell him that. Every time he gets himself into trouble he sends someone here to let me know that he needs me. If it wasn't for that, he wouldn't keep in touch with me at all. I have never bailed him out of jail. Do the crime. Pay the time. I've always believed that and nothing has changed."

"Reggie is not in any trouble, ma'am," Marti explained. "At least not as far as we know."

The woman had her mouth open, ready to say something else. Instead, she closed her mouth, then said, "He's not in trouble," considered that, and added, "Well, that's a surprise to me, especially now that he's taken to robbing the cradle."

"What do you mean, ma'am?"

"Oh, he brought some little underaged teenager over here one night. Just stopped in to use the phone. The phone. Now, I ask you: I told him that was why folks had cell phones, so they didn't have to drop in on their parents asking for something for nothing years after they stopped being children. You think he paid one bit of attention? No. Of course not. Same as always."

"A teenager, ma'am?' Marti asked. The wind had picked up and Marti could see that Garrett-Miller was shivering, but she still did not ask them in.

"He said the child was twenty-three. Must take me for some kind of fool. I'd say seventeen—maybe eighteen, but only because she was wearing so much makeup. Then too, there was the little girl, so I could be wrong. I had Reggie when I was sixteen, and that child's baby must have been somewhere around three . . . so that girl, the mother, must have been at least nineteen, but damn, she sure didn't look a day over sixteen. And Reggie easing up on thirty-two. I told him not to come anywhere near me again with some jailbait girlfriend tagging along."

"When was this?"

Mrs. Garrett-Miller thought for a minute. "One night last week. Thursday? No, Friday. Yes, that's when, on Friday. My husband and I were supposed to go to the casino, but my husband—something came up, he had to work late, got stuck in traffic trying to get out of the city. You know the drill. Only reason why I was even home. And now you're looking for him."

"What did the woman and the child look like?"

Vik took down the description. They still didn't have any photos of LaShawna or her daughter. The description Garrett-Miller gave them sounded close to the one the woman at the temporary shelter had given her. If they didn't find them soon, they would have to get an artist's drawing.

"Do you know where Reggie is staying?"

"No. And I never ask. He still seems to have a few friends

he can hang out with. He's got a disability scam going that keeps him in petty cash."

"How's that, ma'am?' Marti asked.

"Oh, he started a fight with the wrong man one night five, six years ago, and got a good butt whipping. Stayed in the hospital two weeks, went to rehab, claims he has a bad back from it. Long as I've been paying into social security and the way it's about to go bankrupt, his disability is about the only way I'll ever get anything back, but even so, I told him I don't believe a word of it. He told me I ain't got no pain in my back like he does. The pain doesn't seem to keep him from doing most of what he wants to, though. Sure could fool me."

Marti wondered if pimping young girls was another one of his scams, but didn't ask. The uniform in Records hadn't mentioned anything, but there were other ways to find out.

"Do you have any idea of how to reach him?"

The woman's plucked and arched eyebrows went up about a quarter of an inch. "Now, why would I want to do that? Boy's like a bad penny. He'll always turn up."

"But if you did need to get in touch?" Marti persisted.

"There are a couple of his so-called friends who you could check out." When pressed, the woman went into the house, leaving the door ajar, and handed them a piece of paper when she returned. There were two names, G.L. and Joe Boy, written on it along with two phone numbers. "This is the best I can do. Neither of them ever seem to keep their phones turned on for long. Don't be surprised if they are disconnected again."

Marti was shivering as she turned up the car heater and put the fan on high. "I wonder why she didn't want us to come in?"

Vik rubbed his hands together and didn't answer.

"And where are your gloves? I've told you about not wearing your gloves, Jessenovik. I might have some spares in my purse." At least he was wearing a hat consistently, but only since he'd been diagnosed with strep throat. "If you think you can get sick enough to stay home, Vik, think again. With Dirkowitz gone,

Sikich being a mega pain in the butt, and this caseload, you're in this for the duration, sick or not."

She called in the phone numbers and nicknames Garrett-Miller had given her and had addresses for both within five minutes, not because the system was fast or the phones still connected but because the desk sergeant recognized the names.

"Petty drug dealers," the sergeant said. "Nickel-and-dime penny-ante shit. Small buys that they break up into nickel-and-dime bags and pass along to their friends. Both of them need to be locked up for being public nuisances. This G.L. must have two hundred traffic violations. If you catch him behind the wheel of anything including a tricycle, assume he's driving without a license and have him brought in. I used to think that if we paid enough attention to them they would move someplace else, but Joe Boy lucked out when his mother died. She left him one of those starter homes in the Preserves free and clear and he was smart enough not to sell it."

Marti drove over to Joe Boy's place first. It was a small house on a small lot, and painted a deep gold with brown trim.

"I bet it's been in the family a long time," Vik said.

"How would you know?"

"See the siding, how wide it is? Newer siding is narrower. And that siding is cedar, not aluminum. And see the trees?"

Marti looked. They were two or three times the height of the house.

"Chinese or Japanese elms. I forget which. Grow fast, real brittle, give lousy shade. The original developers planted them. Nobody's been that dumb since."

The tree branches outlined a dark sky. Marti didn't want to look at the clock on the dash, but she did. Ten to seven.

"Has Joanna got a basketball game tonight?" Vik asked. "We can probably knock off for the night or at least a couple hours after we check out these two—if we don't meet up with Mr. Reginald Garrett."

"Joanna's got some woman coach coming over tonight to talk to us about playing volleyball in the Olympics."

Vik whistled. "Way to go, Joanna."

"Maybe," Marti said. "She isn't sure that's what she wants to do."

Vik raised his eyebrows. "Our Joanna, not sure about something?"

Marti smiled. He was right. Joanna always knew what she wanted to do, as well as what she wanted everyone else to do, including her mother.

From the flash of recognition in Joe Boy's eyes, Marti and Vik might as well have had neon signs on their foreheads flashing Cop.

"I ain't done nothin', man," he protested. "I'm clean. Swear to God."

He didn't invite them in either. Marti debated pushing her way in, but she didn't want to blow a bust if Garrett was inside.

"We're just looking for one of your friends," she said.

The relief on Joe Boy's face was momentary, but a significant suggestion that he had reasons for not wanting them inside. She thought of what the sergeant has said. Too bad their business was more pressing than a drug bust, even if the quantities would be small.

"Who you want?" Joe Boy asked.

"Reginald Garrett."

Joe Boy shook his head. "Ain't seen him."

"Gee, that's too bad," Marti said.

"Yeah," Vik agreed. "We just asked a couple of narcs to take a pass on you this evening. They're parked right around the corner. We saw them when we were coming in."

A look of panic spread across Joe Boy's face. Like a lot of small-time petty criminals, he lacked the sophisticated, laid-back attitude of the big boys.

"You got any warrants or tickets outstanding?" Marti asked. She turned to Vik. "Maybe we should call that in."

"No, no, no. No, man, I'm clean, swear to God." Despite the cold, he began sweating.

"And you do have some idea of where we might be able to find your good friend, Reginald Garrett."

"Hey, hey, no. I ain't seen the dude since . . . since . . . Saturday. Yeah, yeah, it was Saturday. Him and his woman came over. No, no, Sunday. That's when it was."

"Look, Joe Boy—"

"I know, I know, man but see, I just remembered, on Saturday night I went up to Kenosha with a friend. So it had to be Sunday 'cause Monday I went to the township office to get help with the gas bill and then I went to the food pantry, so I know I didn't see them that day. It had to be Sunday."

Marti looked at Vik and he nodded. Yes, that did make sense to him also.

"So what was happening with them on Sunday?" Marti asked. "They come alone?"

"No, no, man. Had the little girl with them. Cute little thing. I told Reggie it was too cold to have her out at night like that and he got all pissed off and started yelling at LaShawna. Punched her right in the stomach and then a couple times in the back when she doubled over. Mean like that, Reggie is, but he never hits 'em where you can see it. Gives them those body blows. LaShawna could hardly catch her breath and already knew better than to cry. Bit her lip till it was bleeding. Reggie trains them right fast, he does." He stopped talking, shook his head. "I didn't mean to cause her no trouble, honest. And I couldn't do nothing to help her. Reggie only would have hit her again if I said anything else. Nice girl, she was. Quiet. Pretty. I sure didn't mean to do nothing that would cause him to hit her. I wasn't even talking to her. I know it was Reggie who had to come over, not LaShawna."

"Why did Reggie have to come over?" Marti asked. When he didn't answer and got that panicky expression again, she added. "We're not narcs, Joe Boy. We work homicide."

"Homicide? Reggie didn't kill her, did he?"

"Not as far as we know. We just want to find out where she is."

"I don't know, man, I swear to God. I don't know."

"But if you find out, you will tell us, won't you?"

"Yes, ma'am."

"And right away."

"Sure thing. You know I will."

"My name is MacAlister. Detective MacAlister. You know a cop they call Slim?"

Slim worked Vice, not Narcotics, but he had a street rep for coming down hard—legally and relentlessly—on anyone who crossed him.

"Know him real well, ma'am. Went to school with him."

"He and I work together. I'll make sure he knows that I saw you tonight and that you will be giving me your full cooperation."

The sweat was rolling down Joe Boy's face now.

"Detective MacAlister, you got that?"

"Oh, yes, ma'am. I got that. I sure do."

She flicked him two quarters. "Hold on to that so you can make that call."

"Oh, yes, ma'am. Yes, ma'am."

As they walked to the car, Marti said. "Don't you dare mention Joe Boy's reaction to Slim. That man has enough problems with his ego as it is."

She checked her watch. Seven-thirty.

G.L. lived at an address on First Street on the southeast side of town. When they reached the two-flat with the sagging porch and one dog chained to a doghouse, the place was dark. The dog began barking as soon as they approached. Close up, Marti saw that it was a pit bull and not just a territorial mixed-breed mutt. "We'd better get the animal warden to check this one out," she said.

"And soon," Vik agreed.

Ignoring the dog's deep-throated growls and bared teeth, they pushed open a door that was attached to the frame by one hinge, paused to draw their weapons and let the dog calm down, then listened to the wind rattling the shingles and making the house creak for a good five minutes before they knocked first on the door of the upstairs apartment, then on the door on the first floor. Nobody answered. They made a show of getting into their car and driving away, then parked on the street behind the house, walked through an open yard and went to the back door, avoiding the dog, who apparently didn't bother to bark unless he could see someone.

Again they drew their weapons. A porch had been added on to the outside, but they didn't use those stairs. Instead they stood inside the hallway listening to the wind buffeting the house. There was no music, no TV, and they couldn't hear anyone talking. They kept to the wall as they made their way upstairs again. They listened at the door for voices, but heard none. Nobody responded when they knocked. They tried the doorknobs, but the doors were locked. They sniffed, but didn't detect any dead-body odors. No rotten garbage smells either. Or urine stink. The place seemed unlived in. They had no valid reason for a forced entry. There was a missing persons report on LaShawna and her child, but nothing to suggest they might be here.

Downstairs, they found a door that led to the cellar. It wasn't locked and they did confirm that there was no rotting garbage, no rotting bodies, and not much of anything else other than cobwebs, a rusting water heater, and a cement igloo-shaped furnace, that Marti thought must be pre-World War II. Neither the water heater nor the furnace had a gas supply to ignite the pilot light. Nothing happened when she flicked a couple of light switches and no water came out when she turned on a spigot at an old concrete sink.

Outside, Vik said, "We'll have to wait, come back. It's eight o'clock. Let's get over to that temporary shelter."

They agreed that Marti would go inside and see if any of the women there would admit to making the call alerting them to Garrett. That done—unless they got another lead—Vik would check the churches hosting tonight's PADS program for the homeless while Marti went home and met this coach who wanted Joanna on her volleyball team. She called home from her cell phone. The woman hadn't arrived yet. When she did, Ben and Momma would entertain her until Marti arrived. Marti rang off, certain that she would not make it home at all.

Tracy, the same woman she had talked with the day before, admitted her to the shelter. Again Tracy led her into the kitchen. This time, five women sat around two tables. One woman held a sleeping infant. The high chairs were empty, the house quiet. Tracy offered her tea. Marti shook her head. She asked each woman to tell her their name, if they had been here while LaShawna was, and anything they could that might help her find out where LaShawna was now.

"Why?" one woman asked.

"Right," another agreed. "Why should we tell you anything?"

Marti thought for a minute, then said, "I met LaShawna when she was pregnant and homeless and living in a vacant library with four other throwaway children. There was nobody in their lives who wanted them. We did what we could to help; two of the children are fine right now, one is okay, one is about to be accused of a serious crime, and LaShawna and her child are missing.

"I'm a mother, the same as you, the same as LaShawna, so I'm concerned about her child. I'm also a peace officer, and I've found out that the man LaShawna was with just before she came here has a history of physical abuse, and abused La-Shawna last Sunday." She looked at each of the women. She had their attention. "We are looking for that man now. And we are looking for LaShawna and her little girl. We do not know if the crime her friend from the library is in custody for is in any way related to her disappearance, and we need to rule that out. Also, we don't know if this man she was with has found her or has hurt her or her child."

One by one, the women gave Marti their first names and the day they came to the shelter. Marti listened carefully. She was certain none of them was the woman who called in the tip on

Reggie Garrett. Two were here while LaShawna was, three had arrived after LaShawna went missing.

"I knew she was hurt," one woman said. "They way she held one arm, I thought maybe it was her shoulder. But she wouldn't say nothing. Probably afraid of what would happen to her baby if they took her to the hospital. They take 'em from you real quick and it's real hard getting them back."

"Did you check the hospitals?" the other woman asked.

"Yes, why?"

"Her stomach was hurting her something awful. I thought she might be having a miscarriage or something."

Marti turned to Tracy, who said, "She was real quiet, like I said, didn't act like she was in any pain when she was around me. But they're right about why she wouldn't want to go to the hospital. We have a doctor who will see them here, but a lot of the time they're hurt bad enough to need to be admitted. She did ask for Tylenol and I gave her some."

"None of you know where she went?" Marti asked.

The two women shook their heads. Neither of them looked like she was hiding anything.

"You knew she was in pain. Did she tell you anything else?"

"She didn't even tell us that. We just knew. Just by looking at her."

"We don't mind other folks' business," the other woman said. "We're not here to make friends. We're here because we got no place else to go."

All of the women nodded their heads.

Marti left another donation on her way out. "Get them a treat. Whatever a treat is for them. And tell me the name of your pastor. Maybe our churches can do something together."

She left feeling more depressed than she had the last time she was here.

The volleyball coach was still there when Marti got home. The coach, Diana Vickery, was everything Marti expected, and more. She bounded out of the chair in the family room, rushed over and seized Marti's hand with a grip firm enough to bruise, and gave Marti's arm several hard shakes.

"Detective MacAlister," she began, "it's so good to finally meet you. Mr. MacAlister and—"

"Mr. Walker," Marti corrected without explanation.

Vickery paused midsentence, momentarily confused. "You remarried," she said finally.

Marti nodded.

"Well, I'm sure everyone has explained to you the importance as well as the honor of being selected to play on a team with the potential to compete in the Olympics. Can you imagine that, your daughter in the Olympics, on national television, standing on the podium receiving a medal that says she is among the best athletes in the world."

Marti watched the woman closely as she was speaking and could not detect when she took a breath.

"Why don't you sit down, Coach Vickery," Marti suggested. "Since this would be a family commitment, my mother, as well as Joanna's brothers, Theo and Mike, will stay for this meeting."

"Oh, yes, of course." The coach gave her a big smile. "Family support is vitally important, especially during those extended training periods and exhibition tours when you won't see Joanna at all."

Marti glanced at Joanna, who seemed surprised. "Why don't you begin at the beginning," Marti suggested.

"First of all," Coach Vickery began, "Joanna has come to our attention as an outstanding volleyball player with tremendous potential. Most parents think of volleyball as a team sport that their kids play through high school, but there are many college scholarships available for this sport as well. Beyond that, there is the potential for considerable earnings playing competitively. There are professional female volleyball players today making anywhere from seventy-five thousand to three hundred and seventy-five thousand dollars a year. And since I know that all parents put a high priority on a college education, let me assure you that these women, through scholarships, have completed or are completing their postsecondary educations."

"What does this entail now?" Ben asked. "Joanna is fifteen."

"A complete commitment to our program. We cannot guarantee that Joanna will remain injury free, or that she will become a part of this well-paying profession, or that she will make it to the Olympic tryouts or the Olympics, but we can see her potential, help her develop and extend her skills. And she can most definitely compete at a professional level."

"Like a job," Joanna said.

"Yes," Coach Vickery agreed. "In effect, for the next fifteen to twenty years, volleyball would be your job. Isn't that exciting? Instead of trudging off to the office everyday, you get to go to the gym and do something you love, then go to the sports arena and do what you do best in front of thousands of cheering, adoring fans."

Joanna did not seem impressed. "I'm not sure that's what I want to do," she said.

"Of course not, not at fifteen," Coach Vickery agreed. "Many of our girls at your age have tremendous difficulty committing to something that requires so much of them. But you are fifteen, many, many athletes have committed to their sport at five and six and never looked back. And never been as good as you are right now, but through persistence and hard work, they have succeeded. Perhaps not to the ultimate level, but to an economically comfortable level, with the additional satisfaction of doing what they loved, and excelled at."

Marti still couldn't tell when the woman took a breath.

"Tell us about your program," Marti said.

Coach Vickery went on to explain where they trained—Upstate New York and Nevada. The tutoring they received, the special diet regimens and exercise programs they adhered to, as well as the camaraderie among the girls, the personal trainers, the group-home living arrangements, the tutorial program, the state-of-the-art computer and science labs, and finally the cost, which was astronomical. It would take Joanna's entire inheritance, which consisted of investments made with Johnnie's insurance, and some of Theo's college fund as well.

"This is the opportunity of a lifetime," Coach Vickery concluded. "The cost is a bargain when compared to the earning potential of the successful competitor." That said, she whipped out the contract, which looked to be at least a dozen legal-sized sheets of paper with typing on both sides.

"Well," Marti said, "you have certainly given us a lot to think about. You've given Joanna a lot to think about. Ultimately, this is her decision and we will support it, financially and otherwise. However, before I agree to anything, or sign anything, it will have to be Joanna's decision to proceed, and my attorney will have to approve the contract."

"And," Ben added, "assuming that we progress that far, we will all have to tour both the New York and Nevada facilities and speak with the staff and the other girls in the program."

Coach Vickery gave them a wide, toothy smile. "But of course, of course." She handed Ben a business card. "I will be in the area scouting prospective team members for at least another week. I must advise you, though, that we have a limited number of slots available. We can't make this kind of offer to anyone but the best, and we can't work effectively with large groups of girls. So do talk this over and give me a call as soon as possible."

After the coach left, Joanna said, "All I want to do is play volleyball. I do not want to be owned by it." She headed for the steps, turned, and said, "Can you really afford this?" When Marti nodded, she went upstairs.

"That was a little like being chased by a freight train," Ben said.

"Hmmmmm," Momma said. "Hard to believe that very many people get paid that kind of money for getting a ball over a net. And in a game where they dig, block, and kill. At least I think that's what Joanna is doing out there on the court. I go because she's my granddaughter. Hard to imagine someone paying to watch, unless it is at the Olympics. Amazing how silly we've become." That said, Momma mentioned cocoa and cookies to Theo and Mike, and they headed upstairs.

"Guess that leaves us," Ben said, with a grin. "Have you got to go back to work?"

Marti stretched out on the couch. "Nope." Her stomach rumbled.

"No supper yet?"

"Didn't have time."

"How tired are you?"

"Wired says it better," Marti admitted. She felt as though she could do calisthenics for the next three hours.

"Well, candlelight, the hot tub, and some wine sounds good, but since we've already done that this week, want to go someplace nice for dinner and maybe a dance or two? Nothing fancy. You don't have to change."

She thought about that for a minute. She didn't feel the least bit tired now, but when she did, it would come on her heavy and all at once. Meanwhile, it was only a little after nine. The way she felt now, she'd be on this adrenalin rush for the next two or three hours.

"Let's go out," she said. "Long enough to eat and do a little dancing." She reached out and touched his face. "And let's not rule out the possibility of a little candlelight when we get home, although I can't make any promises that I'll be able to stay awake that long."

Ben did a little dance step and began singing "I Got a Woman" in a resonant baritone. His version didn't sound anything like Ray Charles's. Raunchy was the way Momma would have described it.

Adrian stood near the corner of a snow-covered street that looked as if it hadn't been plowed since the first snowfall in November. He was on the south side of the Dan Ryan Expressway. On the other side of the multilaned road, the Robert Taylor Homes stood like warring sentries, each building guarding itself

142

against the daily human onslaught of violence that brick and concrete were defenseless against. Plywood-covered windows were surrounded by smoke-blackened brick. Open windows let in the cold and the snow and provided easily accessed exits for young children, and opportunities for those bent on violent death. Elevators taunted residents who had to walk up flights of stairs, or risk falling to their death if they were too stoned, too drunk, or too stupid to realize they were entering an empty shaft. The hallways beckoned to winos and addicts and the criminals who preyed on them. The tall brick sentries that had once provided security and protection couldn't even promise safe shelter from the cold.

This was no longer the place where he grew up, hadn't been for a long time. Not that it wasn't crowded then, not that there wasn't crime, not that he ever felt safe, surrounded by so many tall buildings built so close together. He always seemed to be walking through crowded hallways, avoiding crowded play-grounds and basketball courts and crossing crowded streets. Crowds. There always seemed to be people everywhere. And noise. The place was alive with noise, even in the middle of the night. When the music stopped playing the sirens began screaming, but always there was the noise.

It was just him then, and Gramps, and Uncle Dudley, and Uncle Rafe. They didn't need any women. His daddy had had a woman, his mama. He caught her with someone else and killed them, then turned the gun on himself. No, they didn't need any women. They cooked, cleaned, washed clothes, did everything themselves.

Everyone, even Gramps, got a little sex—or nookie, as they called it back then. He started taking his when he was thirteen, whether the girl was willing or not. That's what woman were for, lying on their backs and spreading their legs. Women were not important, not even the pretty ones, especially not the pretty ones. Gramps said his mama had been pretty, too pretty for her own good.

Summer and fall, Uncle Dudley would take him south to

Tennessee and they would hunt 'coons and 'possum with shotguns and traps. When they came back their neighbors would line up in the hallway to buy one little taste of home. Gramps liked to fish, but most of the time he just sat and talked about the days when he was young and chased women and drank bootleg. Uncle Rafe was the ladies' man. Love 'em and leave 'em, he would say. Ain't nair one of 'em worth a damn.

Gramps and Dudley and Rafe. Uneducated men, all of them, but they saw to it that he went to school, came home, did his homework and got his butt whipped if he didn't make the honor roll.

One by one, the projects claimed them. Gramps was diabetic. With his toes gone, then his feet, then his legs, he didn't have much reason to live. One night he took Uncle Dudley's shotgun and ended it. He didn't go hunting with them and wasn't as good a shot. It took the ambulance two hours to get there. Took another twenty minutes for two paramedics to walk up twelve flights of stairs with a stretcher. Took another ten minutes for Gramps to bleed to death.

That was when the projects seemed to change. Not long after Gramps died, Uncle Dudley got held up one payday and took a knife through the heart when he wouldn't give up his money. Then, two years later, Rafe got caught in gang cross fire. "Rafe the Rake," Gramps had called him. Rafe was Gramps's favorite. Adrian was glad Gramps hadn't lived to bury him.

He was the only one to make it out of that place, to make it all the way to the Gold Coast. But he was a black man, took that to the Gold Coast too. No way to escape that, no way to pass, or pretend, or hide. He couldn't get smart enough, or rich enough, or important enough to stop being black. And a black man could not prosper in this world. A black man could not prosper at all.

Now he was back. Not to live in the projects anymore but here, where he came from, to kill. This time it was to kill, not to be killed. He was going to kill a cop tonight. He wanted to strangle him, the way the cops strangled the life's blood from this place. He wanted to kill the cop and his son the way he and Gramps had died here, slowly, the way Dudley and Rafe had been killed here, taken by surprise. The cop was white and married and middle class. His illegitimate kid's mama was black, and single, and poor. The cop, Ray Franklin, lived in Hyde Park. The cop's son lived on this side of the expressway, across from the projects his daddy served and protected. Those were the real reasons why Ray Franklin had to die, not just because he had been MacAlister's partner, and one of the cops who'd arrested him.

Adrian felt the smooth metal of the gun in his jacket pocket. He had broken into half a dozen apartments before he found it hidden under a mattress. This was not the way he wanted the cop and his son to die, but it was the only way he would be sure to kill them. There was no way a Chicago cop would let him get closer without perceiving the threat. And this way, with the cop out of uniform and carrying a little black boy in his arms who might not be dead but sleeping . . . well, it would either look gang related or it would look like someone didn't appreciate having that white man invading his territory by using a black woman.

The cop came and took his son out every Saturday. They came home about nine-thirty or ten. It was nine-fifteen now. Adrian walked to the street where the cop's kid lived, two blocks over. This street was plowed, with snow piled against the curb. The sidewalks and walkways and stairs had been cleared. Bungalows, the place to live in Chicago until the condos took over. A house not unlike the one Da Mare, Richard J. Daley himself, had grown up in. Soon the cop's car would pull up. He would get out, go to the passenger side, unbuckle the sleeping boy's seat belt, lift him out and carry him inside without waking him. Too bad he couldn't kill the child first. Maybe he would. He had planned it so that one shot would take out both of them. But the cop . . . it would happen too fast . . . he would never know his son was dead.

Adrian was almost at the corner of the street where the cop

145

lived when four cats ran out of an alley maybe ten feet away from him. Three of them headed in the opposite direction. The last one stopped. It looked like a black cat, but he wasn't sure. The light wasn't that good. Just in case, he called to it. If it came toward him it meant good luck, but if it ran away from him like the others . . . The cat hissed, arched its spine, and backed up. But it was still facing him. Then a fifth cat came out of the alley, the one the black was hissing at, and the black cat turned and ran away. Damn. Double damn. Triple damn. If the cat was black, it had just made his luck turn. He didn't dare risk attempting to kill anyone tonight, let alone Officer Ray Franklin. Angry and helpless Adrian watched as the cop's car turned the corner. He turned up his collar, pulled down his hat, and walked quickly away.

6

José heard the wheels squeaking as they rolled the food cart down the hall. The sound stopped near the door to his room. He turned toward the wall and did not speak when the orderly came in with his tray.

"José, come on, man, eat something for me."

It was the young Latino aide. He was talking in English now, but kept coming in during his shift and talking to him in Spanish, trying to get him to say something back. He would like to talk to this man. He would like to have a friend. But that was not possible anymore. That had not been possible for a long time now. He would not be in this place long enough to make a friend. He would not be anyplace long enough. Better not to bother than to keep saying good-bye.

"José, the food, it gets cold. Pancakes, man, and bacon. Not as good as nopale and chorizo and huevos, the way my mother cooks them, but better than nothing."

José wondered how many years it had been since he had eaten cactus with his eggs and sausage. Not even Mrs. Ramos scrambled eggs with boiled cactus chopped up and mixed in. It had been so long ago since he had eaten that. He could no longer imagine the taste, yet part of him wished for it, wished hard. But for what, the food or whoever had prepared it, or who he had been with while he ate it? He couldn't remember any of that, it was so long ago, and now he could no longer remember the taste or the smell.

"I will be back in half an hour. Surprise me, amigo. Eat something. They will take out the IV when you start eating."

Alone, Jose stared at the wall. If he closed his eyes he would see Graciela the way she looked the last time he saw her. Looking at him. Her eyes wide with fear. All covered with blood. He would see her, just as when he slept he saw her in his dreams and woke up screaming. If only she had not killed the baby. This would not have happened to them if she had not killed the baby.

Despite the surf and turf, and the slow dancing, and then the vanilla-scented soak in the hot tub, with candles, moonlight, and Ben, followed by some intense lovemaking, Marti had not slept well last night. Now Ben was still sleeping, with that little satisfied half smile on his face that she found so endearing, and she was wide awake and tired at the same time. Momma, always an early riser, joined her in the kitchen.

"You all right, Marti?"

She shrugged.

"Well, thank goodness you haven't put on any coffee yet. I'll take care of that right now."

As Momma bustled about, Marti thought of the bright yellow kitchen she had shared with Sharon when she first came here with Theo and Joanna. There was something about the sunny brightness of that room that this wallpaper couldn't compete with.

"Momma, I need to have this room painted yellow."

"That shouldn't be a problem. Want me to check with my church sisters and have someone reliable come in?"

Marti smiled. Momma had been networking long before anyone coined the term. She explained why she was hesitant.

"I don't see why Sharon would mind, if it brings back good memories for you—and the man who invaded that kitchen didn't change that—maybe it still holds good memories for Sharon, too."

"I haven't seen much of her lately," Marti said. Sharon and her daughter, Lisa, who was fifteen, the same age as Joanna, were sharing the apartment over Marti's garage. Each night when she came home, she checked to make sure Sharon's car was there, and usually it was, but she didn't see much of Sharon these days.

"I think Sharon's avoiding me. Does she come over when I'm not here?"

"Usually in the afternoon when she comes home from work. She seems to like teaching third grade. She's talking about taking some teaching course in the summer. I think that will be good for her. She's been through a lot, put herself through a lot more. But you two have been friends since kindergarten. Maybe you should go talk to her."

Momma got some bagels out of the freezer, and also a jar of raspberry something or other that was all natural fruit, without additives or preservatives. Joanna had introduced Momma to it and Momma seemed to enjoy the bagels as much as the delicious, buttery, fruit-filled, sugar-dusted, muffins she used to make at least three times a week. Marti tried not to think muffins as Momma took the bagels from the toaster and smeared on the un-jam. When she had to eat bagels, she preferred to have them slathered with gobs of melting butter, but she didn't have time to be that particular this morning.

Marti made it to the precinct just in time for roll call. Angela Faith Dirkowitz was holding her own in the neonatal unit at Children's Hospital in Chicago with a lung disorder common to premature and low-birth-weight infants. The medication was working. If the baby's condition remained stable, or if she began to improve, Dirkowitz would be in for a few hours a day by midweek. Marti wasn't sure she could hold out that long. Sikich was staring at her from across the room. She stared right back until he looked away, then felt more childish than assertive. Anger rose like bile in her throat. She considered going to the captain or whoever was in charge today if Sikich did not leave her alone.

Sure enough, when Marti and Vik reached their office, Sikich was right behind them.

"Reports?" he asked, as he followed them into the room. "I have nothing from yesterday. No time sheets, no activity logs, nothing."

Slim and Cowboy came in just in time to hear him.

"Baby-sitter's here," Slim snickered.

"Cowboy, Slim," Marti said. "Good morning. So good to see you. Sit down, relax, make coffee."

Slim looked at Cowboy, and said, "Uh-oh." Then he sat down, leaned back, and gave Sikich his best Cupid's-bow smile.

"Reports," Sikich said again, looking from Marti to Vik, then back at Marti.

"There are none," she said. "Nor will there be. I do not have the time for that today nor will I have the time in the near or distant future. I am a peace officer, not a secretary, and not a fool. There is nothing in the current code that requires that I comply with what you are asking for and I do not have the time to humor you."

"MacAlister, you are coming very close to insubordination."

"Good, report me to the chief. Now. Before I report you. If this is not harassment, then it has to be some violation of my civil rights, and if it doesn't stop—now—I will pursue that."

Sikich said nothing. He stared at her for at least a minute before he turned on his heel and walked out.

Slim began clapping. Cowboy joined in.

"Way to go," Vik said. "You've given him something to think about, at least temporarily."

Marti selected a jelly doughnut from the box she had brought in and gave it to him. "There are things to be said for being a former big-city cop, Jessenovik. Sikich never would have survived this long in Chicago. Not because they don't reward incompetence the same as they do here, but because his kind of incompetence would not be tolerated within the ranks. Sikich just needs to understand the meaning of coming to work in a police precinct and having to watch your back while you're there. He had better stay at his desk for a while and do whatever it is that he does, or he's going to find out exactly what that's like."

"Damn, Mrs. Officer Mac," Cowboy drawled. "I sure as hell wouldn't want to cross you when you're having a bad day."

"This is a good day," she said. It was now. For once something would be circulating about her around here that wasn't some kind of a joke.

Over coffee and doughnuts, Marti, Vik, and Lupe compared notes. Everything they had been working on except José and LaShawna had been given to Lupe, which meant Lupe had to work on five cases in her spare time.

"I think we can send two of these to the state's attorney," Lupe said. "We got more forensic reports back on the vehicular homicide. Everything points to the driver of the compact."

"The compact? What about the SUV?"

"Not this time," Lupe said. She summarized the evidence and Marti and Vik agreed with her.

"Good job, Torres," Vik said. Marti was pleased that he complimented her. Like it or not, the compliment carried more weight coming from him.

"And?" Marti said.

"That witness in the hypothermia case is sticking to her story and still more than willing to tell it to a judge."

"Great!" Marti exclaimed. "I think she'll make a credible witness."

"Right," Vik agreed. "One absentee landlord down, who knows how many to go."

"So," Lupe said. "We're down to four cases and one of those is the Graciela Lara case. I saw Ramos, by the way. He made a few disparaging remarks about the department. His ill winds might start blowing this way before long, unless we make some progress."

"Is that a hint?" Vik asked.

Lupe grinned. "These other cases are so cold they'd freeze the . . ." She stopped, and grinned again.

"Well," Marti began, "no change in the Lara case. Forensics has not come up with anything else to prove or disprove that José did it. We've not found the weapon. His public defender has him under wraps now and we can't talk to him. And Denise is working on getting a court order for a thirty-day psych evaluation."

"All we have are the eyewitness reports that he was found with the body," Vik added. "And his clothes that were found covered with her blood."

"Clothing that was very neatly and very conveniently placed in his hamper, Jessenovik. By a complete slob?"

"He hasn't confessed or otherwise incriminated himself?" Lupe asked.

"No."

"What is it about the clothes that bothers you?"

"You saw that room," Marti said.

"So maybe he would fold them and put them in the hamper so you would be sure to find them."

"Or maybe somebody else did," Vik said.

Marti nodded. That was the sticking point. "If he wanted to be sure we found them, all he had to do was keep them on. Her blood was on the clothes he was wearing when they found him, so why bother changing?"

"Maybe," Lupe said, "he was wearing one set of clothes, got them bloody when he killed her, then changed, got blood those also, left the first set where you could find them."

"José wore T-shirts and jeans all the time," Marti said. "That was all he had in his room. He was wearing that when we found him. Why would he change into his school gym clothes to kill her, then change back into jeans and wait with her body until somebody found him."

"So," Lupe said, "the clothes don't tell us anything except that they were his."

Nobody spoke for a minute, then Lupe asked, "What's José got going for him?"

"Nothing," Marti said. "He has a history with Graciela that I'm reluctant to get into, but I'll have to as soon as Denise tracks down someone I can talk to. Graciela got pregnant while they were in the same juvenile facility and had an abortion. According to the Ramos children, they did not get along. José has a history of getting into fights, some of them with females."

"I hate to be the one to say this," Lupe said, "but when you're a Latina, things are different. My mother still gets upset because I'm a cop, goes real dramatic when she sees me in uniform. She's embarrassed to tell her friends what I do. I'm supposed to be an obedient wife, walking two feet behind my husband, and giving birth to a child, or at least having a miscarriage, every year. Also, should this husband backhand me every now and then to keep me in line, my brothers would probably pat him on the back and congratulate him for doing something they never had the guts to do. Not only that, if I were you I would disregard the fights with guys as well. I have seven brothers. Fighting among men means nothing. All male animals are territorial. They all want to be top dog. They all challenge potential rivals. Anything else?"

"Not yet," Marti said. "So far, we know a lot more about Graciela."

"You always say that the victim will lead you to the killer," Lupe reminded her.

"The only thing that Graciela has told me so far is that this is either a random act of violence or an act of sudden rage. Maybe we're not looking close enough."

"According to the Ramoses, Graciela kept close to home, did her schoolwork, didn't associate with others. . . ." Vik said.

"I've talked with a counselor, teacher, and student at the high school. I had a uniform follow up at the public library. Nobody even remembers her there. She's been in so many different placements, and everyone says pretty much the same thing. She was a loner, possessive of whoever the provider was, did not get along with other children, monopolized the adult."

"And," Vik added, "when there were household pets and no other children, she became hostile to the animals."

"And nothing changed at the Ramoses," Lupe said.

"No," Vik said. "Nothing. She called José crazy and stupid, made no attempt to get along with the Ramos kids, and sucked up to Mrs. Ramos."

"Well, you've been trying to prove or disprove a link between Graciela and José that could lead to a motive," Lupe reminded them. "Based on what we know, that makes sense to me."

"I think we're letting LaShawna sidetrack us," Marti said.

"LaShawna?" Lupe asked.

They brought her current on that.

"Missing Persons might jump on this one now that you've got this Reggie guy fingered," Lupe said. "But I've worked with them. When there's a kid involved, and they go missing with a parent, especially the mother, they tend to treat it as a domestic case—an abuse or custody issue—not a potential homicide."

"That's because, ten times out of ten, when parents and kids are involved, either it is a custody or some other domestic issue, or it is a homicide," Vik said. "If it's a homicide, either a family member or friend notices they haven't been a round for a few days and finds them dead, or we find them decomposing miles from where they lived because the killer didn't want the rest of the family to see the body."

"Oh, Jessenovik," Lupe said. "But you are right. If we don't find a missing kid right away, chances are we won't find them alive, but when they're with a parent, the longer it takes to find the two of them, the more likely that they are still alive and hiding somewhere. Do you think LaShawna can give you anything on José?"

"Padgett knows something," Marti said. "And I'm not sure about Georgie. As for LaShawna, she disappeared about the same time that Graciela was killed, and I don't trust those kinds of coincidences."

"Where is Padgett?"

"He's in Lincoln Prairie General, where José is. Different ward, but secured. Alcohol abuse, most likely."

Lupe reminded them that it was time for lunch. Marti looked outside, decided that the grayness of the day was caused by the cloud cover and not just the dirt on the windows. A few snowflakes flew by. The tree across the street was swaying, and for the first time that day she noticed the clanging of the chain that helped secure the flag to the pole just outside the window.

"Let's order in," she suggested.

"Oh, come on," Lupe said. "I don't want to go to the Barrister, but there's this little place just as close that opened a month or so ago. Their sandwiches are great, the ambiance nonexistent, and the prices affordable."

"And," Vik said.

"And?" Lupe asked.

"What's the real reason for going there?"

"Everyone who works there except the manager is mentally ill."

Vik glared at her for a moment, then to Marti's surprise made a noise that sounded dangerously close to being a chuckle. "You don't think I see enough of those kind of folks, Torres? You think I like being around nutcases? You think—"

"I think you'll love their polish sausage and sauerkraut sandwiches. They serve them on this big, fresh-baked roll. They taste great when you add lots of mustard."

Vik managed a pained expression as he gave in.

After lunch, Vik and Marti stopped by the Ramoses' house. Mr. Ramos was at home, but explained that he was busy and his wife and children were still at a nearby Catholic church.

"We just need to clarify a few details," Marti said. "Ask a couple more questions."

"And I suppose if I say no, I don't have the time, I'll seem one, hostile, and two, insensitive."

"Not necessarily," Vik said.

"But that is a possibility," Marti added.

Ramos swung open the door and stepped back to let them in. Instead of going to the company room, they followed him down the hall to an alcove the length of the dining room. From here he could see most of the kitchen. A computer was turned on and papers and manila folders stacked in some kind of order. There were several file cabinets and stereo equipment. Pictures of Ramos and his family as well as other children and adults crowded the mantelpiece above a fireplace that looked unused.

"What do you two want now? It's taking you long enough to charge José."

"Is that what you want?" Vik asked.

"Of course not, but that is what's going to happen. Why prolong it? So that I'll think you have really done your job and tried to find someone else who's responsible for Graciela's death?"

"Do you think our doing that is unreasonable?" Marti asked. "Or unnecessary?"

"I think you are giving false hope to a young boy who has no hope."

"Are you that convinced of his guilt?"

"I was here. I saw him leaning over her body. I saw the blood."

"Did you see the knife, sir?" Vik asked.

"No!"

"We have searched this entire house, sir, and a radius of two blocks, even though there wasn't enough time for José to leave the house to dispose of a knife, and even though there is no evidence to support the possibility that he did leave the house to dispose of it. We have not found the knife, sir."

"And everything else is circumstantial?"

"Right now, yes."

"Damned strong circumstances," Ramos said.

"Yes, sir," Vik agreed. "Sometimes it happens that way."

Ramos motioned toward the computer. "What other questions do you have?"

"How often did Graciela leave the house alone?"

Ramos stared at them with an expression somewhere between annoyance and disbelief. "You interrupted my work to ask me that?"

"Yes, sir."

"One more time, then. Most of the time Graciela was right here. She only went to the library when she wanted to do some special research on some school project. Most of what she needed she could get right here." He motioned to the computer again. "Sometimes she wanted more biographical detail. She had a good mind. She liked to go beyond the obvious, dig into things. She could have done well if she had lived."

"And she never brought anyone home, or mentioned a friend or a teacher?"

"No. In fact, she might have gone to the library that night to avoid going to my daughter's basketball game."

"But there was never any problem at school?"

"Never with Graciela."

"And José?"

"With José there were a few fights and the usual passive-aggressive behavior, but no suspensions."

Outside, Vik put a scarf around his neck, put on his gloves, and pulled his hat down over his ears.

"You okay?" Marti asked as the wind whipped snow flakes against her cheeks.

"Fine," Vik grumbled, then said, "Mildred."

"That's right, Jessenovik. Whenever you show signs of using a little common sense, blame your wife. Is your throat any better?"

"Medicine's working."

"Well, we're going over to Lincoln Prairie General to talk with Padgett now, so if you need to stop by the emergency room, this is the time to speak up."

"Kids," Vik muttered. "Maybe we'll get lucky and not have

any more cases this year involving kids. I know more about Graciela than I ever wanted to know about anyone, more than I know about my own daughter."

"And we're going to have to subject José to that same scrutiny."

"If we haven't, MacAlister, it's not from lack of trying. He kept to himself. We know he did, on occasion, hit females. We know he and Graciela were once at the same place at the same time and that she got pregnant and had an abortion while they both were there. We know she called him crazy and stupid and rebuffed whatever advances he made toward her. Right now there is nobody else to talk to, not about José."

"Except Padgett," Marti said. "And maybe LaShawna."

Padgett looked as though he was having a good time. He and another boy about his age were playing an electronic game. Five other boys were sprawled on the carpet watching television, and four were at an oblong table playing a board game.

"Wait a minute, man," Padgett said, when he saw them. "Looks like I've got visitors."

According to the nurse there had been no telephone calls and no other visits.

"How are you?" Marti asked when he came over and sat beside her on the sofa. "Are you eating okay?" He looked so thin, much too skinny for a boy his age. She could see that he weighed a lot less than Theo, and Theo's weight just made the average.

"Everything's okay, I guess. They keep taking blood and I've got to have some kind of test and a couple of X rays tomorrow."

He looked scared. And this did not sound like a problem involving alcohol.

"Are you in any pain or anything?"

"No, I feel fine. Just tired."

"I need you to tell me what you know about José."

Padgett was wearing hospital pajamas but no slippers. He sat with his hands in his lap and began wiggling his toes, watching them as they moved. "You're trying to help him, aren't you?"

"Yes."

"Maybe you can't this time."

"Things are bad for José, Padgett. What do you know?"

Padgett's toes stopped moving but he kept looking at them. "That he was staying someplace with a girl who had an abortion and he didn't want to be there. He said he was going to get into real bad trouble if he didn't leave. I guess he did."

"Did he say he was the baby's father?"

"No. It wasn't his."

"Then why was her abortion important to him?"

"He believes that it's taking a life."

"What do you believe?"

"That sometimes that's better than what would happen to the kid if it was born."

"Did José tell you anything else?"

"No."

"Can I bring you anything?"

Padgett looked at her and smiled. "Remember that Christmas, when we were all here together in this hospital, after you found us in the library, and we had all of those presents?"

She nodded.

"So do I."

"Do you need anything?"

"No, this is the best its been in a while. Maybe you could let my mother know that I'm okay. She worries about me a lot."

Marti doubted that, especially since she hadn't been worried enough to come home for a couple of days. She said nothing. Maybe his mother didn't know where he was. Maybe she knew where he was and didn't care. Maybe she shouldn't know and there were good reasons for not rushing to tell her. Denise would handle that.

For some reason, after they left the hospital, Marti could not shake the feeling that they were being followed. She circled around several times, stopped, parked and waited to see if the same vehicle passed by more than once. Nothing.

"Mad Sword Swinger syndrome," she said, not convinced.

Vik grunted his agreement.

She drove downtown and cruised around looking for the homeless man. She didn't see anyone who could have been him. Satisfied that if the man was still around, he wasn't following her, or watching her—at least not today—she returned to the house on First Street where the pit bull was still tied up outside. She had reported the dog to the animal warden and intended to follow up as soon as possible. The dog had no water or food. And it was so hostile that she had no intention of getting close enough to give it any.

The house looked as deserted as it had the night before. Again, guns drawn, they entered, listened, and knocked on doors. Again there was no response. Again they sniffed for the odor of death. Again there was not even the smell of garbage or urine. They would have to find out who the owner was and get him to admit them to the two apartments.

Adrian was sitting at the window of a Chinese restaurant on Geneva Street when MacAlister drove by with her partner. He left a twenty on the table, wrapped the last of his sushi in a napkin, grabbed his briefcase and *Watchtower* magazines, and hurried outside. There was no way she would associate a business suit and a top coat with the person she had seen nodding off in a doorway a couple of days ago.

As he watched, instead of turning right and heading in the direction of the precinct, she continued going south on Geneva. Curious, he hailed a cab, explained that he didn't know the town too well yet but, if the cabby would follow his directions, did know how to get where he was going. When MacAlister's car pulled up in front of a house with a dog tied up in the yard, Adrian asked to be let out at the next corner.

He made his way without haste along the street where the cops were, ringing doorbells as he waited for them to exit the building. Nobody wanted to see a Jehovah's Witness, and very few opened their doors. When they did, he handed them a *Watchtower* and wished them a good day.

After the cops returned to their car and drove off, he crossed the street, careful to stay beyond the length of the pit bull's chain. A vacant house. Why would they go in there? The dog snapped and snarled at him. Damned dog. He thought of MacAlister's German shepherd. Careful to remain out of range, he circled around to the side of the house. There weren't many rocks, but he thought there might be enough. Out of view of the neighbors, he began hurling the rocks at the pit bull. The first four times he hit it, the dog yelped. By the time the sixth rock struck, the dog was on the ground. He threw a few more, but didn't get close enough to make sure the dog was dead. Too bad the MacAlister dog wasn't tied up.

When Marti and Vik got back to the precinct, everything was Sunday quiet. They worked at their computers for over an hour without one visit from Sikich. He hadn't even sent an e-mail.

"Think we should send him a copy of these reports?" Vik asked.

"No!"

"Jeez, MacAlister, you sure know how to spoil a guy's fun. I had a rookie all lined up to ride with us tomorrow. Think about it. Five-minute bathroom break from nine-ten A.M. to nine-fifteen A.M.—number three. Belched at nine-twenty-eight."

"I don't want to play games with Sikich. I want him to talk to the chief." She'd had a sergeant like Sikich when she was a beat cop. Watching her, checking up on her, making her meet him for field reports every hour instead of every three hours. Well, she didn't wear a uniform anymore. It had been a long time since anyone could consider her a rookie, and she was not going to put up with that again.

"Oh, well." Vik sounded disappointed. "With any luck the lieutenant will be back in a couple of days. And we're turning over two cases to the state's attorney's office, thanks to Lupe. Who gives a damn about Sikich?"

They decided about six that there wasn't much else they could do. It was Sunday. People they needed to contact weren't available. It was Marti's turn to check the PADS shelters for LaShawna. She would go back out about nine.

"Well, what do you know," Vik said as they walked to their cars. "Sikich is still here." The Saab was parked near the back of the lot, not in his assigned space. "He must be keeping a low profile," Vik said. "I wonder why."

Adrian remained two blocks away from the precinct. Although that part of the street looked residential, the houses had been converted into lawyer's offices and, for the most part, were un-occupied on Sunday. From where he stood, he could see Marti MacAlister's car and her partner's. As he watched, the wind be-gan blowing colder off the lake and the temperature began dropping. He wrapped his scarf around his neck, hiked it up close to his ears, but wished he was wearing a hat. By the time MacAlister left the building his feet were cold and he was shiver-ing.

Adrian quickly walked west to the next corner, because that was the direction he expected MacAlister to turn in when she reached the traffic light. Sure enough, not a minute later, her car passed two blocks away. She was going home earlier than usual, perhaps because it was Sunday. Her departure time was too unpredictable. There were minor deviations in her arrival time. Her daily routine was unpredictable. In order to kill her, he would have to bring her to him.

Momma had served Sunday dinner at four. The kitchen was empty, but Marti could hear the boys' voices and Ben's deep, rumbling laugh. She caught the aroma of sweet potato pie first, then found what was left of the pie on the counter. A plate with half a Cornish hen, acorn and butternut squash, and a big scoop of Joanna's vegetable casserole was covered in foil and waiting for her in the refrigerator. Joanna came into the kitchen before she had time to warm the food in the microwave, which made her think Joanna must have been waiting for her, and also made her glad that this had been a short workday.

"If we didn't leave you enough pie," Joanna said, "there's still some peach cobbler." Joanna had been getting much more lenient about the family having dessert since Momma had come here and started baking.

"Maybe I'll have some with a cup of tea."

Marti didn't know what she should say about their discussion with Coach Vickery. She didn't know if she should say anything at all. She hated it when she wasn't sure how to talk to her own daughter, or couldn't figure out what she should say. Momma would know, but she hadn't had time this morning to ask for advice. She began eating instead.

After what seemed like a long silence, Joanna said, "I want to play basketball."

"You are."

"And softball."

"Come spring."

"I don't want to give up my whole entire life for volleyball."

Usually when Joanna made those kinds of statements, Marti considered it typical adolescent exaggeration. This time, based on what Coach Vickery had said, it didn't seem that far from the truth.

"What do you think I should do?"

That was the question she had been dreading.

"I don't know."

Joanna looked at her for a moment as if she expected her to know everything. By now she must have figured out that wasn't true.

"There are a lot of kids at school who know exactly what they want to be," Joanna told her. "What college they want to go to, what courses they need to take now, what clubs they need to belong to, what kind of community service they should get involved with. I've been existing from one test to the next, happy to be carrying a B average. I don't know what college I want to go to, and I sure don't know what I want to major in when I get there. I thought I'd take general studies at the College of Lake County for a couple of years, get an associate's degree, and go from there."

"And now?" Marti asked. She had learned that at times like this it was best to play it safe.

"Now I've got this coach telling me that I can go to the Olympics, or make tons of money playing volleyball, or both. Volleyball, Ma. She's talking about volleyball. It's just a game. I didn't have a clue that anyone got paid for doing it."

"And?"

"Well, I am going to have to go to work someday. But I thought it would be a real job. I want it to be a real job. I mean, some guy comes up to you and asks where you work, or what you do, and you say, Oh, I play professional volleyball with the Illinois Rockettes. How dumb does that sound?"

"I'm sure all professional athletes say something like that."

"But Ma, volleyball? Get serious. The guys I hang with are into marrying doctors, and lawyers, and engineers, or at least a teacher or an accountant. Professional women, not professional athletes."

That was interesting to know. When she was Joanna's age the guys she hung out with were into getting your clothes off, or at least unbuttoning and/or unzipping whatever they could and copping a feel.

Marti thought about Brianna Laretson, the student she had spoken to at the high school. Joanna might be "just an athlete" and "not intellectual" to a lot of the students there. How would her decision be impacted by that?

"Does anyone at school know about this?" she asked.

"Ma, I'm either a jock at school, or a hero. At least to the kids I don't hang out with, which is most of them."

"And?"

"Being a girl jock is just a little lower than being a guy jock. A good game means more kids talk to me in the hall. Then there are always the wanna-bes hanging around after practices and games, and the guys who want to get in my pants. The kids in my classes know I have a brain. The kids who aren't don't care one way or the other unless a big game is coming up, or we've just won."

"So if you go along with this volleyball program?"

"The kids who care, who play other sports too, will be okay with it. Not happy, if they're on my basketball and softball teams, but okay. A lot of them dream about their big chance. They really want to go to the pros. But, going to the pros for a female is not what it is for the guys. We don't get the attention, we don't get the crowds, we don't get the respect, we don't get the money. Until Coach Vickery came along, I never even thought of going pro, or trying out for the Olympics. And I still don't know what I want to do."

"We can visit these camps, Joanna, talk with the other girls who are in the program. . . ." Marti ventured.

"I suppose," Joanna said, still noncommittal.

"Sounds like you need to think about this some more. Maybe talk to somebody like your coach at school."

"Yeah. Maybe. But Ma . . ."

"Yes."

"Can't you even give me your opinion? You are my mother."

The moment she had been dreading. "I want you to live your own life, Joanna, on your own terms—after you leave my house, of course. I don't ever want to have to hear you saying What if, or If only, because you did something you didn't want to do, or didn't do something you did want to do. And I know that doesn't help, and I'm sorry."

"Have you always done what you wanted to do?"

"For the most part yes, and when I didn't, it wasn't on purpose." She thought of the Job. "That includes what I'm doing now. The only problem is that I want to be a better mother also, and a lot of the time I don't manage that too well. So I guess the real answer is that I don't always do what I want to do, but only when I need to do more than two things at the same time. Sorry," she added. "That sounded confusing."

"No, Ma. It's not. One of the neatest things about you is that you do stuff that's not easy, and you meet life head-on."

Marti didn't know what to say to that.

"Sometimes that's what I ask myself," Joanna said. "What's the easiest thing to do, what's the hardest? Most of the time, what's hardest wins out, because it's more like a challenge, a dare. When that happens, even if it doesn't go like I want it to, I feel like I've really done something, but when I go the easy route, I always wonder—just like you said—about what would have happened if I made a different decision. Momma says I always look a gift horse in the mouth, whatever that means."

"It sounds like you might have just answered your own question about what you should do, or at least figured out a good place to start."

Joanna gave her the biggest smile she had seen since Christmas morning, and a hug and a quick kiss as well. Then, to Marti's delight, Joanna got out what was left of the peach cobbler, warmed it up, and split it between them.

Adrian read the newspaper accounts of his achievements again. "State Representative's Fiancé Dies." He would have preferred that it read "Lureen Stanwick's Daughter Dies," but it did get a big headline and a long obituary, and even Sabrina's picture was included. Not only that, but in another section of the paper there was a police report indicating that they were investigating Sabrina's death. He knew when he did it that there was no way to be sure it would look like an accident, and he didn't care if it didn't. Even better, the police blotter account of Sabrina's death included a mention of another woman, a "young South Side resident" who had been the victim of a robbery attempt Thursday night. Even though they didn't give her name, he knew it was LaPatrice Jenson. Poor LaPatrice, if it weren't for Sabrina, she would never have made the newspaper at all. She wasn't that important to anyone except her mother, poor woman. He smiled.

Douglas Grant rated a write-up almost as lengthy as Sabrina's because he was an executive with a manufacturing company. That was in today's paper also, even though he had died Friday night. His death was considered "an unfortunate accident." Adrian smiled again. If they only knew. Too bad they didn't include a photo of the grieving widow.

Adrian put the paper down and picked up the gun. He stroked the metal barrel and wondered how much of a recoil there would be when he fired it. The first time he pulled the trigger on Uncle Dudley's shotgun, the kick sent him backward three feet. He had planned a different death for the man he would kill tonight, but after being foiled by that cat, he realized that the cat might have brought good luck after all, since he had never used a gun this small and might have made some miscalculation when he fired it.

In fact, the more he thought about it, the more he realized that killing Ray Franklin and his son would have been self-indulgent. It would be much more effective if the cop appeared to be killed in the line of duty and the son was left to mourn him. The girlfriend might not care what happened to Franklin one way or the other, since he hadn't left his wife for her, but his son would always miss him. Then there was Franklin's wife. He had almost forgotten about her. Wait until she found out about the other woman. Too bad Franklin wouldn't be here for that. Not that any of this was important where the cop was concerned. Adrian just wanted him dead.

Once again, the weather was on his side. As he traveled on the city buses and got closer to the lake, the intermittent flurries on the West Side became heavier lake-effect snow in the Loop. That and a strong, freezing wind had cleared the streets from the river to the Lyric Opera House, except for the occasional street person sleeping in a doorway. Adrian tried not to breathe deeply as he unfolded the sleeping bag he had stowed in an old backpack. Both smelled worse than his ragged coat. Everything smelled like rotting garbage. He had borrowed the coat, sleeping bag, and backpack from a junkie not far from where he lived. The owner wouldn't mind if he didn't get them back, he was dead now. Adrian found a spot in the alley where the wind blew the stench away from him, hunkered down and waited. Tonight's performance at the Lyric would be over at ten. Bryan Weinstein would walk this way, taking a shortcut to an indoor parking lot.

Adrian was brushing snow from his face and thinking about the sunny beaches of Mexico when the not-too-distant sound of voices alerted him to the crowds exiting the opera house. He got up, folded the sleeping bag, and stuffed it into the backpack. Then he crouched behind a Dumpster and waited. Poor Bryan Weinstein. He lived alone with his three cats, who hopefully would starve to death before anyone thought about them. His siblings, Barry and Bela, would be devastated. They were triplets. All musically gifted, all artistic performers. Barry the violinist, Bela the pianist, and poor Bryan the tenor, and a good one at that. His father, a mediocre musician who taught because he was not good enough to perform, would be inconsolable. His father, Saul, that pompous bastard, who'd sat there in the jury box with a haughty arrogance that said, I can't wait to find you guilty.

There would never be another Hanukkah, another Passover, another wedding or birthday or bar mitzvah, or any other festive occasion when the three siblings would gather, as they had since childhood, and perform together for family and friends. Adrian smiled. Then he heard the footsteps, muffled by the snow, but audible. He aimed the gun when Bryan Weinstein came into view with his scarf trailing, shoulders hunched, and his head tilted to avoid the brunt of the wind and snow. When Bryan was ten feet past the Dumpster and right in his line of vision, Adrian fired. It sounded loud, and nobody who lived in the city would mistake it for a car backfiring. Adrian, wearing the junkie's tattered coat, carrying a shopping bag, with his back and shoulders bent as if the torn and dirty backpack was heavy, eased along without haste, staying close to the doorways and away from the light. Just as he expected, when he emerged from the alley, the people who were venturing toward it to see what had happened didn't look at him at all. He didn't expect anyone to remember seeing a dirty, ragged, smelly, homeless man.

7

It was snowing when Marti left for work the next morning. Half an inch covered the driveway. She turned on the radio and caught the weather report. Two to three inches by nightfall. There were no school closings. By the time she reached the precinct and walked inside, she was wondering if the weatherman knew what he was talking about. There was at least an inch of new snow in the parking lot, but that could be because they were nearer the lake. She met up with Vik at roll call. Baby Dirkowitz was responding to treatment. She didn't catch Sikich so much as glancing her way. Maybe despite the weather this wouldn't be such a bad day.

Upstairs there was no sign of Slim or Cowboy, but the aroma of freshly made coffee wafted from their office. There was even a coffee cake with a little sign that said Way to Go, Big Mac!!!

"The things one has to do around here to gain a little recognition," she said.

"When do we start terrorizing him today?" Vik asked, meaning Sikich.

"He wasn't waiting for us when we got here and he hasn't shown up yet. Maybe he's decided to leave us alone."

"Fat chance," said Vik. "Nutcases like him just regroup. Our best hope is that the lieutenant comes in by Wednesday and relieves him. Chain of command is one of the few concepts Sikich understands."

Marti called Denise at eight-fifteen. Denise had talked to José's public defender and the woman had agreed to allow José two unsupervised visits, one with Padgett and one with Ramos.

"What's the catch?" Marti asked.

"That no matter what he tells them we won't try to use it in court."

"Not even if he confesses?"

"Especially not if he confesses," Denise said. "The way confessions are being thrown out of Illinois courts these days, sufficient evidence sounds much more reliable."

"Then what do you think these visits will accomplish?" Marti asked.

"Probably nothing for the defense or the prosecution, but maybe something for José. He and Padgett went through some rough times together. And I think Ramos has a much bigger emotional investment in these foster kids than he's willing to admit."

Marti thought Denise might be right about that. "Have you gotten anywhere with the personnel records at the place where José and Graciela were warehoused together?"

"I've got someone working on it."

Several phone calls later, Marti had three previous addresses for Reggie Garrett's friend G.L. She had one address other than his mother's for Garrett. That done, she reached for the stack of papers in her in-basket.

"Hey, Jessenovik, check out this forensic report on that home-invasion homicide. Looks like we've got some fiber matches with the guy who said he'd been to that house twice with deliveries."

"So?" Vik said, flipping through his paperwork.

"So how do you get fibers from your jacket on a rope used for garroting someone if you're just delivering pizzas?"

Vik read the report she was referring to, and said, "Bingo. Let's get him in here."

Two hours later, after being confronted with the evidence, and with a public defender present, their subject gave them a statement, admitting guilt.

"Three down, three to go," Vik said.

"Don't get too optimistic. It'll be a week tomorrow that Graciela was killed. At the rate we've been going so far this year, that's a long time between homicides."

"The homicide rate always goes up right after the holidays, MacAlister. Peace on earth, goodwill towards men brings out the worst in some people. All of that togetherness doesn't agree with everybody either. Then there are those like this pizza delivery victim, who get into the Christmas spirit, imbibe Christmas spirits, and get careless. Right now we might have the weather on our side, depends on whether it keeps people away from each other or has them cooped up together."

"You're in a good mood."

"Three hours, MacAlister, and one bona fide confession, and still no sign of Sikich."

"Scary, isn't it?" she agreed.

She went through all of her reports again, hoping to strike gold twice, but didn't. There was nothing new in the Lara case. If José didn't kill Graciela Lara, the trail leading to whoever did was getting colder than today's wind chill factor.

When the door opened, José was staring at the wall. The Latino orderly had brought his breakfast, then taken it away after turning on the television to a Spanish-speaking station. On the screen a woman spoke in a soft, gentle voice, sounding the way José thought his mother has spoken to him.

"José?"

"Padgett?" he said, without looking. Why was Padgett here?

"Yeah, it's me."

"What are you doing here?" This must be some kind of trick. Padgett was a good kid, but he wasn't too smart when it came to adults. He trusted them sometimes.

"I'm sick," Padgett said.

José turned and looked at him. "You don't look sick."

"Well, I feel sick. I don't feel good at all."

José sat up. Padgett sat in the chair by his bed. Neither of them said anything for a while. Finally Padgett said, "Remember when we were all living together in that library?"

Like anyone could forget.

"It was just us. We all helped each other. Like family."

"Like family," José agreed. "They send you in here to talk to me? To get me to say that I killed her?"

"Who? They said you were here and I could see you . . . after they told me . . . I'm sick . . . My mother will be so worried . . . so scared . . ."

Dumb kid. That's what happened when they let you stay with your relatives. You kept kidding yourself about them. Once you got away from them for a while, you knew better.

"No, she won't, Padgett. Just like she didn't when we were in that library."

Padgett didn't say anything, but he started to cry. José didn't feel too bad about that. Time the kid faced the truth. His old lady probably hadn't even noticed that he wasn't there.

"Look, you got to take care of yourself, Padgett, look out for yourself, the same as you did when we were in that library. You know you can't expect nobody else to look out for you. You know that, Padgett. Are you bad sick?"

"I don't know. I got something, mal, malnur, something. I've got to eat extra, and drink this milk shake stuff, and take vitamins and iron pills."

"Sounds like a good deal to me. You got to do what they say, look out for yourself and not expect anyone else to look out for you."

"I know," Padgett whispered, "I know."

"Can they fix it?"

"Fix what?"

"Fix what's wrong with you, this malnur?"

"I don't know."

"Maybe you'll just have an operation."

"I have to gain weight before they can do anything."

José didn't know what he could do. The kid did look real bony. He was real pale looking too. He could see that Padgett was scared, but Padgett was always scared. He knew that Padgett didn't have anyone but him, just like when they were in the library. And he was locked up in here.

"You feeling okay?" he asked. "Does it hurt?"

"I'm just tired."

"Are you eating like they said?"

"Sometimes. I'm not hungry much."

"You got to eat, and take your medicine and all of that. They're not going to let me out of here to come see you, but maybe if we talk to Officer Mac and Officer Vik, they'll let you come back to see me. I'm in for thirty days' observation. They think maybe I'm nuts. I'll talk to the cops, okay?"

Padgett wiped his nose on the sleeve of his bathrobe. "Okay."

"You scared?" José asked. "I've been scared a lot."

Padgett nodded.

"Yeah, well, whatever you got, they can fix it. Just do like they say.

"My mother . . ."

"Don't worry about her. She's a drunk."

"She's . . ."

"A drunk," José repeated. "Can't nobody do nothing about that."

When Padgett didn't say anything, José said, "You listening to me, Padgett? You gotta listen, man. You gotta make it through this, whatever it is. We gotta stick together, just like we used to."

Padgett nodded. "Okay, but . . ." He started crying again. "I want my mother."

"Yeah, right, we all do, but you're twelve now. You didn't act like a baby when we were in that library. You can't act like a baby now."

The nurse came in and made Padgett leave before he got a chance to say anything else. José asked her to send in the Latino orderly.

"Look, man," José said in Spanish, "me and Padgett been through some heavy shit together. And now he's sick, maybe real sick. And his mother ain't worth a damn. And she can't do nothin' for him. She's a drunk. I gotta be able to see him. I've got to hang in with him. He's just a kid."

"What do want me to do to help, man?"

"There's these two cops. Tell them I want to see them."

"You think the cops will help you?" He seemed surprised.

"Yeah." Like he wanted to owe a cop for a favor. "They helped us once before."

As she drove over to the Barrister for a quick lunch with Vik, Marti felt twitchy again. She didn't have time for the is-anyone-following-me routine, but she couldn't stop checking her rear-view mirror. Mad Sword Swinger syndrome, she thought again. Or maybe lack of Sikich which, she was discovering, was almost as bad as too much Sikich, because she kept waiting for him to show up. Once inside the restaurant, she took up her usual position in the booth, with her back to the wall, facing the room with the front door in her line of vision. When Vik arrived, he slid in beside her.

"Better have a look at this," Vik said, unfolding the early edition of the *News-Times*. He pointed to a headline in the lower left-hand corner of the front page.

Juvenile Justice: Myth or Reality?

Do local police officers ignore state laws that are intended to protect juvenile offenders? Are juvenile suspects questioned without parents being notified? Are parents advised of their right to be present during questioning? Are juveniles told that they have the right to remain silent? Are they advised that not only do they have the right to have an attorney present but that they can have legal representation even if they cannot afford it? These questions are being raised by Joseph Ramos, a local attorney who is also running for alderman. The recent homicide involving a juvenile in Ramos's custody as a foster child, and the charges pending against another juvenile who was also in his care, has Ramos questioning a system that might be more concerned with gaining confessions and getting convictions than with protecting underaged suspects' rights.

According to Ramos, "Juveniles accounted for 7 percent of all people arrested for homicides in Illinois according to the most recent data we have. Despite the fact that 93 percent of those homicides were committed by adults, we as a society are becoming so concerned with protecting ourselves from this small minority of adolescents that we are condoning unconstitutional interrogations that lead to convictions based on false confessions that juveniles are coerced into making."

Ramos's greatest concern is the death of the juvenile in his care and the possibility of another juvenile in his care being accused of homicide. Homicide Detectives Marti MacAlister and Matthew Jessenovik are handling the case.

"Uh-oh," Marti said. "I guess it's our turn to come under fire."

"We don't do things that way, Marti."

"I know that and you know that, but the public—"

"In this town, the buck starts with us, in capital homicide cases, anyway. We conduct those interrogations." The waitress brought coffee and a basket of rolls. "We do everything by the book, but I can't say I blame Ramos for being concerned," Vik added. "Every time Sikich comes in and can't even be bothered getting José's and Graciela's and Ramos's names right . . . it makes you wonder how many people in this city have the same attitude."

Again Marti thought of Brianna Laretson, the student at the high school. Vik was right. Any scrutiny that Ramos could provoke was justified and overdue.

After they ate, Marti spent a few more minutes over coffee. She was tired, and it wasn't from lack of sleep.

Vik pulled a slip of paper from his pocket. "No need to go back to the precinct and face the wrath of Sikich over this newspaper article, not yet anyway. Thanks to the desk sergeant, I've got a couple more addresses for Reggie Garrett and his buddy G.L. And this is the realtor for the place on First Street with the pit bull. She'll come over whenever we give her a call."

It was snowing harder when they left the Barrister. At this rate, the day's accumulation was going to exceed the two or three inches the weatherman had predicted. They went to the house where the dog was. This time, the dog was gone. Both apartments had been vacated, which was news to the realtor. The rent hadn't been paid in several months, but she had been reluctant to start eviction proceedings because of the below-freezing temperatures. A search of the two apartments turned up nothing that Marti could associate with LaShawna or a three-year-old child. She called in the evidence techs anyway, not just for obvious evidence like blood but potential evidence like fibers and hair.

They didn't have any better luck at the addresses for G.L. that Marti's phone calls had netted, but did get lucky on the second of the desk sergeant's two leads. It was a small house, built behind another house that wasn't much bigger. It looked as if it had once been a garage. They could access it from an alley or a narrow walkway that threaded its way along the side of the larger house in front. They opted for the alley access and checked out the place before knocking. There was one door, with one window beside it. The only other way in or out was a window on the opposite side of the house.

The shades were drawn. When nobody answered his knock, Vik pounded on the door with such force that Marti thought the wood might give. He stopped, cussed in Polish, then pounded again. This time a voice from inside said, "What?"

"Police," Vik shouted.

There was a scuffling noise inside. They both drew their guns. There was a sound like wood cracking. Glass broke and Marti rushed to other side. She was just in time to catch a man with one leg out of the window.

"Hi, Reggie."

He looked at the gun in her hand and froze.

Vik radioed for backup and they took Reggie Garrett and G.L to the precinct. There was nobody else in the house, and again, no sign that LaShawna or her child had been there. Once again she called for the evidence techs.

* * *

Snow was coming down in large wet flakes when Adrian reached the school the MacAlister boy attended. At least five or six inches had fallen since he'd left Chicago this morning and the temperature, after warming up a little, had dropped to 20 degrees. He had just about made up his mind to wait and go to the school tomorrow or the next day when he decided that once again, luck was providing him with an opportunity. Not only would the boys be less likely to remember him but with his hat and scarf and his collar turned up, they would not be able to get a good look at him either.

At least a dozen school buses were lined up in the driveway and along the street, with drivers waiting to board their loud-mouthed, runny-nosed, undisciplined passengers. Cars idled as parents waited to pick up their children. A small group of adults was standing near the double doors at the side of the building. Adrian went there and stood with them. When the bell rang, the doors opened. The youngest children came out first. He watched until two older boys, one wearing a Chicago Bears jacket, and the other a Green Bay Packers jacket came out together and ran to a tall mound of snow that had been pushed to the edge of the parking lot by a plow. Adrian walked over to the boys. He wasn't sure which was the MacAlister kid, but he had observed them once before from a distance and they seemed inseparable. Both boys had scaled the snow pile and were at the top making snowballs and seeing who could throw them the farthest.

"Hey," he called, "can you tell me how to get to Armand Drive?"

Both boys stopped what they were doing and looked at him, snowballs in hand.

"There's a crossing guard at the end of that driveway, right by the street," the short, pudgy boy said.

"Or you could ask Officer James," the taller of the two suggested. "See?" He pointed. "He's in that police car right over there behind that school bus. Officer James."

"I'd go ask him now," the chubby boy said. "Before he comes

over here and asks you why you're on school property messing with kids."

Kids were too damned smart these days. Adrian wanted to put his fist in both of their mouths. Instead he turned and walked away.

"No," he heard one of the boys say. "Don't throw a snowball at him."

Both boys laughed.

Marti and Vik decided to talk with G.L. first. Marti guessed that G.L. weighed at least three hundred pounds. He seemed calm as he watched them. His dark, bulging eyes stared out from a face puffy with fat.

"So, G.L." Marti began. "When's the last time you saw La-Shawna Davis?"

"Sunday night," he said without hesitation.

"Where?"

"My place."

"Tell me about it."

"Ain't much to tell. They come over. She's not feeling too good. Holding her stomach kind of." G.L. was soft-spoken, his speech slow and interspersed with gasping breaths.

"Were they staying with you?"

"Reggie picked her up somewhere. She'd been there maybe a week. Ain't but three rooms. They had to sleep in the living room. Reggie had the couch. She slept on some blankets on the floor with the baby. We got up Monday morning. They was gone."

He seemed to be having a lot of trouble breathing. Marti wondered if they should have him checked out at the hospital before they released him.

"Who was gone?"

"Girl and the baby."

"Where was Reggie?"

"Sitting at the kitchen table having coffee when I got up. Said she must have taken off during the night."

"How did he feel about that?"

"Mad," G.L. said. "Real mad. Nobody walks out on Reggie. No need to. He gets tired of them real quick. None of them last long."

"Was the kitchen floor dry?" Marti asked.

"Floor?" He had a puzzled expression.

Marti waited.

"You mean like snow tracked in? No. Nothing like that."

"Was there anything else that seemed unusual?"

He thought for a moment. "Don't know what you're asking. I was the last to go to bed. Don't sleep good anymore. Can't really lay down. Would have heard if the door opened and closed. But it must have, 'cause she was gone by morning. And Reggie mad as hell."

Marti didn't have any problem believing that if Garrett and LaShawna had argued, it would have awakened him. He had to be oxygen deprived, and he sounded as though he had too much trouble breathing to sleep soundly. The question was, was he telling them everything about LaShawna and her daughter disappearing? Would he know if Reggie Garrett had followed them, or found out where they'd gone?

"Was there anything different about the house when you got up that morning?"

"Coffeepot was on. Reggie had made himself some coffee. I had a cup, too."

"How long have you and Reggie been friends?"

"Years, a lot of years. Third grade."

"And you've seen him with women before."

G.L. nodded.

"Have you ever seen him hit any of them, argue with them?"

G.L. grinned. "Reggie's real quick with his fists, but they learn fast not to give him no cause to hit them. Hits them like they was a man."

"How do you feel about that?"

"Me? I don't hit no females. Never. But Reggie? He's been doing it since we was kids. That's just the way he is. Don't even have to be mad at them. They just got to talk back or take too long to do something. Got to train 'em, Reggie says. Guess he knows. He's had lots and lots of women. Don't none of 'em last long."

"And you have not seen LaShawna or her daughter since last Sunday night?"

"No, ma'am. That's right."

"Has Reggie been staying with you since then?"

"Been there every night."

"Has he got a new girlfriend yet?"

"No. He's still looking for LaShawna. They don't walk out on him like that."

"And if they do?"

"Oh, no. He'd hurt them, Reggie would. He'd hurt them real bad."

Marti looked at Vik. He shook his head. He didn't have any questions.

"You don't sound too good, G.L. I'd feel better if you let us transport you to the hospital. We have no reason to hold you."

G.L. didn't object. "Ain't been feeling real good," he admitted. "Got this pain in my chest, comes and goes. And trouble catching my breath."

"So," Marti said, as they waited for Reggie Garrett to be brought into the interrogation room. "We know Reggie hit her, that LaShawna was smart enough to get away from him, that she went to that shelter. That she was hurt but would not risk going to the hospital for fear that they would take her child. And then she disappeared. The question is, did she find a safe hiding place, or did he find her? And did she see or talk with José?"

"Too bad we can't ask José any questions," Vik said.

"Too bad the odds are real slim that Reggie will answer any," Marti added.

Reggie Garrett was tall, at least as tall as Vik. He was thin but muscular, with dark skin. He had shaved his head, and had numerous body piercings. There were five studs in one ear, seven in another, as well as one in his nose and another in his eyebrow. He wasn't that good-looking and Marti wondered how he managed to attract all the women G.L. had mentioned.

"So," she began. "How did you hook up with LaShawna?"

A silver-capped tooth flashed as he gave her a slow-as-molasses smile. "She was waiting in line at that church on Eighth Street. Looked real pitiful with the baby and all. I felt sorry for her, asked her if she needed a place to stay."

The church he was speaking of was located on a one-block, dead-end street off Grant. LaShawna would have either been looking for a place to sleep, a hot meal, or both.

"What were you doing there?"

"Got a friend lives that way."

Marti didn't believe him. He was out looking for someone to pick up, take home and abuse. LaShawna was an easy mark, but apparently smart enough to get away once she understood how the game was played. Marti took him through the same questions she had asked G.L. and got the same responses. LaShawna and her little girl had gone to sleep on the floor Sunday night. They were gone when he woke up Monday morning. He didn't hear them leave.

"Your friend Joe Boy says you were over at his place Sunday night. Says you punched LaShawna in the stomach and again, twice, in the back. G.L. says she was favoring her stomach when she got to his place. You think that might have had something to do with her leaving like that?"

"Bitch," he said. He clenched his hands into fists and brought one down hard on the table.

"Know what I think, Reggie," Marti said. "I think you're going to be here for at least twenty-four hours."

With Slim, Cowboy, and Lupe's help, she might be able to arrange a lineup. Abused women tended to be slow to come forward. Too many of them had such low self-esteem that they felt they deserved to be hit. Most were afraid of being hit again if they complained. Many had been isolated from those who cared and might listen. But it was worth a try. Sooner or later, Reggie was going to hurt some woman real bad, if he hadn't already.

José was eating some cookies the orderly had brought him when his door opened again. He was hoping to see the two cops, but instead it was Mr. Ramos. José was not glad to see him but he decided he'd better try to be nice so that Ramos wouldn't do anything to stop him from talking to the cops about Padgett.

Ramos was wearing his business clothes, a suit and top coat. He held his hat in his hand and stood at the foot of the bed instead of sitting down.

"They told me you're not eating."

"Not hungry."

"Mrs. Ramos is packing some clothes for you. I'll see if we can bring in any food. What they serve here can't be that good."

"Food's probably okay." José thought about cactus mixed in with his eggs. Nopale, chiroza, huevos. He still couldn't remember what it tasted like.

"You've got a public defender right now. She'll take care of the routine stuff until you're out of here. But don't worry, if this makes it to court I'll retain a friend to defend you who's tops at criminal law and the juvenile system."

José thought about being shackled and taken to court, about being locked up in the county jail, about being sent to prison. He swallowed hard, then nodded.

"The detectives handling the case are doing their job, and you're here for thirty days before anything else can happen. The public defender says you're doing as you were told and not talking to anyone. The nurses think you're carrying that to extremes."

Ramos believed he did it. Ramos thought he was guilty. What difference did that make? It was his fault. All of it was his fault. If only she had not gotten pregnant.

"How are you holding up?"

"I'm okay."

"Look, I will see you through this. I'll be here. I'm not going anywhere."

José looked at him, then looked away, He wanted to say, "Why not? Everyone else does," but he had listened to Ramos talk on the telephone, talk on the radio, talk on the local TV show, talk at political rallies. Ramos had to stand by him, or all of that stuff he had been telling people would mean nothing. Yes, Ramos would see him through this, until he was convicted, until he was shipped off to prison and his name wasn't in the papers anymore. When everyone else forgot about him, Ramos would forget, too.

"Thanks," he said. "And thanks for coming to see me." He needed to see the cops. He needed to be able to see Padgett. He couldn't get an attitude with Ramos.

"Do what the the lawyer says, okay?"

"Yeah. I will."

He watched as Ramos walked away. Better to remember what his back looked like than the way his voice sounded, like someone who gave a damn.

This time Sikich was waiting for them when Marti and Vik returned to their office. He was pacing back and forth.

"This, this," he said. His voice shook as he waved the newspaper at them. "This," he said again.

"What about it?" Vik asked.

"Lunes," Sikich said.

"Ramos," Vik corrected. "Joseph Ramos." He hung up his coat and went over to to check the coffeepot. He took off the lid and sniffed the contents, then said, "Still drinkable."

Sikich crushed the newspaper and threw it on Vik's desk. He stood there, with his hand shaking as he pointed at it. "This . . ."

"What are you trying to say, sir?" Vik asked.

Instead of answering, Sikich strode from the room.

"What the hell?" Vik said. "I think he's losing it."

"That was just vintage Sikich," Marti said. Sikich's performance had not impressed her. "He's probably thinks he's being intimidating when he acts like that."

She got busy setting up a quick meeting with Lupe, Slim, and Cowboy to discuss Reginald Garrett. Then she listened to her voice mail. José wanted to see them. She called his public defender and left a message.

José was in bed facing the wall when Marti, Vik, and his public defender came into his room. He turned to look at them, then turned away. Marti walked over to the wall at the side of his bed and stood where he could see her. He kept his eyes closed but he didn't turn away.

"You wanted to see us," she said.

"Padgett's sick."

"What's wrong with him?"

"I don't know. He says it's malnur, or something. I don't know what that is. But he's sick."

Marti looked down at him. He was small for his age, and even though she knew he was a streetwise fifteen, he seemed vulnerable. She wanted to reach out and stroke his thick brown hair, touch his face, comfort him somehow. Do something.

"Why did you call us?"

"Padgett's just a kid. And he's not been out there like the rest of us have, he doesn't know from nothing, never did. Stuff is tough for him that would be easy for me."

"It sounds like he needs a friend," Marti said.

"Well, he ain't likely to get one, not for keeps anyway."

"I think he already has one for keeps. I think maybe he should see you more often while he's here. Like whenever he wants to."

Marti stared at the lawyer, daring her to disagree. The lawyer nodded.

"His mother know he's sick?" José asked.

The lawyer nodded again.

"Yes," Marti said.

"Well, then, I guess you're right. Maybe he should come see me. Maybe then he won't be so afraid."

"Or alone," Marti said.

"You think that, you don't know nothing," José told her.

Marti did reach out and touch his hair then. He stiffened, but didn't speak or push her hand away.

"You need anything else," she said, "just let me know. That goes for Padgett, too."

"Thanks," José said, in a small voice just loud enough for her to hear him.

Adrian found a Lake County edition of the *Chicago Tribune* that had been left on the train. Bryan Weinstein made the lower left-hand section of the front page. He was still alive, but in a coma. Adrian frowned. He had been taught how to hunt by Uncle Dudley when he wasn't much taller than Uncle Dudley's shotgun was long. He had learned to skin, gut, and dissect or fillet whatever he killed, but he was not familiar with handguns. Maybe he wouldn't have to use the gun too often. He'd rather use a knife. He liked the feel of it, razor sharp, slicing open a throat without any more pressure than it took to cut into a hamburger. He had to get close up to use it. He liked that best of all. Unfortunately, the more he thought about it, the more he realized he would have to use a gun on the cops. There was too much risk in getting close enough to use a knife. He just needed a little more practice to get the feel of the .32 and he'd do just fine.

When he opened to the Metro section, there was an article about José Ramos. Marti MacAlister was mentioned as the investigating officer. How appropriate. He read the newspaper article again. What if he gave the homicide detective another case to work on? And threw her a few clues that would take her where he wanted her to go, to Chicago? She didn't know the city anymore, not after four years. And he knew the city very well.

Traffic was heavy as Marti and Vik headed down Route 41 to Chicago. Snow was still falling, but not as heavily as it was when they left Lincoln Prairie. The roads had been sprayed with salt as far as the boundary line between Cook and Lake counties. After that, it was unsalted in most places. Just as well, nobody was driving fast enough to have to brake and slide and the public works trucks would have just added to the congestion.

"I don't know how people do this every day," Vik said as they approached the O'Hare/Kennedy interchange. "This is just a waste of time anyway." They were finally going to meet with someone who knew José when he and Graciela were at the same place at the same time. "We must know all there is to know about Graciela, and who wants to know anything else about José? We've already got enough to hang him." He had been fidgety the entire trip and was getting cranky.

"We don't have a weapon," she reminded him, "and, we don't have a motive."

"Yet," Vik said.

"We've got to control the personal involvement, Jessenovik. Maintain our objectivity."

"I don't think that kid ever had a chance," Vik said. "Every kid deserves a chance."

"Sorry, but in the real world it doesn't work that way."

"Cynic," Vik said.

That, from Matthew Jessenovik, the ultimate cynic? Before she could answer a semitrailer turned on his signal and swung in front of her. There wasn't enough room in the lane for both of them. As she braked and prayed that the driver behind her was paying attention, Vik cussed at the trucker and gave him the finger.

"He can't see you," Marti said. Behind them, the driver, who had not rearended them, was leaning on his horn.

"Let's activate the siren," Vik said. "The hell with this."

"Patience," Marti said, although she felt more like ramming

the truck in front of her than advancing three feet every two minutes. All of that road construction a couple of years ago and nothing had changed. Had there really been a time when she considered driving through the city a challenge? She couldn't believe how many more semis there were these days. And there was no longer a time, night or day, when the main arteries in and out of the city were not congested, although sometimes traffic moved a little faster. She was glad she didn't live here anymore, and even happier that she didn't work here.

They made it through the Loop, past the West Side exits and over to the South Side in only an hour and fifteen minutes.

"What time did you tell this guy we'd be there?" Vik asked.

"Twenty minutes ago."

"Well, call him, for crying out loud."

"You call him, I'm driving. We're meeting him where he works, and his shift ends at nine tonight."

"It's almost that now."

"It is not."

"Well, it will be by the time we get there."

"Don't worry, Vik. He's not going anywhere anytime soon. If nothing else, he'll have to dig out his car."

Nathaniel Madden was working in another youth home, one he described as smaller, that "only" housed thirty-five preteen boys. Marti missed the off ramp, but didn't say anything to alert Vik, took the next exit and doubled back. She parked in front of a large redbrick building that looked as if it had once been separated into apartments. There was no gate, no fence, nothing to suggest that the residents couldn't come and go as they pleased until she approached the front door. Then she noticed the security gate and camera as well as the safety bars on every window, upstairs and down. A uniformed security guard admitted her.

"We're here to see Nathaniel Madden," she said as they held out their badges.

"Sure, just a minute." He spoke into an intercom.

It was an older building, with high ceilings and decorative

moldings and even a few unused fireplaces. The furniture that she could see in what looked like an unused living room was serviceable and sturdy, but didn't match. Floor lamps lit the room. The place was noisy, but the noise wasn't close up. She could hear an argument, although she couldn't make out the words, and knew a television was on although she couldn't identify anything more than the laugh track.

A tall man with skin the color of polished oak came down the curving staircase. He was older than she expected, nearing middle age, but handsome with short, wavy salt-and-pepper hair. He looked muscular and fit, and wore wire-rimmed glasses over dark, intense eyes.

"Hi." He held out his hand. "Nate Madden. You're Detective MacAlister." He smiled at her. "And you're Detective Jessenovik."

"Hey, Mr. Madden!" A boy stood at the top step where the stairs curved. He looked to be eleven or twelve. "Willy said—"

"Tell Willy I said time out if he doesn't stop saying. At least till I get back up there." He turned to them, "We can talk in here."

They went into the room with the furniture that didn't match. It turned out to be comfortable enough to fall asleep in.

"Now, I can't talk long or all hell will break loose around here. So I'll just tell you what I know and try to answer your questions. First, I liked José. Everyone seemed to think he was bad news because he had such an attitude problem, but kids like that can be real easy to turn around if you take the time. The place we were in was a temporary facility, although that's a relative term in this system. This is a permanent facility. I get more of a chance to accomplish something here. The kids aren't waiting to be pushed out the door, and they know they're pretty well stuck here, so they work a little harder at making their lives a little less miserable. That way I'm reasonably happy, and so are they."

"And José?" Marti prompted.

"The system doesn't work for many kids. Personally I think they should bring back orphanages, although that's not a real popular idea. With orphanages kids at least had some permanence and they knew they would have to change before anything else would, if anything else did change. José could have benefited from some kind of permanence, the same as a lot of other kids. He didn't get any stability, and he's the product of that."

"How did you two get along?"

"Better than he got along with anybody else. I told him what Madden's rules were and the consequences of not following them. He knew where he stood with me, and we got along fine."

"And his attitude?"

"Not bad, not like it was with the others. We had some parameters and he could live within them without too much of a hassle. Every war has its cease-fires."

There was thumping and banging overhead and the sounds of an argument. Nate went to the bottom of the staircase. "Hey, Ramon, separate those two. In fact, send Willy down here to the kitchen to help peel potatoes."

He waited until a young boy came downstairs, stopped him and said, "Hey, I told you, this is my house, I live here too, twelve hours a day. And my house rules don't include fighting with a brother because you can't beat him at cribbage, got that? We'll sit down after supper and I'll try to teach you the rules of the game. That's how you'll beat him, by learning how to play."

The boy nodded and Nate stepped aside to let him pass.

When he returned to the room, Marti said, "What about José and Graciela?"

"He liked her. I think he liked her a lot. José was a rescuer. Graciela was his damsel in distress."

"Why?"

"Because she was hanging with some deadbeat at school who got her pregnant."

"It wasn't José's child?"

"Well, I wasn't there, but no, I'm sure of it."

"Did he ever hit her?"

"No, but they argued."

"And after she got pregnant?"

"They argued a lot, right up until she made an appointment to get the abortion, then they stopped speaking to each other at all."

"Do you know why?"

"José had some notion that it was wrong. Morally wrong. I think Graciela just wanted to survive and didn't think she could if she had a child. I remember one day he was yelling at her that everyone did not kill their babies, or even put them up for adoption, that some girls were mothers, not just whores. She asked him how he would know that, made a few derogatory remarks about his mother. José just looked at her and said that he did know someone like that. Someone who loved her kid enough to keep it and raise it herself."

Again they were interrupted, this time by loud shouts and cursing. A man yelled "That's enough," and the argument stopped abruptly.

"Were they still at the same place after the abortion?" Marti asked.

"No. It took the state a week to split them up. The situation was reported to their caseworkers. It had a major effect on hastening their departures. I think the caseworkers thought the kid must be his."

"But you're sure it wasn't. They weren't fooling you, pretending to dislike each other and sneaking around?"

"No, José had a different kind of anger about what happened than being responsible for it would have produced. He was offended by what Graciela did. It wasn't personal, although it wouldn't surprise me if his mother or some other woman in his life had had one. He was relating it to something, but he wasn't the outraged father."

Again there was bumping and thumping.

"Gotta go," Nate said, motioning toward the ceiling. "It's the weather. Barometric pressure dropped because of the snow. Anything else? Make it fast."

Marti didn't have any more questions. She looked at Vik.

"Do you think José would hurt her?" he asked.

"Kill her, you mean. Maybe. If he got angry enough."

"Did he brood a lot," Marti asked.

"Yes. I think so. You want to know if this could have been simmering for a while?"

Marti nodded.

"It's possible," Nate said. "But like I told you, Graciela's abortion wasn't personal on that level. It was something that really bothered José, but there was some other reason for that."

There was more yelling and Nate made his apologies as he hurried upstairs.

"We've got to do more digging," Vik said as they headed back to Lincoln Prairie. "But where? I say we just tell them we've gone as far as we can with this and let the state's attorney take it from here. I don't think they'll try him as an adult with what they have now."

"Maybe we have gone as far as we can," Marti agreed. "But we haven't gone as far as we ought to, and we don't know for sure that we can't go any further."

Vik sighed, "Psychological motivation isn't exactly our area of expertise. What if we just dig a deeper hole for the kid?"

When Marti didn't answer, Vik said, "I know, MacAlister, I know. We play by the rules, we don't choose them."

Marti got on the phone with José's caseworker when they got back to the precinct. The woman sounded more than exasperated when she said, "His mother? Relatives? Friends? Give me a break. What makes you think there are any?"

"Just give me a trail," Marti said. "Anything that will get me to someone who knew José and or his relatives before he came into the system. Where they lived. Anything."

The caseworker laughed. It was a dry, harsh laugh that lacked the conviction that any of this was funny.

The Metra station was crowded when Adrian walked to the long silver commuter train. People hurried along as if it were going to pull out in two minutes instead of ten. He walked alongside it without haste, watching which cars most passengers were boarding, and avoiding them, keeping far enough away from the train to see inside the streaked, dirty windows and across the aisles. The car he entered was empty, at least downstairs. They were double-deckers with a center space from floor to ceiling and an upstairs row of single seats with windows along each side. As soon as he boarded, Adrian walked to the small bathroom at one end of the car, stepped inside and locked the door.

He rode all the way to Lincoln Prairie that way, sitting on the closed toilet seat for over an hour and a half listening to a recording that announced each stop, and told the passengers to be at the doors waiting for them to open. Nobody tried to come in.

Lincoln Prairie was the last stop. He waited for almost half an hour after the train stopped. Then it lurched, moved south toward Chicago, switched tracks and stopped again, wheels hissing and steam making rhythmic belching sounds. Adrian opened the door, and waited for the conductor to come down the aisle to check for anything left behind and stuff newspapers into a large paper bag. When the conductor came into the car and saw Adrian, he opened his mouth to say something. Before he could speak, Adrian showed him the gun, made him turn around, and hit him on the back of his head. Then he dragged him into the toilet and stabbed him, leaving the knife in. He waited until the lights inside the train went out and the hissing and belching sounds stopped, then he pulled open the exit doors located in the center of the train and stepped into the darkness.

He moved away from the tracks and stood under a bridge

until he was certain he was alone and the dimly lit street by the train station and also the parking lot were deserted. He walked up the snow-covered slope to the street, climbed over the railing and walked the two blocks to a central street where city buses converged during the day. Bus service stopped at six in the evening and it was already after eight. At 9:10 another train would leave. Instead of waiting for it, he began walking south toward the Navy Base, missing the 9:10 but waiting on that platform for the 10:43. There were few passengers that time of night. Nobody spoke of a body being found in Lincoln Prairie. This conductor seemed totally unaware.

When Adrian got off the bus at the stop near where he lived, it was still snowing. About five inches had fallen here, less than the amount Lincoln Prairie had received. He stopped at the corner liquor store for a bottle of wine. Cheap wine, but fruity. It was the only kind of wine he could afford now, but he could still remember the taste of good wine, even after all of these years. The money he had salted away in one of his bank accounts that had gone unnoticed for thirteen years had grown with interest. Even so, there wasn't that much, not anywhere near as much as he had once been accustomed to having. And it had to get him to Mexico and last until he could find other sources of income. He had to spend carefully now.

The street he lived on had not been plowed. He doubted a plow had come through since the first snow fell in November. The new snow was soft and mushy, hiding the accumulated snow that had hardened into icy ridges. Tires had made troughs in the snow in the middle of the street. Boots and shoes had beaten down paths on the sidewalk. Here and there shovels had cleared stairs. Not at his building though.

The first thing he did when he went into his apartment was close the window. It had only been open a few inches, but even so, snow had blown in and was melting on the floor. He couldn't think of any bad luck that snow brought, but he couldn't think of any good luck either. Everything brought one or the other. He thought about it for a long time, then he remembered that if you dreamed about melted snow it meant fears would turn to joy. That was it, he decided. He wasn't fearful, but he was concerned about how to get to Marti MacAlister. Not only was tonight a major step toward his ultimate goal but the conductor, Mr. Calvin Ward, had also been on his list. Poor Calvin, hapless bastard. He looked so uncomfortable, so out of place in the jury box. His name had been at the bottom of Adrian's list until his proximity to Marti MacAlister had made him important. Now because he lived in Chicago but died in Lincoln Prairie, Calvin Ward would bring Detective MacAlister here, to him, where it would be easier to kill her.

8

Marti and Ben woke up at the same time when one of their beepers went off. Ben picked up both of them from the nightstand. "Yours," he said, handing it to her. Marti checked the clock, 4:25 A.M. Her first thought was that since the alarm was set for 5:30, she wouldn't lose that much sleep. Her second thought was, not another body. Ben gave her a pat on the butt as she got out of bed. She dressed quickly, then left without so much as a cup of coffee because Momma wasn't up yet. Momma was spoiling her with food and drink in the morning.

"On the train," Marti repeated, and yawned. Her breath became cloudlike in the cold air. The snow had stopped during the night after an accumulation of another six inches, but this close to the lake it was at least five degrees colder than it was when she left home. "The train," she repeated.

The conductor gave her a puzzled look. "Right. The train," he agreed, his face red from the cold. He had been waiting outside for her when she pulled up in front of the train station. The wind was whipping off the lake, less than two blocks away, and even in long coat, ear muffs, gloves, and his conductor's gold-striped hat, he was shivering. "That train." He pointed to a train that was a good distance down the track. Two black-and-whites were parked alongside it, lights flashing. Neither Vik nor anyone from the coroner's office had arrived yet.

"Why don't we go inside?" Marti suggested.

"Cal's dead. Don't you . . ." There was a catch in his voice, as if the enormity of it had hit him. "Don't you have to go down there?"

"Not yet."

"Then why did they send you?"

"I'm in charge," she said. "Me and my partner."

"In charge of what?"

"Everything." She gestured toward the station. It was a modern one-story redbrick building that had been built just a few years ago. She hoped the interior included a couple of candy and drink machines. "There is a coffee machine inside, isn't there?"

"But Cal . . . he's . . ."

"Dead," she said, then, "Inside? Coffee?"

He looked confused. Too much TV, she decided. This was too quiet, too ordinary. No news cameras, no reporters, no crowds, no detective in a wrinkled trench coat. She rubbed her hands together. Her fingers were cold, even though she was wearing gloves.

"There's a refreshment stand," the conductor said. "Jorge's got a pot on." He held the door for her. "Coffee for the lady, Jorge." He still seemed puzzled. She wanted to tell him that there was very little drama in death, except in the telling of it afterward, but said nothing.

Inside, she looked around. It was a one-room station, with the canteen service tucked in one corner, a few plastic chairs near windows with a view of the train tracks, and the ticket booth sectioned off and walled in with a window. Toward the center of the room there was a book rack with paperbacks donated by the Friends of the Library along with the suggestion that if you took a book, you left one next time you came. There were three other men, one behind the counter who must be Jorge, another at the ticket window, and a second conductor. There weren't any customers yet. It seemed as though there should be one or two early birds, even at this hour of the morning.

197

"What time does the train leave?" she asked. Her daddy had ridden the rails, but longer distances, from Chicago to points west. He'd been a porter. She couldn't remember ever hearing him talk about anyone finding a body. She wished she could remember something about trains, like terminology. But she could not.

"This one was scheduled to leave at four-fifty-eight," the ticket master said.

"Where are the passengers?"

"This early they've all got commuter passes. Just board the train direct unless they want coffee or something. See those cars lining up outside? They're waiting for the train to pull up for boarding so they can drop off their passengers."

As soon as Jorge handed her the Styrofoam cup filled with coffee, hot and black the way she liked it, she thanked him, and held the cup in both hands, warming them. The second conductor looked at her, and said, "So I guess this train won't be going anywhere for a while."

She agreed. "No. Can you order another one?"

All four men smiled, but nobody laughed out loud.

She walked over to the ruddy-cheeked man who had met her outside. "Are you the one who found the body?" she asked.

The man paled, shuddered, then nodded.

"Why is the train so far from the station?"

"It came in last night at seven-thirty-five, its last run of the night. Got switched over to the other tracks because it wasn't leaving again until this morning. This is the only station between Kenosha and Chicago where we can switch tracks. We got another train due to leave at five-twenty-eight. Folks wanting this one will take that. Trains run more often in the morning, but the first one coming from Kenosha doesn't leave from there until five-fifty-five. We were warming this one up, getting ready to bring her down. . . ." He got a catch in his voice, stopped talking, grabbed the bill of his hat and pulled it off as he ran his hand over his hair.

"Why were you on the train?"

"I'm part of the crew."

"And you found the body before they backed the train up to the station."

"Well, it's still out there." He seemed relieved that she was finally talking like a cop.

"Where is he?"

"Cal? In one of the bathrooms. There's a knife—" Again he stopped speaking. "Damn."

"Do you live in Lincoln Prairie?"

"No, but not far, Round Lake."

"Did you know the deceased?"

"Of course, Cal Ward." He went pale again, swallowed hard, then said, "Cal lived in Chicago. Should have gone home on the nine-ten out of here last night. Somebody knifed him. A robbery, I bet. Not that we carry enough money to steal, but these days they'll kill you for nickels and dimes." He shook his head. "Nobody's safe anymore. Damned shame."

"How did you know he was dead?"

"Lady, the man had a knife in his back. The train was cold as hell. . . ."

Later, an evidence tech would take him out to the train, go over his actions to determine what he had touched, maybe jog his memory as to something he remembered.

"What time did you find him?"

"About two minutes before I called you guys, or as long as it took me to get from the train to here."

"Did anyone else go out there?"

"No. Too cold. And he's dead. What could anyone do?"

The door opened and Vik came in.

"Train," he said, when he saw her.

"Train," she confirmed.

The two men in the dark uniforms exchanged looks as if there was some significance to that that they didn't understand. And there was. This was the first time since she came here that anyone had found an entire body, in one piece, on a train. There hadn't even been a natural death on a train. Until now there had just been the occasional body parts scattered along the tracks after the train hit someone.

In death, Calvin Ward's tan skin had a grayish cast. His head was twisted away from her so she could only see one side of his face. He wasn't a handsome man; in fact, there was something unattractive about him that wasn't caused by the rigor that had set in. She wasn't sure if it was the filminess of one eye staring without seeing anything, or the scattering of small black moles from forehead to chin, or if it was the waxy mask of death, or the odor of dying and the bodily functions it released. There was something about Calvin Ward that bothered her. She looked at Vik. He sensed it too.

Marti got her camera out of its leather bag, took her usual crime scene photos, walked around the train, inside and out, and followed the evidence tech as he followed the train conductor who retraced his steps leading up to the discovery of the body and then described everything he did next. When the conductor looked at her, and said, "Then she came and we went into the train station while she had some coffee," the evidence tech smiled.

As Marti walked alongside Vik and they headed back to the station, she said, "What took you so long?"

"Mildred," he answered. "She fell again last night, didn't break anything but I didn't want to leave her alone, so I picked up her sister Maisie first, and dropped her off at the house." Vik stopped at the train station long enough to get a jelly-filled and chocolate-creme-filled doughnut. They both got more coffee.

Marti's stomach began churning as she headed for the office. Sikich, she thought. They had missed role call. He was probably waiting for them now. Instead, there was just Cowboy and Slim who reeked of cologne, as usual. Vik made a big deal of whisking open the closet door and looking inside.

"Nope, he's not in here," he confirmed.

Marti took a deep breath and tried to relax. Maybe Lieutenant Dirkowitz would be back today.

"How's Angela Faith?" she asked before either vice cop could say anything.

"Medication is doing its thing," Slim said. "And she's gained back some of her birth weight. Looks like Dirkowitz might be in some time tomorrow."

"Meanwhile," Cowboy drawled, "the captain wants to talk to you. He said either of you could call him. And we've got to schedule a lineup starring the one and only Reginald Garrett."

"You've got some women who will show up?" Vik asked.

"Cleared everything with the captain and the state's attorney."

Vik checked the coffeepot. "Cleared what?" He filled his mug.

"We are relocating all three of them after they testify, and holding him without bail as a flight risk until the trial."

"Damn," Marti said. "Reggie's that bad? What's his MO?"

"Picks them up at sites that provide food and a place to sleep. He has a preference for the church where he picked up La-Shawna Davis."

"Kind of isolated," Marti said.

Cowboy put his feet on his desk. The heels of his boots were making little gouge marks in the wood. "Garrett is nice to them for a couple of days. Then he turns mean. We got one who ended up in the hospital with broken ribs, another with her jaw still wired shut and one who got kicked in the stomach and had a miscarriage. They're scared as hell of him but knowing we can and will keep him in jail alleviated some of that."

"Were there others?" Marti asked.

"Oh, sure, at least another half dozen. No way were they saying anything, not for the record, at least."

"You don't think these three will walk?" Vik asked.

"They'll run," Slim said. "But not until after they testify."

"You're sure about that?"

"We're putting them up in a shelter in McHenry County. Real nice place, state of the art. They leave Illinois as soon as the trial is over, and we're arranging a real nice send-off, a shopping trip for new clothes, and air fare if they don't want to take a train or a bus."

"How did you manage that?" Marti asked.

Slim smiled. "Just a few anonymous friends willing to help out," he said.

Marti thought about LaShawna and her little girl. "You haven't heard anything on LaShawna?"

"Nothing," Slim confirmed. "Got our ear to the ground, but the girl's done a real good disappearing act."

Or Reggie had graduated from battery to murder.

"Keep looking, okay?"

"You got it," Cowboy said. "Heard you caught a dead one at the train station."

She was grateful for the distraction. They talked about the new case for about ten minutes before she remembered to call the captain.

"You and Jessenovik have a ten o'clock press conference this morning regarding Mr. Ramos's comments in yesterday's paper," he advised her.

Her stomach gave a lurch. "Will Sikich be there, sir?"

"No."

She wanted to ask why not, but decided to be grateful instead.

"You two have handled this before," Captain Allendo said. "It shouldn't be a problem. And you don't need any watchdogs." She thought that might be an indirect message. Maybe Sikich had gone to the captain. Maybe that was why he was leaving them alone.

Marti made a few phone calls, made arrangements to meet with Calvin Ward's widow, then got lucky and contacted a counselor who had worked at the facility where José and Graciela stayed. They could drive into Chicago after the lineup, pay a visit to the Widow Ward, then head northwest of the city to a seminary in Libertyville. José's former counselor was now studying to become a priest.

* * *

Marti and Vik met with two local reporters at ten, a veteran from the *News-Times* and a younger man whom Marti didn't know from a newspaper with a primary distribution west of Lincoln Prairie. The room used for the conference was small and crowded with the four of them and a uniform with a tape recorder. When the uniform signaled, Marti began.

"We may or may not be able to answer your questions," she explained. "There are minors involved and no charges have been brought at this time."

"We know," the *News-Times* reporter said. "I'm interested in juvenile justice in general at the local level."

"We can only speak to that in terms of homicide or other death-related cases," Marti advised him.

"We've scheduled a meeting with Denise Stevens also."

"Good," Vik said. He sat back, arms folded.

"How are you handling the Lara case?"

"The same as we would handle any other homicide," Vik said.

"We don't differentiate between adult and juvenile subjects in a death investigation," Marti added.

"Not even when you have a history with one of the juveniles?" The *News-Times* reporter remembered the kids in the library, too.

"We stay focused," Vik said. "It's not the first time we've known the subjects involved in a case. Lincoln Prairie's not that big yet. Hell, I've arrested subjects I went to school with."

"But these are kids."

"And," Vik added, "one of them is a dead kid. Finding out who did it is our job. And we will do our job."

"Doesn't it make you feel different when it involves juveniles?" the younger reporter asked.

"We're parents," Vik snapped.

"So it's a dirty job but somebody has to do it," the reporter said.

"No," Vik told him. "We like what we do and we're good at it."

"When someone dies at another person's hand," Marti explained, thinking of the train conductor, "they no longer have a voice. We become their voice. We look, and listen, we investigate until we can speak for them and tell the state's attorney how they died, who killed them, and hopefully why."

"So you see your job as being as much about who died as who killed them."

Marti nodded. "We don't like it when juveniles are involved, but to us, all victims have the same right—justice. And all suspects have legal rights, too. We have to respect and enforce their rights as well. Detective Jessenovik and I understand those statutes and we comply with every right that is mandated under the law."

"Do you think Mr. Ramos's concern about his ward receiving justice as a juvenile is valid?" the young reporter asked.

"We're glad he's concerned," Marti said. "Every juvenile needs at least one advocate. But I'm not sure that Mr. Ramos's concerns involve us. If they do, he has not been specific."

"Then you don't see his remarks as being addressed to you personally but to the juvenile justice system in general?"

"You'll have to figure that out," Vik said. "We read the article, that's about it. What Mr. Ramos says doesn't affect how we do our job."

"You don't feel any pressure to make an arrest?"

"We don't always make arrests," Vik told him. "We do detain subjects, pending arrest."

The young reporter looked confused.

Marti decided not to leave him hanging. "We present evidence to the state's attorney. If they agree, they obtain an arrest warrant, present the case to the grand jury, bring charges."

"So basically, you investigate."

Marti resisted the impulse to point out that was what they had been saying all along. As her son, Theo, would say, some people are three fries short of a Happy Meal.

"And if your investigation offends or upsets someone like Mr.

Ramos and they make a lot of noise, or have the clout to bring political pressure—"

"Understand one thing," Marti interrupted. "We do not even function at a level where political pressure is an issue. It isn't our job to placate Mr. Ramos or make him feel comfortable with our investigation, or even read about or listen to anything he has to say that is not relevant to this case. Our job is finding a killer."

"And we will do that," Vik added.

By eleven o'clock, Slim and Cowboy had everything in place for the lineup. One at a time, without hesitation, the three women identified Reginald Garrett as the man who had beaten them. Marti was surprised by how young they were, how vulnerable. She didn't want to speculate on how they came to be homeless, but she did hope that Slim and Cowboy's efforts would keep them off the street.

"You're taking them to that place in McHenry now, right?" she asked.

Slim grinned at her. For once it didn't seem like a leer. "Worried about them, tough lady?"

"Maybe," she admitted. In spite of herself she asked, "Don't they have family?"

Slim shrugged. "The youngest was asked to leave home because the mother's new boyfriend paid too much attention to her, the brunette turned seventeen and was no longer eligible for juvenile services. The third has been out there for a while, three, four years. Goes from man to man, started out as a runaway seven, eight years ago. Can't stay away from the life. If one of them is least likely to make it, she's it."

Marti took one last look at the three women. She knew more about them than she wanted to, more than she could forget.

"Two trips to the city in two days is one trip too many," Marti complained as they headed for Route 41 again. She tried not to think about inching her way through traffic again. If it was as bad as it had been yesterday, there was no way she could arrive at the widow Ward's house in an hour and twenty-two minutes.

Vik didn't say anything until they were past Lake Bluff. "Soup kitchens, and warming centers, and PADS for a place to sleep," he grumbled. "Time was when we had a few winos, some nutcases, and maybe a drug addict or two, and we locked them up for the night when it got cold. Now we have homeless women who are still teenagers, and children as well."

She felt depressed about those three young women, too. Her pastor had told them last Sunday that twenty-one children, ages seven months to nine years old, with four and five belonging to each family, and with both parents present, were eating and sleeping in their church basement twice a week. In Lincoln Prairie, those numbers were significant. In Chicago, the shelters would be grateful to have so few to care for.

"I wonder what they do during the day?" she said. For the first time all day, she thought about the vagrant in the doorway of that converted Victorian near the Barrister. What was it about him that had gotten her attention? Why couldn't she put him out of her mind? Instinct? It was like looking at a checkerboard where every checker but one was either red or black. He didn't belong there, especially not in broad daylight. She had never seen a vagrant loitering on that street until she ran across him. At least she hadn't seen the man since. Where did he go?

"I know our church provides coffee and doughnuts before they leave in the morning, Jessenovik. And they give them a bag lunch, but where do they go? How do the children go to school? Do they go to school?"

"I don't know," Vik admitted. "And on top of that, we get predators like Reginald Garrett."

Neither of them said anything else until Vik saw a Dunkin' Donuts sign up ahead.

"Pull in," he said. "I need at least half a dozen jellies and creme filled."

Marti decided she could handle four glazed. They settled into an uneasy silence, ate doughnuts and drank coffee until they neared the O'Hare exchange and traffic came to a near halt, then crept along, stop and go, for half an hour. Marti pulled off at Division and headed west, then north for another seven blocks. They were only ten minutes late when they arrived at the Ward residence. It was a narrow two-story brick with attic, on a block-long street with similar houses, all recently re-habbed. Each had three feet of yard in front and one parking space. Marti circled the block twice before someone on the next street pulled out. "Not one homeless person," Vik commented as they walked down a street with small, trendy eating places and specialty shops and turned the corner.

Unlike other parts of the city, yesterday's snow had been plowed and the steps and sidewalks cleared. There were a lot of yellow stains in the neat pile of snow that lined the curb. "Dogs," Vik said, "and pooper scoopers. Yuppie kids, my son calls them, easier to train than children, and cheaper to raise."

"You better let me do the talking, Jessenovik. You are in a really lousy mood."

Mrs. Ward was wearing a CTA uniform when she opened the door. She didn't look as if she had been crying, which didn't mean much.

"We're the officers from Lincoln Prairie," Marti explained when the woman questioned the shape of their badges. Chicago cops' shields were shaped like, and called, stars. Satisfied with Marti's explanation, the woman unlocked the metal burglar bars and let them in.

Two Pekingese greeted them with high-pitched yelps. One of the little fur balls bared its teeth. Mrs. Ward shushed them and they backed off. The little white ribbons with tiny red hearts that were fastened to the tops of their heads bobbed as they retreated to two baskets in the living room. The entrance way was lit with indirect lighting, the living room was lived in, with a thickly padded couch and matching chairs, television and stereo equipment. Photographs crowded the top shelf of the entertainment center, the other shelves were crammed with videos and more videos were scattered on the floor. Smaller shelving units were filled with CDs.

"I'm not sure I understand what happened," the woman said. She had skin the color of cinnamon and looked as though she might be a little older than her husband. Marti took a closer look at the photos. Most were of the happy couple with dogs. Some were of the dogs in cute poses. There were no pictures of children or young adults, no weddings, and no graduations, except for the dogs posing in pink graduation caps complete with collars that matched the hot pink tassels.

"Are you here alone, ma'am?" Marti asked. "Is there someone we can call?"

"Cal's sister and brother should be here pretty soon. The rest of the family is in Mississippi and Alabama." She motioned them to the two chairs, then sat on the couch and called the dogs over. They jumped up and sat on either side of her and she buried her face in their fur and stroked their heads without disturbing their bows.

"Thank God I've got Beauty and Baby."

She spoke dog talk to them, much as one talked to babies, and they settled down beside her with their heads on her lap. "You're going to miss your daddy, aren't you? Baby waited up for him all last night, didn't you?" She looked at Marti. "I knew something was wrong. Cal always came home, even when he rode the last train north, unless there were blizzard conditions up there, and then he called." She looked down at the dogs again. "We just sat there and worried all night, didn't we? Daddy's Baby was frantic, poor little girl." She stroked the dogs head, then said to Marti, "Cal always walks them before he leaves for work, and fixes their breakfast. My first run is at nine, so I'm not up as early as he is." As she spoke, she kept petting the dogs. "Can you tell me what happened? What happens now?"

"Who have you spoken with, ma'am?" Marti asked.

"His supervisor."

"What did he tell you?"

"Just that Cal was a robbery victim, that he was stabbed."

"Have you spoken with anyone from the coroner's office?"

"Yes, she seemed like such a nice person. Explained where he was, said they had to do an autopsy, and that you would be coming to talk with me."

"We need to ask you some questions," Marti said. "Did your husband have any recent disagreements with anyone, at work maybe, or with some passenger on the train?"

Instead of answering her directly, Mrs. Ward spoke to the dogs. "Daddy didn't come home with any funny stories this week, did he?" Then she looked at Marti. "There was this one guy last week, lost his monthly pass and was pretty upset about it. They are getting expensive." She focused on the dogs again. "Not much Daddy could do about that, though, was there, Baby?"

Marti found the attention shifts from her to the dog disconcerting. Baby must have been Daddy's favorite.

"Were there any problems with the neighbors, any family arguments?"

"Oh no, no, no. We just love the neighbors, don't we, Baby." She looked at Marti. "Especially Barney the dachshund," she said in an adult voice.

"And family?"

"There's just the two of us and Cal's brother and sister." It was Marti's turn again. "They'll be here soon. We're together a lot. Travel, do things. We were going back to Vegas the first week of March. His sister was married but her husband died two years ago. His brother is retired, never married, dates sometimes, nothing serious. Everyone else in the family lives down South, don't they, Baby." It was the dog's turn. "We're going to take Daddy home too, aren't we. We're going to take your daddy home real soon. Everything's going to be all right. Everything is going to be just fine. Mommy's babies are going to miss their daddy, but we're going to be okay. Yes, we are."

"How was your husband the last time you saw him?"

"Excited," she said, without hesitation. "We . . . all four of us, have been taking this genealogy course at Woodson Library, and trying to trace our families back to the Civil War. We've been going through these banking records that the Mormons have for about six or seven months now. Yesterday Cal's brother called before Baby and Beauty even had breakfast. He was sure he had found something."

Marti asked a few more questions, then watched where she walked as she went to the door accompanied by one dog on either side. They were friendly now and so frisky she didn't want to trip over one, or worse, step on little Beauty or Daddy's Baby.

"Say good-bye to the nice lady," Mrs. Ward urged. Their curly tails wagged vigorously. One of them got so excited she left a little puddle on the carpet.

"Oh, Mama's baby tinkled," Mrs. Ward crooned. "That's all right. We'll clean that up right now, won't we."

As they walked the three feet to the sidewalk, Vik said, "I wonder who does the cleaning up. I already figured out who the owner is and who's the pet."

Adrian sat by the window in the coffee shop and watched as Marti MacAlister and her partner unlocked their car doors and got in. This was the fifth local coffee shop he had visited today. He had almost frozen to death walking around, waiting for them to show up, not knowing where they would park, but certain that they would come. This place had a French name, motif, and menu, and wasn't crowded. Most of the people who came in and out were probably regulars, so he was sure he had been noticed. He was dressed in his repairman's jacket and at each place made small talk with the waitress, who brought him a sandwich or dessert, coffee, and then refills. He made sure the waitress knew that his partner, who didn't know the city as well as he did, had gotten lost. He used their pay phones a few times, talking to himself, giving directions that indicated his fictional counterpart was on the far southwest side, then he sat down again to get warm, or stay warm a little longer, and wait.

And then they came, just as he expected them to. He read the newspaper while he assumed they were talking to the grieving widow. Now they took their time buckling up and starting the car. Adrian returned to the pay phone, made a call to his nonexistent co-worker, then another to the make-believe customer to reschedule the job. That done, he left the waitress a nice tip and went outside just in time to see the car turn the corner. He had checked the license number while they were gone. It was the same car they drove in Lincoln Prairie.

Adrian whistled, in spite of the cold, as he headed for the bus stop. The snow melting in his room last night had been a good omen. Detective MacAlister wasn't going to be hard to keep track of at all. He could kill her at will. He just had to decide how. And, since once he killed her the odds would increase significantly that he would at least become a suspect, he had to be ready to leave town. Right now he had to plan tonight's activities.

Marti drove over to the Metra Station at Madison and Canal before leaving the city. Finding a parking place was impossible. She pulled over to the curb where the cabs were lined up and put the Lincoln Prairie police sign on the windshield. Cab drivers stared but said nothing as she and Vik went inside.

The place had changed a lot. The last she had been there it was still the old Chicago Northwestern Station. Now it was more like a concourse at O'Hare, with upscale stores, and boutiques, fast-food places, a bookstore. They took the escalator to the level where the trains boarded and found the gate where the northbound to Lincoln Prairie/Kenosha was berthed. The train was due out at 4:35. As they watched, most of the passengers got on without going to the ticket window, which meant that most of the riders were daily commuters with monthly or weekly passes. When they got back to the precinct, she would call and find out how many one-way or round-trip tickets were purchased on average, and how many of each were bought for the evening commute. They didn't have time to ask now.

"Calvin Ward. Robbery victim," Marti said, as they headed out of the city. "But nothing was taken."

"The body went undiscovered for maybe seven or eight hours, there was plenty of time."

"He was stabbed and whoever did it left the knife in, smart enough to know that would keep the blood from spurting. And what do you want to bet, smart enough to wipe the handle clean."

"Family sounds too close-knit for there to be any problem there," Vik added.

"Random?" Marti asked.

"Too well planned to be totally random. The victim could have been, but not the crime."

"The conductors we spoke to at the train station this morning thought well of him, said there were no problems," Marti said. "He was a Metra employee for twenty-seven years. Excellent record. We'll have to interview the others on his crew when the train pulls in tonight."

"Maybe we should take a ride from Lake Forest or Lake Bluff to Lincoln Prairie, get a feel for what it's like riding in."

It was dark when Marti turned into the long driveway that led to the church and seminary. Vik had called ahead to let the former counselor/future priest know they were running late.

Marti waited in the vestibule while Vik went into the church. She pushed the heavy oak door ajar and peeked in and watched as he lit a candle by some process that did not involve striking a match or igniting a taper. That puzzled her until she noticed that the candle didn't flicker either. None of the candles flickered. They had to be tiny lightbulbs activated somehow when you put the coins into the collection box. To her, this ranked right up there with nuns no longer wearing veils, although she doubted that Catholics took that seriously anymore. If she were Catholic, though, she would miss lighting real candles.

She took a deep breath. The smell was gone, too. The Catholic churches she had sneaked into when she was growing up on the West Side of Chicago smelled of beeswax and blessed oils and incense. It was exotic somehow, and the dark, hushed atmosphere much more mysterious than the Baptist church she attended. At least this church still had real marble altars and not the kind that looked like dining room tables.

There was a cold burst of air as the door opened behind her. She turned to see a middle-aged man wearing jeans and a turtleneck fisherman's sweater under an open pea coat. He had mittens on too, and a hat and boots, but she didn't think he could have walked very far without buttoning up.

He smiled. "Are you Detective MacAlister?"

"Yes. My partner is inside praying. He's Catholic. He'll be out in a minute. You must be Mark Dobrzycki."

"Yes, and I hope you just got here. This seemed like the easiest place to direct you to. Hard to miss it, even in the dark. And there's an office where we can talk."

He spoke quietly but Vik must have heard him because he came out.

Mark extended his hand. "Detective Jessenovik. No need to rush, unless you're in a hurry."

"Where can we talk?" Vik asked. It had been a long day, and it wasn't over yet. Both of them were tired and there was still the 7:35 out of Chicago to catch at Lake Forest.

Mark led them into a book-lined study with statues of Mary and Joseph and several saints Marti couldn't identify. They sat in sturdy but comfortable chairs with wooden armrests.

"You've come to ask about José."

"And Graciela," Marti added. "You're only the second person we've been able to locate who was with them while they were together in that temporary facility."

"How is he?" Mark asked.

Marti told him where José was, and why. When she told him

about Padgett, Mark smiled. She told him about the five children who had hidden in the library and become like a family four years ago.

"That might be what it is, then," Mark said.

"What what is?" Vik asked.

"José did have a family once," Mark said. "Apparently a happy one. A sister, brother, mother. They lived with his grandparents when he was a little boy. Then, for some reason, they moved away and things fell apart. José would never say what happened. I'm not even sure he was old enough to understand. When he ran away, nobody looked for him; when he went back, they were gone."

"He told you that?"

"The children told me many things, especially the younger ones. As they get older, their memories change, things become worse or better than they were, depending on their needs, or their attitudes. Sometimes you know they are telling you what they want to be true, not the truth. José's memories were so fragmented that I believed him. His early childhood was like a puzzle to José, something he couldn't quite figure out or put together."

"And," Marti prompted, "what happened at the library?"

"Amazing," Mark said, "That he would allow himself to become that vulnerable."

"How was he with Graciela?"

"Protective, to the extent that he could be. I think . . ." Mark hesitated, seemed reluctant to continue, then said, "You think he killed Graciela, don't you?"

"We're not sure what happened that night," Marti said. "That's what we're trying to find out."

"And if he did?" Mark asked. "What happens to him then?"

"That's not for us to decide."

"Can I testify for him?"

"Of course you can, I'll give you the name of his public defender."

Mark was silent again. Marti waited. He sighed, sat up straighter, slouched, sighed again.

"There was something about her abortion. I can remember thinking that it would be better for her child if it was not born. That was when I realized what that job was doing to me, and how little I could do to change or make any impact on the lives of those children. That's when I decided to come here. But José, I don't know. It affected him deeply. He became very angry with her, vehement that it was something she should not do. I always felt that it triggered something, some memory, some event. It was a very visceral response." He thought for a moment or two, chin in hand. "Does that mean he killed her? I don't know. There was a level where he felt responsible for her pregnancy, although I'm certain he was not the one who impregnated her. Maybe he felt responsible for the abortion too. I think the José you see with Padgett is the real José, the one he tries to hide. I also think Graciela triggered something from his past that he did not want to think about or remember."

Marti asked one final question. "Is there anything you are not telling me, that you should tell me but were told in confidence?"

Mark hesitated. "Perhaps. A few things were said in confidence, but I don't know how important they are."

"Would you tell those things to his attorney?"

"Maybe. I don't know."

Marti leaned forward. "Mark, it might be important that someone know. It is important that his attorney does not have any surprises, and she will respect your confidentiality. We cannot."

Mark nodded. "Thanks." He seemed relieved. Marti wondered what he wasn't telling her.

They were both silent as they headed back to Lincoln Prairie. Finally, Marti said, "Just what we needed, an amateur psychologist."

215

"He's not an amateur," Vik said. "Read the card he gave you. Mark Dobrzycki, Ph.D."

"That's even worse. I do not want to know what goes on inside José's head. I just want to know whether or not he killed Graciela."

"If he did, the why is inside his head, MacAlister, and finding out what that is, is probably the only way we'll get him to talk. It might even be the only way to get him tried as a juvenile."

"I'm not going there, Vik. I am not going there. He has a shrink to do that."

"So we don't find out," Vik agreed. "I don't see how we can anyway."

"Maybe his doctor should talk with Mark," she conceded.

"Maybe Mark should talk with his attorney."

Marti remembered Mark's relief at the possibility of repeating something in confidence. "I think maybe he will." They might never know whatever it was.

Marti parked their unmarked car at the Lincoln Prairie train station. Lupe drove them to Lake Forest just in time to catch the train that had left Chicago at 7:35, the train Calvin Ward had been on the night before. Marti and Vik boarded as if they were strangers, each entering a different car. Marti walked through, noting that there were few passengers, and that except for a few who were together, nobody spoke or even looked at their fellow travelers. Their ultimate objective seemed to be not to make eye contact. Most were reading newspapers or staring straight ahead. A few looked out the window. She located the bathrooms in three of the five cars. Two were small, like the one Calvin Ward had been found in, one was wheelchair accessible, two of the older coaches had no facilities. When she went into the smaller bathroom and closed the door, she could hear the recorded message just before the train reached the next stop. The killer would not have had to remain in his seat to know where he was. He could have slipped in here several stops before Lincoln Prairie, giving the conductor the impression that

216

he had detrained. With that thought in mind, she stayed inside to see if anyone tried to get in. Nobody did.

She came out before the next stop and did another walk through. Vik was sitting in the car that would be nearest the station when they reached Lincoln Prairie. He wanted to get at least a passing look at everyone who got off. Marti was going to stay in the toilet. She returned to her hiding place. Again, nobody attempted to enter. She could hear the canned message, the wheels clacking on the track, and the doors closing. She could not hear anyone walk by. There was too much noise for that. In order to know someone was out there, she would have to open the door. The killer must have had to open the door to know when Ward was coming.

After the train stopped in Lincoln Prairie, there was spasmodic hissing as if steam were escaping for half an hour. Then the train lurched, headed south moving slowly, and wheezed to a stop. Marti opened the door just enough to see into the coach. After another ten minutes passed, the conductor opened the door. He was holding a large brown bag.

"What are you doing in there?" he scolded. "Everyone got off at the station. We're not even near the platform now. You'll have to walk back."

Nobody had heard Ward speak, so he must not have seen his assailant, or if he did, he did not get a chance to confront whoever it was.

Marti identified herself. The man smiled. "Had me fooled."

"Did you do this last night?"

"No, Cal did. We took turns."

Did that mean it would have been him if it had been his turn, or did the killer know it would be Cal's? Was this random or victim specific? One thing she knew for certain now. It had required a plan.

"Anything unusual happen last night?" she asked.

"No."

"Do any passengers stick out in your mind?"

"No."

"Is there anything different or out of the ordinary that you noticed in the past week?"

He extended his hands, one palm up, the other still holding the large brown paper bag. "We do this every night, ma'am, five or six times a week. Some of the passengers I recognize by sight. I even talk with a few. But I don't know their names. Then there are those you don't notice at all. If it's a Saturday or a Sunday, the ridership is different. Maybe you get an argument, someone who's just having fun, a drunk, more teenagers and young children, a lot of laughing. A few of those people you remember a little while longer. But weeknights, most of these folks are just working stiffs like we are with a ways to go before they get home. There are no radios, a few laptops and cell phones, very little conversation. They just want to go home."

By the time Marti walked the quarter mile to the train station she was chilled to the bone. Vik was waiting inside their warm car.

"Get anything?" she asked as she got behind the wheel, teeth chattering.

"Coffee," he said, handing her a cup with a McDonald's logo.

"Thanks, anything else?"

"Nothing. There was nothing unusual, no disturbances, none of the riders stood out, nothing. They don't even look at each other. Be a shame if one of them did get mugged. Not only would they not be able to describe an assailant, they wouldn't be able to describe anyone who could have witnessed it either."

"Same here," she said, "Easy marks, all of them. But . . ." She described what she had experienced riding in the toilet compartment, as well as what she surmised could have happened last night.

"The Ward autopsy is scheduled for five tomorrow morning," Vik said. "We'd both better plan to be there. I don't want this one to get cold, and we've just about ruled out family, co-workers, and friends, which leaves us with strangers and unidentified enemies. And, oh, I suggested that the conductors might want to think about who wasn't on the train yesterday or today but should have been. Maybe that will bring someone to mind. Your idea about hiding in the toilet ties in with that."

They decided to call it a night and pick up their cars and go home without returning to their office. They agreed that given her experience with Reggie Garrett, it was highly unlikely that they were going to find LaShawna at a PADS shelter, so there was no need for either of them to check them out. Once again, as Marti headed for the precinct, she had the feeling she was being followed. She mentioned it to Vik.

"Mad Sword Swinger syndrome," he said. "We'll get over it in another couple of weeks."

Home was noisy. Everyone was doing something. Momma was in the kitchen with two of her church sisters. Marti walked through, said hi, and kissed Momma on the cheek. Joanna was down in the den with Lisa. They were sprawled on the floor, leafing through magazines and giggling. Grateful for a respite from the Great Olympics Dilemma, AKA the Great Volleyball Career Dilemma, she left them alone. Midlevel, Ben, Mike, and Theo were gathered around the computer. The printer was spitting something out and more printed sheets were on a card table. Marti thought it must have something to do with the Great Spring Mystery Trip. She let Ben know she was there, but spoke from the doorway so that she couldn't see any of the printed sheets. She liked surprises. Sometimes. Upstairs, she fell across the bed fully clothed. The next thing she heard was the phone ringing.

"Weird call, MacAlister," the dispatcher said. "Someone wants to meet you at Ninth and Columbus. Got a hot tip, won't say what it is."

Marti groaned. She didn't think she could get out of bed even to undress. But maybe, just maybe, this was the same person who had called and put her onto Reggie Garrett. Even better, maybe this was LaShawna. Then she thought of that vagrant again.

She requested an unmarked car as backup and told the dispatcher to call Vik. Her snitches had code words. Whoever called this time didn't use one. No way was she going anywhere to meet some dirtbag alone. It took her fifteen minutes to reach Columbus. She circled the block, didn't see anything suspicious, but picked out the unmarked car. When Vik drove up alongside her they parked and waited for a half hour. Nobody showed. Angry at being tricked, she drove home.

"Nobody," Ben said when she told him.
"Nobody."
"Bad night for someone to pull a stunt like that. No matter. You are going to bed. Have you had supper?"
She shook her head, suddenly hungry.
"Come on upstairs."
He drew her bath, added her favorite vanilla bath salts and helped her undress. Then he turned on the CD player. Yanni.
"Don't fall asleep yet," he cautioned as she slid down in the just-hot-enough scented water until it covered her shoulders and reached her neck.
She woke up when Ben kissed her forehead.
"Hate to wake you," he said, "But your skin is going to pucker pretty soon."
The water had cooled.
She let him help her out and wrap a towel around her. He toweled her dry, then led her into the bedroom. Supper was waiting on a tray. Propped up by pillows, she ate, scrambled eggs ribboned with melted cheddar cheese, thick slices of bacon, and buttered toast, real butter, not the fake stuff or the un-jam. She didn't ask where the butter had come from. The last thing she remembered was another kiss on the forehead, the tray being taken away, and the light going out.

The wind was cold and biting as Adrian walked from Lincoln Prairie to the naval base. When he reached the old wooden train station, he stood in the doorway, sheltered from the wind but not the cold. Wood creaked and groaned as he waited. His toes and fingers were numb by the time he heard the train coming. It wasn't cold inside the train, but it was not warm enough either. Adrian shivered most of the way to Chicago, Once there, a McDonald's was still open and he ordered a large cup of coffee. Five minutes later a bus came and he headed home. The bus driver had the heat on full blast. As he settled into the warmth and gulped down the coffee he felt as if he were thawing out.

Everything had been perfect tonight. Everything. He called, she came. He expected her to come with her partner and not alone, and she did. He could take them both out if he had to, as long as they couldn't see him, as long as he didn't get too close. He was certain that the right distance was the key to success. The most important thing that he had found out tonight was that even though he called the precinct and left the vaguest possible message, she responded. She showed up. Now he knew she was his. In his own good time, she would die.

Twice in one day, she had been within his sights, within his power to kill. Better yet, what he had accomplished tonight in Lincoln Prairie, luring her into his space, he could repeat in Chicago. She would come when he called, come where he wanted her to, come where he could kill her. Calvin Ward might or might not be the bait. The gun hidden under his mattress would assure his success.

WEDNESDAY, FEBRUARY 20

It was a little after six in the morning when Marti and Vik left the coroner's office. It was too early to have breakfast at the Barrister, so they picked up a couple dozen doughnuts and sweet rolls at a bakery on Glen Ellyn Avenue instead.

"Okay," Marti said, as they drove to the precinct. "Ward was hit on the back of the head, and had another contusion on his forehead, as well as a bruise and a small cut on his jaw."

"All consistent with being hit from behind and falling forward."

Marti pictured the interior of the train. "Ward could have been hit from behind near but not at the bathroom door, then he could have fallen forward and hit his head on the seat handle, the one you can use to hold on to or change the way the back of the seat is facing. The injury to his chin could have been caused when he fell to the floor. He could have hit the side of his face on the metal seat frame."

"Sounds reasonable," Vik agreed. "The question is, why didn't he put up a fight? There was not one defense wound or abrasion. No bruised knuckles, nothing. There wasn't any bruising on his arm or throat, nothing to indicate he was physically restrained."

"So he was a coward, or a pacifist, or the assailant was too big, or he believed whoever it was when they told him he wouldn't get hurt if he cooperated."

"There were other employees on the train," Vik said. "If he

had called out, one of the other conductors might have come and helped him, and just yelling might have caused whoever was threatening him to run away."

"So he didn't want anyone else to get hurt, didn't want to put them at risk."

"That only makes sense if the assailant had some kind of weapon."

"That might be it," Marti said. "He could have brandished the knife, told him to turn around, hit him on the head with a blunt instrument, dragged him into the toilet. Ward wasn't moved after he was stabbed. The next question is, why was he killed? He wasn't robbed. His assailant either panicked or didn't intend to rob him at all."

"Which brings us to intent. Why go through all that trouble, hiding, waiting, to rob somebody? There are plenty of marks in the city that are a lot easier and faster. Cheaper too. You don't have to buy a train ticket."

"I think you just ruled out random," Marti said. "This was deliberate. But why?"

The aroma of freshly brewed coffee greeted them when they reached their office. It was too early for roll call but Slim and Cowboy had a nine o'clock court call. Both were at their desks, reading through a stack of files.

"How many cases have you two got today?" Vik asked.

"Nine," Slim said.

"They'll be calling this town Sin City in a couple of years," Cowboy drawled.

Neither of them looked up, not even when Marti opened the box from the bakery. Marti poured a cup of coffee, decided on a pecan roll, then retreated to her desk and her own stack of files. Her caseload had dwindled to three, but now, with the Ward homicide, was back up to four. She made as little noise as possible. Vik was quiet too. Slim and Cowboy, for all of their joking around, took the Job seriously. They would spend the next several hours with those files, going over every detail. They had a reputation for being the prosecutor's best prepared and most effective witnesses. Marti didn't think anyone on a jury would doubt what they said. Neither of them so much as looked up when Marti and Vik went to roll call.

Lieutenant Dirkowitz was back. He waved to them as they entered the room. He was a big man, had been known as Dirty Dirk when he played linebacker in college, and he still stayed in shape. Marti was so glad to see him, she could have given him a hug. And, if nothing else, his being there must mean that the baby was holding her own. After roll call, they met with Dirkowitz in his office.

"I'll just be here for a couple of hours," he warned. "We take turns sitting with the baby."

"I hope this means she's okay," Marti said.

"They told us last night that she'll be just fine. She might even be released in a couple of days. She looks just like her mother, and she's gained another four ounces."

"That's great," Vik said.

"Have you held her yet?" Marti asked.

"For a minute. She's smaller than a football and not half as heavy."

They all laughed.

"We touch her a lot, and talk to her. She knows our voices." He was thoughtful for a moment, with a bemused expression on his face. "Amazing, isn't it?" he said, then, "Bring me current on everything except the Lara case."

They brought him up to date, including the three cases they had just closed.

"That interview you did was good."

"Interview," Marti said. "Oh." They had both forgotten. It must have been in yesterday's *News-Times*.

"Joe Ramos and I both went to Southern Illinois, but not at the same time. He's the one who didn't play football." Dirkowitz smiled. "I was known as a Big Man on Campus. Joe was known as a Big Mouth on Campus."

"At least he's not lying about anything," Vik said. "And he's not giving us any hassles."

"I set up a meeting. He'll be here in about half an hour. When I talked with him on the phone, he didn't seem to have any complaints about how you two are doing your job, but he does have some legitimate concerns. The thing with Joe is, he's serious, he isn't just running off at the mouth. He just does it so often that the man and the ego tend to get in the way of the message. Where are we with the Lara case?"

Marti let Vik fill him in.

"You two do have a vested interest in this one. I can hear that. What I don't hear is that it's interfering with your job. Keep it that way. And as for this side issue with LaShawna Davis, stay on it. I'll nudge Missing Persons, because I agree, you do have something to be concerned about, but even with this Reginald Garrett's involvement, it's not going to get a high profile, and not just because of the domestic abuse but because she's a transient, too. Just make sure you've got a line of communication open with MP. Have you got any ideas as to where we could conduct a search for her and the child?"

He meant where they should start looking for bodies.

"Nothing," Marti said.

"Don't hesitate if you get any leads. And let's get something in the newspaper."

"We don't have any photos, sir," Vik said.

"Let the police artist come up with something if you can get a decent description. Let's take this one up a notch or two."

He popped open a can of diet soda and offered them one. They both declined.

"Now," he said, after several long, deep swallows, "this new case, Calvin Ward. You've got everything covered. I don't have anything else to suggest. And good job solving those other three cases. I'm glad you got Lupe Torres involved. I hope the homicide caseload never gets so high that we need a second team, but you two do need a backup with street savvy and experience when the caseload gets this deep."

He finished off the diet pop, crushed the can in his hand, and opened another. "That brings us to Sikich. There is a promotion in the works that will give us a reliable second-in-command. In the meantime, he's your man. However—" He locked his fingers behind his neck, leaned back, and smiled. "The captain did meet with Lieutenant Sikich and outline the parameters of his responsibilities, so if there are any problems and I'm not available, feel free to go right to the top."

Marti hadn't felt this relaxed since Sikich took over. It felt good to have a professional in charge again.

They were wrapping up when the lieutenant's secretary came in to let them know Mr. Ramos was there.

Both men shook hands.

"Joe, good to see you," the lieutenant said.

"Dirk." Ramos nodded toward Marti, then Vik, and sat down.

"Joe," the lieutenant began, "this has nothing to do with anything that has appeared in the newspaper, including MacAlister's and Jessenovik's interview yesterday. It is about a young girl who died while in your care and about the young man who might be accused of killing her."

Ramos nodded. Marti waited for the speech, but he said nothing.

"Now, I think Marti and Vik need to explain their past history with José Ortiz."

Again, Marti let Vik do the talking.

"I wasn't aware of that," Ramos said. "Thank you for telling me."

Marti was amazed by Ramos's lack of belligerence.

"Okay, Joe, your turn," the lieutenant went on. "Why don't you tell us your concerns."

Ramos was thoughtful for a moment, then said, "José's not a bad kid. I know all the rhetoric about bad kids, and kids out of control, and kids who kill."

Now the speechmaking begins, Marti thought, but she listened.

"I know that minority kids get the rap for everything bad or illegal that teenagers do, as if what nonminorities do is an unfortunate aberration. I know many people feel that they must be protected from this dangerous element in society—minority youth. Even when we see the pictures of nonminority children in the newspapers, or see them in custody on television, and they have have killed not just one but a number of people, this assumption about minority youth prevails. That said, it can be terrifying as a minority to have someone you know or care about caught up in a juvenile justice system that is not capable of being color blind."

"Okay," Dirkowitz said. "I hear you. Marti? Vik?"

"We're doing everything we can," Vik said. "I agree with what you're saying, and I think you should continue to say it, but all I can do is my job."

Marti thought that was all that needed to be said, but added, "We are the bottom line here. If we don't do our job right, then the breakdown in the system begins with us. We are damned careful that that does not happen."

"Okay," the lieutenant said. "Are we all on the same page here?"

"I do have one concern," Marti added. "I think Mr. Ramos believes José did it. Even if that turns out to be true, José needs someone who will stick with him, no matter what."

"I've already told him I'll be there for him," Ramos said. "And I mean that, I will."

"Anything else we need to talk about?" Dirkowitz asked. When nobody answered he said, "Good. Joe, my door is always open. If you have any questions or concerns, feel free. If I'm not available, talk to the chief, but come to me first, okay?"

It was the first time Marti could remember the lieutenant ending a meeting without dropping the Vietnam-era hand grenade on his desk to signal that it was over.

Slim and Cowboy were gone when Marti and Vik returned to the office. So was half a box of doughnuts.

"Good, they ate before they left," Marti said. It would help sustain them for their long day in court.

Vik liked it when she said or did something that could be construed as maternal. Now the corners of his mouth turned up just a little. It happened so fast she almost missed it. "Watch it," she told him. "Do that too often and your face will crack."

She checked her in-basket. No reports yet from this morning's autopsy, nothing new on any of their other cases. She pulled the Lara case folder, asked Vik to do the same, and got the folder of photographs out of her file drawer. Without speaking, she laid out some of the pictures on her desk.

Vik watched, then asked, "What's the scenario?"

"I'm not sure. Graciela comes home. As far as she knows she is alone in the house. Everyone else had someplace to go." She pointed to the photo of the half-filled cup of cocoa and the books open on the table. "She goes about her normal routine, which would indicate that she is not concerned about being alone."

"The house has an alarm system," Vik said. "Nobody can come in through the doors."

"I forgot about that. Would she have reactivated it when she came in? Or left it off? Make a note. We'll have to ask Ramos."

"If she reactivated it," Vik said, "then only someone who had a key and knew the code could have come in, at least through the doors."

"Windows, someone could have entered that way, but except for José's, none of them were unlocked or broken or recently replaced. If there was another unlocked window, they locked it after they came in."

Vik selected a couple of outside shots. "The snow by the windows wasn't disturbed. There were no footprints, nothing."

Marti took a closer look. "Then how could someone have come in through a window? José's window is the obvious choice. Even though it was closed when we got there, we know it had been open because the curtains were damp. And look, the way the wind blew the snow on the steps going up to the porch, there are bare spots along the side away from the house."

"No footprints," Vik repeated, then he studied the photos.

"There is a broom on the back porch. See?" He pointed to a darkened area and Marti could make out the handle. The rest was in shadow, but shaped like a broom, not a snow shovel.

"Let's ask Mrs. Ramos if the broom should have been out there."

Marti selected the interior shots of the stairs, carpeting, places where wet spots could indicate snow on boots or shoes. There was nothing, not even a damp smudge that could have photographed as a shadow.

"Graciela sits at the table," Marti went on. "There was no television, or radio or music, no headsets, no noise at all, at least not when everyone came home. Let's make sure that wasn't unusual. Someone else could have turned something off."

"Next," Vik said. "She leaves everything on the table and goes upstairs. What could she have needed that was up there? Everything is right here."

"And that room was so empty, Vik, even the desk drawers. Everything she needed must have been right here on the table."

"So something distracts her. Something that makes her go up there."

"If the house was quiet, it had to be some kind of noise. But not a scary noise. I think Graciela was too smart for that."

"Me too," Vik agreed. "I don't know what she would have done, though."

"What kind of a noise would have got her to go up there?"

Vik pointed. "The window. José left it open. We need to ask him about that, but the public defender isn't going to let us. Maybe Graciela hears something like the wind knocking something over."

Marti went over the pictures of the room after Graciela's body had been removed. "There's nothing here to knock over, Jessenovik. Everything is already on the floor."

Vik considered that. "You're right. But if they got along the way everyone says they did, it wasn't likely that Graciela had ever been in his room."

Marti laid out the pictures of Graciela. "She was facing the

229

window. Someone came up from behind, stabbed her in the carotid artery. She slumped to the floor. No defense wounds. She didn't turn around so she must not have heard whoever it was."

"So it couldn't have been the result of an argument. And it had to be premeditated," Vik concluded.

Marti gathered up the photos and put them back in the folder, returned that to her desk drawer. "José had been angry with Graciela for a long time. According to Mark Dobrzycki, it was set off by something deeper than just the abortion, by some other association that José made. And they were together in that house long enough for José's anger to become rage. She called him crazy, stupid. He called her a bitch. We have nothing concrete to base an assumption of extreme anger on. Nothing that happened to trigger that anger as far as we know. But we can't say that isn't what happened either."

"So," Vik said. "What do we do?" His expression was glum.

"Well, right now this isn't even a prima facie case, it's just supposition. I say we wait it out, see if the psychiatric reports substantiate any of it. And we get those questions answered." There was something Mark Dobrzycki hadn't told her. Not knowing what that was nagged at her. If it was important, and if he didn't tell the public defender, it could blow up in José's face.

Marti looked at the Ward case folder next. It took her three hours to find out, on average, how many round-trip and one-way tickets were purchased in one day for the Kenosha/Chicago and Lincoln Prairie/Chicago routes. And according to the Metra representative she spoke with, there were too many passengers to expect any conductor to recall someone who was not a regular rider unless that passenger did something to call attention to themselves. Also, passengers were responsible for getting off at the right stop. There was no guarantee that if a passenger missed a stop or purchased a ticket for one place and got off at another that the conductor would even notice. The odds of a conductor suspecting that someone might be hiding in the bathroom couldn't even be considered. The bathrooms weren't checked until the trains were empty after the last run of the day, and again before the first run.

"Well, that was a waste of time," she remarked. Vik didn't have to ask what she was talking about. Next she checked to see if there had been any domestic calls to the Chicago police from the Ward's address and came up empty again. "We'll have to drive in tomorrow and talk to the wife again," she said. "See if she can arrange to have the brother and sister there too, and we'll have to smooth the way for talking to the neighbors. We can always say we need to inquire about anything suspicious happening while he was walking the dogs."

She ran a credit check, then got life insurance and pension information. "No problems with debt, and I don't think a hundred and fifty thousand dollars is enough to kill for anymore. Their house is worth more than that."

"You're kidding," Vik said.

"No, they could get half a million at least."

"Could they afford to pay for it and feed the dogs too?"

"Probably not. The trick is to buy before the rehabbing and gentrification begin, get in on the ground floor while the place is still cheap."

"So that's what it's worth now, not what they paid for it."

"Right," Marti said. "But if she holds on to it, it can only appreciate in value. I don't know. Unless we come up with another insurance policy, or a secret lover, I think we're looking in the wrong place, which brings us back to random victim, and I don't believe that either." She thought about Mrs. Ward and her dogs. Or his dogs, at least Baby had been his. "I guess the dogs rule out empty nest syndrome."

She reached for a list of cases outstanding in other Lake County towns to see if she could come up with an MO similar to the ones in the Ward and the Lara cases. While she was perusing that, she ate doughnuts for lunch.

* * *

On days like this, cold, blustery, with sunlight glaring off white snow, Adrian wished for dirty snow at least, to dull the glare. But this was Lincoln Prairie. The fire station where Benjamin Walker worked was located in a combined residential / commercial area. Nice houses, each different from the other, sat back on well-kept lots. A few apartment buildings, small by Chicago standards, and well maintained, were scattered about. And, there were businesses ranging from medical offices to a bakery and a convenience store, a realtor, an insurance agent, and even a travel agency.

The Realtor's office had a Closed sign on the door. It wasn't too far away to observe what went on at the fire station, so Adrian stood there, pacing periodically as if he were impatient for the realtor's return.

The fire station had two bays. Both were closed. He had no idea of what could be going on inside. Eventually, one of the doors went up and after a brief flurry of activity, the ambulance came out, siren wailing. As it passed, Adrian recognized one of the men inside—Benjamin Walker.

He wasn't sure about Walker's shift, but he knew that firemen worked several days—and nights—on, then had several days off. If he came back tomorrow and saw Walker at work, then Walker would still be on duty tomorrow night. He thought about the vacant house with the now deceased pit bull that Marti MacAlister had checked out on Monday. The place wasn't that far from here. This was definitely the nearest fire station. The only problem was that Walker was working as a paramedic, not a fireman. There would be no reason for him to go into a burning house and get trapped inside.

When Marti called Mrs. Ramos, the woman couldn't remember anything about a broom, so they had to drive over to show her the picture. Instead of taking them into the company room, they followed her into the kitchen with its chile pepper red walls and shiny white cabinets.

"You caught me at a bad time," Mrs. Ramos said, gesturing

toward the table. A picture of Joseph Ramos smiled up at them from a stack of flyers. There were four 500-count boxes of envelopes, and a cardboard box on the floor partially filled with stuffed, sealed, and addressed envelopes.

"What is it you want?" she asked. "Something about a broom?"

Marti showed her the picture. She looked at it for a minute, frowning. "I don't know. . . ." she began. "Unless it was the one we keep in the basement. Maybe it was the one in the kitchen, though. I have no idea of why it would be out there."

"Do you remember looking for the broom that was kept in the kitchen?" Marti asked.

"No . . . why . . . it's always in the pantry." She kept looking from the photo to the table. "But . . . I don't know . . . yes . . . maybe . . . yes, I did. It was outside. This must be the broom that I keep in the kitchen. But why was it out there? Everything was covered with snow. They must have put it out before the snow began. . . . It did snow after it was out there. . . . I don't see how . . . I would have swept that day. . . . I sweep every day. . . ." She handed Marti the photo. "I don't know."

"There were a couple of other small details," Marti said.

"What else?" She sounded annoyed.

"When Graciela came in, she had to deactivate the alarm. Since she was here alone, would she have activated it again?"

Mrs. Ramos gave Marti an exasperated look. "What you're asking makes no sense. I have work to do that must be done now. I have to have all of that in the mail before five o'clock. Come back another time. These questions are foolish. You are wasting my time."

"Ma'am, this really is important."

"This is about José, not Graciela, isn't it?"

"Yes, ma'am."

"I don't know what Graciela did that night. I don't know what José did. I don't know."

"Ma'am, what would Graciela have done about the alarm system?

"I . . . I . . . I . . ." Mrs. Ramos threw up her hands. "It doesn't happen that often, someone being alone in the house, other than me."

"What does everyone usually do?"

"The last one out activates it, the first one in deactivates it. They have twelve seconds from the time the door is unlocked. I'm not sure what Graciela would have done that night." She sat down and began folding flyers. "Is there something else?"

"Yes, when Graciela came in, and nobody else was at home, would she have turned on the television, or the radio, or played anything that had headphones?"

Mrs. Ramos shook her head. "No, not Graciela, all business she was when it came to her schoolwork. And it was late, she had to finish quickly, before it was time for bed."

"That was helpful," Marti said when they were back in the car. "To us, at least. But I'm not sure it helped José very much. From what Mrs. Ramos said, my best guess is that either Graciela heard someone come in, or someone was already there and they made enough noise to cause her to go upstairs. But the noise had to be an ordinary noise. Something she might expect to hear."

"Which means it's possible, very possible, that José was already in the house when she got home, and he was waiting for her, and the noise was a deliberate attempt to get her to go up there."

"Until now," Marti said, "I was thinking more in terms of an argument between them. Something confrontational."

But what if José had lain in wait for Graciela? What if he had tricked her into coming to him so that he could surprise her and there would not be a struggle? That made her think of the Ward case. "If this was not done on impulse but premeditated . . ." Then José would be much more likely to be tried as an adult, whether or not there were mitigating circumstances, psychological or otherwise. She wanted so much to prove that

José was innocent, but the deeper she probed, the more it looked as if he was guilty. Unless . . .

"Vik, someone could have used that broom to—"

"The broom doesn't prove anything one way or another. Either nobody disturbed the snow or someone did and used the broom to make it look like they didn't. Whoopee."

Whoopee, Marti agreed, as she turned on the ignition. "It was snowing a little that night."

"Operative words, 'a little,' MacAlister."

Denise Stevens left work early and stopped at Lincoln Prairie General on the way home. She didn't go into the field often enough and seldom got involved with the clients at a personal level anymore, something she missed as an administrator. Today she had followed up her interview with the two newspaper reporters with a one-on-one with Joe Ramos. During their meeting, she had agreed to take a closer look at the Lara/Ortiz case and develop a plan for providing social, psychological, and educational services for José. Ramos had agreed to do whatever he could for him. When Ramos left, he was going home to talk with his wife about the best way to make sure José knew they were committed to seeing him through this.

There were four minors in the hospital under court supervision. She went to see the two in drug and alcohol rehab first. Both were females. They were friendlier than she expected, or maybe just glad to have a visitor, but she left feeling that what her department could do for them was inadequate. She always felt that way. People were more than willing to build jails for them but slow to see the need for educational and rehabilitative services. She had begun an outreach to area churches for volunteer mentors, and thought these two girls might benefit from that.

When she reached Padgett's ward, she found him in the day room, lying on a couch, watching television. Four other boys were playing cards.

"Remember me?" she asked. He nodded. "How's it going?
He didn't say anything. His lower lip trembled.

"They told me you've been going downstairs to visit José."
Another nod.

"How do you feel?"

Tears filled his eyes and ran down his cheeks. He wiped at them with the back of his hand. "I've got malnur. I think I'm going to die."

"Padgett, you're malnourished," she explained. "Tell me what you were eating before you came here."

He did. It was worse than she thought.

"Padgett, you haven't had any protein, no fresh fruits or vegetables unless you count the pickle and ketchup on a Whopper, and you didn't even have one of those very often. Bread and butter sandwiches, jelly right out of the jar, and an occasional can of Spaghettio's don't make a meal. You're body needs more than that, and that's what's wrong with you. You are malnourished. We're going to keep you here and give you a proper diet with some added nutritionals. You're not going to die. You're going to get better."

"And then?" he asked.

"I don't know, but I'm working on it. We'll see. Just eat for now. That's your job. What's next is my job."

"How's my mom?"

"Out there," Denise said. She had found Padgett's mother sitting on a barstool. The woman looked more malnourished than he did, with the potbelly that indicated cirrhosis and a slowness of speech and thought that suggested the alcohol was affecting her brain. When she left, she thought the woman understood that Padgett was in the hospital, but she wasn't even sure about that.

"Can I see her?"

"She has to come here."

Padgett's eyes brimmed with tears again.

"Your mother is sick too, Padgett. She has a disease. It doesn't mean she doesn't love you. It just means the disease is in charge.

It's like getting trapped in a suit of armor with no way to get out. And it's not your fault."

As she spoke with him, she gained a renewed understanding of why her personnel turnover was so high.

José was in a private room with the television turned to a Spanish-speaking station. He was lying in bed with his face to the wall. Denise had cleared an unsupervised visit with the public defender.

"Hi, remember me?"

When he didn't respond, she walked around the bed, folded her arms and leaned against the wall where he could see her.

He didn't open his eyes.

"Padgett isn't going to die," she said. "But he does need a friend. I'll do everything I can to see that you don't lose track of each other again."

His shoulders stiffened but he didn't speak.

"Yes, I know," Denise said. "That promise is right up there with the tooth fairy and Santa Claus, but I remember you guys from four years ago. I tried to do what I could then, but from the looks of it, I wasn't successful. I'll try to do better this time."

As weak as that promise was, she wasn't sure how she was going to keep it.

On the way out, she stopped at Padgett's ward again, and looked into the day room. Padgett was sitting with one of two groups of boys playing cards. As she watched he slapped his cards down on the table. "Two pair!" he said. "Queen high," and racked up the pile of red, white, and blue chips. "I win."

It was after six when Denise got home. She pulled into the driveway without that feeling of dread she usually experienced. Things were beginning to change. This was her mother's first week in an adult day-care facility. Gladys wanted to stay home. Denise almost had to drag her out of the house in the morning. And once at the nursing home, Gladys had at least one tantrum before settling into the daily routine. Although things were not going well, the staff knew how to handle her, and they didn't have any long tales of woe to relate when Denise picked her up in the evening. The only thing that upset her was seeing other clients whose Alzheimer's was more advanced, and knowing Gladys would make that same progression. She had arranged for a church sister to pick up Gladys this evening. On bad days, Gladys fought when Denise tried to get her buckled up in the seat belt. This morning, Gladys had bitten her on the hand. But even on bad days, she seemed to recognize the church members, and comply.

Denise had also decided that her niece, Zaar, needed a life that didn't include too much exposure to her grandmother's illness—especially since Grandma was beginning to confuse Zaar with Zaar's mother, Terri. Gladys did not have a lot of affection for her three daughters. She tolerated Denise and Belle, but saw Terri as a rival for her late husband's affections. Twice this past weekend, Gladys had looked at Zaar, called her Terri, and struck out at her. Twice was enough. Zaar had started going to an after-school program this week. A van would bring her home soon.

The aroma of collard greens greeted her when she opened the door and a pot was simmering on the stove. It had been a while since an odor that homey had filled the house. Belle was the cook, and she only came up from the city every other weekend. Denise inhaled deeply, then felt like crying. She should be cooking more. She should, she should, she should—there was always something else that she should do—but where was the time?

"Denise, I thought I heard you come in." Mrs. Sample bustled into the room. "Sister Gladys just wore herself out today. She's taking a nap in her chair. I hope she sleeps well tonight."

On the advice of the adult day-care director, Denise had installed a voice-activated alarm in Gladys's room so she could just call out if she needed anything, and a childproof locked gate so that Gladys couldn't wander around during the night.

"Thank you so much for picking her up, Mrs. Sample, but you didn't have to cook."

"Them greens was in my freezer. Got more food in there than I'll ever eat, with Mr. Sample gone. It's been four months now since the Lord called him home and I still can't get used to cooking for one. There's some of that spiral ham in the oven thawing out. It was left over from Christmas."

Denise looked at her. Mrs. Sample was a youthful, energetic sixty-four. She had never worked outside of her home, and was the first one to volunteer to cook and serve when there was a funeral, a fund-raising dinner, or a wedding. The woman had time on her hands.

"Mrs. Sample," Denise said. "Would you sit down for a minute?" She explained that Gladys would be at the center Monday through Friday, and that Zaar was in an after-school program, but that there were other things that she just did not have time for, like cooking.

A big grin spread over Mrs. Sample's face. "Why don't I just come over in the afternoon and fix dinner and then get sister Gladys and keep her company until you get home. If Zaar comes home before you get here, I've got eleven grands, she won't be no problem at all. And don't worry none if you have to work late, or go shopping, or go to work on weekends either."

After much protesting by Mrs. Sample, they reached an agreement on her wages.

José listened to the man and woman on the television arguing in Spanish. It was the sound of their voices that he heard, not what they were saying. The words were inside his head.

"Bitch, Bitch!" over and over, and the slaps and the screams, "No, no."

"You kill my baby," he hollered. "You kill my child. My child."

"No, no!" And the crying.

And the thud, when he threw her against the wall.

"You kill my baby, bitch."

Then the crying, softer and softer, and the whisper, "It is my daughter you got pregnant, Manuel, *my* child."

Then the grunts as he kicked her, the cries that became whimpers until there was only the sound of him gasping for breath, and the *uumph,* with each kick, then the slam of the door and silence.

He did not come out of the closet for a long time. He sat in the dark waiting for his mother to call to him, but she did not. He wanted to help her, but he did not want to get beaten again. She would not call him until she was alone and he would not be hurt, so he waited, but she did not call. There was no noise at all, not even the sound of her crying.

When he opened the door, just a crack, it was dark. Mama would not leave him alone in the dark. He listened but didn't hear anything, not the TV, or the radio, or his sister or brother, not anything. They ran out when the fighting began. They were bigger. Mama would not leave him here alone in the dark unless Manuel made her go. He must have made Mama go with him.

He pushed the door open a little bit more, then enough to squeeze out of the closet. The furniture was all broken again, even the TV, and the statue of the Madonna. Always when they got a place to live, Manuel would find them. He would be nice for a few days, bringing them food, giving them coins. But soon he would come to them drunk, beat everyone he could catch, fight with Mama, and break everything, smash everything in the house.

Now there was a pile of clothes in the corner. He saw the dress Mama had been wearing, then one of her shoes, then her leg, then her hair, long and dark. He ran to her, touched her. "Mama, Mama, Mama, Mama, Mama." His chest felt as if someone were crushing him. Blood covered his hands.

"José?"

He jumped. "What?"

"Were you sleeping? I'm sorry if I awakened you."

Mrs. Ramos. Her voice was as soft as Mama's had been, and

she talked all the time, or hummed and sang, and that reminded him, always reminded him, always made him remember, his mama.

"I was not sleeping," he said. He had to be nice to the Ramoses now, nice enough so they would forget that he did not like them. The lawyer said it would be good it they would come with him to court.

"Are you all right?" A stupid question, a woman's question. Men knew things were never all right. But tonight even the sound of her foolish question was better than silence and only the sound of Mama's screams to fill his thoughts.

"I am fine."

"And you are eating?"

"Yes." He didn't bother to add that when he did eat, he threw up.

"Good."

He turned toward her just as she was sitting down. She folded her hands in her lap and didn't look at him. After a moment she said, "It's hard for all of us, this foster-parent, foster-child thing. They bring you to us and we know you will not stay. We know we are not your parents. We don't know when you will leave. And neither do you."

He wondered what she wanted him to say.

"We wanted to help, but the children come and go and we do very little good. And after a while we accept that, and we don't know what we are doing, or why we let you come to us at all."

José stared at the ceiling. This was it, good-bye. Again. They were going away, too. Damn Ramos. He had to send his wife to say what he was not man enough to say himself.

"We forget," she said. "There is so much that we forget. Joseph says things that he does not listen to, things that I do not pay attention to anymore, I have heard them so often. And it is there, in what he says, but we forget."

José had no idea what she was talking about. He wanted to get this over with. Why didn't she just leave? Then the sound of the woman on the television speaking Spanish sounded louder, sounded like Mama, and he wanted Mrs. Ramos, wanted anyone, to stay.

"We forget," she said again. "We are hurt because you destroy your Christmas gifts. We get angry because you turn up the heat and then open the windows, and we forget there is something that makes you destroy, something that makes you angry, something that keeps you from playing the game with Francisco or making friends at school. We forget why you are there and what we wanted to do."

She stopped talking and José wondered if she wanted him to say something now, if it was his turn. What was he supposed to say? Was he supposed to be the one to say good-bye? Was he supposed to be the one to tell her it was okay, that she could leave now, that she never had to come back again?

"So," she went on, "we talked, Joseph and I, we remember what we once wanted to do, help children. And we decided that we still want to do that. We will not leave you, no matter what happened that night. We are going to see this through. All of us, together."

All of that, and she hadn't said anything that Ramos hadn't said. But she said it also. Maybe that meant he could believe them. At least for now. He didn't know what to say. She left before he could say anything.

Alone, he remembered Mama's long, dark hair. Like her, Graciela had long, dark hair. He looked down at his hands and remembered when they were covered with blood and didn't know if the blood he remembered was Graciela's or Mama's. All alone now, he listened to a woman's voice on the television and cried noiselessly into his pillow.

The boys were home when Marti got there. She could hear them just above her head. This was the one night this week that she'd made it home at a reasonable hour and Ben was at work. Trouble's toenails clicked against the tile floor. "Supper, girl?" she asked. The range light was on over the stove. A foil-covered plate would be in the refrigerator, but Marti didn't feel like eating. Her late-lunch doughnuts felt like lumps of clay in the pit of her stomach. Maybe some real food would be good, but not now. Now she wanted to see her children. She took a dish filled with chicken and dog food out of the refrigerator, uncovered it, and put it on the floor for Trouble. Then she went downstairs. The girls weren't there, but Momma was dozing in the recliner. She trekked back to the kitchen and checked the bulletin board. Joanna was playing basketball tonight, an away game. Marti resolved not to think about that business with the volleyball camp tonight. If Joanna accepted, she wouldn't be here when Marti came home, not for a very long time. If Joanna didn't accept, one night, soon enough, she would come home and Joanna would not be here anymore anyway. One night she would come home and Mike and Theo would not be here either. She would be happy that they were out on their own, adults, successful, but she would miss them. She did not want to think about any premature separations now.

The boys were sprawled on the floor playing a board game with Peter and Patrick. During their Christmas break she had realized how much television they watched, how much time they spent with those video games, and decreed two nights a week off limits to both. Now she looked in at them, careful not to let them know she was there. Theo and Mike, with soft brown skin and kinky black hair. Peter and Patrick, with smooth white skin and straight, brown hair. They made her think of a song by Stevie Wonder, "Ebony and Ivory." She was glad the four boys were such good friends.

They were growing up so fast, getting so tall, especially Patrick and Peter. Soon their voices would get deeper and they would stop disliking girls. Soon. Everything was happening too soon and she was missing too much. She leaned against the doorframe, listening to voices that hadn't changed yet and laughter that she hadn't had time to hear in the past few days. She watched them for a long time, until the moment was captured in her mind and would be as clear as a snapshot twenty years from now. Then Theo looked up and saw her.

"Ma! Come play a game with us!" And she did.

Adrian was surprised by how familiar the project halls were after all these years. There hadn't been as much graffiti when he left, or as much destruction. Otherwise not much had changed. He could almost hear Gramps calling to him from the window when he was playing outside and it was time to come in. When he was older, he would look up as he walked home from school and see Gramps watching from the window and wave. A teacher had asked him once what it was like growing up without a mother. "I don't know," he had told her. And he didn't; he couldn't remember a time when there was a mother. But there were times when he thought he knew what having one might be like. When he was in elementary school, mothers would be waiting for their children when he went home. "Boy, tie your shoes before you fall and break your neck . . ." "Lord, look at this child, ain't bringing home nair book. . . ." "Child, you better not never talk like that to your teacher no more . . ." He didn't mind not having a mother at all. He had decided back when Uncle Rafe died that he would not have any children of his own.

When he was in high school, Gramps had insisted that he focus on his grades, concentrate on getting out of here. And he did. It was as if the old man were just waiting for him to leave this place. He no sooner had his high school diploma and his scholarship to Northwestern than Gramps shot himself and died.

He had worked hard all through college. He did everything Gramps had wanted him to, but always he remembered this place, these halls, and Gramps. Gramps, who had told him stories about being a child in Mississippi and living near a small lake filled with fish. Gramps, who chose to live in this project instead of Cabrini Green or Marion Jones, because it was so close to a lake, a much bigger lake. Gramps, who seldom went to Lake Michigan except to fish, and couldn't even do that when they began to amputate. Even now he wished the old man had lived long enough to stay with him in his condo on the Drive, across the street from the lake. He still wished that Gramps could have sat in his wheelchair by the window and looked out at the water. Maybe then Gramps would have had something to live for, or at least not have wanted to die.

Now Adrian stood three floors below the top floor, in the same building where he had grown up, looking out the window at a brick wall. His view of the lake was blocked just as Gramps's view had been. Never once had he told anyone where he came from. He was a self-made man. And never once did the man he made himself into make a mistake. All he did was get caught. Ray Franklin and Johnnie MacAlister were responsible for that. This began with them. This would end with them.

Adrian took the gun and the stolen cell phone out of his pocket. He dialed 911. He reported a shooting, gave the woman who answered the call the address and his location. He hung up before she could ask any questions, then went up another level to wait. This was Ray Franklin's beat. Franklin was the man. If Franklin answered the call, he'd be a dead man.

The wait was longer than he expected. The gun got sweaty in his hand. Twice he heard the sound of sirens approaching, twice the sound veered away. When he did hear a noise, it was heavy footsteps and heavy breathing and no conversation at all until a man's voice said, "There's nothing here. If we had a shooter, he's gone."

"That looks like a bullet hole up there," a female responded.

"Nothing new about that."

Adrian pulled the woolen mask over his face. His hands shook as he held the gun. He made his way down the stairs. As soon as he saw the blue jackets he fired several times. Both officers went down.

The mood was somber at roll call. Two Chicago cops had been shot. Both were still alive, thanks to their vests, but in critical condition. Their names had not been released. Marti returned home as soon as roll call was over. She had to talk with her kids. Joanna had already left for school, but Theo and Mike were still there. She could tell by the way they were laughing when she came in that they hadn't heard the news. The look Momma gave her said that she had.

Marti stood in the doorway and watched as Theo ate hot cereal. He looked so much like Johnnie, same brown skin, smooth and unblemished, like velvet. His face, all planes and angles, same widow's peak, same high cheekbones and dark brown eyes. She looked at Mike, who had lost his mother in a car accident. Mike was a smaller version of Ben, plump where Ben was muscular and solid, but with soft, round features and Ben's gentleness, now that he didn't have to be the class bully anymore.

Theo noticed her first. "Ma!" He jumped up and went to her. "Why are you home?' he asked, alarm in his voice. Was he remembering another day when Johnnie had died and she had come home right after leaving for work? He gave her a tight hug. Mike just sat there waiting, a spoonful of cereal halfway from his bowl to his mouth.

"It's okay," she said. "Everyone is okay. I just heard something at the precinct and I wanted to talk to you about it before you went to school."

"Someone got hurt," Theo said, then louder, "It wasn't Vik, was it?"

"No, no, we're all fine. It was two police officers in Chicago. A man and a woman. They were shot. They were wearing vests. They didn't die. But they are in the hospital. I don't know who they are yet, or if I know them."

Theo kept hugging her. He patted her vest. "A vest wouldn't have helped Dad," he said.

"No," she agreed. "He was wearing one."

"Sometimes nothing helps," Mike said. "Not even seat belts."

Marti walked to the table with Theo clinging to her, and sat down.

"Your dad was doing something dangerous," she said. "Mike's mom was not. That isn't why things happen."

"Grandma said she doesn't know why they died either," Theo said. "She said she just trusts in the Lord to make all things work together for good."

"That doesn't keep me from missing my mom," Mike said.

"And it doesn't stop me from missing Dad, either."

"I miss your dad, too," Marti said. "And Mike, I know your dad misses your mom. We think about them a lot, even though we have each other now. And we do have each other, all of us. We have been blessed."

Neither boy said anything right away. Then Theo said, "A lot of the time now I'm happy. For a long time after Dad died, I was really sad."

"That's good. Johnnie wants us to be happy. Where he is, everyone is happy all the time. He doesn't want us to stay sad."

Theo hugged her, and Mike came over and stood beside her, too. "It's okay?" he said. "Not being mad anymore? I hardly ever get mad now."

Marti gave him a big hug. "Yes, that's good," she said. "That's good. Your mom is in the same happy place where Theo's dad is. She wants what every mom wants for her child, for you to have a good life, and do good things, and make good choices, and be happy, like she is."

Mike buried his face in her chest for a minute, hugging her tightly. "I love you," he whispered.

"I love you, too. Do you guys know how precious you are?"

Theo grinned. "Know what?" he said. "Grandma said that if we ate all of our cereal and a banana—yuck—we could have one of those snack bars to eat on the way to school. Did you have breakfast yet, Ma?"

"No. Do you think I could have a snack bar anyway?"

Theo laughed.

Marti stopped at the high school next, and had them take Joanna out of class.

"I'm all right, Ma," she said as she came into the counselor's office, but she came over to Marti and hugged her.

"You heard."

"A couple of smart-ass kids were talking about it."

Marti wondered if one of them was Brianna Laretson.

"Was it anyone you know?" Joanna was still holding on to her.

"No names yet," Marti said, and stroked Joanna's hair. "Sounds like they'll be okay. They were wearing vests."

"Did you talk to Theo yet? And Mike."

"I went home first, they seem okay. How about you?"

"I'll be all right. It's more remembering what happened to Dad and the funeral and stuff like that than anything else. Now that I'm older, and I see how you do what you do . . ." Her voice trailed off. "I mean, when I'm going to play a game, I might psych myself up, and the adrenalin gets going, but it's more like . . . I know what I can do. A lot of the good players are like that, even if they get a case of nerves, they know what they can do. And that's how I think about you, and your job. That you know what you're doing and you know what you can do. I feel like . . . that . . . if something did happen, it would be because it was supposed to. So I don't worry as much as I used to. But, Ma"—Joanna took a step back and put her hands on Marti's shoulders—"that does not mean I don't know where you hide the butter, and it doesn't mean that it's okay to eat all that fast food when you're at work."

"Yes, ma'am," Marti said. It was her turn to give Joanna a hug.

Sikich was in the office when she got back.

"Unauthorized absence, MacAlister," he said. "I will take this to the chief."

Marti fought back her anger. "Two officers went down in Chicago last night. My first husband was shot and killed in Chicago while on duty. I don't need anyone's permission to make sure my kids hear about something like this from me. The desk sergeant knew I was leaving."

Sikich blinked. "Oh, I didn't know."

"Sometimes when you take your head out of your butt you learn something," Vik said.

Sikich did an about-face and almost marched from the room.

"Stupid SOB," Vik said. "I was trying to tell him that when you came in. Are the kids okay with this?"

"Better than I expected. Did they release any names yet?"

"Not that I've heard. It happened in Wentworth District."

Her old stomping ground, and Johnnie's. "That's the place I used to call home. Department's getting younger, though. It might not be anyone I know." She thought about Jack Zabrowski, one of her training officers when she was on the force there. Crazy Jack, they called him. He took a lot of chances. If he was ever afraid of anything, he never showed it. That was what made people back down, that confidence that said You can't take me out. Zabrowski had taught her a lot, including how to cuss in Polish. "It's a mind game," he would say, "And you're a female. Just look 'em in the eye and say to yourself, 'Are you man enough to try it? I'll blow your ass away.' And mean it. They'll read your mind and roll over like puppy dogs. Crime's easy. None of them got any balls or they'd be productive citizens." She hoped it wasn't Zabrowski. He was close to retirement.

Even Slim and Cowboy were subdued. Slim must have forgotten his morning shower with Obsession for Men because Marti could hardly smell it at all. "How did it go in court yesterday?" she asked.

"Jury's still out on two," Slim said. "Three grand jury indictments and four convictions."

Ordinarily Cowboy would have added four notches to the hand-carved wooden six shooter he kept in his drawer. Today they both looked as if their best friend had died, or was going to.

"You heard anything else about those two cops?" Cowboy asked.

"No."

"Kids okay?"

"They're doing real good."

"Don't you have someone you can call? See what's going on? What went down?"

Marti didn't answer. She was afraid to pick up the phone, afraid that it was someone she did know.

Adrian paced within the circle he had drawn on the floor in his room, careful to stay within its boundaries so his luck wouldn't change. Why wouldn't they give out the names of the cops who were shot? If one of them wasn't Franklin, every cop in the city of Chicago would be so wired that he wouldn't have another chance at him. Why had he panicked? Why hadn't he taken one more minute to be sure it was Franklin before he fired, or stopped to look at the cops' faces before he rushed down the stairs? He stopped pacing and listened when the news about it came on the radio again.

Why weren't they saying anything about who did it, or who might have done it? Why wasn't there any mention of that at all? Why weren't they saying the shooting was gang or drug related? They couldn't know it was him, his face was covered. Besides, even if someone had seen him, nobody in the projects would ever talk to a cop unless it meant saving their own neck, and even then, not many did, there were too many ways to die if you talked too much. "Still clinging to life," the news reporter said now. He hadn't killed them, not yet, anyway. Bryan Weinstein was still in a coma, and he had shot him too. He wasn't good with small guns, not enough practice. Too bad he hadn't found a shotgun to steal. He could get a squirrel at a hundred feet with one of those.

Marti tuned into the news station as she and Vik headed into Chicago again to talk with Mrs. Ward and her in-laws, and possibly a few neighbors, if any of them were home this time of day. She wanted to head back to Lincoln Prairie before the evening commute. Once again, as she was heading for Route 41, she felt as if she were being followed or watched. This time it was because of two officers down, and the memory of an officer she loved who had died almost five years ago.

"No change," Vik said when the report about the two officers came on. "Nothing about any suspects or a motive either."

"Even if they know who it is, or think they do, they won't release that until they've got the subject in custody, unless he's on the run."

"Oh, I didn't know that."

"That's because it's been ten or twelve years since an officer was killed while on duty in Lincoln Prairie, and you knew who did it and mounted a manhunt."

"You're sure the kids are okay? You don't need to be there when they get home from school?"

"They're okay with it. They're handling it better than I expected." Better than she was.

Just as she was exiting from the Dan Ryan onto Division, the names of the two downed officers were given. Ray Franklin and Consuela Jones. Marti felt as if she had been hit the stomach. They were both at the University of Chicago hospital.

"Anyone you know?" Vik asked.

"Just Franklin," she managed.

"Are you all right?"

She shook her head.

"Let me drive."

"No, it's okay. I'll be okay." She concentrated on getting into the far right lane and negotiating a right turn onto Division. "I'm okay," she said again.

"A partner?"

"Johnnie's, way back, ten, twelve years ago at least." So long ago that she could hardly remember what Ray Franklin looked like. "Ray loved Thai food," she said. "Johnnie hated it." Johnnie hated any reminders of Vietnam. "Johnny liked Mexican, which gave Ray indigestion. So they used to eat at this burger joint that neither of them liked. Ray's got two or three kids, at least. They must be teenagers now, or maybe in college or married. His wife's a schoolteacher."

She found a parking place half a block from the Ward house.

"You sure you want to do this?" Vik asked. "We could come back."

"Just ask the questions, okay?"

The little man with the potbelly who opened the door looked a lot like Calvin Ward and was just as homely. It wasn't just the tiny black moles that spotted his face, Marti decided. It was that pinched and pointy weasel look. A woman who bore a strong resemblance to him and Calvin came up behind him. She had a dog in her arms, a Pekingese. Marti didn't know if it was Baby or Beauty or just a visitor. It wasn't wearing a bow.

When she followed the woman with the dog into the living room, Mrs. Ward was sitting on the sofa with Baby and Beauty on her lap. A fourth Pekingese was baring its teeth.

"Hush up, now, Basil," Mrs. Ward scolded. "Tell Daddy to be quiet," she said to one of the dogs on her lap. Marti settled in for another strange conversation, and hoped the other two adults weren't quite as pet oriented.

Vik took them through the usual questions—did anything unusual happen recently, could they think of anyone Calvin Ward might have angered, any work stories that had seemed odd at the time? Were there any traffic altercations near where he lived or worked, any work disputes? All questions were answered in the negative, and neither the brother nor the sister talked to the dogs while answering them. Mrs. Ward butted in periodically, which was how Marti learned that the two additional dogs were Mommy and Daddy to Beauty and Baby. By the time she and Vik left, she had had her fill of dog children, or yuppie puppies, as Vik called them.

Three neighbors were home, two because of the flu. They described the Wards as friendly neighbors who participated in block parties and were conscientious when it came to using pooper scoopers. That, cleared sidewalks or well-trimmed grass, depending on the season, and using one's own parking space seemed to rate high on the good-neighbor list. They all had seen Mr. Ward walking the dogs morning and evening, none could recall him having more than the most banal conversations when they talked with him.

"Zero," Vik said as they returned to their car.

"About what I expected," Marti said.

"You sure you want to drive?"

"It'll keep my mind occupied."

"Hopefully."

"I'm going to swing by the hospital first." She got back on the expressway, continued heading south, and exited on Garfield Avenue, also known as Fifty-first Street. The hospital was a few miles away.

For the second time in an hour, Adrian heard a loud whapping noise and the drone of an engine as a helicopter descended to the landing place atop the roof of Weiss Memorial Hospital. The hospital was part of the University of Chicago medical complex in Hyde Park. Adrian was standing inside the parking garage across the street. Somewhere inside the hospital two cops were close to death. He was on the first level, out of view of the attendant who sat in the booth, but where he could easily see every car that entered or exited. Would Marti MacAlister come here to see Ray Franklin? He didn't know, but he didn't have anything else to do besides watch and wait. If she did show up, would that mean they had made the connection between Franklin and Johnny MacAlister? He wasn't sure. It could just be that cop thing that all of them did to show their camaraderie.

He had known when he shot Franklin that it was a high-risk, high-profile thing to do, but he was so close to taking down MacAlister's wife and immediately heading for Mexico that he wasn't concerned. MacAlister was the only direct link between him and Franklin. He had felt confident that a cop being shot in the Robert Taylor Homes would immediately lead to the assumption that he was either in the wrong place at the wrong time or, as was usual in that part of town, and not just for cops, a target. But so far there hadn't been any speculation as to why Franklin might have been shot. Even if they did suspect a hit, it would take them at least a week or two to work their way through a list of possible suspects. He would be on a tropical beach watching the sailboats and soaking up the sun by then.

Things got a little busy and he walked over to the elevator and pushed the up button to avoid the appearance of loitering. When the elevator came, he went up two floors, then came back down. The elevator moved so slowly that if anyone had noticed him, that gave them ample time to find their vehicles, pay their fees, and leave. There was still no sign of the cop. He decided to give it another half hour and go home. He was certain that Marti MacAlister would drive into the city today to interview Calvin Ward's next of kin. The only reason he was hoping she would come here was because he liked being able to predict what she would do. It would make it that much easier when it came time to kill her. His patience was rewarded twenty minutes later.

"Another one of Johnnie's partners died here," Marti said, as they entered the parking garage. "The one who got pushed off the roof. Remember?"

Marti had all she could do to get out of the car and walk

across the street to the hospital entrance. Johnnie had arrived here without any vital signs, but they had worked on him for over an hour in the emergency room. She had been taken to a small room where she waited until a doctor and her captain came in to tell her he was gone.

This time she went to the intensive care unit. Ray Franklin had made it past the emergency room. There was still hope. As she took the elevator to the second floor, she tried to remember Ray's wife's name. Johnnie didn't socialize with anyone on the Job, just as he never socialized with anyone who had been in Vietnam. Sometimes he did mention names. If he had, she couldn't think of it now.

The waiting room was crowded with half a dozen cops she didn't recognize, two in flak jackets, a couple in plainclothes. The other two wore uniforms. She didn't recognize the women either. She could tell that three were cops. The other four must be wives or family.

It was obvious which woman was Ray Franklin's wife. She was the one with swollen, red-rimmed eyes. The woman who watched the door that led to the ICU. The woman who jumped, then cringed when a nurse came out, then slumped with relief when the nurse walked past her without speaking. She was the woman who was waiting. Marti knew that woman well. She had been there.

"Marti!" the woman said.

Annie, Marti thought, that was her name. Marti opened her arms and Annie came to her. After a few minutes of just holding her, Marti asked, "How is he doing?"

"Thank God for vests, Marti, thank God for vests. Sometimes they work."

"Will he be all right?"

"We don't know yet, but at least he's alive, at least he's got a chance." Annie Franklin took a step back. "Thank you for coming. This had to be hard for you. I appreciate it." She turned to another woman. "Lucille?"

The only other black woman there who was not a cop came over and Annie introduced them.

"Lucille's been with me ever since it happened," Annie said. "I don't know what I would have done without her. Ray is a Big Brother to Lucille's grandson." Her voice broke. "Now that our kids are in college, he missed having someone to play with." She pressed a tissue to her mouth and began crying.

"You can stay strong," Marti said. "You can do this. You have to."

"I know, we'll get through it," she said, sobbing. "He'll make it. He's a fighter."

Marti rocked Annie in her arms as if she was a child. "Be all right," she said. "Be all right."

Vik had stayed by the door.

"You okay?" Marti asked, as they walked down the hall.

"Me? Am I all right?"

"I've done this before," she said. "Several times." Vik had not.

Neither of them talked much on the drive back to Lincoln Prairie.

By the time they reached the precinct, Marti felt exhausted. Her shoulders ached from being hunched over the steering wheel. Her stomach was pumping acid. Someone had left a copy of the *News-Times* on her desk. There was a composite of La-Shawna Davis on the first page. LaShawna had changed a lot since the last time Marti saw her four years ago. She looked older than seventeen and tired, very tired. Again Marti wondered if she was hiding, or dead.

"They haven't charged either of Reggie's friends with anything, have they?"

"Nothing to charge them with."

She put in a call to the state's attorney's office to see if they had any leverage they could use to get Reggie to talk about LaShawna.

"Negative," she told Vik. "If Slim and Cowboy can get a couple more women to testify they might be able to compromise on a sentencing agreement."

She called Ben at the fire station next, something she rarely did, but Ben and his partner, Allan, were out on an ambulance run. Then she called home. All of the kids had made it home from school. Momma was ordering pizza for supper and even though it was a school night, Joanna had organized a sleep-over with popcorn and movies. Patrick and Peter's mom had just taken the boys to Blockbuster. Marti wondered if that meant Theo and Mike were upset or if Joanna was just providing a distraction. According to the news, there had been no change in Ray Franklin's condition, but it looked like the female officer would make it.

Adrian waited until it was dark, then jimmied open a car door, got the ignition turned on, and headed for Lake County. He had better than half a tank of gas, and he would leave the car there when he was finished. He quickly discovered that driving wasn't something you never forgot how to do. It took him ten minutes to figure out how the windshield wipers worked, and where the rear window defogger was, and half an hour in slow-moving traffic to brake without jerking to a stop. The expressway was salted, so he didn't have to worry too much about a major skid, but he did slide a few times. He had always hated driving, bought a BMW because he could afford it, and because the ladies liked being driven around in something expensive. Mostly he walked to work or took the CTA wherever he had to go. It's faster, he told anyone who asked. And he didn't have to waste time looking for a parking lot. Tonight he had decided it was better to take a newer-model car that wouldn't attract too much attention. The owner might notice it was missing sooner than someone driving a car that had been around for a while, but this one wasn't likely to break down. Besides, it wasn't as if anyone were going to put out an APB. He just had to stick to the main roads and the speed limits, and hope some bored small-town cop didn't pull him over because he couldn't turn off the brights.

The first industrial park Adrian went to was west of Lincoln Prairie. There were a couple of one-story office buildings, but most of the buildings were warehouses. He had walked through the area several times at night without being stopped, without seeing anyone, although he was sure there would be a night watchman inside. The building he chose was used to store paper products. It was wedged between two other buildings. He was hoping they would catch fire too. When he used a glass cutter to get in through a window, there was no alarm, which didn't surprise him. Who would want to steal toilet paper and paper towels and cardboard? He went to four different areas, starting fires in each. He expected a guard to challenge him, but nobody did. So he took his time, feeding the fires with more paper until all four were blazing up to the ceiling and beginning to belch thick smoke. Then he went out through a back door.

His next stop was a chemical storage facility north of Lincoln Prairie. This time he took out the gun and knocked. When someone called to him through the closed door, he yelled that he had been in an accident and his wife and kid were still in the car. A uniformed guard opened the door. After he ordered the man outside, made him turn around, and hit him on the back of the head, he went in. This one was really going to go up, and fast. By the time he had fires going in two places, the fumes were making his eyes water and his throat hurt. The heat was making the windows explode as he drove away and a loud alarm was ringing. Fire engines approached with sirens screaming and horns blasting as he turned onto the main road. Next, Adrian headed for Lincoln Prairie and the vacant house he had seen Johnnie MacAlister's wife checking out.

Someone had boarded up the place, but prying the plywood off a rear window was easy. Inside, he looked around. He had got his lessons in arson from an expert, a jailed expert who had

258

been caught. He would be smarter than that. With the fires he had already set pulling in so much manpower, plus the fact that this house was in a densely populated area, the odds were good that Lincoln Prairie would be on standby and Marti MacAlister's husband more likely to suit up as a fireman than to come as a paramedic. Especially if he got the fire going real good.

When Ben arrived at the scene of the fire, the house wasn't fully involved yet. He assessed the situation quickly as he directed a crew setting up hose lines. The acrid odor of burning wood filled the air. The fire crackled and hissed and flared at the windows. The fire command officer directed lines to adjacent roofs. There was a shortage of manpower tonight. They had a call in for assistance, but two other fires had not been struck yet. Ben was in full gear, boots, turnouts—about fifty pounds without oxygen tanks. A private ambulance was standing by. Four volunteer firemen from the next town were assisting. A crowd had gathered.

"There's someone still in there," a man yelled.

"Place is listed as vacant," the FCO told Ben.

"Someone is in there!" the man yelled again. "Get her out! Get her out!"

The crowd took up the chant.

The FCO called a police officer over, and pointed in the direction where they had heard the first call. "See what you can find out."

"Woman," the cop yelled a minute later. "Vagrant. Upstairs. Middle bedroom."

The house was long and narrow.

Ben motioned to Allan, his partner. "We'll get her," he said. "If there's any way to get in."

A two-man crew tried to gain entry for them through the front door but even the two-and-a-half-inch hose couldn't lay the flames and they had to pull back. First-floor windows blew open and dark smoked billowed from the front door.

Ben grabbed the oxygen tanks and a mask and ran to the

side of the house. The ladder crew was attacking the roof and two of the volunteers were making some headway saturating the walls.

"Woman trapped upstairs," Ben said. "Get a ladder up and follow us up with a line."

"It's damned hot in there, Ben," the man with the hose said.

"Get some water on it. Cool it down. We're going in."

Ben secured his mask and led the way up the ladder. Allan was right behind him. He used his ax to break the second-floor window closest to the middle of the house. Smoke came out, but no fire. The crew soaked the side of the building and the interior with water. There was no hissing, no orange flash of flames. Smoke billowed. The smoke was just as deadly.

Ben gave an arms-up signal and jumped through the window. The smoke was thick and the heat intense. The fire below them roared. He motioned to Allan to stay behind him. Their flashlights probed the smoke. Ben tested the floor with each step. It felt like he was walking on a frying pan sizzling with hot grease. He kept to the wall as he made his way around the room. He came to a door, felt it. Too hot. The heat came through his glove. Fire on the other side.

They continued circling the room. Their flashlights penetrated the smoke-filled darkness. He didn't see anyone. He found another door. Not as hot. He opened the door a crack. Hot air. No flames. The heat below them was intense. They were hopping from one foot to the other now. Ben opened the door enough to look inside. Small. Empty. Closet. Nobody here. They might have been given the wrong place. Or the woman had tried to escape. Flames were licking their way through the floor. The fire was coming to them. Ben pointed his flashlight at the window. He gave Allan a push. The floor began shaking as Allan went out. As Ben followed him, he felt the floor beginning to sag. The hose men covered their descent.

At ground level, Ben lifted his mask. "Bathroom," he gasped. That was usually where they ran. "Where is it?"

The FCO shook his head, pointed up. There was a flickering orange glow in the room they had just vacated.

"Another couple minutes and this place is gone," the FCO said.

"That's enough time." Ben argued. Even as he said it, he knew it wasn't.

"No, Ben This isn't Nam. I don't allow suicide missions. You did what you could."

There was a roar as the second floor collapsed.

At 7:25, Marti turned on the radio for the hour-on-the-half-hour news. There was still no change in Ray Franklin's condition. Tired and dispirited, she drove over to the fire station. Both bays were empty. She went home.

After he talked to the cop, Adrian had to move away from the crowd. He stepped into the doorway of a neighborhood bar that had gone out of business and waited. The bright lights from the fire engines and police cars seemed surreal when surrounded by darkness. The beeps and whirls and bangs as the building collapsed, the shouts of a fireman giving orders over a bullhorn could be heard where he stood a block away. Soot settled on the white snow near his feet.

What was happening? What had happened to Walker? The fire department ambulance had been left behind, and the one from a private company stood idle. He was too far away to make out the names on the backs of the firemen's coats. Maybe they didn't send anyone in. Maybe paramedics wouldn't be their firemen of choice for a rescue. Maybe. Too many maybes. It had all seemed so easy when he planned it. He had read three newspaper articles in the library about Walker. In the past two years, Walker had gone into a burning building three times, had saved two lives. Why hadn't Walker gone in tonight?

He had set the fire right below that upstairs room, told them that was where the woman was. The floor should have collapsed as soon as somebody stepped on it. What had gone wrong? What had he missed? Or forgotten? It had been three or four years since he helped that pyromaniac get his GED. At the time, he was just listening to another con making conversation. He hadn't paid much attention. He didn't plan to set any fires. After all the fires he had seen in the projects, fire scared the hell out of him. He had never lit the fireplace in his condo. He had never even smoked. Damn. Killing the others had been so easy. What made killing a couple of cops and a fireman so hard? Was his luck changing? What was he doing wrong?

It was several hours before the fire engines left. Adrian didn't think it would be a good idea to sit in the car. Better to leave it where it was. It would be stripped, then condemned, then impounded. Then maybe one day some cop with nothing better to do would go through his paperwork and match it up with its owner. God, it was cold. He could see his breath and he was breathing through his nose. His toes and his fingers and his ears felt frozen. He wanted to leave, but he could not. He still hadn't seen a coat with Walker stenciled in yellow on the back. The ambulance hadn't moved either. Nobody was injured, unless Walker had been trapped and they hadn't found him yet. When the men did return to the trucks, Adrian was struck by how tired they seemed. Tired people made mistakes. Suppose there was another fire tonight? One where people really were trapped inside?

Ben had just finished taking a shower when the alarm went off again.

"Now what?" he asked, not talking to anyone in particular.

"Oh, shit," Allan said. "Another damned fire. I haven't even washed off the stench from the last one."

This time it was just a garbage fire in the back hallway of a small apartment building. It could have turned serious, even fatal, but the smoke alarms had gone off. By the time Ben got there, two of the tenants had grabbed fire extinguishers and put the fire out with minimal damage.

262

The next call was the one that made it a long night. A man in cardiac arrest who lived in an unincorporated area and was twenty miles from the nearest hospital. Ben heard one of the man's ribs snap as he administered CPR. He and Allan defibbed the man, put him on oxygen, started an IV, and got him to the hospital, unconscious but alive.

Adrian took the last train back to Chicago. For the first time since his release from prison two months ago, he felt depressed. His luck had changed and he couldn't figure out why. There had been no dreams to explain it, no omens, good or bad. He hadn't done anything wrong. He was certain he had not misread any of the portents he had observed. Maybe there was something he missed. As hard as he tried to be observant at all times, everyone had lapses. That must be it. He must have missed something. Now he would have to do something about that so he could kill again. As soon as he got home he would take out the candles and arrange them on the floor, and sprinkle the herbs in the circle. In the morning, he would sweep up the herbs, burn them and bury the ashes with a penny face side up. Then his bad luck would be gone.

11

Marti called Ben as soon as she got to work.

"Are you okay?" he asked.

"Not really."

"Did you know the cops who got shot?"

"One of them. Kind of. From way back." She wasn't superstitious, but something hitting this close to home was unsettling. Even though she hadn't seen Ray Franklin in years, just thinking about Johnnie back then brought back not just memories but sadness, and also the fear that what had happened before could happen again. "You know how it is."

"Yes, I know," Ben said. He did. He had lost his first wife not long before Marti met him. "I tried calling you a few times and got your machine. How did the kids handle it?"

They talked about that for a few minutes.

"I get off in an hour," Ben said. "Can you meet me for breakfast?"

"Why don't I just come home for lunch, so you can get a few hours' sleep. You sound tired. I drove by the station twice and you weren't there."

He began telling her about his night.

"Three multiple alarms? I can't remember the last time that happened."

"And one fatality, a night watchman at a warehouse where they stored paper products. Then we thought we had a vagrant trapped in the house on First Street, but Allan and I couldn't find anyone. The place hasn't cooled down enough yet for the fire inspectors to go in."

"Where on First?" Marti asked. It was the vacant house where the pit bull had been tied up. She didn't know what was going on here, but she did not believe it was a coincidence.

Ben made it home before the boys left for school and fixed breakfast, pancakes the size of a salad plate and half an inch thick. He served them with canned peaches on top and brought four kinds of syrup to the table.

"You smell like smoke," Mike said.

"Well, you know, Allan and I had to go into a burning house last night, see if anyone was in there."

"And they covered you with a hose spraying water and you looked around with your flashlights and came out," Mike said.

"You got it."

"Did you save anybody?"

"Nope. Far as I know, the place was empty."

"Good. I like it when you save people, but it's got to be scary for them until you get there."

Mike poured strawberry syrup and maple on his pancake. His favorite combination.

Theo hardly touched his at all.

"What's up?" Ben asked him.

Theo shrugged.

"Come on, talk to me. I thought we had a deal about that."

Theo jabbed at his pancake with his fork. "A friend of my father got shot."

"Yeah. I heard about that. Makes you remember things, doesn't it?"

Theo nodded.

"Hard sometimes, remembering. Makes you worry, too."

Theo looked down. "Sometimes I wish stuff didn't have to happen."

"Me, too," Ben agreed. "How did you sleep last night? Any dreams?"

"Just one, but it wasn't a nightmare. I was flying over the Grand Canyon."

"Did it wake you up?"

"No, but I remembered it this morning. Sometimes I know I dreamed but I don't know what it was about. This one was cool. I was so high and there were mountains too, with snow on them. I want to go see some mountains."

"Your uncle lives in Colorado, and your mother and Momma Lydia haven't seen him in a long time. Maybe we should plan to go there while there's snow. Your mom and I both need a little vacation. Let's go for spring break."

"Yes!" Theo said.

"Yes!" Mike agreed.

"Colorado!" Theo said. "And the Rockies! Do you think we'll get to see Donner's Lake?"

"Donner's Lake?" Ben asked. These two kids were full of surprises. They knew a lot more than he did when he was their age, and not all of it was about making mischief.

"I'll tell you about it tonight." Theo grinned and reached for the blueberry syrup. "We should have chocolate syrup too, like we do for ice cream. Do they have bears where my uncle lives? And mountain lions?"

"As far as I know. But I don't think we'll get too close to one, unless we go to the zoo."

"Maybe we can camp out overnight," Mike said,

By the time the school bus came and the boys grabbed their backpacks, both were talking about grizzly bears and laughing.

After Marti talked with Ben, she sat with her elbow on her desk and rested her forehead against the palm of her hand. A fire in a vacant building connected with Reginald Garrett and possibly LaShawna Davis. Could Garrett have had something to do with it? She couldn't remember seeing anything unusual when she and Vik checked the place out. The evidence techs had gone through and found nothing. Now Ben had gone into the same building because a man in the crowd said someone was trapped inside. Could they have missed something?

Marti took out the folder on LaShawna. She had put a copy of her notes on the house in there. Concrete floor in the basement. No indications that anything had been buried there. The place was stripped bare. No recent repairs to the walls. No damage. Nothing but a few rat holes. No odor. And death smelled.

Garrett was a sadistic SOB. Could this fire have anything to do with him? Or one of his friends? She called the jail for a list of his visitors. No one had come to see him, not even his mother. She would have to check out Joe Boy and G.L., make sure they had an alibi for last night.

Marti called the arson investigator's office. The house hadn't cooled down sufficiently for them to go in. They would be looking for human remains and indications of arson, and would call with preliminary findings and copy her on their final report.

She talked to the desk sergeant about Garrett and Joe Boy and G.L. He had never heard of Garrett getting into anything but fights. None of them had ever been connected with arson. She went over their sheets again. Nothing. But why that address? Why *that* house? And who was the man in the crowd? Questions nagged at her all morning. The fire gave her a vague sense of unease. She thought of that vagrant. What made her uneasy about him? Or was it something else? Maybe tonight she would start checking the shelters, see if she could find him, ask him a few questions, relieve her own mind about him. A lot of the homeless spent their days at the township office doing small jobs, or at the library pretending to read, she might have time to check that out tomorrow.

She had just decided to go home to have lunch and spend a little time with Ben when the call came in from Chicago. They had made the Johnnie MacAlister/Ray Franklin connection and wanted her to come in to Eleventh and State.

"I'm taking the afternoon off," she told Vik. "I'll get Ben to ride in with me."

Vik looked disappointed.

"That fire on First Street is bothering the hell out me," she told him. "I would really rather you stay here and stay on top of it. If they find a body, it could be LaShawna. If they find two bodies and one is small, we'll know for sure. Joe Boy and G.L. need their alibis confirmed. And I want to know who told the cop someone was in there."

"I'll see if the radio stations or newspapers have any photos or footage," Vik said. "And pay Garrett's friends a visit, now that we know where both of them live."

"Good. Try not to go home until I get back."

"Does this trip to the big city mean they've got somebody fingered for the shootings?" he asked.

"No. It just means they're looking, and maybe they've narrowed the search." She didn't add that they might also think she was in danger, or want to rule that out. From the worried expression on Vik's face, she could see that she didn't have to say anything about that at all.

It had been cloudy when she left for work, now it was snowing again, not fluffy flakes but those tiny icy ones that stung when they hit your face and made little pings on the windshield. When she got home, Ben was sitting at the kitchen table having coffee with Momma.

"I'm sorry I woke you up when I called," she said. "I know you didn't get any sleep last night and—"

He held up his hand. "Actually I did get a good four hours when things quieted down. I just needed a long hot soak and some Tylenol when I got home. Besides, I'm off for the next couple of days. What's so special about the fire in that vacant house?"

"Maybe nothing," she said. Then she explained.

"Who knows," Ben said. He didn't like coincidences either. "Maybe Vik will turn something up."

268

* * *

It was still snowing when they left. They took Ben's SUV, but agreed that Marti would drive while Ben caught another quick nap. She had gotten home early last night and had a decent night's sleep for a change. The salt trucks were out and the roads clear. Traffic didn't slow down until they reached Highland Park. There was an exit off Interstate 94 near Lake-Cook Road and the merging traffic was causing the slow-down. She was driving on the inside lane when she saw a big rusty Oldsmobile swerve toward her. The driver veered away, then lost control again and came right at them. She had no place to go. The car hit her, and they crashed into the concrete dividers.

Marti couldn't move either of her arms. They were pinned to her sides. The SUV was at an odd angle, not quite tipped over but not upright either. There was a lot of weight pressing against her right side. She looked at Ben. His side of the SUV had taken the brunt of the hit and he was crushed against her. He was unconscious, and the sight of him made her panic. She began to scream.

While the firemen used the Jaws of Life to pry open the doors, one paramedic talked to her while the other checked Ben to make sure his airway was clear and he was breathing okay. Then he checked Ben's pulse and took his blood pressure. He relayed this information to someone Marti couldn't turn her head far enough to see to be transmitted to the hospital.

"What's his name?" he asked Marti.

"Ben Walker."

"Ben," the paramedic said. "Ben. Can you hear me? Blink your eyes. Here, squeeze my finger."

The paramedic looked at Marti and shook his head. He wasn't responding.

"Are you an EMT?" Ben was an emergency medical technician and an RN, not that the level of training was always that important if the paramedic was experienced.

The paramedic nodded.

"What's his Glasgow coma score?" Marti asked.

"Less than eight."

Marti didn't know exactly how that was determined, but she did know that less than eight was bad.

While the paramedic worked on Ben, got an oxygen line going, a pressure cuff on, and started an IV, Marti gave a description of the car and the license plate number to a uniformed officer. She hadn't got a good look at the driver, but she remembered a dark-colored watch cap. And his eyes. He had not been afraid or even panicky. She was certain of that. The paramedic told her she might go into shock. He wanted to start an IV on her. She refused. One of them was going to have to be ambulatory when they got out of here, and it wasn't going to be Ben.

"Is he still breathing okay?' she asked.

"Breathing and respiration are fine."

She looked at him. No cuts, no swelling on the parts of his face and head that she could see. There could be neck, back, and spinal cord injuries. But she tried not to worry about that. Ben's being unconscious was more than enough for right now.

"Where are you taking us?"

He named a hospital that she knew was a good level-two trauma center.

"Ben doesn't get to ride in a helicopter?"

"No, not now, anyway."

That was good. Even though he hadn't regained consciousness, he didn't have to be medivaced to a trauma-one center.

Her arm and wrist hurt a lot, but she didn't say anything. She was beginning to wonder if something was broken, but she could wait.

"Ben," she said, even though she wasn't sure he could hear her. "That damned fool ran right into us. I'm fine, but guess what? They are opening the doors with the Jaws of Life and a paramedic is working on you. No helicopter ride, though, sorry. Be nice though if you'd wake up and keep me company, at least until they get us out of here."

She kept talking to him—until the metal gave way, while in-

line traction was put in place, while he was lifted out and im-
mobilized, and all the way to the hospital.

A doctor met them as soon as the ambulance doors opened.
Marti had to get into a wheelchair, but she insisted that she
stay with Ben.

A doctor walked alongside her, asking questions. "Do you
feel faint? Dizzy? No. Good. Anything hurt? Just your arm?
How's your chest feel? Any pain when you breathe? No. Good.
How's your belly? Feel tender? Had the steering wheel or something pressed into it? We'll take a look."

She was taken into a examining room. Ben was right next
door, but she couldn't see him.

"It's okay, ma'am," the doctor said. "Just give me a few
minutes."

The doctor checked her pulse and blood pressure again, then
her abdomen, her neck, and her spine. Ordered X rays. There
was a small X-ray room right by the emergency room, so she
didn't have to go too far away from Ben. When she looked in
on him, the doctor was with him and a nurse. The room wasn't
filled with medical personnel, nobody was giving orders.

"We're just checking him over," the doctor said in a quiet
voice. "So far everything checks out fine. He hasn't woken up
yet, but he should pretty soon. We're going to take him for X
rays and a CT scan. We'll have to keep him at least overnight,
maybe longer. He's sleeping a little longer than I would like, so
we'll take him to the ICU, but all of his vitals are fine." The
calmness as he spoke was reassuring.

Her X rays were negative, but they wanted to admit her for
observation also.

While Ben was in radiology, she called Vik.

"Go see Momma and my kids," she said. "Let them know
what's going on. Make sure they understand there's nothing life
threatening. We're both okay."

"And?" Vik asked.

"And that's all they need to know." That was all she knew
right now.

After Ben was taken to intensive care and put on monitors, Marti refused to be admitted. She told her doctor that they could observe her while she watched over Ben. She would not be allowed to stay in his room, but she could go in every hour for ten minutes on the hour.

A call came in from Lieutenant Dirkowitz. She explained what had happened and what was going on now.

"Okay," the lieutenant said. "I'n out more than in right now. Make sure someone keeps the chief abreast of everything. Whatever you need, Marti. We're right here."

The doctor offered her pain medication, which she refused at first, even though every bone and muscle in her body was beginning to hurt like hell. "Something mild," she conceded, "nothing strong enough to make me drowsy." A nurse took her to a small room with a couch near the ICU. She intended to sit for a minute, then phone home. When she woke up, Vik was sitting in the chair.

"How is he?" she asked.

"Still unconscious, but otherwise okay."

"Did you talk to the kids?"

"They are a little upset. . . ."

"Explain that."

"Your mother is with them, and the next-door neighbors and their boys. Denise Stevens is there, too, and a couple of older women from your church. The pastor stopped by while I was there and we all prayed. So it isn't business as usual, and I think that's making the kids more nervous, but they are okay. Scared and worried as hell, but okay."

"Thanks. Pass me the phone."

Momma answered.

"How is everyone?"

"Upset," Momma said. "But holding up okay. Joanna is a big help. Are you all right?"

"Yes."

"Really?"

"Except for Ben."

"But they didn't admit you?"

"No. No need to. Just bruises, that's all. Have you called Ben's parents yet?"

"Yes. His dad just isn't doing well. I told them I would keep calling and if anything changed we'd come get them. His sister is going to come over and stay with them. I don't think they should make the trip from Kankakee unless they have to. They can come next Sunday for dinner."

Marti spoke to each child in turn, told Mike that his dad was sleeping and promised to have Ben call as soon as he woke up.

"Is that the truth?" Mike asked.

"Yes."

"All of it?"

"No," she admitted. "Ben was on the side that got hit. He was unconscious. He's sleeping now, but he has a concussion." If he didn't wake up by morning, that word would become coma, and could mean he might be like this for days, even weeks. For tonight, it was just a concussion. "We're not sure when he'll wake up. There are no other injuries. I'm staying the night. Everything hurts, but except for that, I'm fine. You'll all come to see us tomorrow as early as possible. Try to get a good night's sleep."

Mike didn't say anything right away. When he did speak, she could tell he was crying. "Give my dad a hug for me," he said. "And tell him I love him."

Marti was crying too when she hung up. Then she got angry. "They should not have to go through this again. If I could get my hands on that idiot . . ." Again, she remembered the look in his eyes.

"Which reminds me," Vik said. "A local detective wants to talk with you, and they are sending someone out from Chicago—didn't say when they would get here. And I'm here for the duration. Mildred will kill me if I leave you here alone. Her sister is with her."

"What time is it?" she asked. There were no windows and her watch had been broken in the crash.

"Six-twenty-five," Vik said.

"At night?

"Mm-hmm."

"Is that all?" It seemed like at least a day should have passed. Everything hurt. Bad. She asked for more pain medicine after checking to be sure it wouldn't make her fall asleep.

"It's not strong enough to do much good either," the nurse told her.

"Then I'll just pretend that it is."

When they were alone she asked Vik, "Find out anything about the house fire?"

"No body inside. Arson. No suspects. I checked the TV station's footage, and the stills the *News-Times* reporter took. No sign of Joe Boy or G.L., but I've got two uniforms out looking for them. Chief says whatever we need."

"Did the uniform ID the man he spoke to?"

"Yeah. Some guy in a black watch cap. Picture was taken from a distance. Can't see much of his face. He was looking down. Had his hand over his mouth. Wearing gloves. They're having it blown up, but they think it'll be fuzzy."

Gloves. The man in the car had gloves on. And a dark-colored cap. She told Vik.

"Do you think this was deliberate?" he asked. "Maybe the same guy for the fire and the accident?

"I don't know. Let's wait until we talk with the local officer here." She debated mentioning the vagrant, then said, "Remember that guy in the doorway of that Victorian near the Barrister."

Vik looked at her and shook his head.

"There was something about him. I'm going to try to locate him when I get the chance."

When the female officer came in, she told them that the car had been located and towed. It was damaged in the front but drivable. Abandoned in Highwood. They had been heading

274

south but the driver turned and went north after the accident. There had to be witnesses, but nobody had stopped and there hadn't been any calls volunteering information. At least someone had called in the accident on a cell phone.

"What do you remember?" the officer asked. Marti wasn't sure of the woman's age. Red hair and freckles made her look young. The Job had given her that edginess that made her seem older.

"He came toward me twice. The first time he veered away. It would have been a glancing blow, but enough to knock me into the barriers. The second time it was more of a direct hit. I thought he must be skidding and couldn't regain control."

"That road wasn't icy at all. Visibility wasn't that bad. There were no skid marks on the road, just the curve of the tires as they came toward you."

"You think it was deliberate."

"Looks like it could have been."

Marti didn't want to agree with her. How in the hell could she pin down someone in a black watch cap, driving a stolen car, who was trying to kill her and her husband?

"I've been a cop fifteen years," she said. "Worked on the Chicago force ten years before I moved to Lincoln Prairie. A lot of people could want me dead. Until now, as far as I know none of them have tried to kill me. I'm not sure anyone is trying to now."

The female officer nodded. "I don't think we'll get much, if anything, from the car. Can you tell me anything else about what this man looked like?"

Marti shook her head. She thought of the photo of the man at the fire but she didn't say anything. Better to wait until she had a look at it. Trying to make a connection now was wishful thinking, or maybe dread.

The officer left and Marti went in to see Ben. He looked as if he were sleeping. The beep noises sounded stable and the patterns on the small green screen looked consistent.

"Wake up," she said. "Please wake up. I need you."

She patted the arm that didn't have any tubes attached.

"I talked to the children. Mike's upset, but doing okay. He sends you a hug and he told me to tell you he loves you."

The beeps and blips continued. There was no change.

It was after midnight when the two detectives from Chicago showed up. Vik was asleep in the chair. Marti made them wait while she went in to see Ben again. If he didn't wake up soon his diagnosis would be changed from concussion to a more serious brain injury. The doctor on duty just said, "No change. Everything's okay for now." She hurt too much to stand there and demand to know more. She needed help. After she talked with the Chicago detectives, she would send Vik out to talk with the doctor.

Both Chicago detectives were young enough to make Marti feel her age, which was only forty, but she felt older, compared to them. The tall, beefy detective with the deep blue eyes and blond hair introduced himself and snapped open his briefcase. He took out a stack of files. "We're using two criteria right now," he explained. "Who Franklin and Jones arrested and got convictions on, and who's been released in the last six months.

Criteria, Marti thought. What were they teaching them in the academy these days?

"Jones has been on the force for five years, but Franklin's been around over twenty. When we got the computer printouts we got a lot of hits for Franklin, so we've got a lot of manpower on this. Your husband was Franklin's third partner. We drew those cases. Eleven subjects have been released in the past six months that Franklin and your husband helped put away. Did you get copies of those lists?"

Marti nodded, but didn't admit that she hadn't paid much attention to them. "They were partners a long time ago," she said. "Those people had to be in jail for years. That's a long time to carry a grudge."

"I know," the blond detective agreed. "But this is what we drew, this is what we look into. Do you remember your husband ever getting threats from anyone he arrested while he was working with Franklin? Not the routine stuff, something that sounded serious."

Marti felt too sore to smile. "Back then they were all serious, at least to me, but no, nothing comes to mind."

"Do you remember any of their cases?"

"Just that they worked Violent Crimes and handled a lot of homicides."

"Eight of these eleven releases were put away for manslaughter. Has anything unusual happened lately, other than this accident?"

Marti told them about last night's fire. "I thought it had something to do with an arrest we just made," she was thinking of Reggie Garrett, "but that black watch cap has me thinking."

"We talked with the detective working this case. They traced the vehicle that hit you to an owner in Chicago. It hadn't been reported as stolen, but the owner is seventy-two, doesn't drive in weather like this. We're checking out family members now, to see if one of them took it."

"We've got a case involving a Chicago resident," Marti said. She told him about the Ward case and they all had a laugh about the dogs.

"That's one I can't tell my wife," the young, blond cop said. "We have miniature dachshunds. She's not as bad as this lady, but I plan to have a real kid real soon."

He gave her a list of the eleven names along with a folder for each. It wasn't a complete case file, but did contain information about the crime along with some of Johnnie and Ray Franklin's notes.

"Is there anything else I should know?" Marti asked,

"I think that's about it. We know that the weapon used to shoot Franklin and Jones was also used last Sunday night to shoot a man named Bryan Weinstein. But there doesn't seem to be any other connection with the two shootings. Weinstein was twenty-four, sang with the Chicago Lyric Opera Company. He was on his way home from a performance."

Marti didn't see any connection either. Weinstein would only have been eleven years old thirteen years ago.

After the two Chicago detectives left, Marti opened a folder, looked at Johnnie's familiar handwriting again, neat for a man, legible. She went in to see Ben, returned to the small room, took another look at Johnnie's notes, sat beside Vik and cried. Then she sent Vik home.

"Get some sleep. And, someone's got to cover for me at work. You've got to try to ID the guy in the photo. And I'm going to go through these files. Maybe I'll come up with something. It won't do me any good if I need information fast and you're sitting here holding my hand. Momma will be here in the morning."

Vik was reluctant to leave her, but he agreed.

Marti went over the files twice, but she had a difficult time focusing on anything. The pain was a major distraction. Finally she went in to see Ben and let him know she wasn't going to leave the hospital but she was going to take a little nap. She warned the nurses to wake her immediately if there was any change. Then she took a stronger pain pill and lay on the couch in the waiting room.

Adrian was so elated he couldn't sit down. Instead, he paced back and forth within the circle. His luck had returned. The cleansing ceremony had worked. Whatever was causing his bad luck was gone. Even though her husband had not died in that fire last night, he had Detective MacAlister right where he wanted her.

He was getting good at setting fires, as much as he feared and hated them. All three fires were in the Lincoln Prairie newspaper. The *Tribune* didn't mention the house fire. Every place had burned to the ground.

He was so wired that he decided a few glasses of wine would help him settle down and get a good night's sleep. He needed to be alert and ready tomorrow. Frost had made designs on his windows. He looked at them and debated whether or not he really wanted to go back out in the cold. He should have thought of the wine when he was walking home from the bus stop. Now he would have to go to an all-night store three blocks away. He thought about taking the gun for protection but that was too risky. He had left his favorite knife, the one he had used on Ramos's foster child, in Calvin Ward's back. He selected a smaller one, razor sharp. Even if he was stopped and searched by the police, they would recognize his need for self protection, and the blade was less than six inches long.

Adrian ran his finger along the edge of the blade. He liked knives. He had always preferred them to guns, even when he was a kid and went hunting. There was something about skinning a coon or a rabbit or a possum, or even going fishing and gutting a catfish while it was still alive and wriggling.

He thought about the list he had made while he was in prison. Almost half of those people most responsible were dead now. He had gotten even with those who did the most to put him there. Other than the cop, there was only one other person he really would like to see dead. He had given it a lot of thought, but the man lived in a house that was built like a fortress, in an area well protected by private security. Maybe now that his luck had changed, maybe it was worth a try. As soon as he shot Franklin, his time here had become limited. By tonight, MacAlister would be dead. Then he would have to run for it. Adrian ran his finger along the stainless-steel blade. Maybe in the morning. Before he went back for MacAlister. By Sunday, he could be halfway to Mexico.

The wind whipped around the corner driving snow in his face. He pulled his watch cap over his ears. He needed a scarf. What a day this had been. What a day. He had planned to just drive to Lincoln Prairie, watch the cop and her partner and figure out the best way to lure them to Chicago. Then she went home, came out with her husband, and the two of them took off, heading south, toward Chicago. Driving along behind them on the highway, it had come to him all at once. Go ahead, hit them.

The car he had stolen was as old and as big as a tank and almost as indestructible when up against those lightweight pieces of tin they were putting on the road now. It was heavier than the first one he stole, easier to control. And it was snowing, road conditions were right. Without any plan at all, it was there, everything he needed to do. Too bad she wasn't driving on the left side of the road where she could have rolled over an embankment, but hitting that concrete abutment had worked just as well. Adrian had called the hospital nearest to the accident. The fireman was in intensive care. And he had her, now he had her. He knew just how she was going to die.

12

Marti didn't know what time it was when the nurse woke her. She came awake all at once, and said, "Ben?"

The nurse nodded, smiling.

Everything—muscle, bone, and joint seemed to hurt as she eased her way up from the couch and walked with the nurse down the hall to Ben's room. His eyes were still closed. Marti tried not to be disappointed. There must have been some change in his vital signs to indicate he was waking up. The regularity of the beeps and the consistency of the lines zigzagging across the green screen had become reassuring.

She went to his side, touched the hand that didn't have a line in it, and he squeezed her fingers.

"Ben!" He knew she was here.

His eyes opened. "Where's my teddy bear?" he asked, and closed them.

"Ben?" He squeezed again, less pressure this time. Then he was sleeping.

The doctor came in. "He woke up and called for you, but he keeps drifting off. We'll be waking him every ten minutes to make sure he's responsive. The injury was caused by the rapid flexion and extension of his head and neck," he explained. "The brain impacts against the skull and rotates. We'll x-ray him again, but from the looks of it, he got lucky. There's no swelling, so I don't expect to find a blood clot in there. It did take him a long time to wake up, so we'll want to keep him under observation for a few more days. He'll stay in ICU at least for today. If his progress continues, we'll move him to the head-trauma unit in the morning."

"You've got a head-trauma unit?" They were at least twenty miles from the Chicago city limits. She knew hospitals there had specialized trauma units. She hadn't expected to find one here.

"You picked a good place to have a collision. We get a lot of car and motorcycle accidents because of our proximity to Route Forty-one, and also, I think, because there are no more stop-and-go lights past Park Avenue."

Marti stayed her allotted ten minutes. Ben woke up when the nurse roused him. He looked at her and smiled.

As soon as she left Ben's room she phoned home.

"He woke up!" she told Momma. "He woke up! Ben's going to be okay! He woke up!"

Then she found a nurse and asked for more pain meds.

"Doctor wants to see you again," the nurse told her. "To make sure everything is okay."

Marti looked at her left arm, the one that hurt the most. It was bruised from the back of her hand to her shoulder. She checked the other arm, same thing. When she undressed for the doctor, most of her body was an angry red or purple. There were no abrasions. Her face hadn't hit anything and looked okay. The doctor decided her left wrist was sprained and had it bandaged.

Adrian took the bus to the lake and got off near the Chicago Yacht Club to watch the sunrise. He could see Navy Pier to his left, the Field Museum, Shedd Aquarium, and the Adler Planetarium to his right. He had loved to go the Field Museum and the aquarium when he was a child. Even as an adult he went there. He would like to go one more time before he left town. He should have thought of that sooner. Now there wouldn't be time.

The wind picked up and he turned and headed into the

Loop. He walked along State Street, then to LaSalle and into the financial district where he stood across the street from the Trade Center. He found the window in the office where he had worked at Wilburton and Associates. Twelve years he had worked there, doing everything right, never making a mistake. Twelve years while he watched the white man come in, get promoted over him, and then had to train him. For twelve years he had done the right thing, and then when the partnership became open, Wilburton chose a white woman with less seniority and a lesser position. Once again, he had to train her. That was when he knew for certain that he was never going to be more than what he was. It was fashionable to have one black man and one Asian—an overachiever just as he was, who spoke English, Vietnamese, Chinese, and French. It was fashionable to bring in a black woman after he had been there for five years and give her a job that should have been his. Like any good black man, he smiled, praised the company, told everyone how pleased he was with his job, and accepted their praise, and even amazement, that he had come so far. Like any black man, he was angry.

Adrian turned and walked away. He headed back to the lake. It was too early to go to the museum or the aquarium, but they opened at nine. He would find a warm place to have coffee, and wait. He went to a McDonald's on Dearborn.

Marti was about to look through the stack of folders when the family came in with Lupe Torres. Lupe was carrying a small suitcase.

"Just a change of clothes and a few personals," Momma said.

"Wait," she warned, "no hugs. Everything hurts."

The boys, faces solemn, came and sat with her, one on each side. Theo touched her bandaged wrist.

"It's just a sprain," she told him.

Joanna sat at her feet on the carpet and rested her head on Marti's knees. Momma patted her shoulder.

"Ben's going to be fine," Marti told them. "You can see him

283

for a few minutes. He'll probably open his eyes when you talk to him, but he might not say anything. He's really tired. And he might not remember what happened. Amnesia is common with concussions."

"That's all it is?" Joanna asked. "They're sure about that?"

"Very sure," Marti assured her. "They took him for more X rays, and everything looked fine."

"Can he come home soon?" Mike asked.

"Soon," Marti answered.

"Will he have to go right back to work?" Theo asked.

"No. Me neither." Vik and Lupe would have to manage their caseload without her. She couldn't go to work like this.

Ben woke up enough to smile at the kids. Mike was the first one to cry, then they all did.

"My teddy bear," Ben said again.

Marti didn't understand what he meant.

"He wants a teddy bear like the ones he gives to kids when they get hurt," Mike explained. "We'll get you one, Dad."

Ben smiled and drifted off to sleep again.

They went to the cafeteria for breakfast.

"Nobody ate last night or this morning," Momma said as everyone loaded their plates.

Then while Lupe shepherded the children in to see Ben one more time, Marti sat with Momma.

"What's going on?" Momma asked. "Anything I need to know?"

"I'm not sure. Maybe nothing. But I think we were run off the road deliberately." She could still see that man's eyes. No fear, no panic. Just determination.

"Should I be worried about the children?"

Marti felt her anger rise again. How dare anyone threaten her, or Ben, or their children. How dare they assume that criminal acts were their right and that anyone who stopped them was fair game. She would not be scared off. She would get them. If this was some idiot who thought he could get even, he needed to think again.

"Why don't you keep them close to home. And I'll call the chief, have the patrol units keep an eye out."

She hated that, hated having to protect her kids, anticipate possibilities that would never have occurred to Momma when she was growing up. All parents had to do that now, but they shouldn't. Children should be safe from harm.

"Ben is going to be okay?" Momma asked.

"It really was just a concussion."

"You look worse than he does."

"And I hurt worse too. I think we're both going to have to take a couple weeks off."

Momma glanced at the folders the Chicago detectives had left with her. "Looks like you've got your work with you."

"Just this," Marti said. "I just have to look into this." She didn't add that she was hoping to identify the person who had run them off the road, and maybe, at the same time, whoever had shot Ray Franklin.

While everyone got ready to leave, Marti motioned Lupe into the hall.

"Thanks for bringing them," she said.

"Anytime. You feeling okay? You look like hell."

"I thought I looked pretty good."

"Vik wants to be here. I thought I could stay by the phone in your office, in case you needed something. Slim and Cowboy want to help too. What needs doing? I saw those folders."

Marti explained.

"Sounds like you're going to need a fax machine." Lupe said. "Maybe the hospital has a room they don't use on the weekends. Vik will be bringing those photos. Slim and Cowboy are out looking for Garrett's two friends. We have nothing on La-Shawna. The composite in the *News-Times* has generated nothing so far. There was definitely no body in the house on First. Vik showed the Ramos photos with the broom to the state's attorney. They're not ready to bring charges. They need the psych report. We've got a little more time on that one. Nothing new on the train conductor homicide. Anything else?"

"I want the black-and-whites that patrol my neighborhood to be conspicuous for the next few days at least. We're in a cul-de-sac, a lot of times they just look that way and don't drive down there."

"You've already got that per order of Chief Allendo."

"Seen Dirkowitz?"

"He's been in and out. Baby Angela comes home Monday. We're chipping in for a gift. I'll put in for you. And I'll bring the family back this evening. You'd better call Vik now if you want him to bring anything with him. He'll be leaving as soon as I get back."

"I'd hug you if it didn't hurt," Marti said.

"You think this was deliberate," Lupe said.

"I'm trying to keep an open mind."

"Well, in this case, it's better to err on the side of safety. We'll be watching your back."

Lupe gave her a light pat on the shoulder. Marti winced, then took her hand and held on.

Adrian took the train to Barrington, got off downtown, walked to Liberty and Hough, then east toward Lake Louise. The Wilburton estate was on several acres of land. The main house sat well back from the road. It was protected with an alarm system and surveillance cameras. There was a security gate and a guardhouse along with an electronic system with codes or keys that had to be used to access the property. Mr. Wilburton felt safe here. Adrian liked it when people felt safe. It made it that much easier to kill them.

It was Saturday. The main streets were busy. Adrian was wearing his repairman's jacket, quilted pants, and carrying a toolbox and a small duffel bag. Even though he would be the only black among many whites and a few Hispanic domestics, his uniform would make him as invisible as he had been the night he wore the homeless man's clothes and shot Bryan Weinstein.

Adrian checked his watch. Mr. Wilburton had retired from

the company, but still prided himself on his fitness and good health. He liked to take a walk after meals, weather permitting. Snow, cold, and wind kept him inside. There was no snow today. The sky was overcast, and it was just below freezing, but only by a couple of degrees. There was no wind to speak of. Assuming Wilburton had ventured outside today, Adrian had missed his after-breakfast constitutional, but was in time for his postlunch walk. If Wilburton did go out, he would head for the lake.

Adrian remembered Mrs. Wilburton as a short, overweight woman who loved food. Apparently she didn't share her husband's enthusiasm for fitness. Adrian had observed Wilburton twice. Both times he had been alone. His noon route would take him into a wooded area that abutted one of the other estates. That was where Adrian waited, behind a tree.

Small birds chattered in the dense evergreen branches. Several squirrels engaged in a loud argument while others scampered across the snow. A pastoral scene, Adrian thought. One that he might have enjoyed one day when he retired, if Wilburton had let him become a partner. If Wilburton had paid him what he paid others with his education, his experience, his responsibilities.

When he heard snow crunching and wood snapping, he took out the knife. As the sounds came closer he tensed. He let Wilburton walk past him in his bright red down jacket. Then he stepped from behind the tree.

"Hello, Mr. Wilburton."

Wilburton started, then turned. "Adrian? Is that you?"

"None other," he said.

"But I thought . . . I thought . . ."

"That I was in prison? Sometimes they let you out for good behavior."

"Oh. I'm glad to hear that."

Wilburton was afraid. Adrian could see the fear in his eyes. He tightened his grip on the knife and took a step closer.

"Nice to see you again, sir."

"Why are you here?" Wilburton demanded. His voice shook.

"Oh, I need a job, sir. Thought maybe you could use a handyman."

Wilburton looked at him for a moment. "Is this some kind of joke?"

Adrian took another step forward. This time Wilburton backed away. Reaching out, Adrian grabbed him by the jacket.

"Now, just a minute, Adrian. I won't have this. What happened—you did that to yourself."

"No," Adrian said. "You did it to me." He took out the knife, snapped it open.

Wilburton opened his mouth. Before he could speak, Adrian slit his throat from one ear to the other. Blood gushed. Adrian let go of Wilburton and he slumped to the ground. Blood saturated the snow. Reaching down, Adrian pulled up Wilburton's jacket and gutted him. Then he went behind the tree, out of sight, slipped off his bloody jacket and removed his quilted pants. He was wearing jeans and a turtleneck beneath them. He unzipped the duffel back and took out another jacket with a company logo, a hat, and gloves. He left his bloody clothes and the weapon where they were and walked back the same way he had come.

Alone again, Marti sat down with the files. She needed a table or a desk, but she also needed to stay close to Ben. She found her favorite nurse.

"There's a small conference room off the ward that nobody will use until Monday."

"Can I set up a fax machine in there?"

"Yes. There's a phone line; I think that's all you need."

The nurse showed her to the room. Marti looked around. There was enough space for at least ten people to sit down. The chairs looked comfortable and there was even a window. She pressed her forehead against the cold glass. A nearby golf course was all white slopes and ridges with crevices of snow. "This is great," she said. "You're sure it's okay if I use it?"

"Sure. But we've never had police actually working here before. Don't be too surprised if a few people find an excuse to come in."

The nurse went and got the files for her, and the small suitcase Momma had brought. "Would you like to take a shower first?"

Hot water. Clean underwear. Toothpaste. That sounded wonderful.

After she showered, Marti changed into sweats. She felt less like a patient and more like a cop as she sat at the table with the list of recent releases and the slim stack of files. She reached for one, thought of seeing Johnnie's precise handwriting again, and hesitated. He would tell her. If the person they were looking for was here, Johnnie would tell her who it was. She just had to pay attention to what he was saying as she read through his notes. She was the only one who could decipher Johnnie's 'one-worders,' those cryptic words and abbreviations that only meant something to him.

She put the folders in alphabetical order and began reading. She read the official forms first, to get the chronology of the crime and arrest, then the forensic reports, then Ray Franklin's notes. She looked at Johnnie's notes last. They were more detailed than she expected. The one-word, one-phrase shorthand must have evolved. Nothing jumped out at her. She compared Johnnie's notes with Ray's. The two men did not think alike.

Ray: "Subject was located at the pool hall. Claimed he was innocent before we indicated we were taking him in. Did not resist. Held out his hands to be cuffed. Laughed when Mirandized. Said he wouldn't say anything without a lawyer." After interrogating him, Ray wrote: "Insists he is innocent. Gave us an alibi. Confident he'll be released." Later: "MacAlister told him too much. Subject laughed in our faces. Thinks we're shooting crappies in a barrel." Then, "Lawyer offered to plead to a lesser charge."

Johnnie: "Not hostile. Knows the drill." After interrogation:

"Too relaxed. Knows we have the right man. Daring us to prove it." Later, Johnnie wrote: "Gave him some of what we have on him." Then, "Ready for plea bargain."

She wasn't used to Johnnie's expansiveness. She had expected his comments to be even more terse.

She took a break, went in to see Ben. Woke him up again.

"What happened?" he asked, but dozed off before she could even begin to give him an answer.

The doctor was at the nurses' station when she left his room. "You're sure this sleepiness is all right?"

"Normal. There's nothing else going on, and he does wake up on command."

"But what if he doesn't?"

"It's a head injury," the doctor said. "We are monitoring him very closely. And, don't forget, he was in an automobile accident as well. His body is exhausted."

She nodded. Ben's brain had bounced around inside his skull. His body had experienced other insults, just as her body had. There were no breaks, no fractures, no bleeding, but his body was still reacting to the total trauma. She hoped that was all this waking and sleeping was about.

After reading through the files twice, Marti selected four that caught her attention. She read through them again, unable to figure out what it was that caused her to single them out. She read through the other seven, decided it was something about the subjects that influenced her choices. She still felt vague about what that was. Other than committing a homicide, they didn't have much in common. "Trust your instincts," Johnnie used to tell her. Johnnie had very good instincts. Marti reached for her notebook. She wished she had a legal-sized pad.

She called Vik. "We've got an office," she told him.

"Good. Lupe stole somebody's fax machine."

"Bring some office stuff. Pencils, big pads, paper clips." Whatever was in her in-basket or on her voice mail could wait.

"What about the files from Chicago?" he asked.

"I'm looking at them now."

"Find anything?"

"Not yet."

She called the Chicago detective next. Bryan Weinstein had regained consciousness. Consuela Jones—Ray Franklin's partner—was doing fine. Neither of them could remember anything. Ray Franklin was still unconscious but breathing on his own. They hadn't narrowed their list of suspects. Three had missed their last appointments with their parole officers. Marti took down those names. One was in her pile of four. The other eight were reporting as required. They had not spoken with any of them yet, but they were in the process of verifying places of residence and current employment.

When Vik came in, he brought a manila envelope, a thermos filled with coffee, and a covered dish.

Marti grabbed the envelope first. "Are these the pictures?"

She pulled out a stack of black-and-whites, and spread them on the table. There were only two shots, both taken from a distance, each blown up five times. She couldn't make out anything from the three-by-five. The nine-by-twelve was too grainy. Nothing in between helped either. The man was looking down.

"If I could just see his eyes," Marti said. "I'll know it's him when I see his eyes."

Disappointed, she turned her attention to the food. She wasn't crazy about Polish or German cuisine, but something smelled good. She lifted the lid, kielbasa and that sweet-and-sour red cabbage she liked, and fried potatoes with lots of onions. Vik had brought paper plates, plastic forks and enough for two.

"Mildred packed this, didn't she? Where's what I told you to bring?"

"Eat. I'll get it."

"Sit down while this is still warm."

He frowned when she winced as she reached for a napkin.

"What's with the wrist?"

"Just a sprain." The sweet cabbage was great with a hunk of spicy sausage. "Mmm."

"I saw the SUV. It looks like someone crushed it the way you take a pop can and crush it. You two got lucky."

Marti ate a forkful of potatoes. "This is good. I didn't even know I was hungry. Who cooked? Mildred or her sister?"

"You should be in a hospital bed, too," Vik said.

"No time for that."

He didn't disagree. "They found a car parked not far from the fire on First Street," he said. "Stolen. In Chicago. Just like the one that hit you yesterday."

"They say what part of Chicago?"

"One was stolen on the West Side, one on the South Side."

"You know what's wrong with all of this, Jessenovik? None of it makes one damned bit of sense."

"I think that if it's just one person, he's smart. Let's hope he's too damned smart and gets cocky."

After they ate everything, Vik went in with her to see Ben. He woke up enough to smile at her, tried to move the hand with the IV, seemed puzzled, or confused, slept again. The sleeping still worried her, but she didn't say anything.

Vik went to the car and came back with a cardboard box filled with things from the precinct. He plugged in the fax machine, then cleaned up from lunch. Then he sat down and she pushed the stack of four files toward him.

"This could be a waste of time," she said. "Maybe what's happening to us and what happened to Ray Franklin are totally separate incidents."

"You don't believe that and neither do I." He tapped his finger on the top folder. "I bet you've got the answer right here. Why don't we come up with a list of additional information we need on these guys, hold off on the others."

Marti began going over the files with him.

"Johnnie cut right to the quick, didn't he?" Vik said, after they went over the first file. "No wonder he was so good. Why do you like this perp?"

She pointed to Johnnie's one-word summary. "Excuses."

"Why that?"

"People who make excuses don't see themselves as responsible for anything. They can cause a lot of damage that's 'not their fault.' This guy's got four priors for battery. First one is a fight, the next a few broken bones and a broken jaw, then the next victim is hospitalized. This time he stomped the guy to death. And none of it was his fault. Who did he blame when he got sent up for manslaughter? Johnnie, for arresting him? The judge for sentencing him? Me vicariously?"

Vik picked up the next folder. They were in alpha order. "And this one?"

"Vehicular homicide. Ran the ex-girlfriend over three times, forward, backed up, went forward. Then he got out to make sure she was dead. And all because she was dating a school crossing guard." She could still see the driver's eyes. Steely. Without fear. Were they the eyes of someone who had killed that way before?

The third folder was that of an arsonist. Johnnie had a one-worder, "coward," and a two-worder, "will repeat."

"An obvious choice," she said. "But people who set fires usually like fires, like to watch them burn, derive a lot of good feelings and satisfaction. Someone dying in a fire can be a real boost to their self esteem."

"Let's find out more about him," Vik said. He picked up the last folder. "Adrian Quinn. What's special about him?"

Again it was Johnnie's one-worder, "Avenge."

"And read Johnnie's notes," she said.

" 'Denial. No guilt,' " Vik read.

"I want to know more about him, too," Marti said.

"What's to know? He denied the charges, said he wasn't guilty."

The word *avenge* held her attention. Getting even. But why had Johnnie used that word instead of revenge?

The Chicago detective had the complete files handy. While she waited for him to fax more information, she went in to see

Ben. Still drowsy, he smiled, squeezed her hand, said "Bear."

"Well, our arsonist should be in a mental institution," Marti said after she read his reports. "Get on his bad side and something is going to burn."

Adrian Quinn didn't have a sheet. He did have several college degrees. "Not your typical killer," Marti said. "Just one victim, a co-worker who fingered him for stealing from the company. No priors, not even a traffic violation."

"Sentence seems extreme, given the crime and the lack of history. Everything they faxed on him is positive. Graduated from Northwestern at the top of his class. It looks like he belonged to damned near every civic and social organization in the city. Got three humanitarian awards for community service. This is the kind of guy they like to slap on the hand and put back in the street. At least that's how it was back then."

"How much time did he get?"

"Fifteen to life for manslaughter."

"Any unusual force?"

"No," Vik said. "He got mad, picked up a bookend, hit the guy over the head. One hit, no bludgeoning."

"Sentence sounds excessive."

"Yeah," Vik agreed. "He was black. Could that have had something to do with it? I know that a lot of what Ramos is saying is true for adults as well as juveniles."

Marti nodded. "Sounds that way. Upstanding citizen. An impulse killing. Unpremeditated." She read through the additional reports. "All of these accomplishments and he embezzled from his firm, threw it all away." She looked at Johnnie's notes again. Denial. No guilt. This was one black man writing about another. What was Johnnie saying? Avenge. Why not revenge? They meant the same thing, getting even.

"I need a dictionary," she said. It took twenty minutes to find one in an office on the first floor that was empty for the weekend.

Avenge and revenge could be used interchangeably, but the definition for avenger was a one-liner that got her attention. A person who avenges a wrong. Adrian Quinn had committed a crime. What if denial and no guilt didn't mean what Vik thought it did? Suppose it meant that even though Quinn did it, he believed it was someone else's fault and not his.

"I need more on this Adrian Quinn," Marti said. She explained what she thought Johnnie might have meant. "Suppose he had to avenge a crime committed against him?"

"The sentence was excessive."

"Let's start there. He's been out, what—" She checked the printout the Chicago detective had given her listing the names and the release dates. "He's been out since before Christmas. Who was the judge?"

She made another call to Chicago and requested a photo of Adrian Quinn and a list of everyone involved in his arrest and trial, as well as a contact at the firm where he had worked.

Adrian boarded the train and headed back to the city. He closed his eyes and thought back to what he had done this morning. He wondered why he had ever liked the Field Museum with its stuffed animals. Even the birds were stuffed and displayed in cases as if they had been stopped midsong, their wings stilled. Now they sat on branches in perpetuity and looked as if they were ready to take flight. Push a button, hear a recording of their song. And the aquarium. That had changed so much. Watching the fish swimming in schools and alone in their little habitats, up and down, back and forth, had depressed him. Trapped, all of them, even the coral was trapped and it was stationary. Everything was trapped, the whales, especially the whales and the penguins. Trapped the way he had been trapped in that prison. In cells, just as he had been. Did they have any memory of freedom?

He used to enjoy watching nurse sharks and turtles swim round and round in that big tank. Now he thought of himself, locked into a routine he had no control over, going in one circle, one direction day after day. He didn't ever want to go back to jail. Another day, maybe two, and he would finally be free of it all. He had been to Mexico before, stayed in a small town where all they cared about was American dollars. A place near the ocean, where the fish were free to swim wherever they wanted, and birds, all kinds of birds, flew free. A place where he would be free also.

Sheets of paper were coming from the fax machine when Lupe returned with Momma and the children. Marti looked out the window, surprised that while she was working, darkness had come. She had been hoping that Ben would be fully awake when the kids returned, but he was still waking and sleeping the last time she went into his room. Momma brought another change of clothes for tomorrow and more food. Mike was carrying a small brown teddy bear wearing a scarf and matching hat.

"They didn't have one with a fireman's uniform," he said.

Marti went with the boys to see Ben. He was awake when they walked into the room. Both boys rushed over to him.

"Are you okay, now?"

"How do you feel?"

"That was scary, you being asleep."

"Does it hurt?"

Mike gave him the bear. Ben smiled and rubbed Mike's head with the hand that was free. He motioned to Theo to come closer.

"I'm fine," he said, almost in a whisper. "See. Not everyone dies." He spoke slowly, as if it took some effort. "God doesn't take everyone. He has to leave some of us here." He took a deep breath. "That trip to the Rockies is still on."

Both boys grinned. Marti didn't ask what trip. That could wait until later.

Ben's eyes were open when Marti returned with Momma and Joanna.

"You're awake," she said. "You're finally awake." She kissed his forehead.

Ben smiled at Joanna. "Did I miss any good basketball games?"

She shook her head. There were tears in her eyes. "We were so scared," she said.

"I know."

Momma went over to him. "You sound tired, baby. You get some rest. God still sits on the throne. Everything will be all right."

Everyone stayed another fifty minutes so they could visit with Ben one more time. Marti returned to his room with some trepidation, but this time he wasn't sleeping when they went in.

Afterward, Lupe said, "Okay, we're out of here. Time for pizza."

When the boys hugged Marti good-bye, their hugs were gentle but extra long. Joanna asked if she could stay.

"You'll miss out on the pizza," Marti said.

"I'd rather be with you."

Marti agreed, but only because she thought Joanna needed to be with her. She wasn't sure how watching her and Vik work would affect her.

"You're using Dad's notes," Joanna said after they had eaten sandwiches from a machine and Vik and Marti got back to work. "This is awesome." Joanna had all eleven files stacked in front of her and was flipping through them one at a time.

"Mmmm," Marti said. She could finally look at what had been faxed.

The phone interrupted.

"Watch your back, MacAlister," the Chicago detective said. "This Adrian Quinn has moved, no known address, and he hasn't shown up at his work site in over a month."

"When are you sending that photograph?" She didn't see any photos in the stack of papers she had just retrieved.

"We've got a file photo, nothing recent."

"Send that."

"You got it."

Marti went back to the faxes. There was a handwritten list

of the names and addresses of everyone involved in Adrian Quinn's arrest and trial.

"Vik," she said. "Look at this!"

"Ramos?" he said. "Graciela?"

Ramos had been Quinn's attorney.

Marti called him.

"How are you?" he asked. "I heard about the accident. Is your husband okay?"

"Doing fine," she said. "What can you tell me about an Adrian Quinn?"

"Name means nothing. What about him?"

"You defended him thirteen years ago."

"I've defended a lot of people."

"My deceased husband was the arresting office. Quinn got paroled a couple of months ago. Now besides my accident, my husband's partner has been shot, and Quinn's disappeared."

"What was the charge?" Ramos asked. "I work mostly on appeals now."

"Homicide reduced to manslaughter."

"What can you tell me about him?"

"Black, well educated, worked for Wilburton Financial, hit a co-worker over the head with a bookend because the man caught him stealing from the company."

"Okay, got him," Ramos said. "I don't represent too many guys with his pedigree. He lied to me about a few things and the prosecutor nailed us for it in court. Quinn was real angry about that. Apparently it wasn't his fault that he lied. Then maybe four, five years ago a couple of his prison buddies were released because of forensic evidence mishandled by a technician. Quinn thought he should get out, too. Trouble was, his evidence was processed by a different technician, and it was very straightforward. His fingerprints on the weapon, the victim's blood was on his clothing, an office cleaner heard the entire argument and saw Quinn run from the office. There was nothing to screw up. Again, he felt that there should have been, that it was my fault, or someone's fault that all of the evidence was in order."

Marti didn't share her suspicion about what might have happened to Graciela.

"I think you should keep that alarm system activated, Mr. Ramos, and that you and your family should be very careful until Quinn is apprehended. If he has shot a cop, he'll take anyone out." She thought of the house fire and car accident. "Quinn might even have an agenda."

When she hung up, Vik handed her another fax. She didn't recognize the man in the photo. "This is Adrian Quinn?"

She shook her head. Quinn was looking at the camera, but his face was expressionless. "The only thing I remember about the man in the car was his eyes." In the photo Quinn's eyes made him look as though he was half-asleep, and lacked that intensity.

She compared the photo to the one taken at the fire scene. Nothing.

Slim and Cowboy came in a few minutes later and put a box of doughnuts and a cardboard tray with four cups of coffee on the table. And there was more food. Thermos containers with soup.

"My mother is big on chicken soup," Slim said. "She thinks it cures everything from depression to diphtheria as well as the common cold. This will stay hot for a while."

"You okay, Officer Mac?" Cowboy asked.

"You don't want to know." She had gotten used to the painkillers fast. They didn't make her sleepy anymore. That and keeping busy kept the pain at a manageable level, but her entire body still hurt.

"We've spent the day trying to find LaShawna," Slim said. "Nothing. I'm sorry. At least we know she wasn't in the house that got torched. We did turn up two more women who will testify against Reginald Garrett. One of them has a permanent disability because of him, tremors, paralysis in one arm, and she walks with a limp. The other young lady is now licensed to carry a weapon. Neither of them wants to relocate. I think if he goes near the one with the gun he's a dead man. I talked with the state's attorney. He says since these beatings were so brutal, they are going to throw every charge applicable at Garrett and go for the max penalty on each."

"I'm beginning to think that maybe LaShawna took off or found some way to go to ground," Marti said. At least she was trying to think that way. Anything was better than wondering if she was dead. "Those kids were pretty resourceful. The system kind of straitjacketed that. But I think they've survived the best way they know how." She thought of Jose. "With plenty of emotional insulation." She wondered if her own kids would be okay. How they were really coping with this, not just how they seemed to be coping.

"We stopped by your place before we drove down here," Slim told her.

"To see how the kids were," Cowboy said.

"It was a little late," Slim said. "But Momma Lydia said that since it was not a school night we could take them to the bowling alley. They took one look at the room with the pool tables and forgot all about bowling and man, those boys shoot a mean game of pool. Kicked my butt. They liked staying out late."

"Thanks. I really appreciate that."

"Cute kids," Slim said. He rubbed his hands together. "Now, what can we do?"

Marti told both of them about Adrian Quinn. "We've got two phone lines," she said. "And a list of people Quinn might have it in for. I need to go and see Ben."

Ben had remained awake all evening, but every time she walked toward his room she became apprehensive. Again she thought of her children. She called home every time she went in to see him, to reassure them that he was okay, but what was this doing to them?

The nurse had propped the teddy bear where Ben could see it. He had a headache but they couldn't give him anything for it. When he tried sipping water, he vomited. Normal, given the circumstances, she reminded herself. But she worried anyway.

The doctor was with him.

"What's wrong?" she asked.

"Oh, he's just fine. We're going to move him to the neuro-logical ward in the morning. It might be a while before I'm ready to let him go home. But at this point, his progress is normal."

Ben gave her a thumbs-up. She gave him a careful hug.

"Let me see the phone," she said when she returned to their makeshift office. The boys were still up. She could hear them whooping in the background when Momma relayed the news.

That done, she turned to Slim and Cowboy. "Got anything?" she asked.

"I don't know," Slim said. He showed her the list. "X means no answer, check mark means a machine. People sure give out a lot of information when they are not at home. No wonder burglaries are up. The caller gets everything but an invitation. "First one, Weinstein machine, Everyone is at the hospital, Bryan is doing as well as can be expected. Leave a message."

Marti felt her stomach lurch. Weinstein was shot with the same gun as Ray Franklin. "How was Weinstein involved with Quinn?"

"A Saul Weinstein was a juror."

"Who's next?" she asked, dreading the answer.

"Ray Franklin, you know about that. Next is Jessica Grant, jury forewoman, machine, leave a message, family in Arizona for Doug's funeral, and funeral details. Phone is listed in Doug-las's name." He continued down the list. "No answer, no answer, everything fine with these folks, then Lottie Mae Jenson, her sister answered, said she was not accepting calls, that there had been a death in the family, Lottie Mae's daughter. When I identified myself as a police officer, the woman wanted to know if we had found the killer yet. The daughter, LaPatrice, was stabbed and beaten on her way home from work on Thursday, February fifteenth. And I don't know about you, Officer Mac, but this is beginning to scare the hell out of me. Have we got a lunatic on our hands here, or what?"

Marti sat down. It was painful, but she rubbed her arms, they were covered with goose bumps. Someone's walking on your grave, Momma would say.

Vik came over and stood beside her. "What in the hell is going on here?"

"Johnnie MacAlister is next," Slim said.

Marti was almost afraid to hear what Cowboy had come up with. "What have you got?" she asked.

"You know Ramos is here."

She nodded.

"I'll skip the no answers, and the 'sorry we are not at home' recordings," Cowboy said. "We're going to have to get more information on the ones that I have—come up with a profile on this guy. First, Lureen Stanwick, prosecutor, daughter Sabrina died a week ago today, snowmobiling accident. Next, Judge Margaret Toner, resigned from the bench due to illness. According to the housekeeper, her husband had a heart attack after he pulled into their garage last Tuesday, Valentine's Day. He couldn't turn off the van, died of carbon monoxide. This next one is familiar, Calvin Ward, juror. And last but not least, Quinn's old boss, Rupert Russell Wilburton the Third, retired. Old Rupert died this afternoon, walking in a wooded area, throat cut and abdomen gutted by an unknown assailant."

Marti felt faint. She put her head down.

"MacAlister?" Slim said.

"Marti?" Vik echoed.

"It's just the pain medication. I'm all right." But she wasn't. She felt sick to her stomach.

She called the Chicago detective.

"Yes!" he said when she began talking. She could hear the excitement in his voice. He had drawn the short straw and got the case of a lifetime. As she continued, the magnitude of what was happening dawned on him. "My God, MacAlister," he said, awe in his voice. "My God. This is incredible. This man is a human killing machine."

"You contact everyone else on this list, ASAP," she instructed. "We're going to call the jurisdictions involved and talk with whoever is handling each case. We need to get a profile on Quinn fast."

"I've got a team here trying to locate him. We're going through everything we've got on him trying to find places to look. I put a call in to Statesville. He taught a class for the GED exam, before he was transferred there from Joliet. We're checking out the graduates and other participants who have been released. Other than that, Quinn kept to himself."

"Sounds good," Marti said. "We'll call whenever we've got something. You do the same."

Ben was sleepy when she went in to see him.

"Nothing to do," he complained. "In the morning I get a room with a TV. I can't believe it's come to that. Have the kids bring me a CD player with headphones and some CDs. Do we have any talking books? If I don't get out of here in the next thirty-six hours, I'm going to go crazy."

"This from a man who didn't know what day it was this morning?"

"And still can't remember anything about yesterday at all," he admitted.

"Just as well," Marti said. "You wouldn't have enjoyed it."

She couldn't worry him now, but wait until he found out about Adrian Quinn.

Marti and Vik decided to work up a profile. Slim and Cowboy decided to go home. Not to their homes, but to hers.

"We'll take Joanna with us."

"Joanna!" Marti had forgotten she was there. She turned, and there was Joanna, in the corner, wide awake, watching, saying nothing.

"I'm not ready to leave yet. I want to stay the night."

Marti nodded.

Slim called the chief at home, confirmed that he had woke him up, and requested duty at Marti's place, with him and Cowboy working in shifts.

"The hookers will think they're in Vegas," Slim said.

"Nothing wrong with a hooker holiday every now and then," Cowboy drawled. "Helps them let their guard down, releases their inhibitions. Makes it that much easier for us to catch 'em in the act."

"True," Slim said. "But what acts?"

"And," Cowboy said, "there is the prospect of having a real breakfast."

Lupe came in as they were leaving. "Had my sister drop me off," she said. "Got a couple hours' sleep and thought I'd drive the old man back to Lincoln Prairie." She gave Vik an affectionate pat on the back. Vik scowled.

"Still awake?" Lupe said to Joanna. "Bored, aren't you?"

Joanna shook her head.

"It's okay if we just forget you're here, right?"

"We already did," Marti said.

"Marti, those boys are so sweet," Lupe told her. "All four of them. We didn't get a chance to tell you when we came in this evening, but we dropped Momma Lydia off after we left this morning, picked up the neighbors' two boys and went ice-skating. They wore me out. I had to go home and take a nap. Is Ben still doing okay?"

"He's bored, restless, and complaining," Marti said.

"Way to go."

"They're moving him out of the ICU in the morning."

Lupe raised her hand for a high five, then realized Marti wasn't in any condition to raise her arm that high.

"So, whatcha get while I was pretending to be in the Ice Capades?" A funny question until she heard the answer.

"Be damned," she said. "Let me help with the profile."

"This is an MO profile, not a psych profile," Vik said. "Even though we might need one of those, too. This guy is a real nutcase."

"Scary," Lupe agreed. "A lot of mentally ill people *know* something is wrong with them. I bet this guy thinks that he's sane."

They got on the phone, woke up a couple of desk sergeants and a few detectives and pieced together what they needed to know.

"He started out with next-of-kin victims. Left the guilty person alone," Lupe said. "I'm not going to analyze that, but it sounds like he wanted to punish them, or make them suffer a lot longer than the time it would take them to die."

"That changed when he killed Calvin Ward," Marti said. "He could have killed his wife or his dogs."

"Then he shot Ray Franklin," Vik said. "And he got the boss this morning."

"Are we including Graciela Lara in this?" Lupe wanted to know.

"I think we have to," Marti said. "At least for now."

Vik tapped his fingers on the stack of folders. "Graciela is stabbed on Tuesday. Toner dies Wednesday, but that's iffy, could be a coincidence. Thursday, LaPatrice Jenson is stabbed. On Friday, Douglas Grant is hit by a train—that sounds straightforward. Sabrina Stanwick—another 'accident' on Saturday. Bryan Weinstein shot on Sunday. Calvin Ward is next—Monday night—stabbed also. This could be interesting. Nobody died on Tuesday, as far as we know. Does that mean he took the day off? Wednesday Ray Franklin and the female uniform are shot. We have the fire Thursday night. Friday you two end up here in the hospital. Today"—he checked his watch. "It's one-fifteen in the morning. Sunday morning. Yesterday—Saturday—his boss got stabbed and gutted. And today?"

"Stabbing is real consistent," Marti said, "The shootings weren't fatal, not yet anyway. The stabbings were. Then we've got two accidents and a heart attack."

Marti consulted her notes. "Charles Toner. Coroner ruled it accidental. The heart attack was massive, but he breathed long enough to inhale the carbon monoxide. Sabrina Stanwick. Still under investigation. Someone stretched a wire across the snowmobile trail. Decapitated her. Could have been kids. Douglas Grant, accidental. Got off one train, ran across the tracks, got hit by another train coming from the opposite direction."

"If these didn't happen so close together," Vik said. "And if we didn't have this connection to Quinn . . ."

"Let's call it a night," Marti said. She was getting a headache.

"A morning," Vik corrected.

"Whatever." The pain in her back from sitting so long was excruciating.

Vik and Lupe both looked concerned.

"I think I need a break."

As soon as Vik and Lupe left, Marti asked for a pain pill. Joanna gave her the couch in the small room, and took the chair.

"You are not going to be comfortable," Marti said. "You'll get a crick in your neck."

"Ma, I went primitive camping when I was a Girl Scout. This is nothing."

Marti was too exhausted to argue.

Adrian sat in the middle of the circle and checked out the map he had drawn of the hospital where MacAlister and her husband were staying. The place was secured at night. He had marked three points on the first floor where guards were stationed. One in the emergency room, another where two corridors intersected, and a third who sat in a room with a window flush to the wall. He concentrated on the third location. The room was in the corridor nearest the elevators. The chapel was right down the hall. He couldn't see any other way to get to her at night.

He studied the map for a long time, trying to figure out another plan in case that one didn't work. He would have to go in before visiting hours were over at ten, hide out in a rest room, and then go to the chapel. There wasn't an alternative plan, and if he didn't get her there, he would have to wait until she and the fireman went home. Then there would be an alarm system and the dog to deal with. He was still apprehensive whenever he got too close to a dog. The dog would smell that. And now that he had met MacAlister's children, he was sure that her dog would be one of those who was trained to disarm and attack. He folded the map.

13

Marti awakened to the aroma of fresh coffee. She sat up too fast and got a muscle spasm in the small of her back. Joanna watched her, face anxious, but said nothing.

"Ben?" Marti asked.

"He's on the third floor now, they moved him. He was complaining about not being able to do anything. His room has a window. I told him that maybe he should just watch the world go by for a couple of days. I don't think either of you have a clue as to how to sit still unless you're completely exhausted. And, oh, I called the boys to let them know everyone is okay."

"Good. I need a shower. My joints feel like they are locked into place. I'm going to see Ben first. I'm sure he's come up with a whole list of complaints by now." She drank the coffee first, and ate a stale doughnut from the night before.

"I was going to throw those away," Joanna told her.

"Nothing wrong with them," Marti said. "Have one."

"Yuck. Too much sugar and way too much fat."

Marti wasn't so stiff after standing under hot water for fifteen minutes. She decided to forgo the pain pill, at least for now, and get to work. Everything in their makeshift office was where she had left it.

"What are we going to do now?" Joanna asked.

Marti raised her eyebrows at the "we" but didn't comment. Joanna had sat without complaint half the night while she and Vik worked. She had to be bored with all of this cop stuff.

"Why don't you write while I think. At least until Vik gets here."

She organized the faxed sheets in numeric order according to when each person died. Joanna was ready, pen poised.

"Tell me if this gets depressing." She picked up a sheet, then said, "Wait a minute. Let's do this by method instead of by date." She resorted the papers, began scanning them.

"We'll begin with the knife victims," Marti decided. "He's very good with a knife. I think that's his weapon of choice. The Lake County coroner's office has the knife used on Calvin Ward." She paused long enough to tell Joanna about Mrs. Ward and their dogs. "We want them to determine if the knife used to kill Ward was also used to kill Graciela Lara and the girl in Chicago, LaPatrice Jenson."

After Joanna wrote that down, she said, "What about Wilburton?"

"The Wilburton and Jenson killings differ from the others in that Quinn seems to have lost control. The other killings are methodical. Those two were brutal."

"Guns, next?" Joanna asked. "Bryan Weinstein, Ray Franklin, Consuela Jones."

"He's not as good with guns. Nobody has died. Yet. It could be the weapon, though."

"How's that?"

Marti explained.

"So," Joanna said. "Even though he seems to be a lousy shot, it could be that he doesn't understand firearms."

"Right," Marti said. The accidental deaths were the ones that interested her the most. "We have nothing in the way of real proof to tie Adrian Quinn to Charles Toner, the heart attack victim, or to the decapitation of Sabrina Stanwick in the snowmobiling accident." She should have worded that differently. "Sorry if that was too graphic."

"Ma."

"Okay, okay. Add the train victim to that list, Douglas Grant." Marti thought for a few minutes, then said, "We need more information about the victims. Without a witness, the victim is the only person other than the killer who can tell us what happened." She reached for the phone.

"What else can you tell me about Charles Toner?" she asked the investigating officer. "There was no gas left in the tank when they found him. The van had to have been running for a long time."

She listened, then asked a few more questions. When she hung up, she said, "Take this down. Toner usually drove the car, not the van. He attended a weekly meeting in Chicago on Wednesdays and arrived home late."

"Why is that important?"

"I don't know yet. Maybe it isn't."

Next, with the receiver tucked under her chin, she reached for the file on Douglas Grant, then dialed. "Grant had been drinking the night he died. His levels were below the limit, but did he do that often? How often did he come home late?"

When she hung up, she told Joanna. "Friday was Grant's night out with the boys. He always made it home on the ten-ten train. No problem with alcohol."

Sabrina Stanwick was next.

"Guess what?" Marti said when she hung up.

"She went snowmobiling every Saturday," Joanna said.

"Close enough. Every other Saturday. On alternate Saturdays, she went skiing."

"What does this mean?" Joanna asked. "Did Adrian Quinn kill them too?"

"There is a pattern," Marti explained. "What is it?"

"Something they do all the time, but . . . ." Joanna hesitated. "That means he would have to know that. He had to follow them or something." She made a face as if she had just seen something crawly. "How weird. That's like having your own peeping Tom. I hate it when people get in my business."

"He studied his victims," Marti agreed. She thought about the house on First Street, about feeling as though she was being watched. She would have to add arson to her list on Adrian Quinn. He set that fire deliberately so that Ben would get trapped. He knew they were on the road Friday because he was following them. Bile rose in her throat. She believed she was his primary target, but thank God Cowboy and Slim were there with Momma and the kids.

Everyone arrived at about the same time; Vik, Slim, Cowboy, Lupe, Momma, and the boys. This time they all went upstairs on the elevator and filled Ben's room with visitors. He was alert and talking now, but still sleeping a lot.

"We brought everything you asked for," Mike said, holding up a backpack.

"Grandma said we couldn't bring you any food," Theo added.

Ben laughed. "Leave it to me to get into an accident after football season," he joked. "I finally get to lay around on a Sunday and I can't even watch a game."

"Okay if some us disappear for a few minutes for a little cop talk?" Marti asked.

When they were all in the temporary office, she said, "I need to fill you in on the latest on Adrian Quinn."

When she finished talking, Vik didn't ask one question. It was the only time since she had known him that he was speechless. He took a couple of deep breaths, then said, "Damn, I've never worked a case like this before."

Marti didn't tell him that she hadn't either. It was time she got a little mileage out of his big-city cop remarks.

"You really think he set up those accidents, MacAlister? Three victims, and you and Ben? Unbelievable. Does this make him a serial killer?"

"Not according to the classic profile," Marti said.

Vik didn't ask what a "classic profile" was.

"Unless he took trophies," she added.

Lupe gave her a thumbs-up.

Marti turned to Cowboy and Slim. "You two are taking this in stride, considering you're our last line of defense."

"Hell," Cowboy drawled, "folks like this Adrian Quinn are

just another sideshow in the drama of life. He's just met up with the wrong people. We got a couple hookers out there who would take that knife away from him and show him how to use it while they castrated him."

"Trouble is scarier than Quinn," Slim said. "That dog would eat Quinn alive if got to close to that house or anyone in it. Dog could jump that fence any time she wanted to. I wouldn't mess with her and she's never even growled at me or bared her teeth."

"She's trained not to trouble unless trouble troubles her," Marti explained. "You have to try to come over the fence or get into the yard or the house. Otherwise, she doesn't even bark. We have visual and auditory commands if we need her for anything."

"Amazing animal," Cowboy agreed. "We were introduced. I shook her paw." He grinned at Slim. "I even petted her and let her take some treats from the palm of my hand. Now, my partner here . . ."

"Dog can tell time," Slim said. "Every four hours she does a complete tour of the house, every window, every room, every door. And let me tell you, there is nothing like waking up at four in the morning and seeing this huge German shepherd grinning at you with her teeth less than six inches from your face."

Cowboy laughed. "What did you do, man?"

"Hell, given those conditions, dog breath be damned, I said good morning. I sure as hell wasn't going to pet her, or make any sudden moves. Me and Trouble have an understanding. The entire house and everyone in it belong to her. No matter how nonviolent she seems, I remain a guest. And I can respect that." Slim folded his arms. "So, Madam Detective, you got a plan for catching this Quinn?"

She had thought about that. "The only plan I have right now is to keep all of us alive until Quinn is caught. Security at the hospital is tight after ten o'clock. The rest of the time there are too many people around, so I feel fairly safe. I'm watching my back, but I think we'll be the most vulnerable going to and from home."

"You carrying?" Vik asked.

"Yes." She patted the pocket in her sweatpants where she was keeping her Beretta. The sweatshirt was bulky enough to conceal the bulge.

"And your vest?"

"I was wearing it when we had the accident. I'll put it on."

"Good. Got a deck of cards?"

"Huh?"

"I'm sticking around for a while and let's get Joanna to go home."

They had supper in the hospital cafeteria. While they ate their salad and sandwiches, Vik announce that he was staying the night.

She didn't argue. Slim and Cowboy were with the kids. There was a black-and-white parked outside of her house and a uniform on foot patrol in her neighborhood. In spite of this, and Trouble, she did not feel that any of them were safe.

When Adrian walked into the hospital, nobody paid any attention to him. It was 9:25. He went to the corridor where the guard's office was, with the window that faced the hall. Luck was with him. The security guard was talking to a Hispanic woman and didn't even notice when he walked by. Adrian turned right when he reached the intersecting corridor, walked over to the elevators but didn't press the button. The rest rooms were right across from the elevator bays. He ducked into the ladies' room and took off the men's coat and hat that he was wearing over woman's clothing, folded everything, put it in the wastebasket and added paper towels until it couldn't be seen. He would sit in the chapel for now. At ten minutes to eleven Officer MacAlister would take the elevator from the third floor where her husband was, to the basement, where the vending

313

machines were just as she had last night and the night before. Tonight she would get on the elevator, but she would not get off.

"Nothing on Quinn yet?" Vik asked, after Marti talked with the Chicago detective.

"Not yet."

"Think they'll find him?"

"Maybe. If he tries to kill again." Or succeeds, she thought. Right now Quinn was invisible. He was a loner, on the move, and if not smart, at least clever.

The increase in the noise level told her that it was almost time for a shift change.

"I'm going up to say good night to Ben."

She timed it so the elevator would be empty and she wouldn't have to stand long enough to get a lower backache while incoming and and outgoing staff got on and off.

When the elevator reached the ground floor, Adrian took a step back as the doors opened. He made sure it was empty, then got on. He pushed the fourth-floor button. In three minutes, MacAlister would push the down button on the third floor. When the elevator came to a stop, Adrian held the doors ajar. He waited until he heard a buzzing noise from the floor below, then released them. He held a tissue to his nose and turned slightly, so that she wouldn't be able to get a good look at his face.

The woman's coat he was wearing had a slit in the pocket to accomodate the unsheathed bowie knife he was carrying. The hat had a brim that was tilted toward his forehead, and a scarf covered his mouth.

The elevator stopped, and the door opened. Without looking up, he could see the white terry cloth robe that MacAlister had been wearing last night. Adrian sniffled, as if he was crying, or had a cold. With his right hand, he gripped the knife handle. MacAlister was leaning against the side of the elevator so that her back was not exposed. Adrian looked her full in the face and smiled as he pulled the knife from his pocket.

Marti pointed her Beretta at Adrian Quinn as the stainless-steel blade flashed. She fired before he could raise it. The doors opened and Lupe was there.

"He changed into women's clothing after he passed Lupe in the hall," Vik said. "And he's barely five feet seven. He was wearing a hat, a muffler. How did you know it was him?"

"His eyes," Marti said. "His eyes."

14

The first thing Marti did when Vik pulled into the parking lot was look for Sikich's car. It wasn't there. Too bad. The next person she got that are-you-man-enough-to-try it? attitude with was going to be him.

When she reached the office, she was as happy to be there as she had been to get home for a few hours. Ben was getting better. She would still be spending nights and most of the day at the hospital, but she could take a few breaks without being worried. She had spent a very long weekend at that hospital. Working in that conference room with a telephone and a fax machine might have got the job done, but it wasn't the same as being here. Now she felt like a cop again, instead of a semi-invalid or worse, a potential victim.

"You okay?" Slim asked.

"I'm okay." One thing about working for a smaller department was that there were fewer officers who had had the experience of killing a subject in the line of duty. "And," she said, "I expect to get a lot more respect around here."

Cowboy grinned. "Damn, partner," he told Slim. "I don't think your Mrs. Officer Ma'am is going to be acceptable around here anymore." Cowboy looked at her. "Is Big Mac still okay?"

"I like that one," she said.

"Good," Cowboy said. "That calls for a fresh pot of coffee."

"Has Sikich been around?" Marti asked.

"Nah," Slim said. "I get the feeling you two are not part of his job description anymore."

Marti scratched her arms, then tried to ignore the itching. It was just nerves. There was something about being followed, being watched. . . . She could still see Quinn dressed like a woman. It was sick, all of it. So much had happened in such a short time. She needed this trip to Colorado that the boys were planning. They all did. She checked her in-basket, trying to regain some sense of normalcy. Just routine interoffice memos. It was too soon for the forensic evidence she had requested on Adrian Quinn's knife. Voice mail was next. She and Vik were going to pay José a little visit at the hospital, then she was going to go home and spend a little more time with the kids before returning to Ben. There were only four phone messages. The last one got her attention.

"This is for Detective MacAlister," a woman's voice said. "Please call this number. LaShawna would like to speak with you."

Marti looked at the phone for a moment. Was this some kind of joke? She dialed the number and got an answering machine with a prerecorded message. She left her name, then gave the number to Vik in case they needed to trace it. "The call came in Saturday afternoon," she told him.

The phone rang while she was inhaling the aroma of a steaming cup of Cowboy's hot black coffee. She didn't know which she would enjoy the most, the anticipation of tasting a real cup of coffee again or the pleasure of drinking it.

She picked up the receiver. "Detective MacAlister."

"It's me," a voice said softly. "LaShawna."

"Girl, where are you? Is that little girl of yours all right?"

"She's fine. Her name is Marti Grace."

"What?"

"You've got a godchild."

"Well, that gives me a good reason to help you. Are you hiding from Reginald Garrett?"

"Yes, but I saw my picture in the paper. Thought I'd better call you."

"Where are you? We've looked everywhere."

LaShawna hesitated.

"Listen, we've got Garrett in jail without bail and half a dozen women who can't wait to testify against him. He can't hurt you."

"Thank you, thank you," LaShawna said. "We're staying with Nessa."

It took Marti a a minute to remember who Nessa was. She always thought of her as the bag lady, even though she knew that was just a disguise to keep people from paying attention to her. Nessa had done her best to protect those kids when they were living in that empty library.

"Nessa! Does she still live in the Preserves?"

"Same place."

"Don't move. I'll be right over. And don't worry—I just want to talk with you. Make sure you're okay. See how I can help. All right?"

Before she left, Marti put in a call to Denise Stevens. "I found LaShawna!" she said. "Or she found me. Now what?"

Denise told her about a program she wanted to get LaShawna into. Then she said, "Guess who got out of the hospital this morning?"

"José?" Marti said.

"No. Not yet. Padgett."

"Where did they put him?" Poor kid. What would he do without his mother?

"He's with Joseph Ramos."

"Ramos? You've got to be kidding."

"No. Ramos didn't think that the two boys should be split up again. You just get that knife matched up with Graciela, and we'll let José complete his thirty days and go home too.I talked with the state's attorney. They think the case against Quinn is strong enough to release José even if we don't get a match with the knife. But I'm hoping we do."

"I'm sure Quinn did it," Marti said. She had seen the look in his eyes.

* * *

Marti sat on the sofa with Marti Grace in her lap and thought she was the cutest little girl she had ever seen, except for Joanna. When she smiled, which was most of the time, she had double dimples. Her eyes were an unusual green gray. La-Shawna had combed her hair in little finger curls fastened at the top with barrettes shaped like balloons. She was a happy, good-natured child. A child who was loved.

"I'm her godmother, huh?"

"I was hoping you would be."

Nessa had opened the door, nodded to Marti, then to Vik, and let them come in. Without saying a word she had left them in the living room with LaShawna and Marti Grace. The room was sparsely furnished, with nothing more than was needed. But, it was clean, smelled of potpourri, and the two cats were not allowed on the furniture. A laundry basket filled with toys was on the floor.

"Do you remember Denise Stevens?" Marti asked.

"The juvie who always wore hats?"

"She's the one."

"Sure, she got me into a good foster home and then a group home after Gracie was born."

"What are you doing on the street?"

"Juvie cut me loose when I turned seventeen."

"And why didn't you come to us?"

LaShawna looked away. "Because I've got to be able to do for myself. Take care of me and Gracie. I got my high school diploma. I just don't know how to do nothing that pays any money. And I can't find no way to get someone decent to take care of Gracie while I work."

"Can you stay here for a few more days?"

"Nessa won't put me out."

"I've had a little family crisis. My husband is in the hospital."

"You don't look so good yourself. You look like you're in pain."

"Car accident," Marti told her. "I talked with Denise right

after you called. There's a program for women with children at a place called Staben House. It's in a beautiful Tudor on a huge lot. Plenty of room for kids to play with their mothers. Denise thinks it will be a good match for you. They only have room for five families. You stay until you're able to leave at least six to nine months. You have to find a job and daycare for Gracie, save money, take classes like child care and money management. Work on self-esteem. You share all of the household chores, and you follow the rules, which are strict. It's a place where you can become self-sufficient and gain the skills to stay that way. They do a lot of follow-up after you get your own apartment.

"And you think I can do that?"

"I'm sure you can."

"And you think they might help me? I don't where to begin. There's so much to do."

"I want you to talk to Denise. I told her that you need to see a doctor. And don't worry, nobody is going to take my godchild away from you," Marti promised.

"Yes, ma'am," LaShawna said.

Gracie looked up at Marti and smiled.

Marti and Vik went from Nessa's house to Lincoln Prairie General to see José. The IV was out of his arm, which meant he must have decided to eat. Someone had opened the curtains. The sun was not shining. The cloud cover predicted more snow.

"So," Marti said, "it looks like you're feeling better."

Jose looked her up and down, then said, "What happened to you?"

"Car accident," she said.

"My lawyer says you got the man who . . ."

Marti waited for him to complete the sentence. Instead he turned away.

"Might have happened sooner if you had talked to us, kid," Vik said.

José put his hands to his ears and shook his head. "I knew

when she had the abortion that she would die."

"How did you know that?" Marti asked.

Jose squeezed his eyes shut. He kept shaking his head.

"She is covered in blood," he whispered. "My hands are covered with blood. I told her not to do it. I told her."

Vik started to say something but Marti shook her head. José was curled up now, tears seeping from his eyes. He began to tremble. "My sister," he whispered. "She had an abortion. My mother . . ." He huddled under the white sheet and thin blanket. "I still hear her screaming. I still see the blood on my hands."

"Graciela," Marti said.

José turned his head from side to side. "Mama, Mama, please wake up. Please wake up now. Please." He began rocking. "Please, Mama, please."

Marti didn't know what he was talking about, but she thought she understood why José had knelt there, beside Graciela, without calling for help, without making a sound. It wasn't the first time he had found someone covered with blood. She didn't know if José was talking about his sister or his mother, but she was certain his hands had been covered with blood before, and that then, just as now, someone else had committed the violence.

"It's okay now," she said.

José shook his head.

"No," he said. "They're dead. All of them are dead."

"It isn't your fault. You know that."

He opened his eyes wide and stared at her. She realized that this wasn't about guilt, or feeling responsible. This was about a child seeing someone he loved who had been viciously murdered. José was one of those victims, the one who found the dead, who got his hands covered with blood without causing the wounds, the one who continued to suffer long after the crime was forgotten by just about everyone else.

15

Marti got Ben settled in the den. It was a little like the crippled being led by the lame. Although most of her bruises had faded, the aches and pains remained. And as Ben had become more alert, he had also became aware of his bruises and sore muscles and aching bones. He groaned as he adjusted his recliner. She winced as she reached for a blanket. He didn't protest when she covered him and brought him the remote for the television.

"Try the sports channels," she suggested. "Or maybe the news."

"Does that mean you're not watching TV with me?"

"Right now I'm going to fix you some lunch. Then I'm going in to work for a couple of hours. Then, when I come home, we are going to soak in the hot tub, prop a lot of pillows on the bed, call all the kids and Momma in to sit with us, put a movie in the DVD player, and recuperate. Tomorrow you and I are going to sleep in, then I am going to wait on you hand and foot—for one day only—then I am going to help Momma with the cooking, pick up the kids after school, take the time to see what they are working on in class, and let them show me how to get on the Internet. I might even help you plan this trip to Colorado to see my brother, since we'll be leaving in another week." She got up and gave him a gentle hug.

"I am so glad to be home for a few weeks."

Ben looked at her with a quizzical expression.

"What?" she asked.

"Are you okay with taking Quinn out or are you just keeping busy so you don't have to think about it?"

She sat in the recliner beside his. She had never killed anyone before. She had wanted to a few times, but there had been other options.

"It is strange," she admitted. "Even though it was self-defense and he killed all those people and he really was a psychopath, he was still a human being, alive if dysfunctional. I don't feel bad about taking him out. I'm glad I did. But it is . . . strange."

As her old partner Zabrowski used to tell her, it was a mind game. From now on when she "looked 'em in the eye" and said to herself, *Are you man enough to try it? I'll blow your ass away*, she could back it up with what she had done to Adrian Quinn.

That night, Momma came into Marti and Ben's room with the kids, sat down, put her feet up and told them stories—about being a little girl growing up in the South, about their great-grandparents and Marti's dad, their grandfather. She talked to them about the civil rights movement, and described what it was like moving to Chicago, and, in Marti's opinion, she told them more than they needed to know about Marti growing up. She even talked about Johnnie. It was reassuring somehow, after what had happened to her and to Ben, to think of continuity, of the past, and the present, and the possibilities still in the future.

Later, after the boys had fallen asleep in their bed where Ben was sound asleep too, Momma went down to the den, to try to stay awake long enough to watch the ten o'clock news. Joanna joined Marti in the kitchen.

"I was going to have some more cocoa," Marti said. "Want some? And more of those oatmeal cookies."

Joanna had substituted dried cranberries for raisins but they still tasted good.

As they sat at the table, Joanna said. "I guess that which we dreaded the most has come to pass."

"Meaning me and Ben."

"Mm-hmm. The boys and I talked about it. We agreed that as scary as it was, now we know that we can hang together and get through things, even bad things."

"Momma said you were a big help with Theo and Mike."

"We helped each other. It was really straight. They're okay for kids."

The cookies were the size of saucers. Joanna broke hers into smaller pieces. "I'm not going to devote my life to volleyball," she said.

"Because of what happened?"

"Yes."

"I'm not sure you should base a life decision on something like that."

"Actually, listening to Momma tonight is what really made up my mind."

Marti stirred her cocoa and waited.

"When I think of volleyball, playing professionally, even going to the Olympics, it's like, is that all there is? It isn't like I'd be the first African American female to win a gold medal at the summer Olympics. Maybe then it would seem more important. But working with you at the hospital that night . . . and helping the boys think positive and not get too upset, listening to Momma tonight . . . I decided there is too much I want to do to tie my life up with an Olympic dream that may or may not come true. And there's too much here, more than I can give up. That's kind of the bottom line, isn't it? What you have to give up to get what you want? Well, I'd be giving up more than I'd be gaining—and for something I don't want that much. Does that make sense?"

Marti nodded. Joanna reached across the table and covered Marti's hand with her own.

Vict
Cara -
- Judg Husband - Juror
- LaPatrice - Juror dgula

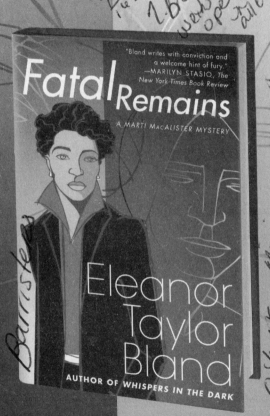